Dear Reader,

This month we a... ...g a little different: *Renton's Royal* is set in 1969 and is more of a saga than anything we've published so far. Do you enjoy this type of romance? Would you like to see more sagas on the *Scarlet* list? Or historical romances? *I'm* a great fan of Regency novels, but perhaps you prefer other historical settings?

Wild Justice is the first part of 'The Beaumont Brides' trilogy, telling the stories of three, very different, sisters. We do hope you'll enjoy the chance to be involved with the same characters over the course of three books. *A Dark Legacy* combines romance with a dash of mystery, while *No Darker Heaven* is the story of a woman torn between two men – father and son!

Do write to us with your views on *Scarlet*, won't you, as it's only by hearing *your* opinion that we can continue to make sure that the books we are offering are pleasing you.

Best wishes,

Sally Cooper

SALLY COOPER,
Editor-in-Chief – *Scarlet*

PS Have you filled in a questionnaire yet? If you haven't, please complete the fom at the back of this book and we'll be happy to send you a free gift as a thank you.

About the Author

Liz Fielding was born in Berkshire and educated at the local Convent school before training as a secretary. At the age of twenty, she took a post with the Zambian Government. Liz met her Coventry-born husband John in Lusaka and after their marriage Liz and John spent some time in the Middle East, Qatar, Bahrain and the UAE before returning to Botswana and Kenya.

After their children were born, Liz remained in the UK and began to write in the long evenings while John was working abroad. The family now lives in a tiny village in West Wales surrounded by romantic crumbling castles and beautiful countryside. Liz's first romance was published in 1992 and *Wild Justice*, the first part of the 'Beaumont Brides' trilogy, is her tenth book.

*Other **Scarlet** titles available this month:*

RENTON'S ROYAL – Nina Tinsley
A DARK LEGACY – Clare Benedict
NO DARKER HEAVEN – Stella Whitelaw

LIZ FIELDING

WILD JUSTICE

Enquiries to:
Robinson Publishing Ltd
7 Kensington Church Court
London W8 4SP

First published in the UK by Scarlet, 1996

A copy of the British Library Cataloguing in
Publication data is available from the British Library

ISBN 1-85487-487-X
Printed and bound in the EC

10 9 8 7 6 5 4 3 2 1

Revenge is a kind of wild justice, which the more man's nature runs to, the more ought law to weed it out.

Francis Bacon

CHAPTER 1

'Luke Devlin?' Fizz Beaumont pushed a distracted hand through the heavy mop of chestnut hair that fell across her face, obstinately refusing to be confined by a pair of delicate antique tortoiseshell combs that had once belonged to her mother. Irritated by their uselessness, she abandoned them on her desk, scooping her unruly hair into an elastic band with one practised movement, before her father's continued silence alerted her to the fact that this was more than a social call to discuss a letter he had received that morning.

She looked up. Edward Beaumont, tall, handsome, elegantly tailored heart-throb to the blue-rinse brigade, looked unusually awkward, and her eyes finally dropped to the letter he was holding in his hand. 'Who is Luke Devlin?' she asked, and then, 'What does he want?'

'I think, my dear, that he's already got what he wants,' her father replied heavily. 'He's taken over Harries Industries.'

'Harries? You're joking – ' she began, then realized with a chill feeling that had nothing whatsoever to do with the February wind finding its way through every

1

corner of the old sashcord window, that he wasn't joking. Her father was in deadly earnest.

'But how could he take over? Harries isn't for sale. Where's Michael? Surely he isn't just letting this happen?' The questions tumbled out, but her father clearly had no answers. 'I've never even heard of the man,' she finished, as if that would put an end to such nonsense.

Edward Beaumont pulled a face, sympathizing with his daughter's bewildered reaction. 'It seems that not many people have, at least not until it's too late. He keeps a very low profile.'

'Low is about right,' Fizz responded, with warmth. 'Positively belly to the ground. There hasn't been so much as a whisper . . .'

'He moved very quickly, according to Michael. Apparently it's something he does particularly well. But since he now owns this radio station's major sponsor, I suggest you keep any opinions about his business methods strictly to yourself.'

Still confused at the suddenness of this turn of events, Fizz clutched at straws. 'Are you absolutely certain? It's not just some misunderstanding . . .?'

'I'm afraid there's no doubt about it, Fizz. Michael phoned me late last night. And the newsroom have just received a press release.'

He threw the sheet of paper embossed with the impressive letterhead of Broomhill Bay's largest manufacturer onto the cluttered desk that separated them, stuffed his hands in the pockets of his superbly tailored jacket and stared at the ceiling as if washing his hands of the whole affair.

'I thought it would take the new man a few days to get around to worrying about details like us. But this was delivered by messenger a few minutes ago.'

A small chill ran through Fizz's veins as she reluctantly reached out to pick it up. It was brief and brutally to the point. In the current economic climate the new management of Harries Industries was forced to 'rationalize' its generous sponsorship of sport and the arts in the town. And, since support for Pavilion Radio was an informal arrangement between Michael Harries and Edward Beaumont, the company would be making immediate changes.

Fizz Beaumont's wide forehead creased in a puzzled frown. 'What does this mean?' she asked. '*Informal arrangement?* Harries have been sponsoring us since we first went on air. Michael was as enthusiastic about it as you were . . .' It had been on the strength of Michael Harries's financial support that she had borrowed so heavily in order to go ahead with her plans for the new restaurant this year.

Her father continued to avoid her eyes but his eloquent shrug spoke volumes. 'It was a gentlemen's agreement, Fizz. Michael and I have been friends ever since school, and a handshake seemed – '

'Some gentleman!' she exploded. 'Some friend, if he's sold us out without warning – '

'It isn't his fault,' her father declared indignantly. 'He didn't have any choice.' His actor's voice vibrated against the walls of her small office, but Fizz had lived with his role-playing for far too long to be intimidated.

'Then whose fault is it? You were the one who assured

3

me that I had no need to concern myself with the details.'

'I know.' He cleared his throat. 'And I'm sorry, Fizz, but I just never foresaw this situation. Apparently Michael's been selling off his shares for months in an attempt to keep the company afloat until things got better. They didn't . . .' He raked his fingers through his thick mane of hair, beautifully distinguished by silvery wings at his temples, and paused momentarily to gather himself.

Her father had played so many parts in his long career on the stage that he simply wore the one that was most appropriate to the occasion. Recognizing the prelude to his 'betrayed Lear', Fizz hurriedly intervened.

'And this – ' she glanced at the letter again' – this Luke Devlin has been buying them?' She felt a surge of anger that someone should so insidiously have been able to gain control of Harries Industries without a fight, without having to stand up and declare himself.

'Michael was so relieved to sell the shares at a decent price he didn't give a thought to the possible consequences.'

'Oh, Lord,' she murmured, suddenly stricken with guilt that in her concern for the radio station she hadn't given her father's oldest friend a thought. Her life was being made more difficult, but Michael had lost a company which had been founded by his family generations ago, and which had been the prop and mainstay of manufacturing employment in the town ever since.

And what about the men and woman who worked at the plant? Would they still have jobs to go to this morning? Tomorrow morning? 'I'm sorry, Dad. I know

4

that Michael's been a good friend to us. This isn't his fault. Everyone's been hard hit in the last couple of years.'

And it was true. The painful fact she had to face was that the fault was entirely her own. If she hadn't let her enthusiasm run away with her wits she would have made certain the generous sponsorship deal her father had negotiated was watertight. But he had made it clear that that was something she didn't need to bother her head over, and she had been sensitive about intruding on an agreement between two old friends. 'Do you think this man realizes the implications for us if he withdraws support?'

'I don't suppose he cares. Why should he? He's an outsider, a stranger.' Her father seemed momentarily to lose his poise, and for once he looked his age. 'Michael asked me to tell you that he was truly sorry. Apparently, when the takeover move came, it all happened so quickly that there was no time to warn you.'

'I didn't realize that the company was in difficulties. Did you know? If only he had given us an idea of the trouble he was in – ' She stopped. There was no point in saying what she *would* have done had she known. She had to deal with the situation now.

Without the new bank loan they could have managed. They might still manage. What she had to do now was persuade this Luke Devlin that Broomhill Bay would be a poorer place without its radio station. And have a convincing answer when he asked, as she knew he would, why he should be expected to support it. She had to be positive.

5

It might all be just a storm in a teacup – a standard letter to all Michael's good causes. And there were plenty of them . . . Over the years the town had come to rely heavily on the Harries family. The Beaumonts, too, were always there to help raise funds, but the big money had always come from the Harrieses – both the family and the company. Not any more. Mr Devlin was clearing the decks and he certainly hadn't wasted any time.

She gestured towards the letter. 'I suppose we shouldn't judge the man before we hear what he has to offer,' she said.

Edward Beaumont shrugged almost imperceptibly. 'Maybe this is all just a formality,' he said, giving voice to her own thoughts. 'I'm sure he'll cut back, but I can't imagine that he'll withdraw his support entirely.'

Fizz re-read the letter carefully, but there was no comfort to be found in the stark words. Michael's cheque had been due within days. Without it the station's own soap opera as well as live coverage of local sports events for the following twelve months would be at risk. And without those programmes the franchise was at risk as well. But the new chairman of Harries Industries made it quite plain in his letter that he expected changes to take place without delay. Changes. Why didn't he just say what he meant instead of playing with words?

'Surely he can't just back out of a commitment at this late stage,' she was driven to protest.' Even an informal one?'

'I imagine that even if it had been a legal commitment he would have been within his rights to change things,'

6

her father replied, and of that she had no doubt. But she would have been a lot happier if that had been the case. If only he had told her the truth. A gentlemen's agreement, indeed! She could hardly believe it. Two dear old-fashioned gentlemen, friends doing business together on a handshake; it had been bound to lead to disaster, Fizz fumed helplessly.

And the radio station franchise was up for renewal within months. If they failed to meet their programming agreement it was possible that they would lose it. Worse, since the relaxation of ownership rules, they were wide open to a takeover bid themselves. She knew of one consortium that had already bought up several nearby stations and was turning out anonymous pop music, so that without the station idents it was almost impossible to tell who you were listening to.

The whole concept of independent broadcasting by local people for local people was beginning to look very shaky. She had been so determined to make her station different, special. With the help of her family and the generous support of Michael Harries she had succeeded. And now, just when she had expanded her business base in order to make the station self-supporting, to avoid having to rely so heavily on sponsorship, she was suddenly in danger of losing it all.

'What will happen to Michael?' she asked, in an effort to keep her own troubles in perspective. 'Will he be all right?'

'He was putting a brave enough face on it – going on about how glad Alice is that he's retiring early, how great it will be to spend the winter at his place in the Algarve and play golf all day. But you know how he felt about the plant. He loved it. Every brick of it and everyone who worked there.'

And now it was owned by some anonymous financier who wouldn't care tuppence about the generations of lives invested in it, wouldn't care about anything except a snappy return on his investment.

She dropped the letter on her desk and walked across to the window, rubbing at the cold glass misted with their breath. The view of the bay curving away into the distance, the town nestling beneath the hills and the sea in all its moods rarely failed to inspire her even on glowering winter days, when the waves battered remorselessly against the pier. But today the sea and sky were uniformly grey, the hills blotted out by cloud, the town misted by a heavy drizzle. February at its most dreary.

'What do you think he means by changes?' she asked finally, turning back to face her muddled little office. It always looked so much worse on the rare occasions when her father deigned to climb the stairs from his own, far more opulent office on the mezzanine floor. Her father, her sister, her dead mother – all had that same star quality that eclipsed everyone and everything they stood near, making the rest of the world look just plain shabby.

'I don't know. Maybe this Devlin fellow just wants to put things on a regular footing,' he suggested hopefully.

'And if he doesn't? If he just wants to be rid of us? Can we fight it?' She had to face the possibility. It was far more than a possibility. Then, as her father's shoulders slumped uncharacteristically, she was sorry she had asked. He obviously felt bad enough without her rubbing salt in the wounds.

'How much can the station stand, Fizz?'

She gave a little shrug. 'The sports coverage and *Holiday Bay* are the major items of expenditure. Given time I might be able to put together a package, but there isn't another local company who could take on the sole sponsorship of one of those, let alone both. Not right now. Not at such short notice.'

'But you can't drop them, Fizz,' he warned. 'It was part of our franchise agreement. Live drama and live sport. It gave us the edge over the competition, and the Radio Authority could fine you or decide against renewal this summer if you drop them.'

'It might not take that long. We still have staff contracts, salaries to pay.' And then there was the loss of advertising revenue. Even if they could drop the programmes, it wasn't a solution.

'Is there any money left from the bank loan?'

'Not to spare. There are enough bills from building contractors to paper my office walls . . .'

'Just as well it's so small, then,' her father said, in an effort to make a light of the situation.

She conceded a smile. 'Yes, I suppose so.' Very small and very shabby. She wasn't a star and she didn't need a glamorous setting in which to shine. 'But it's the bank loan that will be the main problem. If only I hadn't gone ahead with the restaurant. If I'd waited another year . . .'

She let it go. Her father had no interest in the financial side of the station. He lent his name and his stature to Pavilion Radio; the rest was up to her.

'You just need a good season, Fizz,' her father said, trying to be kind.

He continued to run on optimistically, but she wasn't listening; she was too busy trying to think. In a worst-case scenario, assuming Harries's sponsorship was totally withdrawn, it would take a lot more than optimism to keep them going. It would need a great deal of patience and understanding from Julian, the young merchant banker who had been so flatteringly eager to provide the loan for the new restaurant in the restored Pavilion. Flatteringly eager to take their relationship rather further than banker and client, if Fizz had given him any encouragement. Her sigh was imperceptible.

It had seemed such a brilliant idea – how could it possibly fail? They already had an informal chat and music show live from the foyer of the Winter Garden every morning in the summer season and on Saturdays in the winter. It had seemed so simple to capitalize on an audience already in a happy mood, to offer good food with the best view in Broomhill Bay and a gift shop full of locally made souvenirs – including their own Pavilion Radio merchandise to spread the word.

It would make money, she knew it would, but it would take time. She had worked so hard and it had all been going so well. If they could hold on until Easter came, bringing the first visitors . . .

She turned to stare once more at the letter on her desk, then picked it up. 'Devlin has asked you to phone him. Have you done that?'

'Not yet. I thought you should do it.'

'Me? Don't be silly, he'll gobble me up and spit me

out. I'll come with you, of course, but it's probably better that he thinks he's dealing with you.' After all, everyone else thought she was station manager in name only, that she had been given the job by her father because he felt sorry for her. Because she didn't have the talent of her glamorous big sister. Because she was the only Beaumont who couldn't act.

She preferred it that way. And her father's sheer physical presence was usually sufficient to mesmerize people into doing what he wanted. Her father's expression now suggested he had other plans. 'At least until we can work out what his mood is,' she wheedled.

'Fizz, darling, I'm up to my eyes with the joint schools' production of *Much Ado* just at the moment. And my new television series is facing a bit of a crisis.'

'What kind of crisis?'

'Financial. What other kind is there? A couple of the backers have pulled out. I've got to find someone else or put up the money myself.' In other words, Fizz thought, don't ask *him* to help with the cash flow.' And Claudia telephoned last night in a bit of a state over the film with Sean Deveraux, so I've really got to go up to town today – '

'Dad, please!'

'Look, darling, I know absolutely nothing about running the station, and a man like Devlin will see through me in a second. I really think it would be better if you went up there and put all your cards on the table. Michael trusted your judgement, why shouldn't he?'

Michael had just lost the company his family had built from nothing. It wasn't much of a reference. Her father had picked a hell of a time to step back and leave her to prove she could handle it.

Hidden away in her office, she managed the station, made decisions, produced the ideas that kept the advertisers happy. Only two or three people knew the truth, that Pavilion Radio had been her idea. It was her baby, and like all babies it was hard work, but she loved it. The hardest work of all had been to convince a bunch of hard-nosed bankers that they should lend her the money to develop the restaurant. With her father at her side to give the bankers confidence she had pulled it off. But she had known exactly what was required that day. Facing the unknown on her own was something else . . .

'He probably just wants to be buttered up by the famous Edward Beaumont. That might be all it would take,' she said quickly, well aware that her father had a weakness for flattery. 'Even the most hard-boiled businessmen have their weak spots.'

'If he was a hard-boiled business*woman*,' he joked, 'I might be of some use to you. As it is I'm just an old ham actor. If you hadn't coached me I would never have convinced those bankers that I knew what that restaurant deal was all about.'

'I can coach you again,' she pleaded, feeling the tide of panic rising to her throat. She didn't want to step out into the spotlight. He couldn't expect it. She still needed time.

'You're the brains behind this outfit, Fizz. You don't need me, you know. You can do it if you let yourself.' He reached out, lightly touched her cheek. 'And your face is so much prettier than mine – I'm sure you'll be far more

12

effective at buttering him up than I could ever be.' He glanced at his watch. 'Of course, if you need me I'll try and help, but I must go now.' Pausing in the doorway, he turned to her. 'You know this is your station, Fizz. You made it what it is. It's up to you to fight for it.'

She stared at the door he had so carefully closed behind him. Had there been an almost audible snip as he had cut the umbilical cord? He had been pushing her for months, insisting that when the licence came up for renewal she must publicly take on the role of chief executive of Pavilion Radio. She had resisted, preferring to hide beneath her father's famous name, to let him step forward to take the applause and the praise and the awards that occasionally came their way.

Now he was using this crisis to drive her out into the open, make her fight for her station, because no one else was going to do it for her. It was her baby that was being threatened and, knights in shining armour being thin on the ground these days, a girl had to fight her own battles.

Slowly she sank into her chair and reached for the telephone. Gripping the receiver until her knuckles whitened, she dialled the number at the top of the letterhead.

'Good morning, Harries Industries. How can I help you?'

'Good morning. This is Felicity Beaumont calling from Pavilion Radio,' she said, investing her voice with a confidence she was far from feeling. 'I would like to speak to Mr Luke Devlin.'

If it had been Luke Devlin's intention to make life as difficult as possible for Felicity Beaumont, he could not have chosen a better time to drop his bombshell.

'Miss Beaumont?'

Fizz immediately recognized the smooth tones of the local bank manager on the line. 'Mr Nicholson, what can I do for you?'

'Deposit the sponsorship cheque from Harries Industries?' he suggested, without bothering with the niceties of polite conversation.

She had been expecting the call. The takeover had been reported on their own news programmes in great detail, as well as in all the local newspapers. Speculation about redundancies and cuts was rife and the town had a jittery air which had inevitably infected the radio station. Several times in the last week staff had abruptly stopped talking when she entered a room.

'There *is* going to be a sponsorship cheque, isn't there?' Nicholson continued. 'It's ten days until the end of the month, and I don't have to remind you that the salaries will take you a long way over your overdraft limit.'

'I am aware of that, Mr Nicholson, and I have a meeting scheduled with Mr Devlin later this week to confirm the details of Harries's sponsorship with the new management.' More truthfully, she was still waiting to speak to the wretched man, and if her fingers had been crossed any more tightly they would have broken. 'I don't anticipate any difficulties.'

She winced as she replaced the receiver. She hated lying, but she needed time. Despite her determination to see Luke Devlin at the first possible moment, his secretary had been evasive about an appointment,

14

merely assuring Fizz that he would be told of her call. She could do nothing but wait and gather her ammunition.

She had checked and double checked the portfolio that had convinced the financiers to loan her the money for the restaurant and gift shop, and had scrutinized the photographs of what was now an expensive reality. There were pages of careful costings and conservative estimates of return on investment, and she had a sheaf of more photographs and news cuttings showing sponsorship banners at sporting events and listening figures for *Holiday Bay*.

She hadn't wasted her time while she waited. She had been looking for alternative sources of sponsorship from likely companies. But the reaction was the same from everyone. With the future of Harries Industries in question, no one could afford to be relaxed. They were the largest employer in the area, and any cutbacks would hurt local businesses. The station's invoices for the January sales ads wouldn't be sent out by the advertising agencies until the end of the month. Not that anyone would be in a hurry to pay them.

She glared at the phone. 'Ring,' she instructed it. 'Go on, damn you, ring!' It immediately responded with a low burble, and for one disbelieving second she stared at it. Then as it rang again she snatched it up. It was her father.

'I was just checking to see if you had managed to speak to Mr Devlin yet.' He was a good actor, but even so she could detect the note of anxiety on her behalf that had crept into his voice.

'Not yet,' she said, rather more brightly than she actually felt. 'I suppose we must come pretty low on his list of priorities right now. I'll let you know as soon as anything happens.'

'Well, it's in your hands, Fizz.'

Yes, she thought, putting down the receiver. That had been made more than clear to her. But she wasn't complaining. Her father had already done enough, helped her to pull back from the abyss . . . The telephone rang again.

'Fizz Beaumont,' she said, matter-of-factly.

'Good morning, Miss Beaumont. Luke Devlin returning your call.' His voice was cool, distant and not particularly encouraging. He must know why she was calling but he waited, leaving her to do all the work.

She forced her face into a smile, knowing that it would come through in her voice. 'Thank you, Mr Devlin, that's most kind of you, when I know you must be very busy. I received your letter – '

'Did you?' he interrupted smoothly. 'That's odd, I don't recall having written to anyone called Fizz Beaumont. It seems unlikely that I would forget such an unusual name.'

Fizz could have kicked herself. Instead she forced laughter into her voice, congratulating him on his wit. 'I meant, of course, the letter you sent to my father. Since I am the station manager and deal with all financial matters, he naturally passed it straight on to me.'

'I see.' The words conveyed a world of understanding – that her father had been less than polite in passing on his letter to a subordinate, that he, Luke Devlin, wasn't

16

used to dealing with chits of girls when it came to business. And there was something more that she couldn't quite put her finger on.

She dropped the laughter. It clearly hadn't impressed him one bit. 'My father is deeply involved with the city's schools theatre at the moment, as well as other projects that have first call on his time. He prefers to leave all financial matters to me.'

'Even when they concern the fate of his radio station? Dare I suggest that excessive sponsorship has made him just a little flabby in his attitude?' Again there was that dismissive edge to his voice. Fizz felt the slow burn of anger darken her cheeks.

'The fate of Pavilion Radio concerns him very deeply, Mr Devlin. He could come along and give you a convincing portrayal of a high-powered business tycoon if you feel that is your due. But that's all it would be. A performance. He did you the courtesy of assuming you would want to deal with someone who actually knows what they are talking about.'

'And you do?' Once again she caught the undercurrent in his voice. Dislike? She drew the fine arched wings of her brows together in a puzzled frown, but he gave her no time to dwell on the possibility or wonder at it. 'Well, since you have been nominated as spokesperson, Miss Beaumont, I suppose you will have to do. Please be at my office at twelve o'clock.'

'On which day?' she asked, excessively polite.

'This day, Miss Beaumont. If I had meant any other I would have said so.' And with that, he hung up.

Fizz was shaking. So much for putting her cards on the

table and dealing with the man in an honest and straight-forward manner. He had wanted to speak to her father and considered her second best. She opened her mouth to tell the four walls of her office exactly what she thought of Mr Luke Devlin but thought better of it. Instead she replaced the receiver. She had no time for such nonsense. It was nearly eleven and the ring road would be packed with traffic at this time of day.

And she had to change.

She had dressed for the ice-house temperature of her office in the roof of the old Winter Garden, where the heating never seemed to penetrate with any real enthusiasm. She wore thick corduroy trousers, a flannel shirt and an Aran sweater with frayed cuffs that she had bought for fifty pence at a jumble sale. While she was hidden away in her office at the end of the pier her eskimo garb went unnoticed by anyone but the station staff, who were used to it, but it would hardly impress Mr Luke Devlin. She came from a family of actors and was well aware of the importance of putting on a show, wearing the right costume for the part.

The pinstriped business suit that she had borrowed from her sister to wear during her negotiations for the loan with the bank was hanging behind her office door in readiness for Luke Devlin's summons. It had given her the confidence to get through the ordeal of presenting her plans to a group of dubious bankers, hopefully it would carry her with equal success through the coming interview.

Determinedly ignoring the cold, she stripped off her outer garments and stood in her navy stockings and silk teddy, peering into the old cracked mirror fastened alongside the door while she refreshed her make-up and tidied her hair. Then she stepped into the skirt, fastened the jacket about her, slipped into her high-heeled shoes and turned to check her rear view.

Regarding her reflection, Fizz was regretfully aware that the suit didn't have quite the same sharp elegance on her as it had on her sister. But then, she thought, pulling a somewhat rueful face at herself, what did? It wasn't that she was short. Five feet seven inches was a respectable enough height. But Claudia had obeyed Nanny's injunctions to eat her crusts to be sure that her hair would curl and her cabbage for a perfect complexion, and she had drunk up her milk in order to grow straight and tall so that one day she would be a beautiful and famous actress like their mother.

Two years younger, Fizz clearly hadn't tried anywhere near as hard. Not that there was anything wrong with her appearance. Her complexion was fine, apart from a few faint freckles that never disappeared even in the dead of winter, and, although she'd somehow missed out on the curls, she was perfectly happy with the thick chestnut hair that she had twisted into a neat, businesslike chignon. But, although she would never have worn the skirt as short as Claudia did, Fizz was human enough to envy her sister those extra three inches.

Just before twelve, she parked in front of the impressive head office of Harries Industries, running through in her head the convincing little speech that she had been preparing since she had received that bombshell of a letter.

19

It was reasonable, thoughtful, understanding. She would invite Mr Devlin to come and visit the station, see for himself the impressive scheduling, the ties with community projects, the fact that their local sports coverage had won an award that had reflected handsomely on Harries Industries. If he would just give her the chance to make it, she thought, uneasily aware of a distinct feeling that Mr Devlin might not be in the mood to listen to her well-rehearsed arguments. She took a deep breath and headed for the main entrance.

There was a glossy new receptionist in the entrance hall. It hadn't taken long for the new brooms to get to work. 'Can I help you?' the girl enquired, with a professional smile.

Fizz smiled back equally professionally. She had convinced herself she was playing a part and she was glad of a dummy run. 'Felicity Beaumont. Mr Devlin's expecting me.' She signed the visitors' book and while she clipped on a little label that identified herself as such she smiled at the new girl and asked, 'What happened to Edith?'

'Edith?'

'She was the receptionist here for ten years.'

'Oh?' The girl wasn't interested. 'Maybe she took early retirement.'

A secretary looked up from her desk as she entered the chairman's suite of offices. Another new face. Older this time. Michael's secretary had probably taken the same fast track to retirement as Edith. 'Felicity Beaumont,' she said, announcing herself once again. 'I have an appointment – '

'Oh, yes, Miss Beaumont. Please take a seat.' The telephone rang and the woman answered it, listened briefly, then without further acknowledgement of Fizz gathered her notebook and swept out of the suite.

Fizz waited. Ten minutes passed while her nerves frayed, began to unravel, to disintegrate. She began to rehearse her presentation silently to keep her mind occupied. Fifteen minutes. When her watch informed her that it was twenty minutes after twelve o'clock, she knew that it was deliberate.

The man was nothing but a petty little tyrant, she decided, taking pleasure in demonstrating his power. His manner on the telephone had already betrayed his negative attitude towards her and her father. It was almost as if he felt some personal animosity towards them. But that was patently ridiculous. He was obviously just a thoroughly unpleasant man.

Fizz got up and began to walk around the office, taking deep, calming breaths, concentrating on the paintings that decorated the wall, refusing to let the man wind her up with such an obvious tactic. But it took a serious effort of will to uncurl her fingers from the tight little fists that she had unconsciously made of her hands. She was staring at a painting of the pier, constructed in 1835 by the first Michael Harries for the shipment of their goods to the continent, when the door behind her opened.

She turned quickly to face the man who held all their destinies in the palm of his hand, but there was nothing in his appearance to reassure her. His thin, humourless face had the pallor of a man who spent his time hunched over columns of figures under artificial light. He looked as if he had a calculator for a brain and he probably hadn't listened to a radio since the transistor had been invented. But it was her job to convince him of the importance of his support.

Fizz advanced swiftly over the thick carpet before she quite lost her nerve, and extended her hand. 'Felicity Beaumont,' she said, introducing herself confidently with her warmest smile.

'Yes?' He clutched a pile of folders in both his hands and made no move to respond to her gesture.

And he managed with that one dismissive word to make her feel both foolish and angry all at once. Letting her hand fall to her side, she continued to smile even though she thought her face would crack with the effort. 'You asked me to be here at twelve,' she reminded him. 'I realize you must be very busy.' She resisted the temptation to check her watch, to remind him that it was now nearly half past the hour. That would not be a good start.

But he wasn't listening. 'Where is Mrs Meynell?' he asked, irritated.

'Your secretary?' Fizz guessed, trying hard to remain cool in the face of such rudeness. 'She went out a few minutes ago.' He began to retreat into the office. 'Mr Devlin,' she said quickly, before he could disappear again.

'Yes, what is it?' She hadn't known quite what to expect from this man who gobbled up companies for breakfast, but she had imagined someone . . . well . . . larger in body and spirit. Maybe she'd just been hoping for that.

22

'I'm sorry my father can't be here to talk to you in person, but I did explain the reason. And you did ask me come and see you.' She indicated the portfolio lying on the chair beside her. 'Please let me show you what we are doing at Pavilion Radio before you make up your mind to stop sponsoring the – '

'Miss Beaumont, I'm afraid that you are labouring under some misapprehension. I cannot help you,' he said, and turned away, heading back towards his office.

That was it? No chance to put her case, just a few words exchanged in a secretary's office? Oh, no. Not good enough. Not nearly good enough. 'Won't you at least listen to me?'

The man stopped with a sigh, clearly out of patience with her as he regarded her slightly flushed cheeks, the way her breast rose and fell a little too rapidly beneath the smooth navy cloth of her suit. 'I suggest you save your appeals for those foolish enough to listen, Miss Beaumont. I really haven't the time to waste on such nonsense.' With that he disappeared into the office, and for a single shocked moment Fizz remained where she was.

It was a long time since she had come so perilously close to losing her temper. Really losing it and demonstrating the aptness of her pet name, which had started as her sister's lisping attempt at Felicity and stuck because of her habit of going off like a rocket when her emotions were inflamed. Yes, it was a long time since she had lost her temper, but the bubble of outrage that now rose to her throat warned her that she was still quite capable of exploding.

What on earth did the man think he was playing at? He had invited her to his office, kept her waiting interminably and then dismissed her without even the pretence of listening, the courtesy of a hearing. And he had the nerve to criticize her family's manners!

She didn't stop to consider the wisdom of her actions. She had nothing to lose and she certainly wasn't leaving without giving this man the benefit of her opinion. Snatching up her portfolio, she followed him through the pair of tall, ornately carved doors that guarded his sanctum and closed them behind her with a sharp click. Halfway across the vast room he turned, clearly startled by her presumption, but she gave him no time to protest before she launched her attack.

'I realize that a gentlemen's agreement means very little these days, Mr Devlin. But you asked me to come here and the very least you can do is listen to what I have to say.' Fizz launched herself into her ardent plea, her large indigo eyes sparkling as she warmed to her theme.

'Pavilion Radio has given this town real local radio – news, documentary reports, sport, natural history programmes about local ecology, good investigative reporting. It's given the people a voice, and no other independent station has a wider range of programmes. No other station of its size has its own local soap opera, or children's programmes – '

'I have no children,' he interrupted indignantly. 'And if you're so successful I don't see why you need sponsorship at all. If you can't pay your own way . . .' He made a dismissive gesture, clearly considering the matter beneath his lofty attention.

Fizz snapped. She had spent three miserable days poring over her figures, trying to cut everything to the bone. But the truth of the matter was that there was only bone left.

'You might be a brilliant businessman, Mr Devlin,' she said, 'and very plump in the pocket. But I have to tell you that you're very thin in the heart.' The man's eyes did not even flicker, but in any case she was beyond stopping. 'Well, I hope you're happy counting your money. I hope that it will keep you company when the Scrooge mentality has won, and local radio is reduced to endless pop music and the pier has crumbled into the sea. Because it will be your fault. And I'll make sure everyone in this town knows it.'

For a moment after she had finished speaking there was utter silence. Then a slow hand-clap from the door made her spin around, and for a fraction of a second, it seemed, her heart actually stopped.

Then it happened. Light the blue touch paper and stand back. Fizz. Whoosh. Rockets. Catherine wheels. Roman candles. Her insides lit up like a firework display.

The man whose square shoulders appeared to fill the opening was somewhat taller than average, six feet two or three, maybe, and although he was still some way short of his fortieth year there was no doubting the air of authority that sat on his shoulders as easily as the smooth cloth of his elegantly cut grey tweed suit.

His hair, thick, straight, almost black, was brushed back from his face to expose a wide forehead and dark brows that jutted over a pair of slate-grey eyes. His mouth, when it smiled, would be wide, and the lines etched into his cheeks would deepen in a way that would warm the coldest heart.

But he wasn't smiling now. Although a certain sardonic glint in those eyes suggested that he might have gained just a little amusement from her indignant outburst.

'Don't call us and we promise we'll never call you,' he said as he moved away from the door and walked towards her. Rooted to the spot, Fizz remained seemingly bereft of the power of speech while he walked slowly around her, apparently fascinated by the severity of her business suit.

'You've dressed for the role, I grant you,' he said. 'But it takes more than a costume to play a part. And someone should have warned you that there's no room for emotion in business. Tell me, Miss Beaumont, what production was that thrilling speech adapted from? *Little Nell*? *Maria Marten and the Red Barn*? It certainly had all the elements of melodrama.' He paused and finally looked straight down into her eyes. 'Or do I mean farce?'

CHAPTER 2

'Luke. Thank goodness. Will you explain to this young woman that I am not interested in her radio station. I tried to explain, but she wouldn't listen.'

'Don't worry, Phillip. If you'll give us a few minutes, I'm sure I can persuade her to listen to me.'

Luke? *This was Luke Devlin?* Fizz paled, shivering despite the warmth from a more than adequate heating system. She had no idea who the small, grey man letting himself quietly out of the office might be; she knew only that he was not Luke Devlin. And that she had just made an exceptionally large fool of herself – a fact the disturbing man at her side immediately confirmed.

'I'm sorry that the bulk of your performance was wasted on the wrong person, but Phillip is using my office while we decide the future of Harries Industries.' He didn't look sorry. 'I have been told that your father occasionally broadcasts drama on Pavilion Radio. If that was a demonstration of the standard he aspires to, Miss Beaumont, then perhaps the sooner the franchise moves into more professional hands, the better.'

Professional hands? What the hell did that mean? She

made a supreme effort to close her mouth. Devlin was not the kind of man to be won over by her impression of a goldfish out of water. But the fact that he had managed to deprive her of the power of speech twice in as many minutes was a bonus. She loathed rudeness and this man had studied under experts. His rudeness made it so much easier to quell her treacherous body's leaping response to that first elemental power-charge. 'I'm not an actress,' she protested. 'I'm – '

'On that, at least, we are in total agreement,' he agreed, cutting smoothly across her. 'Although the possibility that you were just being yourself is, if anything, even more appalling.'

Fizz opened her mouth to protest that every word she had spoken had come from the heart. But, having paused at the sight of him, that same heart was now galloping in a wild and furious attempt to make up for lost time. The man had simply taken her breath away. Not with his words, although they were bad enough, but there was a rock-hard, unyielding quality about him. And she felt as if she had just run into him at ninety miles an hour.

'You are Luke Devlin.' It wasn't a question. Merely a gambit, an attempt to gain a moment to catch her breath. She had immediately sensed the man's power and now it was clear that he was a two-fold threat. She buried her fear in attack. 'Then why on earth didn't *he* say who he was, instead of letting me blather along?'

'Did you give him the opportunity?'

Fizz felt her cheeks tingle slightly as they responded to this challenge with a blush. *A blush*. This was getting serious. Furious with herself for betraying her discomfort, for letting the situation run away from her and giving him control of the conversation, she attempted to justify her mistake. 'When I called him Mr Devlin he responded,' she said simply.

'That is because we share the same name. Phillip is my cousin. Like the Beaumonts, we Devlins value family ties.' But the twist to his lips suggested that any similarity between his family and hers was purely coincidental. He glanced at the desk piled high with files and littered with spreadsheets, then gestured to a sofa near the window, indicating that she should sit down. 'You *are* Felicity Beaumont?' he continued, when she didn't move. 'Fizz,' he added thoughtfully.

'Two cases of mistaken identity in one afternoon would be pushing coincidence a little far, don't you think?'

'Yes, definitely a Beaumont,' he murmured. 'Your manners betray your origins.'

'And keeping someone waiting for the best part of half an hour is the height of politeness?' she snapped back.

His sharp look warned her that she was pushing her luck. 'A deputation from the staff had asked to speak to me. I took the view that their concerns were more important than yours. Perhaps you disagree with my judgement?'

Fizz positively cringed with embarrassment. The situation had been had enough to start with and she had already made it considerably worse by berating some anonymous accountant. No, not anonymous. Another Devlin, as if one wasn't enough. And now trying to score a cheap point had only made her look stupid. 'No,' she said quickly. 'Of course they were far more important.'

'I'm glad you realize that. Understanding what requires urgent attention and what can be dealt with at leisure is a skill that anyone in business neglects at their peril, Miss Beaumont. Perhaps you should remind your father of that fact.'

Beneath the professional smile she cursed her father. Why on earth had he had to choose this particular moment to throw her into the deep end? If he'd come to the meeting he would have distracted Luke Devlin, given her a moment to study the man, work out what made him tick. 'As I explained, he is very busy – ' she began.

'Too busy to lift a telephone? Spare an hour of his time?'

'He's directing a joint schools production of *Much Ado About Nothing*,' she offered. It was a lame excuse. She knew it.

Devlin's expression suggested that he was of the same opinion. 'A schools production? And that takes the great Edward Beaumont every minute of his day? Or am I supposed to be impressed with his altruism? The Harrieses and the Beaumonts. Public benefactors incorporated, with the town stitched up between them.'

'It's not like that,' she said, indignant on her father's behalf and Michael's. 'I just meant – ' But he wasn't listening to excuses.

'That's just as well. I know very little about the theatre, but I do know that it isn't a twenty-four-hour a day job. He would impress me far more by spending his time managing his business.' His hostility had an astringent quality that stung her, clearing her head like a blast from a bottle of smelling salts.

'He's an actor, Mr Devlin. *That* is his business. The radio station is mine.'

His eyes flickered over her, missing nothing. 'I'm afraid it will take more than padded shoulders to convince me that you know what you're talking about.'

She opened her mouth to protest, then closed it again. She hadn't come here to argue with the man, but to impress him with her business acumen. So far she had made a lousy job of it.

As if to confirm this, Luke Devlin continued irritably. 'For goodness' sake sit down, Miss Beaumont. Now you're here, you might as well say your piece. I'm sure you've been rehearsing for days, but I won't be performed at.'

Despite the lack of warmth with which it was offered, this wasn't an invitation Fizz was about to refuse. Presented with a second chance to state her case there was no point in dwelling on the bad start she had made. Instead she made herself smile. It wasn't as hard as she had expected. 'If I had thought you wanted a performance, Mr Devlin, I would have sent my sister. She's the actress.'

'So I understand.' There was a slightly ironic twist to his voice. 'I look forward to meeting her some time soon.'

Meeting her? That sounded promising. And the sooner the better. Claudia would pull out all the stops for a man like Luke Devlin. In the meantime Fizz wasted no time in obeying Luke Devlin's instruction to sit down, quickly lowering herself onto one end of the sofa.

Its smooth leather exterior was deceptive. The horrid thing swallowed her up, leaving her struggling for her dignity with a skirt that in the mirror had seemed demure enough but was suddenly far too short. Or may be it was just that her legs had rather more thigh than she'd realized.

Luke Devlin relieved her of the portfolio she was still clutching awkwardly and occupied the far corner of the sofa, settling back with the ease of a man perfectly at home with himself and his surroundings. Fizz, struggling with her skirt, wished that she was still wearing her comfortable cords; the suit certainly hadn't made the hoped-for impression. Quite the opposite.

As he flipped through the contents of the folder, outwardly oblivious to her difficulties, she could have sworn that behind that detached expression Mr Devlin was positively enjoying her discomfort. But when he looked up, eyes the colour of rain-soaked slates levelled at her expectantly, his thoughts were unreadable, and Fizz made a mental note never to play poker with the man.

She caught her bottom lip between her teeth. Her mind was wandering again. She didn't have the faintest clue how to play poker. And the idea of playing anything with Luke Devlin was so immediately disturbing that she switched the thought off before it could get out of hand.

'Mr Devlin, you know why I'm here,' she said, dismayed to discover that suddenly her voice was more breath than substance.

'You're here to part me from my money,' he said matter-of-factly.

'I'm here to convince you to continue this company's support of Pavilion Radio,' she replied evenly, refusing to be put off.

'Right now this company doesn't have any money spare to support anyone or anything but itself.' He glanced at his watch. 'But you have fifteen minutes of my time so I suggest you don't waste any more of it.'

Despite his lack of encouragement, Fizz felt the tiniest surge of optimism. Luke Devlin was clearly not a man to prevaricate. If he had decided to cut their sponsorship completely, he would have said so and shown her the door. He wouldn't have wasted even fifteen minutes of his time. He would simply have stated the position in a letter and told his secretary to keep her out of his hair.

Hope blossomed and she resisted the urge to give her skirt another sharp tug. Saving the station from financial disaster was far more important than her dignity. And if a couple of extra inches of thigh would help, she wasn't about to begrudge them.

Instead she briefly outlined the history of her family's involvement with the pier – the disastrous storm that had put its viability in doubt and Michael Harries's determination to save it, calling on his old friend Edward Beaumont for support when it seemed that it might have to be demolished – and the idea of reviving the Pavilion, giving it new life as the studio for a local radio station.

'The idea was dreamed up by the two of them?' he asked.

Public opinion subscribed to that view. There didn't seem any point in disabusing him. 'Michael was excited by the idea. Did you know that it was the founder of

Harries Industries who built the pier in 1835? He used it originally to ship the goods made in his factory to the continent. Before that everything – passengers and merchandise – had to be ferried out to the cross-channel packets in rowing-boats,' she pointed out, but this attempt to win sympathy made no impression on Luke Devlin's lean, hard features, and she quickly ducked her head, leaning across to point out her projections for the next three years.

'What is this?' Luke Devlin pointed to a figure and their hands collided, his cool touch setting off a minor earthquake in her midriff. Fizz almost leapt back, and his curious look at this overreaction did nothing to calm the aftershocks that continued to reverberate through her body. It was ridiculous. Stupid. He might exude the kind of sexual magnetism that could be bottled, but she knew what that was worth. She didn't even like the man, for heaven's sake. 'Well?' he asked, apparently tired of waiting for her answer.

For a moment her mind went a complete blank. Then she dropped her eyes to the point where his fingertip rested lightly on the plan. 'Oh,' she said, collecting herself. 'That's new since we made our original projections to the bank. When we started the restaurant conversion we had to clear the storage area of a century of accumulated junk. We discovered we had far more space than we needed so we've leased part of it to a dance and fitness centre.'

'You've had to spend money on repairs and decoration,' he said, picking up the costs. 'You're not charging enough.'

'It's a new venture. The rent will be revised next year if it's successful.'

'And if it's not?'

'The initial response has been very good.'

He didn't seem impressed, but surely half a rent was better than none? The fitness centre brought people onto the pier to spend money even in the middle of winter, and the chef had ensured that the lunch time buffet in the restaurant included the kind of food that health-conscious women were looking for. Although it was amazing how many then fell for the temptations of calorie-laden puddings. Expensive calorie-laden puddings.

'What do you intend to do with the rest of the space?'

'I'm working on it.' She had hoped that the restaurant would be successful enough to expand into it, but it was too soon to voice that idea. She needed to see how the summer season went first.

He nodded thoughtfully. 'You don't appear to have missed anything.' He tossed the portfolio onto a nearby table. 'Except, of course, for the possibility that your cosy relationship with Michael Harries might not last.'

'I . . . That is, we . . . my father and I . . . hope that you will want to continue to support us for the coming year – or at least until we can find other sponsors.'

'I'm sure it's rather more than a hope. If you don't fulfil your programme commitments the Radio Authority is not going to look favourably on the renewal of your franchise,' he said. She was surprised he knew about the Radio Authority, or the way it worked. She was equally surprised that he was interested in the running of a very small radio station. But then she supposed a man didn't reach his dizzy heights of success without taking the smallest detail into account. And it was the small details that got you every time.

'Our programme commitments were made before you took over our sponsors,' she reminded him. 'The Radio Authority will understand our problems.'

'Will they?' He knew she was bluffing. 'Let us hope for your sake that they do, because the repayments on the bank loan for the new restaurant must be making heavy inroads into your profits. You have no experience of the restaurant business?'

The question was purely rhetorical. He knew the answer. It was clear that he knew all the answers. She had assumed he would be too busy with Harries to worry about the details of the radio station it sponsored, but it had been a mistake to underestimate the man. He wasn't too busy for anything that interested him. But why on earth should he be interested in Pavilion Radio? He was either going to support them or he wasn't. It couldn't be worth so much of his time.

'It's a little early in the season to start counting profits from that direction,' she replied, answering a question he hadn't asked. 'Although local reaction so far has been good.'

'Didn't it occur to you to lease it to someone who knew what they were doing? To let them take the risk?'

Of course it had. Once planning permission for the restaurant had been granted she had been inundated with offers from every kind of fast food chain wanting to install pizza parlours and burger bars. But she had wanted more than that.

'I wanted to keep it under my control, to provide something more than a repeat of every other cheap and cheerful seaside café. I've a first-class chef, an excellent staff – '

'And a wages bill to match, I have no doubt.'

'And as soon as the season begins – ' She ploughed on, refusing to be sidetracked, but Luke Devlin had other ideas.

'That's usually Easter isn't it? It's late this year, but I'm sure you've taken that into account.'

It was as late as Easter could be. Ten weeks away. Ten long weeks before the invasion of people eager to throw off winter. Seventy long days before the Easter holidays brought children bursting out of school and families down to the coast to fill the caravan parks and the guest houses. 'People will start arriving as soon as the weather picks up a little. The antique shops in the Wynds bring them long before it's warm enough to sit on the beach.'

'And why should they venture out along a cold and windy pier when the Wynds can offer them any number of attractive little bistros?' He leaned towards her, fixing her with a stare that pinned her back against the sofa. 'Let's drop the pretence, Miss Beaumont, and admit that without my support you're in deep trouble.'

It took all her self-control to keep her voice pitched low, thoughtful. 'The loss of sponsorship from Harries would be a serious blow, Mr Devlin. I would be a fool to pretend anything else. It will take time to find new sources of support and it's a setback. But since you kept your activities very discreet, and Michael preferred to keep his problems to himself, I had no reason to suspect anything was wrong. After all, if your takeover had been a week later, the money would have been in the bank right now.'

'You think you've just been the victim of bad timing?' He shook his head. 'Let me disabuse you of that fantasy. The truth of the matter is, Miss Beaumont, that if my . . . activities . . . had been delayed, even for a week, there would have been no money to put in the bank. In business, as in drama, timing is everything. And even a local radio station has to be run as a business if it's to survive.'

Fizz clamped down hard on her lip at this. That was precisely why they had needed to spend so much money on diversification . . . If only she had known, had been given some warning when things had started to go wrong . . .

'Yes, of course it must.' She lifted her chin a little. Luke Devlin was right. She should have known. It was her job to know that their sponsorship rested on a handshake, that their sponsor was about to go to the wall. 'As you can see from the figures, the reason for our expansion is to do precisely that. I wanted to give the station a broader base to avoid just this kind of difficulty.'

She remembered her intention to issue an invitation. 'Perhaps you would like to come and look around, see for yourself what we're doing? Saturday morning is always lively and you could have lunch with us in the new restaurant. As the station's guest, of course.'

'No. Thank you.' Those disconcerting eyes could apparently read her mind. 'Harries Industries is in trouble because the previous chairman ran it like a philanthropic society, and it will take considerable cost-cutting to put it back on its feet. It would be quite wrong of me to encourage you to squander your financial resources on entertaining me, since there is no possibility that I will change my mind once it is made up.'

Fizz swallowed. 'And is it made up?'

'Yes. It was made up long before you made your touching little speech.'

'I see.' Could she have been so wrong? Time was money to this man. Why would he have wasted it listening to her?

'I will continue with the sponsorship for the time being subject to certain conditions.'

'All of it?' The words escaped before she could bridle them as her heart performed a somersault of pure relief mixed with joy. The emotion was intense, but short-lived.

'You might not care to take it when you've heard my conditions,' he continued, in the same careless voice.

Conditions? 'Within the guidelines, we'll be happy to provide you with any additional advertising messages, of course – '

'Miss Beaumont, I have no doubt that you'd put my name in lights above the Pavilion if I asked it.'

'Only if the borough council approved,' she replied, unable to stop a grin from widening her generous mouth. She felt glorious, as if some great weight had been lifted from her shoulders, and she was perfectly willing to forgive him his earlier rudeness. Good grief, she'd walk on her hands down the pier, somersault its length if that would make him happy.

'I won't bother the borough council on this occasion,' he assured her. 'My conditions have nothing to do with advertising.' His voice, cool, distant, brought her crashing back to earth.

Conditions again. What a horrid word that was. She lifted her hand in a small gesture, inviting him to continue. 'Perhaps you'd better tell me exactly what you do want,' she suggested.

'As you must realize, Miss Beaumont, Harries is in no state to give money away.'

'It isn't entirely a one-way street,' she protested. 'The public relations aspect has been very valuable to Harries in the past. Perhaps you don't understand . . .'

'Don't I?' His voice hadn't changed much. Just the tiniest inflection to warn Fizz that she had said something rather silly. 'That argument might be a little subtle for the men and women who will be made redundant, don't you think?'

Her eyes widened. She hadn't realized things were so bad. 'Will there be many?' she asked. 'Redundancies?'

'I can't say until Phillip has made his report.'

His cousin? That dry, humourless man. She looked towards the door he had disappeared through. 'Then heaven help them,' she murmured.

'Phillip might not be your idea of fun, Miss Beaumont, but I can assure you he has a highly developed sense of what is right. He won't lightly waste a well-trained workforce.'

'I hope you're right.'

'In this instance you can trust me.' Fizz, fastened by his intent gaze, was compelled to believe that he meant exactly what he said. In fact, she was sure that he never said anything he didn't mean. And he had said that they could have their funding. She frowned slightly.

'And the sponsorship money? You said we could have it. Can I trust you in that instance too?'

His eyes mocked her doubtful tone. 'I am prepared to write you a cheque now. My personal cheque. And I can assure you that I won't require any public relations, corporate entertainment or personal publicity in return. Quite the reverse, in fact.' He paused briefly before adding. 'And if I do decide to visit your restaurant I will be more than happy to pay for my own lunch.'

Fizz wasn't fooled into heartstopping gratitude a second time. 'But there are conditions attached to your generosity?' Of course there were. Nothing about Luke Devlin suggested that he was simply an easy touch and she had a sudden ominous sense of foreboding. 'Conditions that I'm not going to like?'

For a long moment Luke Devlin said nothing, but subjected Fizz to an intense and level regard from the coolest pair of eyes she had ever seen. Clear, incisive, ransacking eyes that made her feel transparent. The eyes of a man who would be very hard to fool, and who would make you pay with everything you had if you ever succeeded.

She held his glance for as long as she could, matching his determination until she began to feel slightly dizzy, as if leaning over the edge of a precipice. 'I think you'd better tell me.'

He turned away abruptly, as if he too had found the intensity of that exchange uncomfortable. 'Perhaps, after

41

all, it would be better if I discussed it with your father. I'm sure that he will be able to take a less emotional view of my proposition.'

Edward Beaumont thrived on emotion, it was his life-blood, but Fizz didn't think it advisable to say so. Luke Devlin had used the word in a manner that suggested he didn't much approve of emotion. There was no place for it in business. He had said so. 'But he is not here, Mr Devlin,' she pointed out. 'I am. And I can assure you that I am fully empowered to make any decisions on behalf of Pavilion Radio.'

Her determination must have filtered through because he turned back to face her and she met his questioning glance head-on, determined not to be the first to back down this time. Fortunately he did not put her strength of will to the test, but after just a moment nodded. 'Very well.' But he didn't immediately explain his proposition. First he took a chequebook and fountain pen from his inside jacket pocket, then, casually propping one ankle on his knee and using his leg as a table, he proceeded to write a cheque, which he tore from the book and handed to her.

Fizz took it almost reluctantly, with a feeling of apprehension. Luke Devlin was showing her the money. Putting it into her hand. She recognized the technique. They both knew how hard it would be to give it back, no matter what he asked. He was banking on that and that made her nervous. It suggested that he thought she might say no. She glanced at the cheque and her heart sank further. It was nowhere near the level of sponsorship she needed.

'Cheer up, Miss Beaumont. That is just the first instalment.'

'Instalment?'

'I realize that in the past the sponsorship money was paid in a lump sum. However, this will help you to keep the bank manager happy.' And it would keep Luke Devlin in control, make sure that she kept him happy too.

'This is for one month? But that means you will be giving us more than Michael agreed – ' she began.

'The additional sum is to cover the cost of employing another member of staff.'

Fizz met his impassive gaze. 'Only one? It's an awful lot of money for one person.'

'Only one,' he confirmed. 'But I think you'll be happy enough to take her on.'

Her. Of course it would be a woman, but why on earth had Fizz's heart plummeted at the word? She should be relieved. She recalled the moment she had set eyes on him, her body's explosive reaction. She'd experienced that instant, almost cataclysmic sense of recognition only once before. She looked again at the cheque. At least if Luke Devlin was involved with someone who meant this much to him she would be safe from him. From herself.

'I think perhaps you had better explain exactly what you want in return for such overwhelming generosity,' she said.

He paused for just a moment. 'There is a young woman, Miss Beaumont. An actress. You may have heard of her. Melanie Brett.' He paused pointedly, clearly expecting some reaction. Not to have heard of her was apparently unthinkable.

43

Her forehead wrinkled in concentration as she tried to remember where she had heard the name. 'She's in one of those Australian soaps the teenage girls love so much, isn't she?'

'You admit to watching the opposition, Miss Beaumont?' Unexpectedly, he smiled. His mouth, as predicted, became wide, the lines drawn into his cheeks deepened, and as for being heartwarming it would have melted permafrost – a highly dangerous ability that could undermine the strongest foundations. Deep inside her she could almost hear the ice cracking.

'Of course,' she said quickly, determined to ignore the thaw. 'It's essential. Don't you keep up with your competitors?' She didn't wait for him to answer. Of course he did. 'Tell me about Melanie.'

'She arrived in England this morning.' He glanced at his watch. 'In fact she's due in Broomhill within the hour, which is why I'm on such a tight schedule myself. And she has expressed a wish to guest in your own little soap opera.'

'She wants a part in *Holiday Bay?*' To have said she was surprised would have been the understatement of the year.

'Just for the summer.'

Fizz laughed; she couldn't help herself. 'You're joking!'

His face remained impassive. 'Why should I joke about something that is going to cost me a small fortune?'

'But surely she'll be appearing on television while she's here? Doing the chat shows, that kind of thing?' He neither confirmed nor denied it. 'Oh, come on, Mr

Devlin, I don't believe she's even heard of *Holiday Bay*. I know the limits of our transmission, so you can't tell me she's been picking it up on her tranny in Australia.'

He responded to her disbelief with the faintest smile, the smallest shrug that confessed he had had his bluff called. 'Maybe not. But she'll be in Broomhill Bay for the summer and I don't want her to be bored.'

Relief that it was something so simple relaxed her face into a smile. There had been something about his manner that had made her certain he was going to ask for much more. Something impossible. Even so, it might not be as easy as he seemed to think.

'If you can organize a work permit for her, I'm sure we can fit her in. The publicity would be more than welcome.' With Melanie Brett in their daily soap they would be fighting off sponsors for the programme, not begging for them. Luke Devlin must know that. She quickly dropped her eyes in an attempt to conceal her excitement and looked again at the cheque. 'I'm afraid we can't possibly pay her this kind of money, though. It's strictly Equity rates at Pavilion Radio.'

'Although she has lived most of her life in Australia, Melanie was born in England and has a British passport. A work permit will not be necessary. And you'll pay her whatever I say you'll pay her.'

Fizz was puzzled. She had already agreed to take Melanie on board. Good grief, she'd be an idiot to refuse. 'We'll find a place for Miss Brett in the cast, Mr Devlin,' Fizz said very slowly, very carefully. 'But I meant what I said about Equity rates,' she continued, before he could interrupt. 'My sister, my father, every member of the cast is paid the same fee. I couldn't possibly allow any exceptions. You must see that.'

'Must I?' Cool, impassive, Mr Luke Devlin regarded her with mild amusement. But she refused to crumple. Claudia considered herself a star, and took part in *Holiday Bay* with grudging condescension only because Edward Beaumont insisted upon it. As it was, the scripts had to be written around the times she was available. If she discovered another, younger actress was being paid more than she was, she would walk out – and Fizz wouldn't blame her.

'Your interest in the show is really very flattering, Mr Devlin,' she said, with an attempt at a smile. 'And we'll be delighted to include Miss Brett . . .'

His smile was merely a display of strong white teeth. 'I never doubted it for a moment.'

'The problem is, I'm not quite sure why you feel you have to pay us for the privilege.' She made a small gesture with the cheque that now weighed like lead in her hand.

'All pleasures have to be paid for.'

Fizz was very glad that her cheeks were already pink, so that her blush shouldn't betray her. She remembered her initial relief that all this was to do with impressing a woman. But Melanie Brett? The girl was so young, so very tender for a man like Luke Devlin. Thirty-five or six years old, rockface-hard, he didn't seem to be the type to lose his head over a pretty face – at least not that of a girl very nearly young enough to be his daughter. Or maybe not. Some actresses specialized in playing teen-agers well into their twenties, and the episodes of her

46

soap currently being shown in England would be at least a year old.

Besides, it was absolutely none of her business. If he was so besotted that he would use his money and power to buy her what she wanted . . . well, she supposed it demonstrated a kind of humanity behind that ruthless exterior. Heaven alone knew that she could understand why Melanie Brett would be attracted to the man. She had once fallen head over heels herself for that heady mixture of dangerous good looks and sexual magnetism when she was too young to realize the dangers . . . and she had just learned that she still wasn't as immune as she had imagined herself to be.

'Anyway, I'm sure that the scripts will have to be rewritten, and that will involve you in some expense,' he pointed out.

'Well, yes. That's very thoughtful of you. I hope Melanie will be suitably grateful.' She swallowed – hard. She couldn't believe she'd said that.

But Luke Devlin apparently hadn't noticed her embarrassment. 'You'll find Melanie is very enthusiastic about radio – very keen to widen her experience in the medium.'

'There isn't a radio station in the country that wouldn't give her a guest spot, as I'm sure you know.'

'But I want her here with me, in Broomhill Bay,' he said, very softly. 'So it must be your lucky day, Miss Beaumont.'

Lucky? On the surface, maybe. Yet she preferred to suspend judgement on her luck for the present. She had the feeling that nothing was quite that simple where Luke Devlin was concerned.

'And Melanie greatly admires your father,' he continued smoothly. 'I believe he has something of a reputation for bringing on young actresses.'

Something about the way he said that set her teeth on edge. 'My father is a busy man,' she said quickly. 'He hasn't time for coaching.'

'Well, maybe once he's met her he'll make the effort to set a little time aside for her from his hectic schedule.'

'I'm sure she's charming, but I would advise against raising her hopes.'

'I could make it a condition of the sponsorship.'

'That, of course, is up to you.' That she didn't have any choice other than to accept such a condition she left unsaid. Unless something else turned up, and quickly, she would have to accept *any* condition he put on his generosity, and she had the uncomfortable feeling that Luke Devlin knew that as well as she did.

She wanted to run to the bank right now, pay in the cheque and make Mr Nicholson a happy man. But something, some inner voice, was urging her not to do anything without thinking very carefully about what he was offering and what he wanted in return. If he wanted Melanie on the show badly enough to pay for the privilege, a day or two wasn't going to make any difference.

'It's an interesting proposition, Mr Devlin,' she said finally, holding the cheque out to him. 'But I think it would be better if you kept this until I've spoken to my father.' Her hand remained extended, but he made no move to retrieve his cheque.

'So your boast that you have full authority to make

decisions is an idle one? I'm disappointed in you, Miss Beaumont. You've wasted my time.'

She refused to rise to his taunt. 'On the contrary. You have wasted mine. I came here to discuss finance. I'd be happy to accept the portion of your cheque dedicated to sports coverage . . . unless, of course, you know some other young person who is anxious to join the commentary team . . .?' His eyes gleamed dangerously, but he didn't answer. 'No, of course not. You did say just one extra member of staff. Unfortunately my father is the casting director of *Holiday Bay* and the decision must be his.'

'You'd better make sure that he knows it's a package deal, Miss Beaumont. The sponsorship and Miss Brett. You can't have one without the other.'

Somehow that didn't come as a surprise. She made a move to stand, but the sofa clung to her possessively. He ignored her plight.

'Then we must hope that my father is as enthusiastic about Melanie as we both are,' she said politely.

'Are you telling me that casting rests entirely upon merit? That it has nothing to do with finance?'

'*Holiday Bay* is a soap on a small, independent radio station, Mr Devlin. Hollywood it isn't. But courtesy requires that I speak to my father before I agree to this.'

'Courtesy? If that's all it is then we already have an agreement,' he replied, with the suspicion of a smile that sent her treacherous pulse cartwheeling. 'I'm sure you are bright enough to realize that there are occasions when artistic decisions are too important to be left to the artists. And even if you don't it's all academic anyway.

You are out on a limb, and I'm afraid that sooner rather than later someone will come along and saw it off.'

A threat? It sounded horribly like one. 'You?' she demanded. 'or are you simply content with providing the saw?'

'You climbed out along the branch all by yourself, Miss Beaumont. Does it really matter who lops it off?'

'It's really not as bad as that,' she said, with every appearance of calm conviction.

His smile deepened and she remembered, far too late, her earlier feeling that trying to deceive this man would be futile. It *was* that bad and somehow he knew it as well as she did. He knew too damned much. But for the moment he was generously prepared to give her the benefit of the doubt.

'I'll believe you, Miss Beaumont, if you'll just tear that cheque up,' he said. And he waited.

Fizz saw with a jolt that she had been wrong when she'd decided that Luke Devlin had no feelings. Quite wrong. He was actually enjoying this, she realized, her hackles rising dangerously at the thought of him playing with her, with the fate of her station.

As if he sensed her intention to tear the wretched cheque into a million pieces and consign it and him to the devil, he stretched out his hand and fastened long, cool fingers warningly about her wrist. 'I won't write another one, Felicity Beaumont, so I suggest you think twice before you do anything . . . melodramatic.'

It was almost as if he was determined to goad her, to sting her into an unwise retort. Why? She wanted to ask him, to demand that he tell her, but she had been imprudent enough for one afternoon. To lose her temper in the face of his disquieting authority just for the amusement of this infuriating man would be too shaming to bear.

Instead she managed a laugh – small, and little breathy, it was true, but still a laugh. She was driving herself beyond the limits today. Her own career as an actress might have been shortlived, but the techniques she had learned at RADA came in useful from time to time. When she wanted to hide emotion, for instance, or to cling onto her self-control, and at this moment they were both being tested to the limit of endurance.

'You're right, of course, Mr Devlin,' she said. 'But I'm afraid I couldn't impose this on my father without his agreement. He might not be prepared to accept it, and then we would be in real trouble.' She fervently hoped he hadn't noticed the tiny wobble in her voice. Sometimes technique alone was not enough.

'I'm glad you realize that,' he said, and he opened his fingers to release her hand.

She wanted to snatch it away. Instead she quietly laid it back in her lap, where it trembled very slightly from the sheer effort of holding onto the small slip of paper that represented the future of the station and all its employees. Tear it up? She might as well attempt to tear up a telephone directory.

'And if, as you boasted, it were your decision?' he persisted.

It *was* her decision, and hers alone, but she needed time to think. To work out what his motives were. *Holiday Bay* was a popular programme that more than

51

justified the hard work that had gone into it, but with Melanie Brett in the cast they would draw a vast teenage audience away from the national commercial stations. And that would be a tremendous boost for advertising.

The obvious choice would be to grab his money and run. But that was what bothered her most. He wasn't the kind of man who would pay for something that he could have had for nothing. There was something more to this than a simple trade-off.

He saw the conflicting emotions in her face. 'In the end, the toughest decisions have to be made alone, Felicity Beaumont,' he warned her. 'It divides the men from the boys. The winners from the losers. So? What do you say?'

CHAPTER 3

Luke Devlin did not wait for her answer but stood up and, apparently satisfied that he had made his point, magnanimously offered her his hand to help her to her feet. He didn't move back as she rose, so that she found the tip of her nose uncomfortably close to the smooth tweed lapel of his suit, her senses stirred by a combination of elusive masculine scents: good soap, the faintest woody top-note of expensive cologne, the rich leather interior of an expensive motor car.

He was playing power games with her, demonstrating that he was stronger than her in every sense. With the sofa tight behind her calves she was unable to retreat, to put some distance between them, and she felt trapped.

She was normally so careful to avoid any physical contact other than a handshake with men she did not know well, who did not understand the inviolate circle of space she kept around her. It made it easier to keep relationships distant, to avoid misunderstandings. But she had been angry when Luke Devlin had made his entrance and anger had shattered the protective bubble, made her vulnerable.

53

Now the cool touch of his hand as his fingers locked with hers was a jolting reminder of how different it had once been. A painful reminder that her skin had once tingled with excitement, that the clamour of her pulse had pounded in her ears, that longing had ached between her thighs.

An almost audible sigh of relief escaped her lips as he released her hand and stepped back to pick up her portfolio. The relief was shortlived as, his hand lightly at her back, he escorted her to the door. 'You have until next Friday, Miss Beaumont.'

Next Friday. Friday was the day the salary cheques would have to be signed and payment was due on the loan.

There was still that long, slow post-Christmas period to get through before the holiday season began – a time when local businesses traditionally cut advertising to the bone. And now the town was holding its collective breath, waiting to see what would happen at Harries. This couldn't have happened at a worse time. Did he know that? She risked a glance at his hard profile. Yes, she decided. Luke Devlin knew altogether too much.

She would have liked to know how he had got his information, but there was little point in asking him. He would simply smile, threatening the permafrost once more, and then he'd change the subject. Well, she would have to do her own homework. Find out everything she could about him. Maybe he had some weakness that she could use to her own advantage.

She caught herself. She had come out of the meeting with her sponsorship intact. It was far more than she had hoped for and his one condition could easily be coped with.

She should be happy. Over the moon. But she had a deep gut instinct that Luke Devlin was trouble. Not just because of her own almost overwhelming response to him – that was personal and she would have to deal with it – but something else . . . a feeling so nebulous that she could not have put it into words. She was probably being foolish, but happy was the last thing she felt.

She pulled herself together. 'Friday?'

'At twelve o'clock. You can give me your decision then.'

'I will. You'd better look after this in the meantime,' she said, offering him his cheque.

He smiled. Was it deliberate? she wondered. Did he know that when he made the effort to smile he radiated enough power to light up the national grid?

'I'd like you to keep it, Miss Beaumont. It will help you make up your mind.'

'No – '

He look it from her, folded it neatly in half and tucked it into the breast pocket of her suit. She swallowed, her entire body trembling as the pressure of his knuckles through the broadcloth brought her breast to singing life, bringing painful memories surging back from the place they had been buried so deep that she had almost managed to forget.

'You shouldn't do that,' she said hoarsely, her eyes firmly fixed on his tie. Burgundy. With the insignia of some professional organisation. Silk. Well it would be, wouldn't it?

One dark brow rose just a fraction. 'Do what?' he asked, as if he had no idea what his touch was doing to her, though she was sure he must be only too aware of her painful blush, of the stammering incoherence to which he was reducing her.

'Banks . . .' she began, but the word was more throat than voice.

'Banks?' he prompted gently.

Drat the man. He had apparently left her incapable of stringing a simple sentence together. She dug her nails hard into the palm of her hand.

'Banks,' she said, with almost grim determination, 'hate you to fold cheques. It messes up their electronic systems.'

'Really?' His fingers seemed to burn through the treacherous suit – heavy enough to keep out the cold and the wind, but no protection against his casual touch, and he knew it. His smile verged on an insult. 'I've never had any complaints.' She didn't think he was referring to banks. Was certain of it. God, the arrogance of the man. The sheer bloody nerve. She took a swift step back, retrieving herself from his mesmerizing touch.

'Are you that sure of yourself?' she enquired, her emotions veering wildly between a furious urge to slap his face and an equally urgent desire to rip her clothes off and pull him down with her onto the thick carpet and make violent love to him. Well, that would certainly wipe the smile off his face.

The thought provoked an almost overwhelming desire to giggle. In fact she realized she was in grave danger of hysteria. Taking a firm grip of herself, she asked, 'Aren't you afraid that I might pay it into the bank? Once the salaries are drawn and this month's loan repayment made, I won't be able to give it back to you if I change my mind.'

His mouth tightened into a thin, dangerous line and he dropped his hand to his side. 'I wouldn't advise anything so rash, Miss Beaumont.'

Tension finally overwhelmed her and she giggled. 'I was *joking*, Mr Devlin.'

'Were you, Miss Beaumont?' He handed her the portfolio, his eyes expressionless. 'I'll see you here on Friday at twelve. We'll see who's laughing then.'

Luke Devlin did not turn as the door opened behind him and his cousin joined him by the window. Fizz Beaumont was crossing the car park and the two men watched her. She had a natural, unstudied grace that even the stark lines of the pinstriped suit could not disguise.

'I'd say she's a bit of a handful on the quiet,' Phillip said, breaking the silence.

'Quiet?' A wry smile twisted Luke Devlin's mouth. 'That's generous, considering the way she went after you.'

Phillip shrugged. That wasn't what he had meant, and he was pretty sure that Luke knew it. 'She's a good-looking girl. Vivid.'

'She certainly wasn't what I expected,' Luke agreed, turning to watch as the old but still dangerous-looking sports car she drove roared throatily into life.

The report he had commissioned on the Beaumont family, now safely locked in his desk, had described

Felicity as being quite different from the rest of her family. She was apparently reserved, leading a quiet life mainly involving the radio station owned by her father, and had no theatrical ambitions. Having met the girl, he could certainly see that she wasn't like the rest of her family. But 'quiet' and 'reserved' seemed way off line.

Both her parents were well-known actors, famous for playing opposite one another in long-running West End hits and much loved by the public at large until her mother, Elaine French, had retired. Edward Beaumont's career had taken a downturn then, until Elaine's death had generated waves of public sympathy and the kind of publicity that had suddenly made Edward Beaumont good news.

Luke's mouth tightened as he recalled the newspaper clippings showing the apparently grief-stricken Edward at her graveside with his two daughters. Claudia, by then already making a name for herself in television, had been over-the-top tragic in black. Felicity, about fourteen years old, gawky and awkward, had been unreadable, private. And her life had stayed private. His file was full of photographs of the rest of the family, but she appeared in very few, and even then, it seemed to him, only as an afterthought.

She lived alone in an apartment in Broomhill, with no obvious romantic attachments. She had the title of station manager at the local radio station franchised to her father, but the general opinion seemed to be that the job had been manufactured for her by him because she had not succeeded in a theatrical career despite a brief spell at RADA.

Compared to her Technicolor family, Felicity came across on paper as oddly monotone and anonymous and he had almost dreaded what he planned to do to her.

But in person she wasn't monotone. She had a golden butterscotch voice, an excitingly generous mouth, eyes like hot sapphires. And a disconcerting habit of trembling when he touched her. Vivid. Yes, it was a good word to describe Felicity Beaumont. His researcher had got her quite wrong. But then he hadn't uncovered other things about Edward. The Beaumonts were good at covering their tracks. He'd just have to dig deeper. There had to be something to account for the difference between appearance and reality.

'It's not too late to drop this, Luke.' Luke Devlin turned and looked down at his cousin. The older man's face showed real concern. 'Why don't you just let it go? Forget it. Juliet would have never wanted this.'

Luke peeled himself away from the window and crossed to the desk. 'Come on, Phillip,' he said impatiently, when he saw his cousin still staring down into the car park. 'I need your figures. Just how much is Harries Industries going to cost me?'

Phillip Devlin turned away from the window. 'Too much,' he said flatly, then he shrugged. All the Devlins had a stubborn streak, but Luke made the rest of them look like putty. 'The whole place needs refitting with modern machinery,' he said. 'It'll cost a fortune. I don't know why you bought it.'

'Yes, you do.' For a moment the two men's eyes clashed. 'And we have to pay for our fun.'

'Revenge is a wild justice, Luke. Unpredictable. Take care the price you pay isn't more than you can stand.'

Fizz did not return to the pier. She didn't want to see her father. She was in no fit state to see anyone. The confrontation with Luke Devlin had left her wrung out, emotionally drained. After seven years without so much as a flicker she had thought, in her innocence, that she was quite safe from that kind of overwhelming charge of passion. She had been so certain that no one would ever have that effect on her again.

She gripped the leather-wrapped steering wheel until her knuckles showed white, and clamped down on her teeth to stop them chattering. But the trembling was unstoppable and as she edged the car forward into the traffic her foot slipped on the clutch and she stalled. There was an immediate chorus of horns from impatient drivers behind her. For a moment she didn't even hear them. She just wanted to get home. Lie in a warm bath until the shivering stopped.

She reached forward and restarted the engine, but the traffic was backed up from the ring road, and once caught in the one-way system there was no escape. She switched on the radio. Andy Gilbert's familiar voice immediately filled the car, warning drivers to stay off the ring road if at all possible.

'Police are in attendance and traffic should be moving shortly. In the meantime for those of you stuck out there, here's something soothing . . .' He moved smoothly into his patter and a few moments later the car was filled with music.

Fizz dug about in the glove compartment for a scarf. Her car, so old that it was a classic, had once been a glamorous head-turner, but now its shabby soft top let in a draught that today seemed to come direct from Siberia, and the heater only worked when it felt like it. She knew she should give serious thought to buying something small and sensible that cost less to run. She would, she promised herself. Once she had sorted out her sponsorship problems.

There was no scarf, so she turned her collar up and, chilled through by emotional stress as much as the cold, continued to shiver as the traffic edged slowly forward a few feet at a time until she reached the cause of the problem – a commotion in front of the town's leading hotel.

A white limousine was drawn up before the entrance and a pack of photographers and reporters were clustered about it, as well as an enormous gathering of excited girls.

A gasp went up from the crowd as the occupant of the limousine emerged and with the most brilliant smile, framed by golden hair that spilled around her fur-clad shoulders, turned and waved enthusiastically to her fans. For a moment Fizz stared at the young actress. So that was Melanie Brett – genuinely youthful, fresh and heartbreakingly pretty. It was, she discovered, painfully easy to understand why Luke Devlin would want to give her everything her heart desired.

Once clear of the traffic, she headed up the hill to her apartment in an old house that overlooked the bay and the town that rimmed its shore. Everything looked so uncomplicated from up here, so simple: neat rows of beautifully preserved Georgian houses lining the pebble-dash of the south beach, the clean black lines of skeletal winter trees that made the town's famous parks seem almost dead from this distance. She knew that there would be deep drifts of snowdrops close up under the bare branches and that the grassy banks would show promise of soon being spread with a purple, white and yellow carpet of crocuses.

Beyond the parks spread the tangle of the town, with the new shopping mall at its centre and further east the Wynds, narrow alleyways full of exciting little shops that sold exotic and precious things from all over the world and were a popular hunting ground for collectors even in the winter. She remembered Luke Devlin's disparaging comparison of her new restaurant with the cosy bistros in the heart of the Wynds. Had she really been that wrong?

As she walked down the road to the shop on the corner to pick up the evening paper her eyes came to rest on the long arm of the pier, stretching out above the golden sands of North Beach, its elegant ironwork tracery gleaming under a new coat of paint. At its furthest point the domed shape of the Pavilion, now the home of Pavilion Radio, stood out bright against the grey of the sky. Of course she had not been wrong. People loved the pier, and no trip to the sea could ever be complete – even in winter – without a bracing walk along its sixteen hundred feet.

'Hello, Fizz, you're early today. Just the *Post*, is it?'

'Please, Arthur. No – wait.' She picked up a bar of chocolate from the display and grinned self-consciously as she handed over her money. 'I'm in need of a little comfort. This is the closest I'm likely to get.'

'Comfort – that would make a good name for a chocolate bar,' he said with a grin, walking with her to the door. He nodded down at the pier. 'It's a grand sight these days,' he said.

'Yes, it is.' Her father and Michael Harries had set up the Pier Trust, and both of them had worked so hard to restore it. Grants, money-raising concerts – anything to raise the funds. After she had abandoned her fledgling film career and run home to lick her wounds in private, her father had dragged her along to help, refusing to allow her to hide away at home, moping.

She still remembered the ache of her hands and back from painting what had seemed like miles of wrought-iron tracery. But the hard, back-breaking work had given her a purpose to get out of bed each morning, and when the local radio franchise had been announced the pier had seemed to her the obvious place for it to be – visible to the entire town and a constant reminder that the pier was not just some museum piece, to be grumbled over as a costly reminder of bygone days, but a living part of Broomhill Bay.

Fizz and her father had often joked that they each supported the other. The rent the radio station paid to the Trust for the pavilion that had once housed the Winter Gardens was used to keep the pier in good repair, and the pier held up the radio station. But for how much longer?

She turned to the newsagent. 'Can I ask you a question, Arthur?'

'Fire away.'

'If someone offered to pay you to employ a really good-looking girl – '

'Oh, yes?' he said, heavily sarcastic.

'No, listen. Someone really glamorous – a girl that would bring men out of their way to buy the morning paper from your shop just for the chance of a smile. What would your reaction be?'

Arthur looked at her a little oddly. 'Pay me, you say?'

'To give you her salary and some more money for yourself.'

'Why would anyone want to do that?'

She raised her eyebrows and he shrugged.

'No one ever does anything for nothing, Fizz,' he said. 'I'd have to ask myself what he was up to. What was in it for him. Is that what you mean?'

'Yes, Arthur. I rather think it is. Thank you.'

Once inside her apartment, Fizz flung off the un-accustomed suit, filled the bath and submerged herself in the deep, scented water. A shower would have warmed her just as efficiently, would have washed away the disquieting scent of Luke Devlin that seemed to have seeped into her very pores, but she needed more than that. She needed to rid herself of his touch, with its skin-prickling sensation of heightened awareness. A bath was comforting and she needed to be comforted. She reached for the bar of chocolate, broke a piece off and let it slowly dissolve in her mouth.

Not that she was in any real danger. It was obvious that the man was utterly wrapped up in Melanie Brett. And why not? It was easy to see how the girl had captured

64

what passed for Luke Devlin's heart. But Fizz wasn't particularly keen on letting him use her radio station as a toy, a plaything for his lover. Not if she could help it. Of course she would like to have Melanie in *Holiday Bay*. But on her own terms. She broke off another piece of chocolate. If she could raise the money some other way, maybe she could . . .

Later, warm but guilt-ridden at her self-indulgent chocolate binge, Fizz made some tea and carried it to her small desk set in the bow window overlooking the sea. Then she took a deep breath and reached for the telephone.

'Julian? It's Felicity Beaumont.' She wasn't used to phoning men and asking them out, so she didn't give herself time to funk it. 'I'll be in London tomorrow and I wondered if we might have lunch?'

The young merchant banker almost fell over himself to accept. 'I'd love to see you, Fizz. Any time.' He sounded so eager that she felt a complete heel. It wasn't that she didn't like him. She liked him very much. He was good-looking, charming, had all the attributes any girl might seek in a partner. The trouble was, she wasn't looking for a partner. She knew he liked her, and it was unfair to use him like this, but life wasn't fair and she didn't want him to back out. 'Where would you like to go?' he asked.

'Oh, it's my treat,' she said quickly. 'But could you suggest somewhere? It's a while since I was in London.'

He mentioned a restaurant that Claudia had been raving about and she winced. It was bound to be horrendously expensive, but information didn't come cheap. 'That sounds lovely. I'll book a table for about half past twelve, shall I?'

'Great. Are you staying in town? I've got tickets for a new show.' He was like an eager puppy scenting a treat, and she wasn't prepared to take the responsibility for raising Julian's hopes any further.

'I'm not quite sure of my plans, Julian,' she said. 'Can I let you know tomorrow?' After lunch he might not want to speak to her ever again.

'I can't wait.'

'I'll see you tomorrow,' she said, before things got out of hand.

When she walked into the restaurant at a little after twelve-thirty the next day Julian looked less like an eager puppy than a disgruntled basset hound. He rose to his feet as she approached the table, but his smile was perfunctory.

'You've heard,' she said without preamble, sinking into the seat the waiter held for her.

'About the Harries takeover? Yes, I've heard. And I imagine this lunch is not because you wanted to see me, but because you wanted to talk about your loan.' He was stiff with hurt pride.

'So why didn't you telephone and cancel?'

'I tried, but you had already left your office.'

'Oh,' she said flatly, then, 'Oh, do sit down, Julian, everyone's looking. We can have lunch, surely? And if you insist I won't say a word about the takeover.' He sat, but with an ill grace. 'You did say that I was to ring you, night or day, if I needed advice or help,' she reminded him. 'You appointed yourself my personal banker, remember?' She put her hand over his on the table and for a moment he stared at it. 'I'm asking for your help now.'

'Then why didn't you tell me what you wanted when you phoned?'

'I'm sorry. The truth is I wanted to see you face to face. It is important, Julian, and if we get into trouble . . . well, you did recommend acceptance of my proposals to your board.'

'You mean, it's my head on the block as well?' The idea did not seem to bother him much, but then he bore the same name as the bank – even if it was at some remove. Indeed, he surprised her with a sudden grin. 'What if I pay for lunch and we forget business? Who knows? I might yet dazzle you with my wit, stun you with my charm, tempt you into bed with my winning smile . . .'

'Your wit and charm are undeniable, Julian.'

He turned his hand and grasped hers. 'Then come with me to the theatre tonight,' he urged. 'You can catch an early train back in the morning.'

He'd missed out the bit in between. The important bit. 'Your wit and charm are undeniable, Julian,' she repeated, 'but I'm not so sure about your plan to tempt me with your winning smile.'

'You've got to give a guy a chance.'

'I can't think why.'

'Well, forget the winning smile. I won't put a hand out of place if you'll come. Promise.'

'That rather depends on your definition of "out of place",' she pointed out. 'And I'm staying with my sister tonight. She wants to talk to me.'

'That won't take all evening.'

He was right about that. When she had phoned to tell her sister she would be in town, Claudia had been almost desperate for her to stay over, but she had probably already forgotten, and Julian deserved something for being treated so shabbily. 'All right, but I'll hold you to your promise to keep your hands to yourself.'

'You do realize that tickets for this show are like gold-dust? You've no idea what I could get the girls in the office to do for them.' He waggled his eyebrows at her.

'I've a fair idea,' she said, giggling despite everything. 'Perhaps, after all, you'd better save them for a rainy day.'

'Actually, I think I'd rather have your company – even with the embargo on my hands. Of course, if you should suddenly feel so overcome with gratitude that you change your mind, just say the word.'

'And what word is that, Julian?'

For a moment their eyes locked, and then Julian shook his head, releasing her fingers as he admitted defeat. 'I don't know who broke your heart, Fizz, but if you don't pick up the pieces and at least try to glue it back together he's won.'

'Love isn't a contest, Julian. There are no winners or losers. And sex is no substitute.'

'But it's fun,' he assured her eagerly. 'Try it – you might like it.'

It was odd, thought Fizz, how he reminded her of some soft little puppy. A golden labrador. Luke Devlin, on the other hand, was pure Dobermann.

The waiter, sensing a hiatus in the conversation, stepped in. 'Are you ready to order, sir?'

Julian ordered for them both and insisted on treating her to champagne, refusing to talk about business until they had eaten. Afterwards, as they warmed themselves on brandy, she brought up the subject of the take over again. She outlined the terms of Luke Devlin's sponsorship and her own feelings of disquiet.

'Look, Fizz, if you want to talk about rescheduling your loan I'm warning you now that you are wasting your time.' He sounded genuinely sorry.

She tried to ignore the small cold spot in the pit of her stomach that the brandy couldn't seem to reach, and invested her voice with good-humoured banter. 'Before you've even heard what I have to say?' He didn't answer. She tried a small laugh. 'Come on, Julian. You would have loaned Pavilion Radio twice as much when we originally came to you. Money in the bank, you said.'

'I know that.'

'Three month's delay on starting repayments. Two, even. It's not much to ask. With Melanie on board the advertisers will be begging us for air-time.'

'But you could have it all,' he reminded her. 'Devlin's sponsorship, Melanie Brett *and* the advertising.'

'Maybe I just don't trust my luck. Maybe I just don't trust him.'

'I don't understand why. The guy's rock-solid – gold-plated.'

'I have this feeling, Julian. Nothing I can put my finger on . . .' She shrugged awkwardly.

'Just a gut reaction that there's something up?'

'I was going to say feminine intuition, but I suppose gut reaction will do just as well.' But it was more

69

complicated than that. She couldn't trust her own judgement where Luke Devlin was concerned.

'It's human nature to distrust generosity from an unlikely source. Something to do with having the story of the Trojan horse drummed into us at school, I expect. But the truth is, I can't help you, Fizz. When I realized why you were coming I made some tentative enquiries about rescheduling. They were blocked. Your first repayment is due next Friday and the bank won't take no for an answer.'

'You mean they had already decided? Before I even asked?'

He shrugged. 'Harries was your major sponsor. It had to be a possibility that you'd come back to us.'

'It's still a bit quick off the mark, isn't it?' Julian didn't deny it. 'What is it? Does someone on your board fancy starting his own media empire at a knock-down price?'

He stiffened. 'I couldn't say.' Back in his banker's hat, he was deeply affronted by such a suggestion. Perhaps she had gone a fraction over the edge, but she still couldn't believe what she was hearing.

'Oh, come on, Julian. Don't be pompous – it doesn't suit you. I wasn't really suggesting dirty work on high.' She hadn't expected Julian to leap with joy at the suggestion that she reschedule the loan, but although it was a lot of money to her, it must be peanuts to his bank; their refusing even to discuss the possibility sounded . . . well . . . unusual.

'I'm really sorry, Felicity. It's been lovely having lunch with you, but there's nothing I can do about the loan.'

70

'At least you're being honest with me.'

'Tempting as it is to try, I'm not stupid enough to think you'd fall into bed with me if I promised to help.' His smile reappeared. 'And I prefer not to have my eye blacked for suggesting it.'

'Oh, Julian!' she declared, moved to laughter despite her worries.

'Not all us City folk are as black as we're painted,' he said. And that, at least, gave her an opening to ask a favour.

'There is one thing you can do for me. Nothing to do with money,' she added quickly. 'Can you get me a full list of your directors?'

'Why?'

She didn't know. Just another gut feeling perhaps. 'It's not a state secret, is it?'

'We're a private bank, Fizz.'

'And I'm a client. It must be on record somewhere, surely?'

'If you know where to look. Oh, what the heck? I'll get it for you and bring it when I meet you this evening. You are still coming to the theatre with me?'

'Only if you're paying,' she said as, despite his protestations, she insisted on signing the credit card slip for lunch.

Claudia was in a foul mood and made no effort to hide it. She never bothered to put on an act for her sister – Fizz knew her too well to be fooled – but even she was surprised by such an open display of temper.

'The man is a vertically challenged jerk,' she declared,

before Fizz had even drawn breath to ask what had upset her.

'Who?' she asked, barely managing to suppress a sigh as she followed her sister into her sitting room. Whenever Claudia had problems she never accepted that *she* might bear some of the responsibility, preferring to load the entire blame onto someone else's shoulders.

'*Who*?' Claudia turned to face her, throwing her hands dramatically in the direction of the ceiling, and groaned. 'Don't you ever listen? Sean Deveraux. That's who.'

'Oh.' Sean Deveraux was the hottest thing in tight pants on the box, a cover pin-up on every television magazine since his smouldering portrayal of Heathcliff a few months earlier. Claudia had been drooling on about him *ad nauseam* since she'd landed a plum part starring with him in a bodice-ripper designed to show his tanned torso to its best effect. He was a little too self-conscious in his manliness for Fizz's taste, but if he'd offended her sister, she pitied him.

'You begin shooting in Spain in a couple of weeks, don't you?' She'd have to check her scheduling, make sure that the recordings for *Holiday Bay* were made before Claudia left the country. As if her life wasn't complicated enough at the moment.

But Claudia was demanding her full attention. 'I *was* shooting in Spain, with Sean bloody Deveraux as my leading man,' she said. '*He* still *is* shooting in Spain. With someone else as his leading lady. Some totally unknown, talentless trollop he's fallen in bed with,' she said, claws at full stretch.

'But he can't do that. What about your contract?'

'There was a delay in signing. My agent wasn't quite happy with one or two of the details.' The defensive toss of the head spoke volumes. Claudia had probably been holding out until the last moment, hoping to squeeze a better deal when it was too late for the film company to change their minds. 'Do you know what excuse he made? Why he's insisting on a different leading lady?'

'No.' But she was going to be told. At length. With all the actions. And for that she would need the fortification of a strong cup of coffee. As she filled the kettle Fizz grinned. Luke Devlin had described her own performance as melodramatic. If her sister ever stormed his office intent on making her opinion felt the man would discover the true meaning of the word.

She quickly straightened her face as Claudia loomed in the doorway. 'He said . . . he said . . . I was too *tall*.'

'Too tall?' Fizz frowned. 'But surely that's not a problem? Sean Deveraux is – '

'You don't think so?' Claudia laughed unpleasantly. 'Everyone thinks he's six foot two. It's in all the press hand-outs. But he's not an inch over five feet eleven. I swear it,' she proclaimed angrily, as Fizz looked doubtful. 'He's just been lucky so far. He's had shrimps to play opposite him. I'll bet they've scoured the casting books looking for short men too, just to make him look good.'

Well, they had succeeded, but Fizz, who suspected there was more to the re-casting than height, knew better than to say so. Claudia, however, was waiting for some response. 'Why doesn't he just stand on a box?' she suggested. Her sister stared at her. 'Or get the rest of the cast to stand in a trench?' Fizz enquired. 'Isn't that what they used to do in the good old days in Hollywood?'

'You're not taking this seriously, are you Fizz? Don't you understand? I've lost twelve weeks of filming work. I turned down other roles just so that I could do this. It was going to be really big – a chance to break into feature films.'

She sat down quite suddenly on the kitchen stool and began to cry. Not noisy, unpleasant, eye-reddening tears, but huge drops that rolled with controlled pathos down her cheeks and made one want to cry in sympathy. It was an act she had used to stunning effect on many occasions, and although Fizz should have been immune she still found herself sniffing.

'But surely everyone knew how tall you were when you were cast?'

'Of course. It's just an excuse to get rid of me and get that woman on the set. Twelve weeks in sunny Spain, bonking at the expense of the production company.

Fizz hid her exasperation. The last time she had been home Claudia had declared Sean Deveraux to be gay. It was, after all, the only possible reason why any man she set her cap at should resist her. Female pride as well as the threat of damage to her professional career was fuelling this outburst.

'Oh, Claudia, look, I am sorry – truly. But there'll be other parts. Better ones, you'll see. Everything happens for a reason.'

'Well, this happened because that little squirt didn't want to be shown up for what he is.' She stood up as suddenly as she had collapsed on the stool and turned off her tears with equal facility. 'Oh, what do you know about it, Fizz? I can't expect you to understand. You've *never* understood. It's just a waste of time talking to you about the profession.'

She swept into her bedroom to check her reflection, repair the damage. 'All you're interested in these days is that stupid little radio station.' Satisfied with her appearance, she pulled a coat from the wardrobe. 'At least David will understand.'

David Hart, a lovely man with a private income that allowed him to play at being an actor without having to worry about where the next meal was coming from, glowed in the reflected glory of Claudia's friendship, and never failed to provide her with a sympathetic ear and a warm bed when she needed her ego massaged. She used him shamelessly. But then Claudia used everyone shamelessly.

Now, having apparently forgotten that she had begged Fizz to stay overnight so that they could have a good long talk, she waved in the direction of the kitchen. 'You don't mind if I leave you, do you? I expect there's a yoghurt or something in the fridge if you're hungry.'

'But, Claudia, I wanted to ask – '

'Help yourself to a drink. Anything,' she said impatiently. 'Don't wait up for me.'

'Your advice,' Fizz finished quietly as the front door banged behind Claudia. Even if she had been listening in the first place she would not have heard that. 'But don't worry about this evening . . . fortunately I've made other plans – ' So much for feeling guilty about accepting Julian's invitation.

She wandered back to the kitchen, picked up her mug

and began to sip her coffee. 'Well, this is cosy,' she said, addressing her sister's vacated stool. 'I do love these long, sisterly heart-to-hearts.' A mischievous grin teased the corners of her lips as she recalled her sister's parting remarks. 'Let me tell you all about my date this evening. Yes, I knew you'd be surprised. Me with a date. He's not Prince Charming, of course, but he's kind, good-looking and well-mannered.

'Actually, I was going to ask you . . . and please don't be afraid to say no . . . if I could borrow your black dress – you know, the Herve Leger that you prize above rubies? After all, you did say to help myself to anything, didn't you? I'd give my fairy godmother a ring, but it's a busy time of year for her; she's still in panto.' She took another sip of her coffee, half expecting the very walls to vibrate at such an outrageous suggestion. But nothing happened. 'Well, that is kind. I knew I could rely on sisterly devotion to see me through . . .'

But in the end she settled for something a little less revealing. It would be unkind to put too much strain on Julian's good intentions in a dress apparently held together by safety pins.

As promised, he didn't put a hand or word out of place all evening. He treated her like a Dresden shepherdess, making her feel fragile, valuable and very desirable. And at the end of the evening, when he had seen her to her sister's door in a taxi, he produced an envelope.

Fizz hooked her thumb beneath the flap, but Julian stopped her. 'Don't. Not now, Fizz. Let me pretend that at least some of today was just for me.'

She looked up, surprising him with a smile of real

warmth. 'I can't remember when I last had such a lovely evening. Truly.'

'Then why don't you kiss me goodnight?' he said, his voice not quite steady. She stiffened slightly. 'I don't bite, Fizz.'

No. He didn't bite. He was a thoroughly nice young man who deserved a great deal better than the way she had used him today. A kiss was a small enough price to pay for his kindness, yet . . . She looked up at him, hoping that she could explain, and surprised a look of such tenderness that before she could change her mind she nodded in mute agreement. Maybe, just maybe . . .

As he took her into his arms and lowered his head to kiss her lightly on her mouth she held her breath, waiting for something, some reaction, a repeat of the lightning strike she had experienced in Luke Devlin's office. But there was nothing.

Curious at her own lack of response, she obediently opened her mouth when, encouraged by her acceptance of his embrace, he deepened his kiss. But when his hand strayed to her breast and still nothing happened she pulled away. To allow such an intimate touch was to encourage him to hope when there was none – for either of them. 'I'm sorry, Julian.'

'That was just an experiment, wasn't it?' he said, staring down at her. 'God, I thought for a minute – ' He broke off as a tear began to slide down the side of her nose. She put up her hand to dash it away, only too aware that she had never learned to cry as prettily as Claudia.

'I'm sorry, Julian. I thought perhaps . . .' Thought perhaps he could wake her body from the coma, the living death by betrayal into which it had slipped so long ago. She hadn't realized how completely her senses had been numbed until her unexpected, almost shocking reaction to Luke Devlin. Hadn't been aware of what she was missing. And now she was, and apparently there was only one man could help her. The wrong man.

Julian pulled her gently into his arms and held her briefly. 'No, sweetheart, I'm the one who's sorry. I'm sorry that I can't fix it for you, whatever it is. But someone will one day, you'll see. Don't give up.' He dropped a kiss on the top of her head. 'Goodbye, Fizz. Good luck.' Then he released her and turned to walk swiftly away.

'Oh, Julian.' She leaned heavily against the door arch. 'Don't you know you mustn't ever say good luck?' she murmured to his retreating back. 'Don't you know that it's tempting fate?' It was one of the first things she remembered her father telling her. Even before she had properly understood what a performance was, she had known that she must never say good luck before one. You had to say 'Break a leg . . .'

'Break a leg, Fizz.' Her father had risen with her long before dawn, insisting on seeing his little girl off on her first exciting job, filming in Italy. There were tears in his eyes as he hugged her now, holding onto her for a moment.

'I just hope I don't make a fool of myself,' she said anxiously. Plucked, untried, from RADA, she felt the idea of such a major role a daunting responsibility. 'Suppose I can't do it?'

'Of course you can do it. You're a Beaumont. And you'll be a star,' he said. 'I know it.' Then he walked her down the path and hugged her again. 'Ring to let me know you've arrived safely,' he instructed, 'and stick to mineral water. Too much wine will show in your skin and the camera is never kind. And stay out of the sun. You won't be popular in make-up if your skin keeps changing colour.'

'I know,' she said, standing on her dignity. 'I'm eighteen, not a child.' Then she grinned, realizing that her father was winding her up, jolting her out of her uncertainty.

She had been chosen over dozens of other girls with more experience for a major film role, and no director would risk that if he wasn't convinced she could deliver the goods. Of course, everyone was saying that she got the part because of her name, because she was a Beaumont. It was only to be expected. Claudia had been through it before her. And, like Claudia, she would just have to prove them wrong.

'Eighteen and she thinks she's all grown up,' Edward Beaumont remarked to no one in particular, before looking down at his youngest daughter. 'You're a baby, and I must be mad to let you out of the country with a bunch of randy actors and technicians without me or your sister to look after you.'

'You're both working and I'll be fine,' she said, then threw her arms about him. 'I'll be fine.'

'Will you?'

'You said it. I'm going to be star.' She laughed delightedly, her fears forgotten for a moment.

'Well, just . . . you know . . . be *careful*,' he said meaningfully as she climbed into the car.

'Don't worry! Claudia's given me a huge packet of condoms and a major lecture about safe sex,' she giggled, paying him back in kind.

'Your sister – ' But the car began to slide away from the kerb. 'Don't forget to ring me,' he called as she leaned out of the window to wave.

She didn't forget. Not at first. But then for a while she forgot everything . . .

Fizz sat in her sister's flat and for the tenth time studied the sheet of paper on which Julian had listed all the directors of his bank. It was a surprisingly long list of names, but she hadn't needed to look far to find what she was looking for. One name leapt off the page at her. Julian had underlined it as if it meant something. Luke Devlin. The new owner of Harries Industries. It certainly meant something. But what? She had been trying to work it out ever since she had first seen it.

She had tried telling herself that it could just be chance, but she was forced to acknowledge that that would be stretching the long arm of coincidence just a little beyond credibility. She picked up the list of directors' names once more. Luke Devlin. He was very neatly placed to push Pavilion Radio off the air if that was what he wanted. Julian's underscoring suggested that he had used his position at the bank to ensure that the station wasn't helped out of its financial difficulties. She wanted to pick up the telephone right now and ring him, ask him. But he had done more than enough.

The trouble was, nothing about Luke Devlin's interest in Pavilion Radio made any real sense. If he wanted to take over the station all he had to do was cut off sponsorship and wait. But he had written a personal cheque, offered her a way out. Just to prove to Melanie Brett that he could give her anything she wanted? Why did she find that so difficult to believe? Because she didn't want to believe it?

Fizz found herself dwelling on the memory of a pair of forceful grey eyes of a mouth that smiled so slowly that before you knew it it would have stolen your heart. She gave a little gasp, then, pulling a face at her own stupidity, stared at the sheet of paper she was holding as if that could give her the answer. But it couldn't. She threw it down and walked across to the window. She stared down at the lights of London.

Could it be that she was making too much of the whole business? Looking for problems where none existed? Why couldn't she just thank her lucky stars, take Luke Devlin's money and welcome Melanie with open arms?

She didn't understand why she was hesitating. She had gained a little thinking time by convincing him that she would have to speak to her father, but she could have agreed to Devlin's conditions on the spot. In retrospect, she had been mad not to. Yet some instinct had warned her to play for time. Why, she couldn't say. Except that his attitude to her, to her father had seemed so . . . personal.

She took the cheque he had given her from her bag and laid it on the windowsill, smoothing it out very carefully, studying the strong, masculine handwriting. There was determination in every thick downstroke, but with the occasional telltale flourish to warn that the writer had a strong imagination. It seemed to her a very dangerous combination.

'What are you up to, Luke Devlin?' she asked out loud. 'What do you really want from Pavilion Radio?'

The cheque, if it knew, wasn't talking.

CHAPTER 4

At seven-thirty the following morning Fizz put her head around the newsroom door. 'Have you got a minute, Jim?' she asked.

Jim Ryan, a burly man in his late thirties, was sitting behind his desk organizing the bulletins and cartridges for the major news and local current affairs programmes on the hour. 'Two minutes for you, Fizz, my darling,' he said easily, without looking up from his task. 'What can I do for you?'

'Tell me everything you've heard about the takeover at Harries Industries. Everything you've heard about Luke Devlin.'

'The long version or the potted one?'

'Which would you advise?'

'Since nobody knows much, they're much the same,' he said, throwing her a grin. 'Apparently we're lucky the whole lot didn't just go down the pan, and if anyone can dig Harries out of the red, Devlin can. The workers – at least, those who have met him – are impressed, although naturally there have been rumblings of discontent. Everyone expects there to be some job-losses.'

'When are you going to do a feature on him – his plans, what it means for the town, that sort of thing? I assume you *are* planning one of your awesome face-to-face interviews?'

Jim, the manager of news and current affairs at the station, had been with her from the beginning, and was one of the few employees who knew that she, and not Edward Beaumont, was the boss. It didn't stop him from pulling a face at her blatant flattery. 'I'd certainly like to. I've been trying to get hold of Mr Devlin all week, but his secretary is a positive dragon.' He finished organizing his bulletins and swivelled around in his chair to give her his full attention. 'Any particular reason for your interest?'

Fizz sidestepped the apparently innocent query. Jim never asked innocent questions, as many a local dignitary attempting to bluff his way through a budgetary fiasco had discovered to his cost. 'I was certain you would have assembled a vast amount of information about him from your contacts.'

'And information is power?' Jim grinned. 'What I've got is in that folder, but I warn you it's not much.' He pointed to a disappointingly thin file. 'You'll not find any scandals that you can use to blackmail him into sponsoring the station.'

Fizz remembered the slate-grey eyes, the warning not to do anything rash. But she hadn't needed any warning. From the first moment she had set eyes upon him she had known that Luke Devlin was not a man to cross. She buried that knowledge beneath an amiable grin. 'Now, why would anyone need to be blackmailed into supporting the best local radio station in Broomhill, Jim?'

'It's the only local radio station in Broomhill, Fizz.'

'I rest my case,' she said, laughing. 'But thanks for this.' She picked up the file, then paused in the doorway. 'If you can't get Luke Devlin at his office, Jim, you might try the Metropole. I've a feeling he might be staying there.'

'Where else would a man of his means and style lay his head? Unfortunately he doesn't answer his telephone – or he has the receptionist as well trained as his secretary.'

Maybe that's because he isn't in his own room to answer it, she thought. But that wasn't news, that was gossip, and she kept her thoughts to herself. 'And I thought Maggie Church was deep in your pocket, Jim Ryan,' she teased him.

'So did I. I guess I'll have to buy her a bigger box of chocolates next Christmas. If the budget will run to it?'

'We can afford the chocolates, Jim. It's the red roses and candlelight supper when you hand them over that disturbs the accountant's blood pressure. Why don't you marry the woman and be done with it?'

'Just to save you a few quid on expenses? Besides, she's got more sense than to lumber herself with a liability like me.'

'You have asked her, then?'

'That's privileged information.' He grinned. 'According to Maggie, this way she gets all the fun and none of the dirty washing.'

'Clever girl – I must remember that.' But she felt a momentary pang of sadness for Jim, who was a truly kind man – although, having carefully avoided any kind of relationship herself, she was in no position to criticize Maggie for keeping hers at a level of commitment she was happy with. 'In the meantime, don't worry about Luke Devlin. When he's ready to talk, he'll call you.'

'Is that the voice of experience I hear?' Jim's eyes narrowed as the faintest blush heated her cheeks. 'Well, well.' He sat back and regarded her thoughtfully. 'You are a dark horse.'

She was rescued from the need to reply by the click of the huge reel-to-reel tape recorder starting up and the warning of an interview coming in that Jim was waiting for. She escaped as he turned to slide in a cartridge, ready to record it for the upcoming bulletin.

Back in her office, as she flicked through the folder he had given her, she acknowledged that he had been right about the scarcity of solid information on Luke Devlin. There were a number of news clippings, but most of them were several years old. It was quite clear that the more money the man had made the less forthcoming he had become about his private life.

The very early clippings were all from Australian newspapers and showed him out on the town with the kind of glamorous young women who like to get their pictures in the newspaper. The more recent articles were dry-as-dust pieces from the financial papers about acquisitions and mergers of interest only to those involved in the City, without even a photograph to enliven them.

The takeover at Harries had been reported as the unresisted buy-out of a company in difficulties. There was some speculation as to how it would fit in with Luke Devlin's other interests and whether he would invest heavily in the company and push it into the twenty-first century, or whether he would simply redevelop the site. Informed opinion seemed to favour redevelopment. It made depressing reading.

Jim had written a summary of the information he had gleaned from the cuttings and Fizz read this with interest, hoping for some clue as to his interest in her radio station.

Luke Devlin was British, although shortly after taking a degree in geology he had gone to Australia where, either by luck or good judgement, he had made a great deal of money prospecting for minerals. Then, still only in his twenties, he had not been content simply to invest his wealth, sit back and let someone else do the work. He had diversified into electronics in the Far East and the USA and had taken an interest in Eastern Europe.

He was now involved with a number of forward-thinking companies although, she was interested to notice, his connection with a seriously heavy merchant bank had been missed. The takeover of Harries Industries was just the latest in a long line of business coups. Jim, more interested in the ramifications of the takeover than Luke Devlin's social life, hadn't dwelt on anything personal. Not that she discovered much more in her own reading of the material beyond the fact that he was thirty-four years old and unmarried.

Younger than she had thought, then. Perhaps making money in such quantity wore one out.

And there was nothing to provide a clue as to his motives. No indication that he had any ambition to move into the media at all – although even if he had, a small south coast radio station would have been an odd sort of place for a man of his means to start. But then his move on Harries had taken everyone by surprise. Jim had warned her not to expect too much. It was just as well.

Of course, there was one person in Broomhill Bay who knew all about Luke Devlin. Having ascertained from Luke Devlin's secretary that he was unavailable for the rest of the day, Fizz telephoned the Metropole, chatted amiably to Maggie for a moment or two, then asked to be put through to Miss Brett, as if her call was expected.

She knew she was taking a risk. Luke Devlin might be expecting something like this and already have put Melanie on her guard, warned her not to speak to anyone, especially nosy radio station managers. But it was a risk worth taking. Fizz wanted to find out what Melanie Brett was like, whether she really wanted to take part in a minor radio soap, and she didn't want Devlin at her elbow prompting her. And if she could find out some background on Devlin at the same time . . . pillow-talk . . .

As she waited to be put through she had a sudden vivid image of the young actress lying in his arms, the darkness of his hair in contrast to the bright, sunny spread of hers against a pillow, the tanned skin of his fingers stroking her breast. The same strong fingers that had so recently been fastened about her own wrist. Her nipples tightened involuntarily at the memory of his touch, the feel of his skin against hers . . .

'Melanie Brett.' The breathy little voice with its new-world accent brought Fizz back to earth with an almost painful jolt.

'Miss Brett,' she began quickly. 'This is Felicity Beaumont from Pavilion Radio. Forgive me for telephoning so early, but I understand from Mr Devlin that you are interested in working with us during the summer. I wondered if you would like to come and have a look around the station this morning? If you have no other plans?'

There was a squeak of pure pleasure that could hardly have been faked. 'Luke told me he'd asked you, but I didn't dare to hope Mr Beaumont would agree.' She was really that keen? That naïve? Surely she must know her own worth? 'I just can't wait to meet him.' Oh, Lord, but she sounded so young. How could a man like Luke Devlin take advantage of such innocence?

Easily. Without a second thought. 'I'm afraid my father won't be here today,' she said, which was just as well, as she hadn't yet explained the situation to him. 'But he'll certainly want to meet you as soon as he has some time to spare.' Nothing but the truth. Her father was as susceptible to a pretty young fan as the next actor. According to her mother's vitriolic outpourings, he always had been.

'Oh, I do understand. And I would really love to come to the studios.'

'Don't expect too much,' Fizz said, with a small laugh that might have been of sheer relief at it all having been so easy. 'Actually, we're recording some episodes of *Holiday Bay* this morning, at about eleven-thirty. I thought perhaps you'd like to sit in?'

Another squeak of pleasure, an offer to send a car for her at eleven and her mission was accomplished.

Melanie Brett, fresh as a May morning and twice as pretty, caused a minor sensation as she walked along the pier, stirring the heart of every male lucky enough to have decided to go fishing that morning.

Fizz, watching for her arrival from her office window, had seen the easy way she stopped to sign odd scraps of paper thrust at her, perfectly happy to chat with perfect strangers. The girl was a natural, and worth twice her weight in listening figures. Fizz's fingers itched to ring the advertising agencies and tell them about her prize. Instead she hurried down to the foyer to greet her visitor.

'This is so kind of you, Miss Beaumont,' Melanie said, shaking hands with a convent school politeness that reminded Fizz painfully of herself just a year or two younger – eager, wide-eyed and utterly innocent.

For a moment Fizz felt a twinge of conscience at her deviousness, then realized that the innocence, at least, had to be an illusion, although the girl was certainly as young as she looked. Then there was another feeling. Alien and uncomfortable. A feeling that she couldn't identify, or perhaps didn't want to admit to.

She buried it under a warm smile. 'Actually, I have to admit to an ulterior motive in asking you to come to the station. Since you arrived in town everyone has been dying to know what your plans are. I wondered if you might be prepared to sit in on a radio phone-in later? It would give your local fans a chance to ask you a few questions. Only if you would like to, of course.'

'Oh, I love phone-in programmes. But I should really ask Luke.'

No, you shouldn't, she wanted to scream at the girl. You don't have to ask anyone. Be your own person. Don't let him take you over and break you apart so there's nothing left.

Instead she kept a polite smile fixed to her lips. 'You could telephone him from my office if you like?' She held her breath and hoped his instruction to his secretary to say that he was unobtainable for the rest of the day included Melanie. It didn't seem likely.

'Phone Luke at work!' Melanie looked horrified. 'Lord, no. He's always so busy, and he *hates* being dragged out of meetings.' Fizz could well believe it. And she doubted if he kept his feelings to himself. 'And if I don't ask him, he can't say no, can he?' Melanie giggled.

'That's true.' And perhaps because of the sudden relaxation of tension Fizz giggled too. 'I'll introduce you to Andy Gilbert later.'

'Oh, I've heard him. He's really good.'

'He's certainly very popular with our female listeners,' Fizz said, drily. 'If you're not too busy perhaps we could all have lunch together and you can discuss what you're prepared to talk about. He'll field anything difficult – after all, we do want you to have fun.'

'Oh, I will,' Melanie answered. 'It'll be my first public appearance since I arrived in England.'

'Then we're very honoured. I would have thought

you'd have been snapped up by the chat shows the minute you set foot here.'

'Oh, there are some booked,' she said vaguely. 'In a week or two, I think. But radio is such fun.'

'You've done a lot? In Australia?'

'I've been a guest on a few shows – you know the sort of thing. Music and chat. I haven't done any drama myself, but my mother used to take me along sometimes when she made recordings.'

'She's an actress too?'

'Was.' The girl's face clouded momentarily. 'She died last year. In an accident.'

'I'm so sorry.' Melanie didn't say anything else, and after a moment, Fizz said, 'Shall we go through to the sound studio so that you can meet the cast of *Holiday Bay*? They'll be having coffee and a run-through of the script before recording.' She smiled encouragingly. 'We'll have to give some thought about how you're going to fit in. An unexpected arrival at the end of an episode, I should think. Like a bolt from the blue. The listeners will love it.'

She introduced her to the cast, who instantly absorbed Melanie into their group, keen to quiz her about working in television and life in Oz. She might be a celebrity, but she was still an actress – one of them. Fizz excused herself. No one noticed her leave.

She picked up the telephone and began to work. Twenty minutes later she leaned back in her chair, well satisfied. She had drummed up an extra five minutes of advertising time for the phone-in and re-scheduled one or two others in order to earn a few brownie points at a time when agencies were spreading their budgets ever thinner.

Luke Devlin flipped the intercom on his desk. 'Get hold of Melanie for me, will you, Liz? And book a table for two at the Angel up at Broomhill Gate.'

'Of course, Mr Devlin. I didn't know you were back in your office.' There was the hint of reproach in her voice.

As a secretary, Liz Meynell was top of the tree. As a mother figure, she could be a man's worst nightmare. Most of the time Luke was happy to put up with the one for the sheer efficiency of the other. But not today.

His meeting at the council offices had not been a barrel of laughs. They hadn't much liked what he'd had to say and he didn't blame them. Without Harries Industries the town would have a serious unemployment problem.

It wasn't his fault, of course. It probably wasn't anyone's fault. Harries was a company running out of markets. It hadn't diversified, kept up, retooled. But the residents of Broomhill who relied on the factory for a wage every week wouldn't see it like that. They would never be convinced of the inevitability of what had happened. They would only see the effect, not the cause. Michael Harries was apparently considered something of a saint in Broomhill, while he had found himself cast in the part of devil.

It wasn't a comfortable role to play, and he knew things could get a lot worse before they got better. So he'd needed a quiet place to think, and as the choice was between his office, and the ministrations of Liz Meynell, and the Metropole, where there were hordes of teenage girls camped on the doorstep, he'd let himself quietly into his office and had been sitting there for the last hour trying to sort things out in his mind.

When he had gone after Harries it had just been a means to an end. He had seen his objective in black and white – two dimensions. Now it had been made very clear to him that he was responsible for the fate of nearly a thousand families. Good people. It was a complication he hadn't anticipated caring about.

'Did you say something, Mr Devlin?'

'What? Oh, no.'

'I'll get Melanie straight away. Oh, and Miss Beaumont called earlier. I told her you weren't available for the rest of the day. Do you want me to get her back?'

Luke Devlin frowned. Felicity Beaumont. She was another problem. Ever since he had found the woman berating Phillip her presence had seemed to cling to him. It was her eyes that had bothered him. One moment looking at him as if she would devour him whole, the next almost as if she were afraid of him. Not of what he could do to her father's precious radio station – although that clearly worried her – but of him, personally. Try as he might he couldn't get to the bottom of her.

She was a mass of contradictions. One moment convincing him with her grasp of figures that she was a totally efficient businesswoman, the next behaving like a schoolgirl who had to ask her father's permission to grab the best offer she was likely to get this side of the millennium. But she wasn't a schoolgirl; she had been playing for time. For some reason she hadn't trusted him.

Her personal life was equally incomprehensible. She lived alone, and, while her sister still kept an apartment in Edward Beaumont's roomy house, Felicity had moved out when she was twenty. Yet, if his researcher was to be believed, she was the closest thing to a nun outside a convent. Except for those eyes.

And now she had telephoned him. He had been certain he wouldn't hear from her until the dot of twelve on Friday. She had wasted no time in contacting the bank about her loan and had drawn a blank, as he had known she would. But he knew she wouldn't give in until she had exhausted every other possible alternative source of finance. She wanted Melanie, but she wanted her without him pulling the strings. Which was interesting, since he had been careful not to attach any strings – only money. It suggested Fizz Beaumont possessed a highly developed sense of danger.

'What did she want?' he asked now.

'She just asked if you would be in today and I explained that you were in meetings all day and not available.'

'Did she leave a message? Ask for an appointment?'

'No.'

Then why had she called? 'Tell me exactly what she said, Liz. Word for word.'

'Well, let me think. She said, "Good morning, is that Mr Devlin's secretary?" I said yes, and could I help. She said, "Can you tell me if Mr Devlin will be in the office today?" and I said you had a number of meetings today and were unavailable. I offered to take a message, but she just said that it didn't matter. Something like that.'

'You didn't ask who was calling?'

'I didn't have to. I recognized her voice.'

'I see. You said I would be in meetings all day. Then what?'

'She said thank you and hung up.' She waited. 'Would you like me to get her for you now?'

'No. Don't bother. Just call the Metropole and see if Melanie is there.'

Melanie, Liz reported a moment later, had gone out at about a quarter to eleven. He wasn't a bit surprised.

The recording of the soap went remarkably smoothly, mainly because Claudia was still in London. They always had to make allowances for Claudia, in more ways than one, and Melanie's arrival would undoubtedly cause a fit of the sulks. Well, that was something her father would have to deal with, as director. She'd have to tell him about Melanie soon – her thinking time was running out. For heaven's sake, her reluctance was ridiculous. She should be shouting it from the rooftops.

It was just the feeling of helplessness that so rankled. The feeling of having her arm twisted. She had spent the last seven years making sure that every single strand of her life was in her hands, in her total control, and she was sure she had succeeded. Yet the moment she had met Luke Devlin she'd felt as if she had stepped into quicksand.

She sighed. It wasn't just the sponsorship, or taking on Melanie. It was more personal. It was the flash of recognition, the electric charge that jarred the senses, the raw desire for a man even before you had spoken to him, even before you knew his name. The sensation of having the air knocked out of your body. Leaving you breathless.

She had excused herself from lunch with Andy and Melanie. One look at Andy's starstruck face had reassured her that he would behave himself. Not that he was likely to prove any competition for Luke Devlin. But then, who would? And she couldn't pump the girl for information with Andy in attendance.

After the phone-in she would invite Melanie for tea in the Green Room. On an emotional high after the programme she would be less careful about what she said. Susie would make sure they weren't disturbed. She smiled to herself. Luke Devlin wasn't the only one with a dragon for a secretary.

Instead of going to lunch she had returned to her desk to catch up, and she was, on the whole, pleased with her morning's work – and partially reassured by the fact that Melanie was genuinely interested in taking part in *Holiday Bay*. Now, her coffee cooling, her sandwich untouched beside her on her desk, she tried to work out just how much extra advertising she needed in order to avoid taking the sponsorship money from Devlin.

'Did you get that information, Susie?' Fizz asked as the door opened. But the hands that were placed on her desk were not those of her secretary. They were large, darkly tanned and bore the scars of too many close encounters with sharp rocks.

'Where is Melanie?' Luke Devlin asked, in a low growl that shivered against her skin.

Fizz jumped. Not physically. The snap as the point of

her pencil broke was the only outward sign of a reaction that began as an internal explosion somewhere about her midriff and rippled in a series of shock waves until her entire body seemed to be shaking. Inside.

She had made a life's study of hiding her feelings and right now it was being put severely to the test. Because her reaction to Luke Devlin hadn't been a one-off. This time it was worse. She didn't need to look up to read his expression, to see the clamped down jaw, the angry line of his mouth. They were all engraved for ever on her memory, playing havoc with her nerve-endings, unravelling them . . .

Fizz took another perfectly sharpened pencil from a pot at her elbow and, waving to a chair, said, 'Good afternoon, Mr Devlin. Do sit down. I won't keep you a moment.'

Without looking up from the page in front of her, she continued to run her pencil down the column of figures. Although she lost count after the third figure, she refused to let him see the effect he was having on her. But who could be expected to add up anything more complicated than two plus two with an earthquake going on in parts of her anatomy that should have known better?

She continued to the end before she jotted down the first figure that came into her head. Only then did she look up to discover that his face was inches from her own. He had not availed himself of her invitation, but was still on his feet, filling her tiny office with his overlong legs and quite unnecessarily broad shoulders. And he was still leaning over her desk, his hands placed before her. All macho threat. His eyes, however, glinted with something

98

that might have been amusement, although for the moment his mouth was refusing to join in.

'I suggest you use a calculator in future, Miss Beaumont.'

She didn't normally need one, but refused to be intimidated by his apparent ability to calculate upside-down. 'There's nothing wrong with my figuring,' she declared.

'The correct answer is twenty three thousand, six hundred and ninety-seven pounds and ninety-two pence,' he said quietly. 'Write it down and check it later if you like.'

'I will.' She did. He was just as capable of bluffing as she was. She glared at him. He didn't back down.

'Can I get you some coffee?' she asked, using the excuse to slide her chair back towards the coffee-maker behind her, and taking her time to pour him a cup. 'I didn't expect to see you before Friday,' she said, her back firmly towards him.

'I'm sure when you enticed Melanie along to your office, you must have been concerned that I would follow close on her heels. Why else would you telephone my office to assure yourself that I was otherwise occupied for the day?'

For one crazy moment Fizz was going to deny it, but even as she opened her mouth she knew that it would be a mistake. A man who could add up a column of figures upside-down was not a man to trifle with.

'How did you know that I rang your office, Mr Devlin?' she asked, marvelling that the hand holding out the cup and saucer did not shake.

'When you didn't leave your name? You have a very beautiful voice, Miss Beaumont. My secretary recognized it.'

He ignored the cup and she quickly put it down as a tremble threatened to betray her at this totally unlooked-for compliment. After all, he need only have said that his secretary had recognized her voice.

'So I return to my original question. Where is Melanie?'

Fizz rose from her chair and walked across to the window, partly to disguise the heat that had rushed to her cheeks, partly to put some distance between them. 'She's down there,' she said, indicating the sparkling white dome of the new restaurant. 'Having lunch. I gave her the grand tour of the studios, then she sat in on a recording session for *Holiday Bay*. I thought she might be bored alone all day at the hotel.'

'How thoughtful of you.'

He didn't believe her. Well, if she was honest, she hadn't expected him to.

'She was keen to come and I'm sure she's had a good time.' Feeling more in control, she half turned, only to find that he was at her back and she was staring at his tie. Again. Navy with tiny red spots. He had a nice line in restrained silk ties, she decided. And it was safer counting the number of spots to the square inch than looking up, risking his eyes. 'I would suggest that you join her, but I know you would insist upon paying for your own lunch, and since Miss Brett is my guest . . .'

'She's on her own?' His concern was immediate.

'She's with Andy Gilbert. One of our presenters,' she

added, since there was no reason why he should recognize the name. Fizz realized she had better come clean. 'She's agreed to sit in on his programme this afternoon and chat to callers. They're discussing it over lunch.' She finally gave up on the spots and looked up. 'You needn't worry; he's young, but very experienced – '

'So I've heard,' he said, interrupting her with a wry twist to his voice that suggested he was well aware of Andy's reputation. And yet it seemed unlikely he would have time for local gossip, or would even be interested in such trivia. Except that he seemed to be interested in everything to do with Pavilion Radio. She had the uncomfortable feeling that his file on her family and her radio station would be a great deal thicker than Jim's meagre dossier on him.

'I hardly think Andy would have much attraction for someone like Melanie,' she said coolly. In fact he had seemed unexpectedly overawed by her. Almost tongue-tied. It had been amusing to see the tables turned for once, and the local Don Juan reduced to a state of stammering incoherence by a girl, but right now Fizz had her own problems with co-ordinating thought and speech, and she suddenly felt a great deal more sympathetic towards Andy. 'Of course, if you object, I'll stop the announcement going out.' She turned and reached for the telephone receiver, but he placed his hand over hers, trapping it there, keeping her his prisoner.

'Melanie has done enough radio and television interviews to be able to take care of herself, and she knows nothing about Harries Industries or sponsorship, Miss Beaumont.'

'Since the average age of our callers is likely to be around fourteen years old, I don't imagine they would be interested in either, Mr Devlin. Or associate Melanie with them.'

'Probably not. I made the point in case you considered slipping in a question or two of your own.'

'If there's anything I want to know about you, Mr Devlin, I promise you I'll ask you myself,' she said sharply, reacting without thinking. A bad habit.

'And is there anything?'

'I'd like to know why you're taking so much interest in my radio station,' she replied.

'No doubt,' he said. And finally he removed his hand from hers.

She quickly stuffed it into the safety of the pocket of an old, but very warm pair of trousers that were a long way from the tailored elegance of the business suit she had worn for their first meeting. If Luke Devlin was going to make a habit of turning up unexpectedly in her office, she would have to make a little more effort with her dress.

She suspected the tightening of his mouth was the beginning of a smile and too late realized that her gesture had betrayed her vulnerability to his touch, but he lifted his face to the window before she could be sure. 'You have a spectacular view of the bay from up here,' he said.

So, having duped her into asking the question, he wasn't going to answer. She should have known better. But scenery was neutral ground; she could cope with that. 'It's why I chose this office.'

'There couldn't possibly be any other reason,' he

murmured, dragging his eyes from the distant horizon to look around at the tiny attic room with its awkward sloping ceiling that forced her to duck every time she stood up. They came to rest on the heavy cream sweater she was wearing over a brushed cotton shirt in a deep blue. The same colour blue as her eyes.

'Do you feel the cold, Mr Devlin? I find it keeps me on my toes,' she said, with an attempt to lighten the atmosphere. 'Of course I usually meet *important* visitors in the comfort of the Green Room.'

'Is that where you met Melanie?'

'No, I saw her coming along the pier and went downstairs to meet her.' It was a pity she hadn't seen *him* coming. She could have diverted him to it, perhaps improved his opinion of them. Maybe it wasn't too late. 'Perhaps you'd like to go down and see it? You appear to have some interest in my father and it's lined with photographs of him in his more memorable roles. My mother too. She was Elaine French,' she explained.

'Yes, I know.'

'And my sister, of course.'

'Ah, yes, the beautiful and talented Claudia. I can hardly wait to meet her.'

'It's a common condition.'

Devlin lifted one speaking but silent brow. It was a family joke that men caught a dose of Claudia as frequently as the common cold, but too late Fizz realized that to an outsider it would sound as if she were jealous. Oh, well. It shouldn't matter. It *didn't* matter.

He looked away. 'Did Melanie meet your father?'

'I'm afraid not. He's in London today.'

'And Claudia is busy rehearsing for a chocolate commercial.'

'How do you know that?' she gasped.

'Wasn't it in all the newspapers that the chocolate company was going for sex appeal in its first major advertising campaign?'

'Was it?' It hadn't been in all of them. The PR people had done a pretty thorough job, but even they hadn't managed to interest the financial papers. 'You seem to have gone to a great deal of trouble to find out everything about us, Mr Devlin.'

His eyes dropped to meet hers. 'I don't know everything. Miss Felicity Beaumont, the only member of the famous family to shun the limelight, has turned out to be something of a surprise. I'm particularly interested in – '

'There is nothing the least bit surprising or interesting about me, Mr Devlin,' Fizz said abruptly, determined to interrupt him before he could tell her what he found interesting about Miss Felicity Beaumont. 'I'm the practical one.'

'The one who can add up a column of figures?'

'That's a bit below the belt,' she protested. To discover that he was capable of teasing her was unsettling. To discover that she enjoyed it was far more disturbing.

'Possibly. But I'd like to find out just how practical you are. Are you game?'

Fizz was almost lost for words at the unspeakable nerve of the man. But not quite. 'What did you have in mind, Mr Devlin? I'm rather too busy for games.'

Luke Devlin didn't answer immediately, instead regarded her thoughtfully for so long that she began to heat up under his dark eyes, the warmth beginning as a small, intense spot that swiftly spread through her body until the chill of the room was forgotten. Then his gaze flicked back to the white-flecked sea that swelled around the huge legs of the pier, and she almost staggered with relief as the cold rushed back, sending a little shiver through her.

'There's no need to look so concerned, Miss Beaumont. It's nothing too difficult. I'm not going to set you a maths problem. I want you to come and look at some houses with me.'

'Houses?' Fizz hadn't known what to expect, except that his cool, assessing glance had suggested something far more demanding of her nerve. The sheer ordinariness of house-hunting was such an anticlimax that she was left feeling rather stupid. 'Does that mean you're planning to stay in Broomhill Bay?' she asked.

'You sound surprised. Or is it that you're disappointed? Were you hoping that I'd be out of your hair in a week or two?'

'That would be – ' A relief. It would be a relief if he just went away. She could cope with Melanie Brett, but she wasn't at all sure she could handle Luke Devlin breathing down her neck day in, day out. She had barely stopped herself saying the words, but she could see from his expression that he knew exactly how she felt.

'I'll be around for a while, Miss Beaumont.' He seemed to take pleasure in telling her that. 'It seems my work in Broomhill Bay has hardly begun, and hotels are very public places. I've decided to rent somewhere for a while.'

'And what about Melanie?' The words tripped over her tongue and had escaped before she could stop them, but he didn't seem to notice her confusion. 'Is she expected to stay in Broomhill as well?'

'Melanie has no choice in the matter.'

Who would want one? Her wits seemed to be wandering and she hauled them firmly back into line. Melanie Brett might have the manners of a well-behaved schoolgirl, but she was clearly a full-blown woman if she could keep a man like Luke Devlin in thrall. 'In that case I'm sure she'd prefer to look at the houses herself.'

'That was the plan, but on consideration Mel is hopelessly romantic. She would yearn for an English cottage with thatch, and roses around the door – '

'And you are not romantic?'

'Like you, Miss Beaumont, my taste runs more on the lines of practicality. And efficient heating,' he added, throwing another disparaging glance about her office. 'Presenting Melanie with a *fait accompli* will avoid any possibility of the sulks.'

She dared to *sulk*? 'But surely she should have some . . .?' Her voice petered out. It was obvious that Melanie's taste, good, bad or indifferent, did not interest him. Their relationship was undoubtedly on an altogether earthier plane.

'Besides,' he continued, as if she had not interrupted, 'thanks to you, Melanie is not available. She's having a working lunch with Andy, which she will doubtless enjoy a very great deal more than an afternoon looking at houses – none of which are likely to live up to her expectations.' He didn't appear to be in the least concerned about that. 'And being "the practical one", you'll make an excellent substitute.'

'I'm afraid on this occasion you'll have to excuse me, Mr Devlin.' Fizz indicated her sandwich. 'As you can see, I, too, am having a working lunch.'

'That's not lunch,' he said, regarding her sandwich with distaste. 'And it has not escaped my notice, Miss Beaumont, that you are shivering. I think you should have something hot and nourishing to sustain you in this ice-box of an office. I've booked a table at the Angel, and as your reward for help in navigating me around Broomhill, and offering your no doubt pithy views on the houses available, you are most welcome to join me.'

It was true. She *was* shivering – although not with the cold, but he mustn't know that. Fizz forced a little smile to her lips. 'I've been threatening to buy some thermal underwear,' she began, 'perhaps it's time I did – ' His finger flew to her lips, cool against her skin, playing havoc with her self-possession, raising her pulse so that she could feel it ticking at her throat, inducing the low, shaming ache . . . Was there such a thing as lust at first sight? she wondered unhappily. She certainly didn't find Luke Devlin in the least bit lovable.

Sure now of her undivided attention, he smiled. 'Shall we try lunch before you do anything that drastic?'

The touch of his fingertip against the fullness of her lips somehow made protest seem impossible. But the moment he released her she tried. 'I'm really too busy, Mr Devlin – '

'Luke,' he said, taking her ancient fleece-lined leather flying jacket from behind the door. He held it out, inviting her to slip her arms into the sleeves. But she had had enough of dancing to his tune like an obliging puppet. She ignored the jacket.

'No, Mr Devlin. I'll see you on Friday, as we arranged.' As *he* had arranged, she mentally corrected herself. She hadn't had anything to do with it. For a moment he remained quite still, the air between them strung out like a tennis net. Then the door burst open.

'Oh, sorry, Fizz. I didn't know you had someone with you.' Susie gave Luke Devlin a long, appreciative look, the kind of look that a happily married woman didn't feel the least need to hide. Immediately sensing an ally, Luke Devlin smiled back. It was a real smile this time, the whole works, with the little pouches beneath the eyes that couldn't be faked. Permafrost began melting as far away as Siberia.

'Luke Devlin,' he said, offering his hand as he introduced himself. 'I'm trying to persuade Miss Beaumont to spare me a couple of hours of her time. I've even offered to throw in lunch, but she says she's too busy,' he said, shamelessly encouraging Susie to rat on her employer.

Susie, her hand still held in his and always a sucker for a smile from a good-looking man, duly ratted. 'Nonsense,' she said, before Fizz could stop her. 'She could do with a good lunch and an afternoon off. She works too hard.' She gave Fizz an outrageous wink as she leaned over her desk and put down the file containing the figures that Fizz had been waiting for. 'Off you go. I can hold the fort here.'

'I've an appointment at two-thirty,' Fizz reminded her pointedly.

'I am perfectly capable of interviewing a cleaner,' Susie said treacherously.

Devlin held out the coat. 'Please, Miss Beaumont.' Humility did not suit him, and she was not in the least bit convinced. She knew the 'please' was purely to impress Susie. 'A couple of hours of your time isn't much to ask. You know the area and I would value your opinion.' A moment ago he had been demanding her company. Now, Fizz thought, butter wouldn't melt in his mouth. But she knew when she was beaten.

'Very well, Mr Devlin. But I must be back by four. I've promised Melanie afternoon tea.'

'Luke,' he invited.

'Luke.' She repeated his name obediently.

'Thank you, Felicity.'

'Oh, grief, don't call her that,' Susie warned him as he settled the sheepskin about her shoulders. 'She hates it. Call her Fizz.'

'Haven't you got some filing to do, Susie?' She glanced pointedly at the heap of papers in the filing basket with a layer of dust on them. She didn't wait for Susie's pained expression, but opened the door and swept through.

'Do you really prefer to be called Fizz?' Luke asked as he followed her down the steep flight of stairs that led from her office to the public areas.

'If we're going to spend the next two hours together, Miss Beaumont would be tedious.'

'Why Fizz?'

Fizz, bang. She wasn't going to admit to that. 'My sister couldn't manage Felicity and it just stuck, I suppose.' Not without reason.

'I see.' He didn't quite buy it, she could see, and his look was thoughtful as he opened the huge glass door at the entrance for her.

'Fizz!' The receptionist waved her back, phone in hand. 'Susie wants you. She says it's urgent.'

'A reprieve, do you think?' Luke enquired.

Knowing Susie, she doubted it. 'Will you excuse me for a moment?'

'Of course. But only for a moment.'

She walked back to the reception desk and took the telephone. 'What is it, Susie?'

'Look, Fizz, I don't really have to do this filing, do I?'

That was more like it. 'No, Susie. On second thoughts filing isn't nearly punishment enough. I'm going to fire you instead.'

Susie chuckled. 'Rubbish. After an afternoon with the delectable Mr Devlin you'll give me a rise. Have fun looking round other people's houses. But do be careful in the bedrooms.'

Fun? She glanced across to the dark figure waiting for her in the doorway. Susie had it all wrong. Delectable he might be, but an afternoon in his company was not her idea of fun. Luke Devlin burned bright and strong, and in his presence she felt horribly like a moth flying too close to the flame.

Furious at her own weakness, Fizz fastened the zip of her flying jacket and tugged it up. What did it matter if she was singed a little, so long as Pavilion Radio was safe?

CHAPTER 5

The day was bright, the very best kind of winter day, with a clear blue sky trailing thin, high, storm-teased clouds. The wind was whipping up white horses as the sea ran up to the beach and the pale sun gave just a hint of the promised warmth of spring.

The weather had brought out the locals, well-wrapped against the wind, to promenade the pier, and the restaurant appeared to be doing a brisk trade in early lunches. It was encouraging, an affirmation that Fizz had made the right decision. Unfortunately success could not come quickly enough to stave off disaster if she refused to accept Luke Devlin's sponsorship.

'We could eat here,' Fizz offered, pride pushing her to show him that she was not quite the commercial innocent he seemed to think her, to show him that she had made the right decision, impress him.

'You'd feel safer on home territory?' He glanced down at her. 'Why? Are you afraid to be alone with me?'

Impress him? Who was she kidding? He was treating her like a silly girl six feet out of her depth without a lifebelt.

111

Afraid? Why wouldn't she be afraid? Anyone with a well-developed sense of self-preservation would be afraid of Luke Devlin. He was the shark in the calm water. And when a shark invited you to lunch he only laid one place at the table.

And his threat wasn't just to her business. It was on a deeper, more personal level. He had jolted her out of her quiet contentment and stolen her peace of mind. But she didn't like him speculating about the state of her nerves, so now she gave him a look that suggested bemusement.

'I was merely being polite, Mr Devlin . . . Luke. Since you were looking for Melanie, I assumed it was her you wanted to take out to lunch?'

'I did.' His jaw tightened ominously. He might be a mind-reader *par excellence*, but he didn't much like the tables being turned, Fizz thought. 'But my plans didn't include watching her steal your presenter's heart.'

'Will she do that?'

'Oh, yes. Quite unwittingly, of course.' His glance flickered to the restaurant, but Melanie and Andy were not visible through the windows etched with delicate line drawings of Victorian ladies promenading with their beaux.

'And you don't mind?'

'Should I? I'm sure Mr Gilbert will survive. But I've seen her do it too many times to enjoy the spectacle.' With that, he turned and strode along the pier.

Fizz, quite shocked, remained rooted to the spot. Such a casual attitude bordered on the heartless; or was that bitten-down emotion as close as Luke Devlin came to betraying his feelings? She shrugged. Maybe he was just

112

so arrogant in his hold over the girl, the power that money had bought him, that he didn't even consider the possibility of competition.

Realizing that she was not beside him, Luke stopped and walked back to her. She started as he took her hand.

'You should be wearing gloves,' he said. 'It's cold out here.'

She swallowed as he drew her hand into the warm crook of his arm, against the bulk of his body, so that she was protected from the wind that ruffled his dark hair. She looked back to the safety of the restaurant.

'Don't worry, Fizz, Andy will survive.' Of course he would. He'd had years of practice. She wasn't worried about Andy. 'And so will you,' he added.

'Me? Why should I be worried about myself?'

'I can't think.' And under the sudden heat of his smile, with her hand firmly grasped in his long, warm fingers, Fizz discovered that she couldn't think either, and quite unexpectedly she smiled back.

As they approached the entrance to the pier Luke Devlin slowed. When he had left his office his only concern had been to make sure that Melanie was safe. Out in the town, with no one to protect her if a crowd gathered, the situation could so easily get out of hand. He'd seen it happen once in Sydney. He'd left her for a moment and still remembered his fear as he'd had to fight through a mob to get back to her.

He'd realized the moment he reached the pier that he had overreacted. Everyone was going about their business in an orderly fashion. There were no hysterical fans, no seething masses of reporters. He should have turned around and gone straight back to his office; he had more than enough work to keep him pinned behind his desk until evening. But Fizz Beaumont had taken him by surprise and he didn't like that. Not one bit. It suggested that he had underestimated her.

He still wasn't sure why he had insisted on her help in house-hunting. He wasn't even sure he wanted a house. It had never been part of his plan to stay in Broomhill Bay. He had acquired Harries at a ridiculous price, planning to redevelop the site, put up small industrial units where satellite companies could assemble electronic units manufactured cheaply in the Far East. Once the dirty work was done he had intended that he and Melanie should shake the dust of Broomhill off their feet and never return.

He glanced down at the girl beside him, breathless in her attempts to keep up with his long strides. She looked vital, full of life, with her hair blowing about her and the colour whipped into her face by her wind. He had thought, from the photographs he had seen of her, that she was a fragile little thing. But, while there *was* a vulnerability about her, she had strength too.

If her secretary hadn't come in at that moment, taking the ground from beneath her, he doubted if he would have moved her from her office. Not without resorting to some kind of threat. And he didn't want to threaten her; he wanted her to trust him. But she didn't. Which was odd, since he was going to considerable expense to make life easy for her. She turned and looked up at him and something inside him seemed to contract. Abruptly he stopped, looked back at the ocean.

The oriental domes of the Pavilion were sparkling white against the pale winter blue of the sky, and the sea was broken by hundreds of tiny wavetops running before the wind. 'I love the sea in winter,' he said.

She stopped looking at him and turned to face the sea. 'You should try it when there's a gale blowing,' she said.

'Don't you feel vulnerable out there at the end of the pier?'

She shrugged. 'The Trust has spent a fortune strengthening the underpinnings, as well as restoring the deck and the Pavilion. It's a constant job to keep it up, of course, but we're safe enough at the moment . . .' her smile was slow, wide, oddly seductive '. . . at least from the weather. Now that Michael has retired to Portugal we'll be needing another trustee. As the new chairman of the company that built the pier you do realize that you are almost duty bound to take his place?'

Even when she was struggling, at her wits' end, she couldn't resist the temptation to provoke him. He liked that. Under other circumstances he realized he could have liked Fizz Beaumont very much indeed. It was an uncomfortable thought.

But become a trustee? It was a twist he hadn't considered. Maybe he should, but he didn't say so. Instead he favoured her with a look so dry that she could have sandpapered the deck with it, just to keep her on her toes, before turning her through the elegant arched entrance and onto the promenade, where his car was attracting admiring glances from people arriving at the pier. He unlocked the door for her and she slid into the leather-scented interior.

'Well, an Aston Martin. What a treat,' she said brightly. 'Is it?'

The weather, the scenery, his taste in cars? Maybe he should take his cue from her and stick to safe subjects. When she didn't answer he turned and found himself confronted by a tormenting little smile, and for a moment he had the feeling that he was walking on quicksand, that being with Fizz Beaumont was never going to be safe.

'My heap has more rattles than a first-born babe,' she confessed, her smile deepening, and he suffered the stomach-lurching sensation associated with taking a humpback bridge too fast. 'I don't imagine this car rattles?'

For a moment his eyes rested on the elderly E-type Jaguar parked alongside them. Old it might be, but it had been well cared for and was still very beautiful. 'Your heap was a fine car in its day,' he said. 'Unfortunately its day was over twenty years ago.'

'Twenty? That recent? You can be honest with me, Luke, I can take it. Don't feel obliged to be kind.'

The smile abruptly left his face. Kind? What did any Beaumont know about kindness? 'I don't feel obliged to be anything.' She threw a startled glance in his direction and he cursed inwardly as he turned away to slide the key into the ignition. With an effort he forced his face into a smile before he looked back at her. 'Certainly not kind to your car. Shall we go?'

Fizz had almost felt the anger boiling up from somewhere deep inside the man. It had only been for a moment, like the heat from an oven door as it was opened and closed again quickly. Now the smile was back in place and, try as she might to see beyond the mask, the hard cheekbones, the hawkish flare of his nose and the passionate line of his mouth gave her no clue as to his real feelings. But she knew she was right to distrust him.

She would be wise to remember that Luke Devlin wasn't about to sponsor Pavilion Radio out of the kindness of his heart. If it hadn't been for the evidence that Melanie Brett was capable of stirring the passion damped down behind eyes dark as wet slate, Fizz would have considered it entirely possible that he didn't have a heart.

Or could it be that the girl was just another attractive acquisition for a man wealthy enough to indulge himself with expensive playthings? Like the car she was sitting in. Like the wristwatch he wore. Made from tough stainless steel, rather than gold, it would still cost enough to put down a deposit on a small house. And quite suddenly, although she could not have explained why, she pitied Melanie.

She took a deep breath. 'Right. If we're going to the Angel for lunch, we should be able to look at some houses on the way. Have you got the details?'

He took a sheet of paper from his breast pocket and handed it to her. 'The estate agent gave me this. It lists everything available to rent, although I don't suppose they'll all be suitable.'

'No. I don't suppose they will.' The list was still warm from his body, and for just a moment she wanted to put it to her face to see if his scent had penetrated the paper. Then, certain that she was going quite mad, she snapped it open. 'What exactly are you looking for?'

'Something comfortable, easy to run, secluded, with a view of the sea,' he said, waiting for her to scan the list and suggest which direction they should take before pulling out into the traffic.

'The sea view is easy,' she said. 'Any property of consequence in Broomhill Bay has a sea view.' And he wouldn't be looking for anything else. 'As for the rest . . .' Fizz found a pen in her bag and proceeded to strike through two-thirds of the houses listed as totally unsuitable for a man of his means and a girl who would certainly require a considerable degree of privacy.

His hand closed over hers. 'Perm any three from four,' he instructed.

Fizz firmly ignored the battalion of butterflies that stampeded through her body at his touch, devastating the cool, self-assured indifference to anything but work that she had cultivated with such care over the years. Why should she suddenly lose it? And for Luke Devlin of all people? Why couldn't she be bowled over by someone like Julian, who was kind and thoughtful and would never hurt her?

It had been the same with Patrick. Fizz, bang, light the blue touch paper and retire. Except she hadn't retired. She had been like Melanie, young, bright, full of life and ready for love. For a second the print blurred before her eyes as she remembered how she had been. Then she blinked hard. She had reinvented herself, changed her life, and eventually the pain had faded into the background. Older and wiser, she *wouldn't* let Luke Devlin take anything from her. Not her radio station. Certainly not her heart.

'I've left all those properties that meet with at least two of your requirements,' she informed him, in control of her voice if nothing much else.

'You think I'm being unreasonable?'

His smile was back in place. Not quite up to the standard of the one that he had turned on Susie, but still dangerous. It was so much easier to hang onto her wits when he was being just plain rude.

'Not unreasonable,' she said, keeping her eyes firmly on the list. 'And I'm sure you're prepared to pay well to get exactly what you want. But Broomhill isn't a large city with an enormous choice of houses to let. I think that unless you modify your requirements you might be living at the Metropole for some time.' With Melanie Brett.

That thought made it much easier to turn and look at him, confront the slightly puzzled expression with which he was regarding her. She even managed a smile of sorts. 'Shall we get on?' she suggested. 'This is still a working day for me, no matter what Susie said, and I don't have time to waste.'

'I'm sure you consider this as work, Fizz. And, since you want me to sponsor your radio station, I'm afraid that you'll have to waste just as much time as I think necessary. I never said you had to enjoy it.'

It was just as well that she was – finally – lost for

words. Anything she said right now she would be sure to regret.

He didn't want to get out of the car and look at the house and it wasn't a comfortable feeling. He was having to face the fact that he had manufactured an excuse to get Fizz Beaumont to spend the afternoon with him. Not so that he could flirt with her, tease her, ultimately take her to bed. But because he wanted to be with her, to find out what made her tick. And, despite his harsh words, he did want her to enjoy his company, although for some reason she seemed to be fighting him every inch of the way. Perhaps it was simply because she *was* fighting him every inch of the way.

'But it's beautiful,' Fizz declared, with barely cloaked irritation at the waste of her time.

She had already made it quite obvious that in her opinion the other houses had been quite adequate for a temporary stay. But Winterbourne Manor was a great deal more than adequate. It was a house to dream about. To dream in. A place to raise children, to grow old in, to spend a life in utter contentment. All the things that had evaded him. But he'd had no example of happiness. His mother had been abandoned by his father when he was a baby. His sister . . . Well, Juliet hadn't even got that far.

Luke stirred. 'Don't you think it's a bit isolated for Melanie?'

'I thought the whole point of this exercise was to present Melanie with a *fait accompli*?'

'Would you like to live out here?'

'It's only five miles from Broomhill, Luke, and I'm

120

sure Melanie can drive. You did ask for seclusion, and in the height of the summer you'll be glad of the privacy. Both of you.' She didn't wait for him to agree but opened the car door, swinging her long legs out, apparently determined that he should look at the place properly.

He had hated the suit she'd worn when she came to his office, but right now he wished she was wearing it. He had enjoyed her struggle with the skirt, the briefest glimpse of a stocking-top. For a moment he watched as she walked across to the edge of the drive. She had a great walk, swinging her legs from the hips in a smooth, fluid action. It made him wonder what she would be like in bed. He remembered her hot eyes and knew. God, he wanted to feel her beneath him, her thighs opening to welcome him. The knowledge was like a kick in the midriff, robbing him of the ability to breathe.

She leaned over the stone parapet. 'It's even got a little beach of its own, Luke,' she said, impatient with his reluctance to come and see. She turned and looked back over her shoulder at him. 'For heaven's sake, Melanie will love it.'

He climbed out of the car and walked over to where she was standing. The beach was a pale yellow postage stamp of sand where the dark, spray-soaked rocks parted to form a tiny bay.

'Little is right,' he agreed. 'And is it ever warm enough to swim?' She was intent on the little beach, on a pair of gulls trawling a rock pool in search of lunch, and he was content to look at her small white hands curving over the top of the parapet. Her nails were perfect little ovals; even without nail polish they were as pink as the inside of seashells. His own hands, beside them, were permanently darkened by the sun, scarred and hardened – a legacy of his short but glorious career as a field geologist. 'Well?'

'You know it is,' she said, lifting her eyes to meet his, not backing down at his silent challenge. 'Unless, of course, you've gone soft in the warm waters of the Pacific?'

He knew then that he'd made a serious mistake. It had been a mistake to allow her to take her father's place in the negotiations, to fill his mind with questions to which there could be no answers. Felicity Beaumont was to have played a supporting role in his scenario, to have provided the last little twist of the knife in his destruction of Edward Beaumont. But she was beginning to assume an importance out of all proportion . . . 'Don't rely on it. When was the last time *you* swam off this coast?'

'Me?' For a fraction of a second she hesitated. 'I can't swim.'

And she hadn't even crossed her fingers as she lied. 'Isn't that a little foolhardy for someone who works at the end of a pier?' Luke asked.

'I hadn't thought about it.'

She was so damned cool. 'Maybe you should. It's a dangerous place.' The implication that she was at the end of the pier without a lifebelt was too obvious to be missed. There was no need to press the point. Instead he turned, resting his elbows against the stonework, and looked up at the house. 'According to the agent, Winterbourne Manor has a heated pool. Perhaps you'd like me to give you some lessons?' he offered, very gently. He saw her swallow nervously. That would teach her not to cross her fingers.

'That's very kind of you, Mr Devlin,' she said, abandoning his given name in an attempt to shoehorn the formality back into their relationship.

'Luke,' he prodded her, not allowing her to get away with it.

'But you haven't taken it yet. And, as you pointed out, it *is* quite isolated.' He didn't disagree; he didn't do anything. He just let her keep talking. 'And I suppose it would be very large for just two people,' she persisted, in the manner of a child who had just learned to swim and was determined to make the width of the pool, sinking further with every stroke but refusing to give up. 'It's sure to cost a fortune to heat.'

'Particularly the swimming pool.'

'Yes,' she said. And she blushed. And so she should. Although he had enjoyed the performance. It had been plucky, full of grit. He had particularly enjoyed his own comparison of it with a child learning to swim. It fitted very nicely with some old publicity photographs of Elaine French swimming with her two daughters in the private pool of their London home. Fizz must have been about four and she had been like a little fish.

'Actually, the house does have two of the features I was looking for. You seemed to think it would be foolish of me to expect more.'

'Two?'

He generously upgraded isolated. 'It's secluded and it has a view of the sea.'

'But it won't be easy to run. And it's bound to be terribly draughty . . .'

'Why don't we go inside and find out?' And, taking her gently but firmly by the arm, he led her towards the huge studded oak door.

Winterbourne Manor was one of those warm stone houses that looked as if it belonged in the landscape, nestling into a natural contour, taking advantage of the shelter it offered and sitting low against the sudden storms that could whip up the channel and batter themselves out on the Downs. Built long ago of the local buff-grey stone, the house had weathered until it blended so perfectly with its surroundings that nothing jarred or looked out of place.

Fizz reached for the bell but Luke forestalled her, producing a key.

'Where are the owners?' she asked, surprised.

'In America, apparently. They inherited it over a year ago. They've kept on the housekeeper but she's visiting her sister for a couple of days.'

'And the agent handed over the key? Just like that?'

He gave her an odd look. 'He's desperate to let the place. Or sell it. And perhaps he had the good sense not to offend me by suggesting I might run off with the silver.'

'If you did he'd know where to look for you.'

'Perhaps that was it,' he agreed softly, and discovered that making her blush was a pleasure he hadn't anticipated. She turned away, making a great performance of looking at the house. But he didn't need to look at it. Winterbourne Manor exuded a warmth that had nothing to do with the efficient central heating and the ruthless exclusion of draughts. Fizz was right. It was beautiful.

'Well? Where would you like to start?' she asked.

'You're the practical one, where do you suggest?'

'The kitchen?'

'I'm disappointed, Fizz. The housekeeper is part of the package. I'll leave the kitchen to her, thanks all the same. Really practical people look at the plumbing first.'

'The *plumbing*? You want to hunt for stopcocks?'

For just a moment he cherished the delightful picture of the beautiful Miss Beaumont covered in cobwebs and dust as she braved the spiders in some back scullery. 'Not stopcocks,' he said. 'But I do insist on a shower that does more than dribble.'

'Oh.' She looked up the broad oak staircase that had been built, like the house, to last centuries. 'Upstairs, then.'

The sudden wobble in her voice surprised him. Despite her inclination to snap, she was clearly as aware of the sexual tension between them as he was. Maybe that was the reason for the snappiness. He would have to be careful or she would shy away like a skittish colt.

'Upstairs,' he agreed, with a smile that caught him unawares and found a brief answering echo in her eyes. Then she turned quickly and ran lightly up the shallow steps.

He let her go, taking pleasure in the swing of her neat bottom beneath the short leather jacket, imagining those twin cheeks cupped in his hands as he pulled her hard against him. The strength of his desire for her took him by surprise and he caught his breath, swallowed.

She had paused on a half-landing to glance out of a tall stained-glass window. The winter sun filtered through the leaded panes, spattering the wall behind her with coloured light, turning her chestnut hair to dark copper, and he felt the life force stir within him.

He hadn't expected seducing Edward Beaumont's daughter to be difficult. It wasn't that he was especially conceited, but his enquiries had produced no evidence of a recent relationship and he knew that girls who lived in the shadow of a glamorous sister were usually grateful to be noticed. And he hadn't expected to enjoy it. The hair stirred on the nape of his neck as he realized that he was in danger of enjoying it too much.

He refused to think about it. He had done his thinking. It was time to act, and he took the stairs two at a time until he was standing behind her, but taking care not to actually touch her, so that he could see what had caught her eye. A hundred yards or so away, where the formal gardens gave way to woodland, snowdrops had colonized the area beneath the trees – drifts of delicate white flowers that sparkled in the thin sunshine.

'Pretty, but not practical,' he chided gently. 'And admiring the garden definitely comes under the heading of time-wasting.'

'Some things are never a waste of time.' She turned her head on her long neck to look up at him, her eyes wide, her lips slightly parted in unconscious invitation. He felt an almost overwhelming longing to kiss her, to taste her, to gather her up and feel her tremble against him. He restrained the urge with difficulty. He wanted her to fall in love with him. Making her wait would bring her into his arms all the quicker. The trick would be to keep a clear head. It was an exciting and oddly disturbing prospect.

He smiled. 'Perhaps we could exchange notes on our favourite ways to waste time over lunch. In the meantime, enjoy your snowdrops. I'll check upstairs. It doesn't need two of us.'

He looked. The bedrooms had a faded elegance that could only be the real thing – each one furnished by generations of occupants, each generation discarding this, adding that. But some pieces must have been bought when the house was new.

In the master bedroom, the four-poster bed had sufficient gravitas to make even the most sceptical believe that it might have been slept in by the first Queen Elizabeth. A second suite, with its own luxurious bathroom and a small dressing room, was similarly furnished, although in a lighter, more feminine style. It was all quite lovely, and, looking around, Luke was saddened that such a wonderful family home should be reduced to being let out on a short lease.

'Luke?' He stirred as Fizz appeared in the doorway. 'Is everything all right? You were rather a long time. Does the shower work?'

'It's fine.' He arranged his face into a smile and turned to face her. 'What do you think of this?' he asked, with a flourish towards the smaller four-poster. They both looked at it. 'It's entirely possible that Melanie will never forgive me if I deny her the chance to sleep in a genuine four-poster bed,' he prompted.

'If you don't tell her, she'll never know. Besides, it's a

bit on the short side,' she said disparagingly. He'd expected a bit more enthusiasm, but she barely glanced at the bed before looking at her watch. 'Have you seen enough, Luke? Time's getting on,' she said. Then he saw the faint flush that heated her cheeks and he smiled to himself, deep inside. She rather fancied the bed herself. He would do what he could to accommodate her.

'I haven't looked downstairs yet, but I'll be quick, I promise. You must be hungry.'

Twenty minutes later they pulled up outside a small inn high on the Downs. 'I thought you only wanted to rent something temporarily,' Fizz said, flicking at the list crossly.

Luke Devlin seemed determined to waste the afternoon touring around the rest of the houses on the list, and right now she would have traded any amount of roast potatoes in return for her sandwich in the safety of her little office at the end of the pier. Except it was no longer safe. Luke Devlin had invaded it as surely as he had invaded the rest of her life. But she had had enough of hearing about what Melanie would like. The bed had been the final straw.

'Winterbourne had absolutely everything you asked for. It might not be the easiest place on earth to run, but it has a housekeeper who will do it all for you.'

'And its own private beach.'

He caught her eye. He was teasing again. 'A very small one, admittedly,' she said stiffly.

'You don't have to sell it to me, but I still think Melanie would rather have something close to town.'

Melanie. 'I told you, you should have brought her with you,' she said. 'If she'd seen it I'm sure she would have fallen in love with it.'

'Like you,' he said drily. 'Although it would probably have been the four-poster bed that swayed it for her, not the gardens.'

'Four-poster bed?' she queried blankly, as if she hadn't even noticed it. The truth was that everything about the small Tudor manor house had been quite beautiful, right down to the wood panelling glowing with the patina of centuries of caring hands as the sun had streamed through the windows in long, raking beams. Their eyes met and Luke's brow rose so slightly that she might have imagined it. But she knew she hadn't. 'It *was* beautiful,' she conceded.

'Very picturesque,' he agreed. 'Even if it was on the small side.'

'I meant the house.'

'I suppose we could always go back and try it for size,' he suggested, thoughtfully. 'You're about the same height as Melanie.'

Fizz turned quickly away and buried her head in her list to hide the slow burn of anger that darkened her cheekbones. The man had her at his mercy, for heaven's sake. He didn't have to flirt with her as well, did he? Wasn't possession of a prize like Melanie Brett enough to satisfy his ego? 'There's nothing else here that you will like,' she said stubbornly.

'You can convince me over lunch.' He climbed out of the car and opened the door for her. Lunch. Lunch would mean sitting opposite him with no possibility of escape for at least the next hour. And discussing the merits of four-poster beds did not seem to be a very sensible way of keeping her head.

'A rather late lunch,' she said, glancing at her watch. 'I really should get back. I've a dozen things – '

'Keeping me happy is your number one priority right now,' he reminded her, taking her elbow and easing her out of the car.

The top of her head barely came to his chin. 'You're not our sponsor yet,' she said, addressing his tie.

He cupped her chin in the palm of his hand and tilted it until she was looking up into his eyes. 'You've found someone else?' he asked, the low, husky tone of his voice rippling through her, the intimate touch of his fingers scrambling the message systems that kept her body on an even keel.

'When you're being so generous, Luke Devlin,' she offered, with a show of spirit she was far from feeling, 'why would I be looking?'

'Why, indeed? But you are. Not that you're having much success. I don't imagine anyone in Broomhill is eager to throw that kind of money about at the moment. They are all waiting for the announcement of redundancies at Harries.'

So, he had been checking up on her. She wondered how. Had he employed a private investigator? Tapped into her phone line? Planted a spy in the radio station itself? She would have given a good deal to know. She'd like to use the same techniques on him. 'Will there be many?' she asked. 'Redundancies, I mean?'

'I'm not going to tell you that, Fizz.' He almost smiled.

'And I'm sure you don't expect me to.'

Of course she didn't. But if she didn't ask . . . 'News that Melanie is to join us will bring in the advertisers,' she reminded him.

'How much extra business did you manage to drum up for this afternoon?'

'Nearly five minutes. But I didn't have a lot of time.'

'Bank my cheque and you'll have all the time you need.'

'Hadn't we better make it official – sign the agreement first?' she asked.

'Friday at twelve. Of course, if you don't sign it, Melanie will not be joining you.'

'Isn't that her decision?' she countered.

'No.'

Not maybe. Not perhaps. No. 'I see.'

'I'm glad you do.'

Could he really be that ruthless? The answer was staring her in the face. There was no doubt about the determination in those dark eyes and a nervous tremor shot through her. But she made a fair stab at a careless shrug. 'Why shouldn't I sign? As far as I can tell I'm getting the best of the deal.'

'Then that's a very good reason to keep me happy, wouldn't you say? And Friday will be a very good day for both of us.' The provocative curve of his mouth was so close that for a moment she thought he was going to kiss her. The knowledge that she wanted him to kiss her, that he would almost certainly be able to read the desire in her eyes, was as chilling as a winter dip in the sea, and she stepped sharply back from the warm touch of his fingers, his thumb brushing against the down on her cheek.

Then, as his brows rose slightly, she attempted a small laugh to cover her confusion. After all, with Melanie Brett to warm his bed, the idea of him kissing her was surely quite ridiculous.

'Lunch, you said?'

He smiled slightly, as if satisfied with this evidence of her obedience, and ushered her into the inn. The bar was low, beamed, very old. 'I really must bring Mel here,' Luke said as Fizz looked about her. 'She can't get enough of this olde worlde stuff.'

'I told you, she'd love Winterbourne Manor. It's even got a rambling rose growing round the front door. In the summer you'll be glad of its seclusion. And before you ask,' she hurried on, 'I don't know the estate agent and I shan't be asking for commission.'

'Now you've got all that off your chest, what would you like to drink?' he asked.

'A tonic water, please.'

'Nothing in it? You're not driving.'

'I'm working.'

'Do you really find my company that difficult?' He seemed to take it personally, and she was glad – because personally she found him extremely difficult to be with.

'I had the feeling that you wanted it to be,' she said.

'Then I really must make more effort to put you at your ease,' he returned, the softness of his voice not entirely cloaking an altogether darker undercurrent. 'Especially since you're spending so much of your valuable time helping me.'

'I didn't have a choice.' The colour rocketed to her

cheeks as she realized how far she had allowed her personal feelings to intrude into what was, after all, a purely business arrangement. 'I'm sorry. I didn't mean . . .' She stopped. She didn't know what she meant, but she knew that an apology would only make things worse. 'The station doesn't run itself, Luke. I should be there.'

'Should you? But that's your father's responsibility, surely?' Something about the way he said that made Fizz pause before denying it.

It was true that it was her father's name on the franchise document. And Edward Beaumont had an office at the Winter Garden, far more opulent that her own little cubby-hole, from which he conducted his affairs with the help of a part-time secretary provided by the station in return for his appearances on *Holiday Bay*. It was an arrangement that suited them both very well.

To the outside world, to all but a few of the station staff, who had been with them from the beginning, Pavilion Radio was the brainchild of Edward Beaumont. After all, who in their right mind would have considered giving the franchise to a nineteen-year-old girl who was trying very hard to build herself a new life, a new career from the ruins of her dreams?

'Your father *is* the franchise holder?' Luke persisted.

Fizz felt that it was important to him, and she was suddenly afraid that if he knew the station was her baby, not that of the well-respected Edward Beaumont, he might not be so keen to prop it up.

'My father?' she said, staring into her glass. *Say yes, Fizz,* her subconscious prompted her. *Say it quickly.*

133

It was nothing less than the truth, after all, but it had been Fizz, suffering the misery of a broken heart, who had seen the possibilities one afternoon, when her father had persuaded her to go along with him to the pier to see the renovation work – anything to get her out of the house and into the fresh air. To put some colour back into her pale cheeks.

The town had been buzzing with the news that they were going to have a local radio station, and suddenly the Pavilion, run-down, deserted, had seemed to Fizz to be the perfect place. And, seeing at last a spark of enthusiasm coming back to her face, Edward Beaumont had thankfully encouraged her, agreeing to lend his name to the scheme if she could raise the finance and prepare the bid. The finance had been the least of her problems. She and Claudia had inherited her mother's estate between them. – though it had not been so very much for an actress who had been at the top of her profession for a long time. She had always been extravagant, of course, spending a fortune on clothes and jewellery. And it had taken her nine expensive years to die after her accident. But it had been enough . . .

Fizz stiffened. *The jewellery*. Safe in the bank. Half of it hers.

Fizz realized that Luke was looking at her a little oddly, as if sensing her reluctance to confirm her father's role. She wasn't happy that he had chosen this moment to push her out into the cold, hard world, yet despite the problems she had faced over the last few days there was a growing reluctance in her to keep up the pretence. It had been *her* hard work that had made the

134

station such a success, and when the franchise came up for renewal she would be glad to take the reins openly into her own hands. Assuming she wasn't swallowed up by some media monster first. No, she wouldn't allow that to happen. She would smile and sup with the devil first.

She raised her eyes to meet those of her particular devil. 'Why are you asking me, Luke' You seem to know everything about us; I'm sure you know the answer to your question as well as I do.'

The lines of tension about his mouth visibly relaxed. 'Not everything. Why, for instance, didn't you join your illustrious family on the stage?'

Fizz blinked quickly. No one had asked her that for so long that she had forgotten how much it hurt. 'I'm surprised you have to ask, Luke,' she managed, on a breathy little laugh. 'You were singularly unimpressed with my performance at your office.'

'A little over the top,' he conceded, 'but full of passion. And you must have been tempted – after all, you went to RADA.'

She felt a stir of unease at this further evidence of his interest in her family. RADA had been a very long time ago. But her shrug was convincing enough. 'Everyone expected it. One of my father's few regrets in life is that he didn't have three daughters so we could play to his Lear.'

Luke Devlin's head came up sharply, his eyes narrowing. Then he gave a little shrug. 'An interesting idea,' he said drily.

'It wouldn't have worked. The truth of the matter is that I was not cut out for the stage.' He nodded, and the fact that he had accepted her word without question was a demonstration of how very good she could have been.

'Shall we eat?'

'Will they still serve us this late?' she asked, glancing towards the almost empty dining room.

'I telephoned our order through from the car while you were still slavering over the garden.'

'I was not slavering,' she objected. 'I have never slavered in my life.' She caught his eye, and without warning a bubble of laughter escaped her lips. 'Well, perhaps just the teeniest little slaver.' He had practically had to drag her away from the old herb garden she had spotted from the window and had gone in search of while he took a quick look through the ground floor. 'But it wasn't just the garden. The whole house was wonderful.'

'It should be lived in by a family who will care for it, not rented out like some anonymous apartment.'

'It must be very different from your home in Australia,' she said as he held a chair for her. 'Overlooking Sydney Harbour, isn't it? All glass and steel?' she added, remembering something she had read in Jim's file.

'You must have been reading some very old press cuttings,' he said, with the barest shrug. 'I sold that place four or five years ago.'

'Old press cuttings were all I could get my hands on,' she informed him. They were both toying with the cutlery, avoiding the other's eyes.

'I prefer to conduct my personal drama on a private stage.'

'Is that the reason you're so anxious to leave the Metropole?'

He looked up then. 'Melanie has a rather higher profile than I can comfortably live with,' he agreed. 'Hordes of teenage girls camping on the doorstep is not my idea of fun.'

She grinned. 'It could be worse.'

'I can't think how.'

'It could be hordes of teenage boys,' she said, then caught her breath. It was hardly tactful to point out that Melanie was young enough for teenage boys to find her desirable. But since meeting Luke Devlin her tact quotient had become dangerously depleted. He didn't seem to notice, however, but turned to smile at the waitress who had brought their food, and Fizz had time to catch her breath while it was served. 'This is wonderful,' she said, tucking into a succulent slice of roast beef. It was infinitely safer than discussing his living arrangements.

'You haven't been here before?'

'Not for ages. I don't have too much time for eating out. The station takes every minute of the day.'

'And night?'

She looked up, surprised by the deep query in his voice. Why would he be interested in her personal life? 'We're a twenty-four-hour a day station, Luke,' she reminded him.

'That can't leave much time for . . . other things.'

'Not a lot.' And that suited her just fine.

'It can be a mistake to get too involved in your work. You can lose your sense of perspective. What would you do if your father lost the franchise, for instance?'

'Why should he lose it?' she asked, sensitive to every

137

nuance in his voice. 'Do you know something we don't?'

'Probably quite a lot, but if you think I'm interested you can forget it. I've no use for a radio station.'

'You're using Pavilion Radio for something. What, I don't know, but you're not telling me everything.'

'Whilst you, of course, are the soul of probity?'

'I've nothing to hide.'

'Maybe not. But this station seems to mean a great deal more to you than to your father. He couldn't even be bothered to pick up the telephone to call me.'

She had been right. The man was a typical male chauvinist, who wouldn't knowingly put his precious money into the hands of a slip of a girl. The knowledge that she had kept her secret was deeply satisfying. This wasn't the moment to declare war, to stand up for her rights. Her time would come. Fizz swallowed her pride and fixed an earnest expression upon her face.

'I can assure you that my father is totally committed to Pavilion Radio.' She tried to remember what he had said the night they went on air. He had been playing the role of public benefactor to the hilt – she had teased him about it for months afterwards as she'd been swept along on the high of their success. 'Broomhill is his home, and when the franchise was put out to tender he fell that the town deserved better than the usual pop station with advertisements.' That was the absolute truth. 'He wanted to ensure the widest possible choice of pro-grammes.'

'That was what *he* wanted. What about you?'

'Me? Oh, I just do the books, keep the place ticking over. Anyone could do it.' She was well into her part now. 'If we lost the franchise I'd get another job,' she said earnestly. 'But Dad . . .' At this point her father would have laid his hand very gently over his heart, but then he was an accomplished actor and was allowed the occasional over-the-top gesture. Fizz refrained from anything quite so dramatic, contenting herself with a telling little shrug.

'Then I take it that there's no question of you turning down my offer?' Luke said, very, very softly. The more softly he spoke, Fizz decided, the more dangerous he was, and she was grateful that her hands were fully occupied with her knife and fork so it was quite impossible for her to slap that infuriating look of satisfaction from the man's face.

Instead Fizz made herself smile. She was certain Luke could hear her jaw creaking with the effort it took. 'It would be a shame to spoil a good lunch talking about business. I'd much rather listen to you tell me how you made your millions.'

'Why? Are you hoping for some ideas to make your own fortune?'

'Oh, I don't need a fortune. Just enough money to keep the radio station above the waves.'

'I'm already offering you that for nothing.' Not for nothing. He was taking and taking and taking. A one-man invasion force.

'I don't think you'd give me the shavings from your pencil for nothing,' she said, with exquisite politeness.

'Don't you?' His smile was just a little forced, she thought. She had touched a nerve. 'I can assure you that I don't expect you to pay for your own lunch.'

'And I wasn't planning to charge you a consultancy fee for helping you to find a house. Shall we leave it at that?'

'Until Friday.'

'Until Friday,' she agreed.

CHAPTER 6

The Pier was a heaving mob of youngsters. Luke groaned audibly as they climbed from the car and saw hundreds of girls blocking the way through. 'Oh, God, it'll take hours to get Mel out through that lot.' He clearly wanted to be somewhere else – anywhere else.

Fizz thought that an excellent idea too. Three hours in the company of a man she found in turn ruthless, disdainful and frighteningly attractive, and her attempts to disguise her own feelings in turn, had left her utterly wrung out. 'There's no need to wait, Luke. I'm sure you've got a great deal to do.'

'Yes,' he agreed. But he didn't make any move to go.

'You shouldn't have insisted on looking at that last house. I told you you wouldn't like it.'

'No doubt it gives you enormous satisfaction to know that you were right. I'm afraid it will have to be Winterbourne.'

'Melanie will love it,' she said, resting a reassuring hand on the soft sleeve of his overcoat. *Reassuring*? She was reassuring Luke Devlin? She removed her hand,

141

very slowly. It took every ounce of self-control not to snatch it back.

He glanced down at her. 'Yes, well, thank you for sparing so much of your time.'

'You'll be late for your meeting,' she prompted.

He was still reluctant to leave and she was intrigued. If he was really concerned that she might tempt indiscretions from Melanie's young lips, it could only mean that there were indiscretions to tempt. 'I'll get her back to the Metropole as soon as things quieten down. She'll be quite safe, I promise.'

He seemed to gather himself. 'Yes, I'm sure she will.' Nevertheless, he regarded the pier with misgiving. 'What will you do, call out the lifeboat?'

Fizz grinned. 'I'm sure the crew would enjoy it enormously, but the coxswain might have other ideas. Don't worry, the cold will drive these girls home for their tea soon.' She turned up the fleece collar of her jacket against her cheeks. The sun was sinking fast, and taking with it all pretence that spring was near.

'You'd better get out of the cold yourself,' he said a little gruffly. 'Will you tell Melanie not to wait dinner for me?' Fizz lifted her brows in gentle query. 'If she wants to know why, say I'm working late, making up the time I spent looking for somewhere for her to live.'

'I'll think of you while I'm doing the same.'

'Will you?' For a moment they simply looked at one another. Then, as a crowd of girls who had noticed his Aston began to close in on them, clearly hoping that it was their heroine's transport, Luke surrendered to Fizz's prompting and climbed back behind the wheel before he

142

was inundated. 'I'd be grateful if you can ensure that she gets back to the hotel in one piece, Fizz.'

'No problem.'

'And thanks for this afternoon.'

She lifted her hand in a small gesture, too small to be called a wave, before turning away and, taking a deep breath, preparing to tackle the pier.

'I told you it wasn't her car,' one of the girls was muttering as Fizz eased passed the knot of fans at the entrance. 'She's got a white stretch limo.'

'Don't be stupid. That just brought her from the airport. And anyway, he's definitely her boyfriend.'

The first girl scoffed. '*Him*? He's as old as my dad.'

'I don't care. My mum works at the Metropole and she *knows*.'

'Well, who's *she*, then?' she said, staring at Fizz.

'She just works at PR. A secretary or something. I've seen her before.'

'Oh.'

Of no further interest to the girls, and happy in her anonymity, Fizz slipped easily through the milling crowd of girls. But the front door of the Pavilion had been locked and the foyer lights turned off, presumably to discourage Melanie's fans. She had her keys, but the girls behind her began to surge forward as they sensed she might provide them with a way in so she rattled the door, then turned and shrugged in a general gesture of helplessness before taking refuge in the restaurant, now busy serving afternoon teas to matrons who had also come in to escape the mayhem on the pier.

'Hello, Fizz.' The young chef she had chosen to run

her newest project was in the kitchen, laying out knives and boards in preparation for the evening.

'Hi, John. You're busy today.'

'We've had a rush on afternoon teas,' he agreed. 'I just wish I had a hot dog concession out there. Those girls could do with something to spend their money on.'

'They could have come in here.'

'If you'd decided on a burger bar they might have. Although frankly I doubt they'd risk missing Melanie Brett.'

'Mmm. Well, we stock chocolate in the shop if they're hungry.' She would have to find out whether they could have the 'I listen to *Holiday Bay* T-shirts overprinted with Melanie's name or picture, and have some new mugs made.

Melanie was keen to take part and apparently stuck in Broomhill Bay for the summer. Despite Luke's warning, Fizz was sure she would still do the show even if she could pull off a last-minute lifesaving act and keep Luke Devlin out of the picture. The young soap star could be a real money-spinner for the station, and Fizz swore silently that she would take every penny available. She was determined that if she got out of this predicament she would never, ever be held hostage to fortune again.

She suddenly realized that John had just said something. 'I'm sorry, what was that?'

'I said chocolate doesn't have the same sensory appeal as frying onions on a cold afternoon. Is this going to happen on a regular basis?' He nodded in the direction of the pier.

'There's no reason why it should,' she said, anxious to

dampen any entrepreneurial ideas John might be nursing. He was a young, talented chef, keen to open his own restaurant but for now happy to learn the business and make his mistakes at someone else's expense. She had no illusions about keeping him for more than a year or two at the most.

He gave her a sideways look while he began to count lemons out of a box. 'Janice must have got it wrong, then.'

'Janice?'

'One of the waitresses.' Fizz knew who she was and made an impatient little gesture. 'She overheard Melanie Brett telling Andy that she was going to be joining the cast of *Holiday Bay* for the summer.'

Yes. 'Did she tell anyone else?'

'The waitress or Miss Melanie Brett?' John, who spent most of his working life with women, took great enjoyment in winding them up, but something in her expression made him think twice about teasing Fizz any further and he straightened. 'What do you think?' he said. Fizz thought it was likely that the news would be all over town by closing time. 'It is true, then?' John persisted.

There was no point in denying that there was something in the wind. 'If I can pull if off. Nothing definite. Will you speak to your staff, John? Tell them . . . no, *ask* them, very politely, to be discreet.'

'Let me put a hot dog stall out there and I'll guarantee your secret.'

She hid her irritation. 'Oh? And how would you do that?'

'Simple bribery. I'd be able to afford it.'

145

Fizz wondered how much money a hot dog stall would take on a busy day. Not everyone wanted to come in and sit down to eat. And if it was sited far enough away, down by the bandstand, perhaps, it wouldn't interfere with the restaurant. It was certainly an idea. Not that she was in a position to give John what he wanted. The Pier Trust controlled concessions, and even if they were prepared to consider such a thing it would have to be put out to tender. By the time that could be organized it would be too late for her. Too late to keep Luke Devlin at bay. So she allowed the smallest expression of regret to cross her features.

'Unfortunately, John, I refuse to work with the constant smell of frying onions. Or with blackmailers.'

'Only kidding, boss.' He shrugged. 'But if you should ever change your mind . . .'

'You'll be the first to know, I promise. In the meantime will you send a tray of tea up to the Green Room?'

'Muffins, sandwiches, cake?'

'Oh, anything you can spare. I'm sure a seige mentality has taken over upstairs, and whatever Melanie doesn't want the gannets in the newsroom will devour.' She glanced at her watch. 'Now, if you'll excuse me, since this appears to be the only way into the station, I'll help myself to your back door.'

She found Melanie already at home in the Green Room, chatting to Andy and a new girl Jim had taken on. Fizz groped in her memory for her name. Shelly? Something like that. 'Had a good day?' she asked Melanie, shrugging out of her jacket.

'Wonderful. I can't wait to start. Have you got next week's scripts for me to read?'

'Yes, they're about somewhere. Of course, we're going to have to make some changes to ease you into the cast. We've got a wedding coming up. It's been put off twice already,' she said with a grin. 'This time I really thought it might go ahead. But, as you may have heard, everything happens in threes.'

She turned to the young reporter – Kelly, that was it. 'Kelly, I think we should embargo the news that Miss Brett is joining the cast of *Holiday Bay* until Friday afternoon.' She was certain rumours would be flying thick and fast by then, but at least Melanie had heard her give the instruction. It was up to her whether she owned up to her own lack of discretion.

'Perhaps I could do an interview with Melanie for the Friday afternoon magazine programme, Miss Beaumont?'

The girl had quickly learned to grab herself a slice of the limelight. If she was tough enough she would go far. 'Call me Fizz, everyone does. I'll let you know, Kelly.' And Kelly was dismissed.

Andy didn't take the hint. 'Did the show go well this afternoon?' she asked him.

'It was really good. Lots of calls.'

'Good.' She glanced at her watch again. 'Haven't you got a disco this evening, Andy?' Most of the broadcasters had more than one string to their bow, and Andy was in great demand – not just in Broomhill, but right down the south coast.

'I was keeping Melanie company until the crowd outside got a bit thinner.'

'I don't think it will be too long; it's getting very cold.'

147

She turned to Melanie. 'And I've promised Luke that I'll see you safely back to the Metropole.' Fizz gave Andy a look he shouldn't have been able to ignore.

He ignored it.

'Andy's already promised to drive me home, Fizz.' Melanie seemed perfectly happy with the arrangement and Andy looked positively smug.

'You could come along to the disco, if you like,' he offered – a throwaway line that could be grasped or not, without loss of face on either side. But there was a brightness about his eyes, a sharp eagerness that sent a tiny quiver of alarm feathering along Fizz's spine.

'Andy! Are you mad? The poor girl would be mobbed.'

'But I'd love to come another time,' Melanie said, without the slightest coyness. 'Once people are used to seeing me about and I can fade into the background a bit. It won't take long, will it, Fizz?'

Fizz released her breath very carefully. 'No, it won't take long. Just make sure you have someone with you for a week or two, and a portable phone to call for help if you need it.'

'I'll be happy to keep you company if you want to get around a bit,' Andy offered, and received a smile to put the sun in the shade for his trouble. 'I have plenty of free time.'

Fizz, realizing that she had made a mistake, ploughed on. 'Of course, if you wear a woolly hat to cover your hair and the kind of nondescript clothes that don't attract attention you could probably walk through Broomhill without anyone recognizing you right now. Or at least they wouldn't be sure enough to risk making a fool of themselves.'

She felt like a universal aunt dispensing wise advice to the young, and she wasn't much enjoying the experience. Besides, she was only too aware that Melanie was a full-grown adult. Luke Devlin might treat her as his personal property, but Fizz was in no position to forbid the girl to drive home with Andy. She only hoped Luke would see it in the same light.

Tea arrived, with just two cups, and Andy was dispatched to check on the state of the siege. Having established his right to take Melanie home, he didn't protest. 'Luke asked me to tell you that he might be late for dinner. He said you shouldn't wait for him,' Fizz said, as soon as he had gone.

'Oh, you've seen him?'

'We've been house-hunting for you.'

'Poor you.' She took a muffin, smothered it with butter and sank a row of small, even white teeth into it. 'Luke's not very easy to please, is he? I suppose he settled on some gloomy great place miles from anywhere?'

It seemed Luke had been right about Winterbourne Manor. 'I don't think he's made any decision yet,' she hedged. 'He seemed more concerned about what you would want.'

'Did he?' Disconcertingly Melanie blushed, as if she had been scolded. 'Oh, gosh, I don't really mind where we live. I just wish . . .' She glanced at Fizz and then away again. 'I just wish Luke could spend a bit more time with me. I've hardly seen him since I arrived.'

149

She was still such a child, Fizz thought, angry with Luke Devlin for being so selfish. Melanie should be with someone like Andy. Someone who would take her to exotic little restaurants in the Wynds, to discos and the cinema. Someone to make her laugh. Someone to flirt with her. She had the feeling that Melanie could do with some fun, and the thought of her rattling around the Metropole, as stuffy as it was expensive, or alone at Winterbourne Manor, waiting for Luke to come home was very depressing. 'He did try to find somewhere close to town, but there really isn't anywhere that you'd like,' Fizz said, more gently.

Andy stuck his head around the door. 'It's fairly quiet out there now. Just a few determined fans who won't go until they've seen you. It might be kind to go out before they actually freeze to the deck.'

'Finish your tea, Melanie. Andy can fetch your coat. It's in my office.' She stood up and offered her hand. 'I'm so glad you want to join us. We're all looking forward to working with you.'

'I can't wait. And tell Kelly to give me a ring if she wants to tape an interview for Friday.'

'I will. Perhaps you'd like to do a few promos as well?'

She caught Andy on the stairs. 'Straight to the Metropole, Andy, and keep your hands to yourself.' She might think it a very good thing if Andy whisked Melanie off to his disco and gave her the kind of good time a girl of her age should be having, but she had her station to think of.

'She's over the age of consent, Fizz.'

She knew that. Oh, God, she knew that. But she kept her feelings to herself. 'Maybe, but Luke Devlin will have

Melanie out of here faster than the Broomhill Thunderbolt if anyone upsets him. And neither of us wants that.'

Andy grinned. 'And when were you last on the Thunderbolt, Fizz?' The Thunderbolt was the pride of the funfair and a white-knuckle ride bar none.

'Me? I wouldn't go on that thing for a king's ransom.' For the money to pay off her bank loan was another matter.

'You should try it. It might shake a few of the rivets out of your corset.'

'When I want my rivets loosened, I'll consider it. In the meantime – '

'Straight to the Metropole. Hands to myself.' He repeated her instructions. 'This time.'

She hesitated. 'It never hurts to play the gentleman, Andy.'

He grinned. 'Leave them guessing, eh? Is that what works with you?' She knew he was puzzled by the fact that she found him utterly resistible, but this time he was nearer to the truth than he knew.

Once. Just once it had worked with her. Patrick March had been a lot like Andy. A little taller perhaps, his eyes meltingly dark. That first morning on the set – when she'd been eighteen and with a part any young actress would die for, a bundle of nerves at the thought that she might make a fool of herself, ruin her career before it had even begun – that first morning he had played the gentleman to perfection.

He'd been broodingly handsome. Heathcliff, Romeo, Mr Darcy – with his dark good looks and tousled curls, he could have played any one of them. At twenty-six he'd been almost too old to play the part of an out-of-control youth living off petty crime who had lost his heart to the young daughter of the most powerful family in town, but he had once appeared in a film made in America and had been noticed. The company making that low-budget adaptation of *Romeo and Juliet* to be filmed in modern Verona had wanted to cash in on his moment of fame before he was forgotten, or became too expensive.

Fizz had seen the film. And she had recognized the talent that had simmered just below the surface, contained only by the fact that the actor/director starring in the film had made certain anything that outshone his own performance had ended up on the cutting room floor. But Patrick had still been noticed. And now he was noticing her. The knowledge had gone to her head faster than champagne.

On her arrival in Verona, it hadn't taken her an hour to discover that the rest of the cast assumed she had been given the part because of her illustrious family connections. A few of them had been openly hostile, more fawned all over her – neither of them comfortable experiences. Patrick had simply taken her hand, held it briefly, given it the smallest squeeze her a reassuring smile. She hadn't so much melted as dissolved.

He had spent time explaining what would happen so she didn't feel quite so lost and confused. He'd gone out of his way to make her look good for the camera, never stealing a scene. And when they'd kissed for the camera he had broken away the minute the director called a halt. Leaving her wanting more. A perfect gentleman. A very clever gentleman.

He had rehearsed her in the evening, when the crew and the rest of the cast had been out having a good time. He'd taken her to see the galleries and the museums, holding her hand as they walked through the city, had taken her through the film script, comparing it knowledgeably with Shakespeare's play. He'd seemed oblivious to her family, oblivious to her melting desire for him, until she'd begun to wonder if he was gay. How different her life might have been now if that had been the case.

'Fizz?' She jumped. 'You were miles away. I said, we're just going.'

She stared at Andy and Melanie. 'Oh, yes. Take care, both of you.'

She could see them making their way down the pier from her office window. They were followed by the faithful band of fans who had stuck it out despite the cold and the dark. Melanie was laughing. Fizz could see her breath, little puffs of vapour, her hair a golden nimbus in the glow of the lamps as she signed the last of the autograph books thrust out to her, not hurrying, all charm. And Andy waited patiently. Then Melanie slipped her hand under his arm and, still chatting to the girls who had waited so long to meet her, walked slowly off the pier with him.

She sat down, her cold hands stuffed hard into her pockets. Why had she told Andy to play the gentleman? She, of all people, knew that any actor worth his salt could play the gentleman if you gave him a script. It took more than a script to make the genuine article. The problem was, it could be hard to tell the difference.

There was a tap at her door and she looked up to see her father watching from the doorway. 'Can I come in?'

'Of course, if you can stand the cold. I really will have to do something about the heating up here. It's not fair on Susie.'

'I understand that snow has been forecast.'

She nodded. 'I heard. We don't usually get it down here on the coast, though.'

'Is everything all right, Fizz? You looked . . . distant.'

'Fine.' She found a smile for him. 'Mr Devlin has agreed to carry on sponsoring us provided we find a part for a young actress he knows in *Holiday Bay*.'

'Really?' He sounded pleased. 'Well, that shouldn't prove to much of a problem.'

'No. None whatever. She's a delightful girl. She's something of a celebrity, in fact, and I'm sure listening figures will rocket. Having her in the town should be good for local trade too.'

Edward Beaumont beamed. 'There, now,' he said, delighted with the world. 'I said you could handle it without me.' Then he shivered. 'Why don't you come down to my office and have a glass of sherry to celebrate?'

'I'll leave it until the weekend if you don't mind. Is Claudia coming home, do you know? I'd like to talk to her, explain what's happening.' Before she picked up some second-hand gossip.

'I am expecting her. She phoned earlier, still sounding thoroughly fed up about losing this film. We really ought to do something to cheer her up. A little party, perhaps? You haven't had an official opening of the restaurant yet – '

154

Fizz suddenly realized that her father's visit was to discuss Claudia's problems, not hers. 'Dad, would you mind if we talk about this tomorrow? I really have a million things to do.'

He hesitated for just a moment, then gave a little shrug. 'Of course. I'll see you tomorrow.'

She waited until the door had closed behind him and then quickly checked a number in her book. Taking a deep breath, she reached for the phone.

'Julian? It's Fizz. I need to sell some quite valuable jewellery quickly,' she rushed on, before he could say anything. 'Will you help me?'

Rather to her surprise he said yes.

Just over an hour later Julian met her at Victoria. He was standing at the end of the platform waiting while she walked down the platform, his expression guarded.

'I'm sorry,' she said, quite simply. 'I didn't know who else to ask.'

'I guessed that. Although I can't say I'm flattered by your assumption that I would know where to pop the family jewels.'

'Pop?'

'Pop, pledge, pawn.' He turned her away from the station, leading her to where his car was parked. 'Don't look so shocked. Even the best people do it. And its tricky to get a good price for jewellery unless you can wait for the right buyer. This is your mother's stuff, right?'

'Yes.'

'Then I'd recommend an auction. She still has an army of adoring fans, you know – middle-aged men who would fork out a mint just to possess a necklace that had adorned the neck of the great Elaine French.' He looked at her, slightly baffled. 'I'm still not sure why you feel you have to do this if Devlin has agreed to sponsor you.'

'I'd rather be in charge of my own destiny.'

He shrugged. 'In that case pawning it will cover your immediate problems.'

'Will it?' She was horrified by the idea. 'But could just one pawnbroker handle something like this?' Fizz had a sudden terrible vision of trailing around the backstreets of London, hocking a necklace here, a bracelet there in dingy little shops.

'Don't worry about that. Just tell me where we have to go to pick the stuff up.'

Fizz gave him the address of the depository where, at the insistence of the insurance company, her mother's jewels were kept in a safety deposit box. They were stored in London for Claudia's convenience. Her sister wore hers frequently but Fizz scarcely ever took hers out, except to wear at one of her father's rare first nights, or to one of the media award dinners. She certainly wouldn't miss them. The fact that it had taken her so long to come up with such a simple solution to her problem was ample evidence of how rarely she even thought of them.

She showed her identification to the guard, went through a complicated checking procedure with the clerk, and then she and Julian were taken to a small room and the safety deposit box was brought to them. She opened it.

'Good grief.' Julian's expression said it all.

'There is rather a lot, isn't there? My mother liked

beautiful things. Of course it isn't all mine; half of it belongs to Claudia. Mother made a list of who was to get what so we wouldn't quarrel.' She had never quite been able to shake off the feeling that if her mother had known she wasn't going to make it on the stage she would have left all of it to Claudia.

Julian opened one of the boxes to reveal a diamond pendant and earrings. 'I can't think of another girl I know who would part with this without throwing hysterics. Are you really so certain that it's necessary? Devlin can't possibly want to take Pavilion Radio from you.'

'I keep telling myself that. Then I keep asking myself what he does want.'

'Tell me about it.'

She told him, and afterwards he sat back, deep in thought.

'Well, what do you think?'

'Honestly?'

'Honestly.'

'I think you've got yourself worked up over nothing. But . . .' He hesitated and she looked at him. 'Well, sometimes when I'm negotiating a loan, when everything seems perfect and common sense tells me that nothing could go wrong – you know?' She nodded. 'For no reason at all I get this feeling . . . my gut instinct suddenly tells me that we're being had.' Fizz waited. 'I suppose what I'm saying is, if your gut instinct is telling you that Devlin is up to something, and if this stuff really doesn't matter to you . . .'

'It doesn't.' He shrugged and Fizz produced a plastic

carrier bag from her handbag, loading in the leather-covered boxes that belonged to her, double checking the contents as she went, with about as much interest as she loaded her shopping each week at the supermarket. 'Right. Where now?'

The London traffic was chaotic with roadworks and late shoppers adding to the rush hour bedlam. And with every foot of ground covered Fizz wound herself up just a little more tightly for the coming ordeal. It was nearly half an hour before Julian parked in front of a surprisingly modern, brightly lit building. It was a far cry from Charles Dickens, although the traditional three balls of the pawn broker were plainly visible.

'Is this it?' Fizz demanded.

Julian grinned. 'What did you expect? Some dark back alley and a pawnbroker in fingerless gloves and a greasy hat?'

'You know I did. I was dreading . . .' She laughed as the tension flowed from her. 'You're a rat, Julian.' She looked up at the building. 'This doesn't look so bad – more like a bank.'

'The most basic kind. You hand over your jewels and they hand over some money in exchange, and when you want your jewels back they ask for their money, plus interest.'

'And if you don't come back?'

'They keep the jewels.'

'I see. Well, I never wear them anyway.'

'This is only a short-term solution,' he warned her. 'They won't give you anything like the full market value and the interest rate will be high.' He looked at her. 'I wouldn't have brought you here, but you sounded so desperate when you phoned. It's still not too late to change your mind.'

'I know, but if I can raise the money to pay off the loan, I shall never have to go to anyone cap in hand again.'

'And you can tell Luke Devlin what to do with his sponsorship.'

'I wouldn't be that rude. I'm hoping that Melanie will still join *Holiday Bay*.'

'In other words, you want to have your cake and eat it.'

'It would be nice, just for once, but I don't want to be greedy. To be honest, if I can just get my life and my radio station back under control it'll be enough.'

'Go for the cake, Fizz,' he advised her gravely. 'You might just end up with the crumbs, but always go for the cake.' He climbed out of the car and opened her door. 'Do you want me to come in with you?'

'Would you mind?'

A quarter of an hour later they were both sitting in a small office, with the glittering collection of Elaine French's jewellery laid out before them on a desk. The broker picked up each piece in turn and examined it carefully, looking at the stones through a jeweller's eyeglass. Finally he sat back and looked at Fizz. 'How much do you hope to raise on these pieces, miss?' he asked.

'Well, I'm not sure – '

'As much as possible,' Julian intervened.

'Well, they're very nice sets. A bit old-fashioned, perhaps. If they were genuine stones, of course, they could be re-set, but it would hardly be worth it – '

'If they were genuine? Of course they are genuine.' She threw an anguished glance at Julian. 'They were my mother's . . . She was Elaine French, and I can assure you that she wouldn't have been seen dead in fake anything.'

'Elaine French?' The man's face lit up. 'Good Lord, I saw her in *Private Lives* with Edward Beaumont the year before she retired. What a wonderful actress. She illuminated the theatre.' He came back from his memories and looked at Fizz. 'I'm really very sorry, but I imagine the insurance company insisted on copies. They wouldn't have been keen to cover them when she was travelling. Even the copies have a value, of course, especially because of their connection with your mother . . .'

He continued talking. Fizz was aware of his voice a long way off, but it didn't matter. She just had to get out of that claustrophobic little office before she fainted. She was vaguely aware of Julian packing the jeweller's boxes into the carrier bag as she began to rise.

She made it to the pavement before she sank down onto the cold, concrete step and flopped forward, her head between her knees. Then Julian came and helped her back to the car.

'Oh, Lord. What an idiot. What a fool. I'm just so sorry to have involved you . . .'

'Oh, my dear Fizz. Don't you know that I'd rather make a fool of myself over you than anyone else.' And he gathered her into his arms and let her cry.

It felt so comfortable to be held like that, to feel her cheek against the soft, dark wool of his overcoat, for once not to have to pretend that everything was all right. But to hang on too long would be self-indulgent, and after a while she pulled away and took the handkerchief Julian offered without a word.

'Sorry. I'm making rather a habit of this. Shock, I suppose.'

'You've had a bad week.'

She sniffed, tried a smile, and found it wasn't so difficult provided she concentrated very hard. 'I'll survive. I always have.' He looked doubtful. She tried even harder. 'But no cake this week. Not even crumbs.'

'What do you suppose happened to the original jewels, Fizz? Could they have been switched by someone? You know, stolen?'

'Oh, no.' She shrugged. 'They were probably sold when my mother was so ill.'

'Ill?'

'She didn't just retire. She had a bad car accident. She . . . she wanted everyone to remember her as she had been. Dad looked after her. He couldn't work for a long time.' She shrugged. 'He sold the house in London quite soon after the accident and took her home to Broomhill. I always assumed he lived on that money, but my mother was an expensive woman. If I'd thought about it I suppose it would have been obvious that the jewels would have to go too. He probably didn't even tell her.'

'Why do you say that?'

'Because he would have known how upset she'd be.' And if he had told her, everyone within a half-mile radius would have known it too.

'I'm sorry. Really sorry.'

161

'Oh, well. It was just a thought. Nothing's changed after all.'

'That's very philosophical of you. I don't think I'd be quite so calm under the circumstances.'

Calm? She wasn't calm. Not because she didn't have her bagful of precious jewels. They were just the same. She could still wear them and no one would ever know the difference. The only difference was that she wouldn't bother putting them back in the vault; she could at least save herself the cost of that. She wondered briefly if Claudia knew. What her reaction would be when she discovered her beloved sparklies were fake.

But it would have been wonderful not to worry any more. To be back in control. 'Oh, Julian, I'm sure you're right about Devlin. I've just got an overactive imagination. Everything will be just fine.'

'Of course it will. Come on, I'll take you home.'

'You've done more than enough already. I can get a taxi back to Victoria.'

But Julian was insistent. 'You're not going back to Broomhill tonight, Fizz.'

'I can't stay – '

'You can, my dear. In fact, I insist. You're being very brave, but you've had a shock and you need looking after. So I'm going to take you back to my place and cook you supper.'

'But – '

'If I can't be anything else, I'm happy to be your friend, Fizz. I think you could do with one right now.'

She subsided. 'I really don't deserve you.'

'Probably not.' She giggled. 'That's better. Now settle

162

down and be quiet while I concentrate on getting through this traffic.'

It was a blessed relief to have someone else making decisions for her, just for a while. So she did as she was told and said very little at all until Julian placed her supper on the table. She stared at it.

'Baked beans on toast!'

'Comfort food. There's nothing to beat it.' Julian grinned. 'And when you've eaten all that, I'll make you some cocoa. Then you can have a warm bath, borrow a pair of my pyjamas and fall into bed.' He intercepted her look. 'I'll take the sofa.'

Friday arrived with unnecessary haste, it seemed to Fizz. And yet it was just as well. After the nightmare of the jewellery fiasco, Thursday had offered no comfort.

She had spent the day contacting advertising agencies, hoping that when they heard about Melanie they would buy some extra time. She'd had high hopes after the good result on the phone-in programme, but this time the reaction had been disappointing. Worse, she had received confirmation that one of the station's regular advertisers would not be renewing their contract.

So, there were no other options open to her. And once the agreement with Luke Devlin was signed it would be over and she could stop worrying about some totally imaginary threat. What could he do, after all? Her gut reaction was probably due entirely to her out-of-control hormones racketing about like an electron in a particle accelerator. She was getting her knickers in a twist over nothing. Nothing.

As she parked her car in front of Harries' impressive headquarters building she glanced at her watch. Two minutes to twelve. She had started out in plenty of time, but her unwillingness to arrive had apparently communicated itself to her right foot resting lightly, very lightly, on the accelerator.

But it wouldn't do to be late, so Fizz locked the car and, throwing the hood of her teal-blue coat over her hair against the sleet-laced rain, hurried into the building and upstairs to Luke Devlin's office. The outer office was unexpectedly empty, and for just a moment she wondered if he meant her to cool her heels there as she had done on the previous occasion. A test for her temper, perhaps, after the way she had so unceremoniously upbraded Phillip Devlin on her last visit. It would probably serve her right, she thought.

She bent to pick up a sheet of paper that had blown onto the floor as she had walked in, and when she straightened Luke was standing in the doorway watching her. The shock didn't seem to lessen. Even when she was prepared for him, expecting to see him, the pulse-jolting reaction that rocketed through her like an out-of-control express train still knocked the breath from her.

'Shall I take that?' She glanced down at the letter she was holding, absently registering the familiar logo.

'It fell on the floor,' she said lamely as he took it from her and replaced it on his secretary's desk. 'When I opened the door.' She stopped. She had done nothing to apologize for, it was just that he had a disconcerting habit of not answering, knowing that if he waited she would keep talking, make a fool of herself. Anything rather than listen to the deepening silence that loomed between them, full of questions that would one day have to be answered.

'Come along in, Fizz. This won't take long.'

He ushered her into his office and took her coat, shaking off the raindrops before hanging it on his coat-stand. Then he joined her by the window, staring out of the window at the grey, rain-lashed town spread out below them.

'There were days,' he said, 'in Australia and later in California, when I longed for just this kind of weather. I must have been mad.'

'Without a doubt,' she agreed, then turned to offer him a bright smile, her pulse very nearly under control. 'But it'll soon be spring.'

One corner of his mouth lifted in the smallest of smiles and her steady pulse missed a beat, skittering danger-ously off on some wild adventure of its own. 'Remind me, Fizz, will that make it stop raining?'

'No,' she said. 'But it will be warmer, the woods will be scented with violets and the fields will be full of new lambs.'

'Ah, yes. I remember.' And for a moment he remained very still as he regarded the softly draped jersey dress she was wearing in the same blue as her coat. She hadn't forgotten his scathing comments about the suit she had worn on her previous visit to his offices, and this time she had dressed to please herself, rather than to impress. It seemed to have worked because he made no comment, instead his glance flickered back to her face. 'But I've a good mind to make the sun a part of the contract.'

165

'But it's always there, Luke. It's just that sometimes you can't see it for the clouds.' Fizz was being mesmerized by the disturbing impact of his eyes, drawn towards him. Abruptly she shifted her glance, turning to his desk and the document that lay upon it. 'Is that the agreement?' He nodded. 'You're very confident that I'm going to sign it.'

'Why wouldn't you?' He walked across the room and held out a chair for her. 'Sit down. Read it very carefully. Then, if you've no questions, I'll get Liz to witness your signature.'

He retired to the sofa, leaving her in solitary grandeur behind the broad expanse of his desk on which lay a single document.

She was aware that it would have been wise to have the radio station's solicitors look over the document. But she instinctively knew that this was a take it or leave it situation, and if they said it would be unwise to sign what would she do? So she had done her homework, spending hours going over other sponsorship documents her father had signed on behalf of the station during the last five years and letters from solicitors pointing out problem areas. She had familiarized herself with the language, the get-out clauses, the traps for the unwary. They all seemed to be fairly standard documents and she was confident that she would spot anything odd that had been slipped in. She began to read.

But it was his powerful figure relaxed against the soft leather that drew her eyes. He was far away, lost deep in thought. Wherever he was she was certain it was not a happy place, and despite her determination to be calm and businesslike there was, deep within her, an urgent and unfamiliar longing to go to him. Comfort him.

He looked up and caught her staring at him. 'Can you manage, Fizz, or do you want me go through it with you clause by clause?' His voice was gently seductive, as if he could read the weakness that was invading her bones.

'No.' Luke Devlin was dangerous enough at a distance. If he was sitting at her shoulder she knew she might sign anything, do anything. 'Thank you,' she added, somewhat belatedly.

She ducked her head, grateful for the heavy curtain of hair that fell forward to hide the quick blush that stained her cheeks. She read on, anxious to get the whole thing over with as quickly as possible so that she could get off this crazy rollercoaster and return to some semblance of normality.

The majority of the agreement was straightforward enough – standard clauses. He didn't want a great deal from them. No sponsor's message, no display boards to proclaim his generosity in supporting local sporting events.

There was a clause forbidding any other advertising immediately before or after *Holiday Bay*, which was a little harsh, but since he was sponsoring the programme he was entitled to make that stipulation. Then she turned the page and alarm bells began to ring.

CHAPTER 7

Fizz looked up and was disconcerted to discover that Luke was still watching her intently. It was almost as if he had been waiting for this, expecting it.

She cleared her throat. 'What does this mean?' she asked. 'All cast changes to *Holiday Bay* to be cleared with you first . . .?' She used the excuse of checking the wording of the document to look away.

But he rose from the sofa and crossed the room to her. With one hand on the back of her chair and one on the desk, he leaned over her to read the wording for himself. 'It's clear enough, isn't it?' He turned his head and looked down into her eyes.

She felt trapped by the contact, caged by his body even though he wasn't touching her. 'I understand the words, Luke, but I would hardly have thought the casting of a minor soap opera constituted a serious concern for a man as busy as you.' He waited, but she had finally learned not to fall into that particular trap. 'That's all.'

'It's not an objection on principle, then?'

Fizz knew she had made a mistake. It wasn't all. Not

by a country mile. But she hadn't seen the danger and now he was toying with her, making the point that since she had accepted the principle that he could impose Melanie Brett on the cast, she was being petty on this particular issue. But she wasn't.

'Suppose one of the cast were taken ill suddenly and had to be written out?' she asked.

'Just keep me informed. I wouldn't want anyone having a diplomatic illness simply to avoid working with Melanie.'

'To avoid working with Melanie?' She could scarcely believe her ears. 'Why on earth would anyone do that? The cast are only too glad of the work.' Most of them. She dropped her eyes. He wasn't talking about most of them. He was referring specifically to her sister. She appeared in *Holiday Bay* somewhat grudgingly at the best of times, considering it beneath her dignity as a 'serious' actress. With a soap queen to steal her thunder, she was likely to prove even more difficult, a fact that Fizz was well aware of. She decided to confront the problem. 'Are you specifically referring to Claudia?'

'Your sister?' Fizz didn't bother to answer. He knew well enough that it was her sister. He knew too damned much. 'Is she likely to prove difficult?'

'She does drop in and out of the cast to suit her other commitments, sometimes at short notice. Occasionally she has to record her lines wherever she happens to be and they are edited in. I wouldn't want there to be any misunderstandings.'

'Just make sure she doesn't make a habit of it and there won't be a problem, Fizz.'

'You'll really enforce this?' She turned and looked up at him. 'If I don't adhere to the letter of this agreement you will stop the sponsorship money?'

'Naturally. When you explain the situation to your sister I'm quite sure she'll rally to your cause, go out of her way to help.'

Fizz had her own views on that subject, but refused to be drawn. If the worst came to the worst she could play Claudia's character herself; their voices were enough alike and she had done it before in an emergency. If it was edited in afterwards Melanie, and therefore Luke, would never know.

'I'll get Liz in, then, shall I?' His chest brushed against her shoulder as he reached for the intercom switch and she jumped, her whole body responding to his touch. 'Unless there's anything else?'

Fizz shook her head briefly. It wasn't true. There was a question burning on her lips. Why? Why was he doing this? It simply wasn't logical, and every fibre of her being was screaming out *beware* in neon letters ten feet high. But as he leaned over her, and she caught his elusive man-scent, the signals became terribly confused. She couldn't be sure if it was her head that was afraid of Mr Luke Devlin, or her heart. Not that it made any difference. She needed him and he knew it.

Ten minutes later it was over. The agreement signed. The deed done. Pavilion Radio was, for the moment, saved. But at what cost? Even if he had no ulterior motive, her peace of mind had been wrecked beyond recall.

'I think this calls for a little celebration,' Luke said as

he walked her to her car beneath the shelter of an umbrella borrowed from his secretary. 'Melanie is throwing a house-warming party tomorrow evening. Will you come?'

'I've made other arrangements for tomorrow evening,' she said, without hesitation. To stay at home with a good book and try and forget Luke Devlin existed.

'I'd like you to come and so would Melanie. And a night out will do you good.' She glanced at him sharply. What did he know about her private life? Or lack of it? 'You spend too much time worrying about work. Who knows? Perhaps your father could find a window in his busy schedule to come along as well,' he added, with just a touch of irony. 'And your sister too, if she's in Broom-hill. Naturally the invitation also extends to the staff at the radio station, but I think Melanie has already covered that.'

'You've found a house, then?'

He shrugged. 'I took your advice and settled for Winterbourne Manor.'

She steeled herself. 'Does Melanie like it?'

'You saw the alternatives, Fizz. We're moving in today.'

We. Luke and Melanie. They were a pair. An odd pair – not right for each other. He was too dominant; she was too young. But it was none of her business. *For heaven's sake girl, get a grip.*

'And throwing a party tomorrow? That takes stamina,' she remarked, with a careless ease that she dredged up from some deep well of strength.

It certainly fooled Luke because he smiled. 'No, we

just hired a good firm of caterers. And we have a housekeeper whose middle name is efficiency.'

We. We. 'And did Melanie throw hysterics about the seclusion?' she asked, jabbing herself with the girl's name.

'I told her that *you* thought it the best available.' His smile was slow, wide, oddly seductive. 'But it was the four-poster that clinched it.'

Fizz swallowed. 'It'll work every time.'

'Will it?' They had reached the car. Luke took her car keys and as he bent to unlock the door for her he glanced up, his eyes directly level with her own. 'I'm sorely tempted to put such a bold assertion to the test.'

A little gasp escaped her before she bit down hard on the anger that welled up in her throat. How dared he flirt with her with his lover's name still warm upon his lips? Her heart pounding so loud beneath her coat that she was sure he must hear, she raised a well-shaped brow.

'Are you, indeed? Won't Melanie object?' she asked, hoping to shame him.

'I won't tell her if you don't.' He touched her lips lightly with the tip of one finger, his dark eyes heavy-lidded against the sudden shaft of sunlight that sliced almost horizontally through the lowering clouds. Then he took her hand and dropped her keys into her palm, wrapping her fingers about them before stooping to open the door for her. Stunned into silence, she slid quickly behind the wheel without a word, just desperate to get away. 'Until tomorrow, Fizz,' he said. And she wasn't sure whether it sounded more like a threat or a promise.

She banged the door closed and raindrops showered her from the leaky canvas roof. She didn't even notice.

Luke stood for a moment in the car park and watched her drive away. He should be feeling elated at how smoothly his plans were going. Instead he felt oddly frustrated. Coming to grips with Fizz Beaumont was like trying to catch scotch mist. She was elusive, defying him to work out just what made her tick. She lived like a nun and yet the way she looked at him when he caught her off guard made him catch his breath, driving an urgent heat through him. But when he attempted the mildest flirtation she shut up like a clam. He was confused, and that made him angry.

Liz Meynell looked up from her VDU as he returned to his office. 'The report you were expecting arrived while you were with Miss Beaumont,' she said, retrieving her dripping umbrella and handing him the envelope unopened, as instructed. 'Shall I get your call to Germany now?'

'Not yet, Liz. There are some private calls I need to make first.' He bent and picked up a letter that had blown onto the floor and put it on her desk. 'Does this happen every time the door is opened?'

'Not always. I think it must be a combination of events creating a wind tunnel.'

'Get someone in to sort it out, will you? We can't have confidential letters blowing about the place. And I'll let you know when I want that call to Germany.'

He shut the door to his office.

'Fizz?'

She stirred at the sound of her name. She had spent the

173

remainder of the afternoon looking through the scripts for *Holiday Bay*, trying to find the right moment to introduce Melanie. Anything to distract her mind from Luke Devlin, the touch of his finger against his lips, the look in his eyes.

The on/off engagement of the two main characters was winding up to a wedding. The arrival of a beautiful young Australian could be used to tighten the suspense, the anticipation that something would go wrong. But how? It was important not to waste such an asset . . . Now, at the sound of her name she eased her neck and sat back. 'Hello, Jim, come in. What can I do for you?'

'It's more what I can do for you,' he said, sitting down and accepting her offer of coffee. 'You know how little information we were able to come up with on Luke Devlin?' She nodded. 'Well, I thought I'd try another approach. A friend who works in one of the press agencies pulled the file on Melanie Brett for me.' Fizz looked up sharply from pouring the coffee. Her relationship with Luke was common knowledge? 'Not that I found anything useful about Devlin, but I came across this, and since Melanie's joining the cast of *Holiday Bay*, I thought you ought to see it.' He pushed a photocopy of a press cutting across the desk.

'That's official now,' Fizz said, picking up the sheet of paper. 'Did Kelly record an interview with Melanie for the magazine this afternoon?'

'Yes, she edited it last night. It's a good piece. And all the presenters have their instructions about running the promos.'

'Good. We want to get the whole of Broomhill Bay talking about it.'

'You may not be quite so eager for everyone to be talking once you've read that, Fizz.'

She looked down at the photocopy in her hand. 'What newspaper is this?'

'A Sydney daily. That's from the gossip and entertainment page.'

'But this is Claudia,' she said, puzzled, staring at a blotchy photograph of her sister smiling from the page alongside a picture of Melanie.

'She was over there last year touring Shakespeare with your father, remember?'

'Was she? In Australia?'

'Australia, New Zealand, Hong Kong, Japan. And a couple of other places.'

'I knew they'd gone to the Far East, but I hadn't realized . . . I suppose I should listen more.' But when Claudia and her father started talking theatre, she tended to switch off. It was a defence mechanism. Automatic.

Australia. The word had an ominous ring to it, and as Fizz began to read the press cutting she realized that she had been right to expect the worst. The cold that ran through her veins as she scanned the reporter's words had nothing whatever to do with the ambient temperature of her office.

After her triumphant portrayal of Portia to her father's Shylock I went backstage to talk to Claudia Beaumont and I was immediately struck by her likeness to our own sweet Melanie Brett, a point I mentioned to the

175

actress. Miss Beaumont seemed amused by this and remarked that it would always be possible to tell the two of them apart . . . Melanie was the one who played in soaps while *she* was the one who could act. Miss Beaumont is certainly a fine actress, but her likeness to Melanie is, after all, illusory . . .

'Your sister may look like an angel, but she has a tongue that could cut skin at twenty paces,' Jim said, when Fizz remained silent.

'Possibly, but she isn't stupid enough to make a remark like that. At least not to a newspaper man.'

'On a high after the performance she may just have been careless.'

'Or he might just have made the whole thing up.' She stared at the fuzzy pictures. They hadn't been great to begin with, and photocopying hadn't helped. 'Are they alike?' she asked after a while. 'I hadn't noticed any particular resemblance. It's hard to see much from this.'

Jim considered. 'Not really. But Claudia had her hair dyed blonde for Portia, remember.' He took the clipping from her and studied it. 'There's a superficial likeness, I suppose. Something about the mouth, perhaps. I suppose this guy spotted it and thought it would make a good story. It wasn't likely that Claudia would ever see it.' He glanced at her, frowning deeply at the photographs. 'Does it matter? The likeness?'

'How can it possibly matter?' she asked, firmly ignoring the prickle of apprehension that shimmied down her spine. The tightening of Julian's famous gut reaction. 'And since there is absolutely nothing we can do about it

176

you might as well go ahead and put out the news bulletin.'

Jim rose heavily to his feet. 'You're the boss.'

'Right now, that isn't a comfort, Jim, but thanks for bringing this to me. Forewarned is forearmed.'

'Weapons will be fingernails at point-blank range. Perhaps you should sell ringside seats for the first recording session,' he said, trying to raise a smile from her.

But Fizz barely noticed. 'You won't have to wait that long. I've a feeling the match has been arranged for tomorrow night, and everyone's invited.'

But by eight o'clock on Saturday evening her sister had not arrived in Broomhill. She had her own, self-contained apartment in their father's home that she used when she was in Broomhill. Fizz had called there in the afternoon, hoping to see her, talk to her before the party, warn her what to expect. But if she wasn't home by Saturday afternoon it meant she must have a date in London; it was unlikely that she would be home until some time on Sunday, if then. A reprieve.

Fizz dropped in again just after eight, to pick up her father, who couldn't see the point in going to a party and not having a drink. But he wasn't ready. 'You go on, darling. I shan't be staying long, and it'll be easier if I get a taxi.'

'I can wait.' She wasn't in any hurry to arrive at Winterbourne Manor.

He glanced at his watch. 'No. You get off and have some fun.'

Fun! She anticipated it being about as much fun as a visit to the dentist, but she didn't say anything. If her father had decided to take a taxi, nothing on earth would move him.

'Fizz,' he said as she turned for the door.

'Yes?'

'I like your dress. It's a treat to see you looking so thoroughly grown-up.'

'I am twenty-five, Dad.'

'I know. But you always seem so unsophisticated compared to Claudia. Sometimes, because you didn't become one of us, I think perhaps we've undervalued your talent. But you've done a great job at the radio station. I'm really very proud of you.'

'I couldn't have done it without you.'

'Oh, I know that.'

'You needn't be quite so quick to agree with me,' she laughed.

'I only meant that you'd never have got the franchise. But everything else is down to you. I really think it's time for me to step back and put out the word that Miss Felicity Beaumont is the boss. When you're looking like that no one could doubt your – '

'No, Dad.' Edward Beaumont raised a pair of well-honed eyebrows at this unseemly interruption. Having prepared his little speech, he didn't expect to have his thunder stolen. 'I need your name to help me through the next three months. I suspect that Mr Devlin is an old-fashioned male chauvinist. I don't think he'd be happy handing his money over to a mere woman.'

'But I thought you were going to tell him.'

'Trust me, Dad. It really wasn't a good idea.'

Winterbourne Manor was ablaze with lights as Fizz edged her way down the long curve of the drive and found space to park a little way from the house. For a moment she sat there, quietly gathering herself. She rarely went to parties unless they were business functions that couldn't be avoided. Not because she was naturally unsociable, but because she had long ago realized that the women sought her out in the hopes that they might be introduced to her father and the men because they wanted to meet her sister – or, worse, remembered her mother and wanted to reminisce about seeing her perform one of her great roles. No one ever seemed to be aware of her as an individual. She had got used to it, but she didn't put up with it unless she had to.

But at least tonight wasn't going to be as bad as she had feared. She leaned back against the worn leather seat and thanked whichever kindly god watched over radio stations and younger sisters for the fact that Claudia had decided to stay in London for the weekend. She had no illusions about who would have to persuade her glamorous sister into making some kind of public apology to Melanie, but it wouldn't be easy. She had been trying to get hold of Claudia ever since Jim's bombshell had landed on her desk, so that she could warn her, but she wasn't at home and hadn't bothered to switch on her answering machine.

It should have been a relief to know what to expect. Once she had seen the newspaper clipping, Luke's motive for making Melanie a part of *Holiday Bay* had become all too obvious. But it was difficult to know how much had been planned and how much was simply chance. Whether the opportunity had presented itself when Devlin had taken over Harries . . . or whether he had taken over Harries to get at Claudia.

No. That was too ridiculous for words. No one would carry a grudge to that length, that expense. It had to be chance. And when the sponsorship question had arisen, and he'd discovered that Claudia was involved with Pavilion Radio, the opportunity to put the two girls together in the same cast must have been irresistible. But to achieve that he had to be sure that the station stayed on the air. He *couldn't* allow it to go under. She felt like laughing. Oh, Claudia. Bless you and your big mouth.

Another thought whirled and took hold. The whole thing might even have been Melanie's idea. Sweet, innocent little Melanie – that most unlikely lover for Luke Devlin – was, after all, an actress. Could it be that she was playing the role of her life?

The door beside her opened, letting out the respectable fug of warmth she had managed to build up and letting the freezing night air in. She gave a little shiver as she turned her head and found herself staring into Luke's dark eyes. 'I was beginning to think you were going to stand me up,' he said, folding his long legs until he was down on the same level as her.

'Stand you up?' Easy to loathe him when he was out of sight. When he was so close conflicting emotions crowded in.

But Fizz reined in the giddy thought that he had been watching for her arrival. More likely he had seen her headlights through the window and recognized her car, wondered why she was taking so long to leave it. There weren't many like it, certainly none among the mixture of solid saloon models and the more exuberant four-wheel drive vehicles of the younger guests parked along the drive. And when she hadn't immediately appeared at his front door he had come to find her. He couldn't wait to get on with the show.

She shivered. 'I doubt that you've ever been stood up in your entire life, Luke Devlin.'

'Could that be a compliment?' He regarded her face gravely, then his face creased in a smile that might have reached his eyes, or might not; it was difficult to tell. The small light that had come on when he opened her car door threw his features into deep shadow. 'No. Not a compliment,' he said, after a moment. 'But the night is young. And now you've arrived things can only get better.'

She refused to dwell on what he might consider 'better'. Instead she allowed him to help her from the car and offer her a steadying arm as she stumbled on the gravel driveway in her ridiculously high heels.

He ushered her into the warmth of the hall, his hand at her back. The house had seemed welcoming enough on her last visit, but now the bare black and white marble squares of the hall floor had been softened by a jewel-bright Persian rug, there were flowers everywhere and the hearth was ablaze with a huge log fire, the firelight glinting warmly on the polished balusters of the great oak staircase. 'The house looks wonderful. No one would ever guess you had just moved in.'

'I'm glad you approve. It was on your advice that I took it.'

Aware that his hand was still nestling in the small of her back, she moved quickly across to the fire and held out fingers, thoroughly chilled even in the short walk from the car. 'I think we might get the snow after all,' she said, turning to Luke.

'Do you?' His eyes sparkled. 'Well, since I'm assured that the roof is sound, perhaps you'd care to risk taking off your cloak?'

She pulled at the ties and he lifted the heavy floor-length black velvet cloak from her shoulders, and his look brought a blush racing to her cheeks.

'I'm glad you've given up power-dressing, Fizz. The role of hard businesswoman didn't suit you at all.'

She made a small movement, feeling awkward at being the object of such open admiration, and the simple lines of the long black crêpe dress shimmered over her body. It wasn't the kind of dress she would normally wear, but for this party she had needed more than a dress – she had needed a costume that would send out all the right signals, say that she was sure of herself, smart, in control of her business and her emotions. That she was someone who dealt in the adult world of figures, black and red, profit and loss, and had long ago abandoned the ephemeral fire and air of the theatre for the sham she knew it to be.

Before Luke Devlin had arrived in town it had been true.

As she caught a glimpse of herself in the heavy mirror over the fireplace, saw her sleek chestnut hair glowing in the warmth of the flames, the long gold drops, like falling leaves at her ears and throat, she knew she looked the part. Only the close observer would have noticed the uncertainty that marked her eyes.

Luke handed on her cloak to a girl who bore it away and, resting his hands lightly on her naked shoulders, stood behind her, staring at their twin reflections. 'Allow me to tell you that you look quite stunning, Miss Beaumont.'

His hands, featherlight against her chilly shoulders, sent heat fusing through her body, flaring into her cheeks. But Luke Devlin was the kind of man who would exploit the slightest sign of weakness and, despite the fact that she found him as compelling as iron filings for a magnet, she didn't intend becoming a sideshow in his affair with Melanie. No Beaumont had ever played a supporting role, and she wasn't about to start.

She had worked it all out when she was choosing the dress, breaking everything down to the parts they were playing. Melanie Brett was the innocent *ingénue*, certain to have her heart broken by an older, cynical man of the world. That was easy. She had been there, done that, got the scars to prove it.

Luke Devlin was a rich, heartless man who thought he could manipulate everyone, and in the moral world of the drama he would certainly get his comeuppance sooner or later. In life, nothing was ever that simple.

And the role she had assigned herself was that of a young career woman who had her life planned down to the last detail and was far too wise to get drawn into some dark game by a man who had turned her on like a light switch the moment they had met. So long as she remembered that the brighter the light, the quicker it burned out, she would be safe. So long as she played her part, stuck to her lines, everything would be fine.

Fizz turned and gave him a cool, appraising look. His hair, dark and thick, curled onto the collar of a dinner jacket that stretched across an acre of shoulder; his shirt was plain, the black silk tie a perfect bow. 'You look pretty stunning, yourself, Luke,' she told him. 'But you could do with a haircut.'

A dangerous glint kindled in his eye, but before he could retaliate Melanie erupted into the hall in a delicate silver tissue creation that stopped about a yard short of her knees, and the dangerous glint immediately softened.

'Fizz! You've arrived. What on earth are you doing keeping her out here, Luke?'

'Taking her cloak, paying her compliments, everything that you would expect . . .'

Melanie threw him a glance that was pure exasperation. 'Keeping her to yourself, you mean.' She looped her slender arm possessively through Fizz's and drew her into the main reception hall. 'Come on through and meet everyone while Luke gets you a drink.'

He raised an enquiring brow in her direction.

'A fruit juice, please,' she murmured, before being claimed by a number of locals who wanted to talk about the Harries takeover – how it was affecting business in the town, whether it was affecting the radio station. She merely smiled and took grateful refuge behind her father's name, directing all enquiries to him.

'Where is your father?' Luke asked as he handed her a drink.

'On his way. I'm afraid Claudia is still in London.' She took a sip of freshly squeezed pink grapefruit juice fizzed up with soda. The man had taste, she had to admit. 'She'll be sorry to miss your party,' she couldn't resist adding. It was the truth, after all. Claudia loved parties; they gave her the opportunity to play the role she had been born to: leading lady. But one leading lady at a party was enough.

'It doesn't matter. You're here.'

'I was coerced.' Now that the pressure was off, and she understood the game being played, Fizz discovered that she was actually beginning to enjoy herself.

'You wouldn't have come if I'd given you a choice?'

'Perhaps not.' Fizz gave him a sideways glance before taking another sip of her drink. 'I don't usually enjoy parties.'

'Then I shall have to make it my duty to ensure you enjoy this one.'

'There's no need to go to any bother,' she assured him.

He took no notice. 'First, I think we should dance.'

'I'm afraid I've got two left feet.'

He bent and, taking her skirt, twitched it above her ankles. He regarded the pair of narrow feet encased in strappy high-heeled sandals for a moment, then looked up. 'Have you got a doctor's note to that effect?' he asked.

Shaken out of her poised sophistication by this casual hijacking of her dress, she discovered herself staring into his eyes. They were laughing, inviting her to laugh too. And she did, out loud, so that several people turned to look in her direction and smiled too.

Having won the round on points, he took the glass she had been holding before her almost like a shield to keep him at bay and placed it on a nearby table. Then, taking her hand between both of his, he looked down at her and said, 'I should very much like to dance with you, Fizz I won't tread on your toes, I promise.'

She wasn't worried about her toes. Her toes could look after themselves. But she was terrified by the surge of longing that swept over her; she wanted to be held in his arms, to mould herself to him, to wind her arms about his neck. She should have remembered. Iron filings stood no chance when there was a magnet about. 'I can't promise the same for yours,' she said, a touch huskily, as without another word she surrendered.

He led her across the hall to a large room from which all the furniture had been removed for the party. It was now home to a small band of musicians who somehow managed to play pop music without endangering the eardrums of the dancers. They were playing something lively, a dance with actions that all the youngsters knew, and for a moment they stood and watched. Safe for the moment, Fizz wasn't sure whether she was relieved or sorry.

'They're good,' she said, leaning closer so that he could hear. 'The band. They're not local. Who are they?'

'Friends of Melanie's. Most of these people are.'

She turned in surprise. 'But I thought she'd only just arrived in England?'

'London is apparently full of Australians. And they all seem to know Melanie,' he said, somewhat drily.

But Melanie wasn't with her Australian friends. She

186

was with Andy, her face flushed and excited as she stood with her hand upon his arm, whispering in his ear as they waited for the music to begin again. Fizz saw a frown temporarily pucker Luke's brow, but then the band moved into a slower number and, turning back to Fizz, he smiled down at her, his hand at her waist, drawing her into his body as he moved with her to the haunting strains of a dreamy song that was currently being played endlessly on all the music programmes.

For a moment she held herself rigid, distant, her breathing constricted with panic. But Luke made no move to pull her closer, to dominate her. On the contrary, his touch was so light that it was with no sense of danger that she gradually began to relax into his arms. Her own body seemed to mould to his as they moved in perfect rhythm, and her cool, sophisticated inner voice assured her that laying her head against the lapel of his jacket was the most natural thing in the world. Not that it would have mattered if it had screamed warnings of doom. It felt right. Perfect. And he hadn't trodden on her toes once.

Yet the flutter of a thousand butterflies stampeding through her veins at the steady thump of his heart beneath her ear warned her that she was treading a dangerously narrow line between the role she was playing and a reckless disregard for her own peace of mind. He was the wrong man, it was the wrong place, and as the banked-down fires of desire threatened to burst into flame she knew she was in imminent danger of making a fool of herself.

But not yet, because as soon as the dance finished he

released her and excused himself without ceremony, moving in to break up a serious clinch between Melanie and Andy that hadn't stopped when the music faded.

Thanking providence for small mercies, Fizz took the chance to escape to the relative safety of the drawing room, where she was immediately buttonholed by a local councillor who wanted to know if Claudia had been invited to the party. She told herself that she was grateful for this rude imposition of reality. But, when, a few minutes later, she caught a glimpse of Luke through the open doorway, crossing the hall with Melanie in tow, her young face defiant, her pale lips almost petulant as she was forced to listen to what Luke was saying, she turned away as a pain like acid shot through her.

She had no right to feel jealous. She knew the situation. She had known it twenty minutes after she had met the man. But it had been too late by then. He'd already thrown the switch.

Almost as a punishment, she forced herself to look at the scene being played out in the hall. Luke had put his arm around Melanie and was leading her towards the stairs, but she pulled away from him and flounced up them, not looking back.

Agitated, Fizz turned away, unable to bear it. As she did so her eyes met Andy's, his jealous reaction a mirror image of her own. She gave a rueful little shrug. 'I'd keep your distance if I were you, Andy. He seems to be the possessive type.'

'Possessive?' The only thing he was interested in possessing a few minutes ago was you,' Andy replied tersely.

To her shame, Fizz found herself blushing. 'We were just dancing, Andy. That's all.'

'Just dancing.' His smile was deeply sceptical. ' ". . . the vertical expression of a horizontal desire . . ." to quote the inimitable Mr Shaw. He knew a lot about human nature.'

Andy hadn't bothered to lower his voice, and several people turned to look. Horrified that they might have been overheard, even more horrified that what he said was no less than the truth, she pushed him into a corner. 'For heaven's sake, Andy, she is his . . .' She couldn't say the word. It stuck in her throat, a great big lump that wouldn't budge. 'Responsibility,' she hedged.

Andy gave a look of utter disgust. 'For heaven's sake, Fizz, I know you've been in the deep freeze ever since the Ice Age, but I've never thought of you as a killjoy.'

'I am not – ' But her protest was cut short.

'No? Well, let me tell you that right now you sound like some Victorian pedagogue. Melanie's nearly twenty and no shrinking virgin.' He glared in the direction of the hall. 'So there's no need for him to take his responsibilities so damn seriously.'

'He seems to be aware that you have something of reputation, Andy,' she said, in a low urgent voice. 'And Melanie isn't any girl you can bed without a second thought. Just . . . watch yourself.'

Andy looked at her, his chin as stubborn as a board, and her heart sank. 'This is different.'

'Very different,' she agreed. 'Please, Andy? It's important.'

'What is? Why are you so interested anyway?' Then

his face cleared. 'Oh, I get it. You're after the big guy's money for the station and you're afraid I'll queer your pitch. I always wondered what it would take to defrost you. Well, I guess you've just answered that question.'

Fizz blenched. It was a long time since Andy had made a ritual pass at her. It was an almost automatic reaction to every girl he met, and an awful lot of them fell for his charm. He gave them a good time while he was interested, but it was never for long. She had declined a dalliance, as she had declined a dozen others over the years, politely but firmly and had thought nothing more of it. It must have hurt his pride a great deal more than he had let on at the time, but that was no excuse for such insolence.

'I think you'd better go outside and take a few deep breaths, Andy,' she said sharply. 'It might clear your head and remind you of just who you're speaking to.'

He looked as shocked as if she had slapped him.

Satisfied that she had made her point, she swivelled on her high heels and walked away. She was in the hall before she remembered Luke.

CHAPTER 8

Luke propped his foot on the fender, and with his arm resting on the great beam that formed the mantle stared down into the pulsing heat of red caves burned into the big logs by the flames. The fire had died down, was simply glowing, smouldering hotly on a thick bed of embers. Thoughtfully, he put out his foot and gave one of the logs a prod. It fell apart, sending sparks flying up the chimney and into the night.

Fizz Beaumont was like that; he was convinced of it. He had seen her eyes when, kindled by anger, she had dropped her guard in a moment of passion. Beneath that touch-me-not quality, the cool, apparently detached exterior, she was smouldering like the log. And the man who took the trouble to stir the embers and release the spark would be rewarded with the collapse of her defences and ultimately achieve melt-down.

But what would stir her? Would surrender be a slow process, a brick by brick dismantling of the barriers? Or if he stormed them could it be that the collapse would be as sudden and complete as that of the log? To understand what would bring the defences down, he would first have

191

to know why she had erected them. Prompted, his investigator had uncovered a mystery, a silence so thick on the subject of an ill-fated film that Fizz was to have co-starred in with Patrick March, that there had to be something. Somehow he would have to discover what Patrick March had done to her. Or what she had done to him. Perhaps, if he was very careful, she would tell him.

His body stirred at the memory of the way she had come into his arms. That had taken care. Care not to take before she was ready to give, so that the initial stiffness, the determination to hold him at bay, had gradually yielded, and she had melted against him and laid her head against his chest. It had been a moment of triumph. A moment to cherish. He frowned as he remembered what had disrupted it. Damn Melanie. She knew better than to throw herself at the first smooth-talking man who came her way. He didn't need a complication like that right now.

The sharp tap of heels on the marble floor brought him back to the present. He knew it was her. She had been in his head for days and he had become so attuned to her that he could recognize the lilting cadence of her walk, pick her scent out of the very air. 'I was just thinking about you,' he said, and smiled.

'Were you?' Her confident step faltered as she saw him. Something had driven her from the drawing room, he could see it in her heightened colour, the brightness in her eyes, but the last person she wanted to see was him. He might have been offended if he hadn't been so certain that she was more afraid of herself than of him. That only served to heighten his interest.

'I wondered where you'd gone. Are you, despite all expectations to the contrary, managing to have a good time?'

'Yes. Thank you.'

'I hope you crossed your fingers before you said that, because it's fairly obvious that you'd rather be anywhere else right at this moment.' She had already told him she didn't like parties and, despite the sophisticated dress, the casually assumed air of confidence, she was as nervous as a kitten. Her air of assurance had momentarily fooled him when she had arrived. But she had the theatre in her blood. Putting on a performance was part of the family show, and she was putting on a performance now as, with a beautifully judged little gesture, she put her head to one side, offered him a smile.

'I'm sorry, but I did warn you,' she said.

'So you did. Perhaps we should dance again. You seemed to enjoy that.'

A delicate pink suffused her cheekbones. 'Where's Melanie?' she asked, looking around – any excuse to avoid his eyes.

A door opened; the noise of the band filled the hall as a group of youngsters spilled out. Luke glanced at them irritably. The party had been Mel's idea. She had been getting restless cooped up in the Metropole and it had seemed like a good idea to let her invite some friends down from London; also the party would be an opportunity to offer hospitality to some local people. But it really wasn't his scene. He glanced at Fizz. She was trying to find some way to escape him without actually being rude.

'Do you want to rejoin the fray?' he invited. 'Or would you rather find somewhere quiet?'

'Shouldn't you be looking after your guests?' she offered.

'You are my guest. And since I have no intention of dancing with his honour the mayor, or the president of the chamber of commerce, I shall look after you.'

'You could talk to them. I'm sure they'd be interested to hear your plans for Harries.'

'I'm sure they would. But if they want to discuss business they must come to my office. As I've just reminded Mel, this is her party, and amusing the civic dignitaries might keep her out of Andy Gilbert's amorous clutches for a while at least.'

'Or drive her into them. She doesn't know anyone in Broomhill, Luke, she needs you to be there for her.'

She was lecturing *him* about his duty? That was rich, coming from a Beaumont. But he had succeeded in capturing her full attention, although her consideration for Melanie would have impressed him more if she hadn't been using it as a stick to beat him with. But it had lit the promise of a spark in those big dark blue eyes. 'And if I'm not, someone else will be happy to take over? Someone like Andy Gilbert?' he suggested, fanning it gently.

'He's a very appealing young man.' It was, after all, one of the reasons she had employed him.

'Personally, I can take him or leave him.' He straightened, dragged a finger and thumb down the length of his long, straight nose. 'But maybe you're right. She needs some company her own age. I realize I'm going to have to let her go, but I wouldn't have believed it would be so hard . . .' He stopped as he saw genuine concern in her face. He didn't want that. He wouldn't be able to handle that. He lifted his shoulders in a careless shrug. 'I guess I'm beginning to realize that I'm just not cut out to play nursemaid.'

She didn't like 'nursemaid', he noted with interest. The sparks had brightened considerably. 'That's a bit unkind, Luke.'

Restrained. She was working very hard to keep a lid on her emotions, but he wanted another glimpse of the Fizz Beaumont who had stormed his office, refusing to take no for an answer. 'Is it? Well, I never promised to be kind.'

'Just what *did* you promise?'

The promise he had made to Melanie had been too deep for words, too personal to share. It was in his head and only he knew it. 'You're very free with your tongue now you've banked my cheque, Miss Beaumont.'

'Your cheque has nothing to do with it, Mr Devlin. Melanie is young; she needs a little fun.'

'And I'm sure Mr Gilbert will do everything in his power to see that she gets some. In the meantime I'll allow you to lecture me about my failings at length, but over something stronger than fruit juice. Come on, the study's out of bounds to the rabble and no one will miss me for a while.'

He took her hand before she could think of any excuse and headed to the back of the house, away from the incessant thump of the band's bass note, the murmur of voices and the sudden bursts of laughter coming from the drawing room. Her hand felt so small in his, so fragile, that conscience momentarily pricked at him. Then he remembered another hand that had held his, clinging to his fingers . . . He shut the door and they were blanketed in silence. Beyond the heavy oak door the party might never have been happening.

The study was dim, lit only by the flames licking over the logs, and the warm red underglow of the cinders made hot reflections in the glasses standing on the sideboard. He released her hand and she moved quickly away from him. He made no attempt to hold her, waving her to the sofa in front of the fire before picking up a decanter. 'Brandy?'

'No, thanks. I'm driving,' she said, looking anywhere but at him. 'And the roads are going to be treacherous tonight.'

He smiled as she remained on her feet. 'Are they? I suppose you have the most up to date weather information coming into the station.'

'All the time. The latest was definitely for snow.' She wandered across to the window and pulled back the curtain. 'I don't suppose Melanie has ever seen snow.'

Melanie. She never missed an opportunity to bring up the girl's name. If she only knew how dangerous that was. But he smiled, put down the decanter and joined her at the window. A few flakes were drifting onto the lawn. 'She'll be like a big kid. She'll want to build a snowman, have a snowball fight, get a toboggan up on the hill.'

He looked down at the top of Fizz's head, the smooth cap of chestnut hair, bright as a new conker. He wanted to stroke it, slide his fingers through it, feel it trailing

196

over his skin. He swallowed. 'You know. I think you're right. She definitely needs someone like Andy to make sure she has a good time.'

She turned her head, looked up at him. 'So you've decided to pass on your nursemaid's cap?'

'Cap, apron, ceremonial rattle if he'll take over playground duties. But somehow I doubt if Andy has quite that role in mind.'

'I think Andy can be relied on not to do anything reckless.'

'In other words, you've read him the riot act?'

She let the heavy velvet curtain drop back over the window. 'I can't have him upsetting our new star. But he's only human. If Melanie takes the initiative . . .'

Her breathing was getting ragged. The ice was beginning to thaw. She was fighting it, but she wasn't winning. It was time to turn up the heat a little.

'I hope you're as careful with your new sponsor.'

'He's more than capable of looking after himself. I think I ought to be going, Luke. I've only driven in snow once before, and it made me feel dizzy.'

He reached over her head and lifted the curtain. The snow was beginning to swirl thickly. 'Then it's already far too late. You'll just have to stay here.'

'And taste the pleasures of your four-poster bed?'

Luke didn't immediately answer. She had shocked herself, he could see that. The words had spilled out before she could stop them, like champagne into a glass. Fizz. He smiled deep inside as he cracked the code. Yes. Fizz. God, but how it suited her. Best kept chilled. Inclined to erupt when shaken. The thought of making love in a four-poster bed had been simmering in her head, fanning the damped-down fire. Her deliberate lack of interest had alerted him, and he had known then that he would take her there, that she wouldn't, in the end, be able to resist the romance of it.

But while he had thought to melt the ice just a little, it seemed that unwittingly he had used a blow torch – because now she had said the words there was no way of taking them back.

Desire did something to her face, lighting it from within, and she looked unbelievably beautiful. Without a word he let the curtain fall and reached for her, lifting his hands to cradle her face gently, slide his fingers through the silk of her hair, twisting it around his wrist, and she came to him, as he had known she would. Dancing with her had simply been a prelude to making love.

For a moment he held her. Nothing more. But everything more. Beneath his fingers he could feel her pulse throbbing at her temple, and the edge of his thumb brushing against her cheekbone raised the fine down as she shivered against him, as if every minute contact of his skin against hers was an agony of pleasure. He understood. The sensation was a two-way passage and he wanted to touch all of her, to feel her touching all of him.

She clung to him, boneless. Only his strength was supporting her and he could see his twin reflections silhouetted against the firelight in the bottomless depths of her eyes. And then, when his lips were so close that they were all but touching hers, she closed her eyes. He had never seen such a look on a woman's face, such complete surrender.

It was a moment to cherish, and for long seconds he simply looked at her. Fizz Beaumont was an original. She didn't play games, demand promises, expect declarations of undying love. She wanted him, and as he bent to kiss her his very personal vendetta against the Beaumont family was entirely forgotten. She wanted him and the feeling was wholeheartedly reciprocated.

His lips touched hers, barely a kiss, more a gentle exploration of the possibilities. He didn't know how he kept himself under such control, knew only that he mustn't frighten her now. He had to give her an opportunity to draw back, shrug, laugh a little at such foolishness. Foolishness. This was worse than foolishness. It was crazy. There was a party on the other side of the door. People. Melanie. His teeth tugged gently at the fullness of her lower lip, teasing her lips apart, and he dipped his tongue into the honeypot of her mouth. The taste of her was delicate, enticing, intoxicating. He wanted more. He wanted it all. Then she was kissing him back and everything beyond the door was forgotten.

For a single stunned moment he drew back to stare down at her. It was there, the look that had been haunting him since he had first set eyes on her. Hot desire. And, abandoning any idea of carefully fanning the sparks into flames, he let his mouth come down on hers like a naked flame on gunpowder, torching the need he had seen hidden beneath the ice, inflaming a response so intense, so emphatic that when he raised his head long moments later she mewled an anguished protest.

'Patience, sweetheart,' he murmured as she tugged at his tie, dealt ruthlessly with his shirt-studs, scattering

them on the study floor in her haste to undress him.
'Let's go upstairs – '

But she wasn't hearing him. She stepped back, and
with a single smooth movement she slid down the zip at
the side of her dress. It slithered down the length of her
body and pooled at her feet. Then she stepped out of the
black circle of cloth, kicking it to one side, and she was
naked before him but for the smallest triangle of black
lace at her hips, the sheerest lace-topped black stockings
that clung as if by magic to her long legs.

A soft expletive left his lips. An ember dropped in the
grate. Nothing else moved in the entire world while he
stared at her, mesmerized by the glow of her skin in the
firelight, the dark tight buds that tipped her breasts, the
glorious flare of her hips. Then he reached out to touch
her, the pad of his thumb tracing the fine skin drawn
tight at her temple, the hollow of her cheek, the long,
elegant column of her neck. His lips followed this tender
homage, lightly grazing her skin, the tip of his tongue
tasting her smooth, firm flesh, his teeth teasing the
sensitive lobes of her ears. She was quivering beneath
him and she whimpered softly.

'Tell me what you want, Fizz,' he encouraged her. He
knew what she wanted, but he wanted to hear her say the
words. To surrender to him utterly.

'Hold me, Luke. Touch me . . . please . . .' He liked
that. No, he loved that. To hear the want in her voice
made him feel a hundred feet tall. The tips of his fingers
stroked across the satin skin of her shoulders, but she
wanted more and she reached out, swaying towards him.
But his other hand tangled in the hair at the nape of her

neck, holding her away from him while he explored the tender hollow of her throat, his hand flattening out as it stroked down over the slope of her breast. She gasped as his palm grazed its peak, which hardened in eager anticipation, reaching up to him, begging for his touch.

'You like that?' And as his thumb momentarily brushed that impulsive bud she shuddered as the invisible thread that tied it to a deeper, more urgent need tugged at the very core of her being. He felt her knees buckle as he caught her to him. She closed her eyes and a low growl of desire came from somewhere undiscovered within her.

His eyes flickered to her face, watching the fleeting expressions that chased across it as he continued his slow, fascinated exploration of the contours of her body. The gentle swell of her stomach, the flare of her hip, the triangle of lace that covered the fluff of hair that marked her sex. 'Beautiful,' he declared, sinking to his knees, his mouth exploring the smooth white skin at the top of her thigh, exploring the gap between thigh and sex, his thumbs stroking lightly over her silk-clad legs until he was almost overcome with the scent of her arousal. Then he tugged down the tiny lace panties and buried himself in her.

She gasped with shocked delight, driving her nails deep into his back, arching her hips against him, and with a sense of triumph that made him want to beat his chest he knew that it was the first time for her, that he had given her something new.

'Luke.' Her voice was strangled as she clutched at his head, not wanting him to stop but wanting more, demanding more. As he drew back to look up at her she sank to her knees and kissed him, tasting herself, her breasts flattening themselves against his chest. Then it was his turn to groan as she grazed his nipples with the tips of her nails and they leapt to attention beneath her touch until he too was lost and out of control.

That was when he pushed her back onto the floor and pinned her beneath him, just where he had always meant her to be.

'I've wanted you, Fizz,' he said as he saw the intensity of passion glittering in her eyes. 'God knows how I've waited.'

'So why are you?' Her voice was thick with her own need. 'Waiting?'

'You have to ask that?' he groaned. 'We can't . . . not here. What I need right now is upstairs.' But Fizz wrapped her legs about him, imprisoning him and smiled like a cat.

'I like it here.'

'You think I don't?' She tightened her grip and he began to sweat. 'For heaven's sake, Fizz . . .' He suddenly realized that she was playing with him and he laughed. 'You little witch, behave yourself.'

In answer she reached up, and her little pink tongue licked at the hollow of his neck, her teeth nibbling at his chest. Luke decided that he didn't have to suffer alone, dipping his head to seize a nipple between his teeth, roll it around his tongue so that she drew up her legs in an unconscious gesture of longing, threw back her head and moaned.

'Now,' he enquired, 'do you really want to make love on the carpet?'

'It's a very . . .' she gasped as he touched her, '. . . nice carpet. And as an alternative to walking naked through the hall, it has a lot to commend it.' She reached down to unfasten his trousers, slide down his zip, and for a moment he surrendered to the sensual delight of her touch.

Then, the pulse beating hard in his temple, thrumming in his ears, he struggled to reassert himself. 'No, Fizz. Please. There's a door hidden in the panelling, a staircase – ' He groaned as she arched against him, the thrumming was growing louder, knocking, knocking . . .

'Luke? Are you in there?' Melanie's voice from beyond the door brought him crashing back to earth, and for a moment they stared at one another.

'Melanie!' Fizz whispered. He saw the sudden flare of realization in her eyes and knew that he had, for the moment, lost her. As the doorhandle turned he put his hand over her mouth, afraid she would call out.

'It's all right, the door's locked. She can't get in,' he murmured softly, reassuringly, but instead she bucked furiously beneath him and rolled away.

'Luke?'

'I'm on the telephone, Mel. Give me a minute.'

'It's all right. It's just that Claudia has arrived and she's looking for Fizz. Do you know where she is?'

He swore softly. Then rose to his feet, attempting to straighten his clothes with fingers that shook like a boy's. 'Fizz was dancing when I last saw her,' he called out, gathering his wits as Fizz scrambled about the floor in a panic to find her clothes. 'I'll be with you in five minutes.'

After a moment he turned, but any thought that they might ultimately retire to the privacy of his bedroom and resume their delicious foreplay was immediately dashed. The barriers were back up and he could see that it was going to take a lot more than a blowtorch to burn them down next time. 'Fizz, I'm sorry . . .' She ignored him, and, clutching her dress against her, quartered the floor, looking for something. 'Can I help?'

'Haven't you done enough?' Her voice, the merest whisper, conveyed outrage. Outrage? Anyone would think he had pinned her against the wall and ripped the dress off her back. He didn't kid himself that his intentions had been honourable, but she had led the way.

'Here.' He opened a narrow door concealed in the panelling. Beyond it was a flight of stairs. 'This goes straight up to my room. You can take your time to get dressed properly.'

'Properly?' she snapped furiously. 'Properly? How can I get dressed properly when I've lost my knickers.' He found them beneath the drinks cabinet, damp with the dew of her desire, and handed them to her without a word. She snatched them from him and then blushed crimson. 'And an earring. And my handbag. I'm quite sure I'll need a comb.'

'Not for me, sweetheart. Don't change anything for me.' Indeed, as she stood in the doorway, her hair gloriously tousled, her eyes blazing, her cheeks flying bright flags, she looked more beautiful, more desirable than any woman he had ever known. Unable to help himself he moved to hold her, but she flinched away from him.

'No!'

He silently cursed both Melanie and Claudia in the same breath. 'I'll find it and bring it up.'

'Don't you dare come near me.'

He was beginning to lose patience. 'I'm sorry, Fizz, but I need a fresh tie, and I don't plan to crawl about on my hands and knees looking for my shirt-studs either.' He looked down at himself. 'Of course, I could just go back to the party like this, if you would prefer, but I can't imagine what kind of telephone call would leave me in a state like this, can you?' She didn't answer. 'Go on, now. Before she comes back. These stairs lead straight to my room. I'll be up in a minute.'

She turned and fled up the stairs, leaving him with a glorious view of her backside. He smiled briefly, then shut the door and looked about him. He found her handbag and a couple of his studs before abandoning the search. He crossed to the foot of the stairs, then returned to the sideboard and poured a measure of brandy into a large glass before following Fizz up the stairs.

She was in the bathroom. He could hear the shower running and he didn't disturb her. There didn't seem to be any point. Instead he found a fresh shirt, fitted another set of studs and, with hands that lacked his usual rock-steadiness, made a less than perfect job of tying his tie. Then he went back down into the study, picked up his jacket, unlocked the door and rejoined his guests.

It's all right, the door's locked. All right? What was so damned all right about the door being locked? It suggested premeditation, forethought, planning. For a moment she had been lost in wonder and joy at the rediscovery of herself, but those six little words had sent splinters of ice down her spine. How could she have been so stupid?

Fizz stood beneath the fierce shower, her face flaming in hot shame at the wanton way she had just unzipped her dress and stepped out of it.

These stairs lead straight to my room. Ice-cold inside, Fizz had heard the words and known exactly what they meant. Straight to his damned four-poster bed, he meant. She had lost more than an earring in Luke Devlin's study. She had lost her pride, her self-respect, and quite obviously her head. Claudia was right; she had never been cut out for the stage. She had never been able to pretend. The poised, cool young woman she had been playing had crumbled the moment Luke had touched her.

She might have been able to live with that. Just. After all, Luke Devlin had it all. Money, good looks, the kind of power that was a real turn-on for some women. He must be used to women throwing themselves into his bed. But she had stepped out of her dress and thrown herself into his arms with a casual ease that suggested a lifetime of practice. And afterwards . . . Where had she learned to do those things?

Fizz closed her eyes and groaned, her whole body trembling with mortification. She had had one lover. Only one. And that had been seven years ago. The irony of it was that she had flung herself into Patrick's arms too. The speed of it had left her bewildered, unsatisfied, but Patrick hadn't seemed to realize that anything was wrong and she had been young and inexperienced and quite ready to believe that any shortcomings were her own. They had to be. After all, Patrick March was sex on a stick. But suddenly she was not so certain. Patrick had never made her feel the way she had felt in Luke's arms.

She leaned against the tiles and let the water beat against her skin. She had never indulged in casual sex. But then there was nothing remotely casual about her feelings for Luke Devlin. She hated him and yet she had wanted him since the first moment she set eyes on him. And she was quite old enough to know that such a combination was lethal.

Thank God that Melanie had given her breathing space to restore the carefully constructed barriers that Luke had somehow managed to crash.

She began washing herself from head to toe, scrubbing herself to try and rid herself of the taste, the scent of him. But using Luke's soap made it quite impossible, and in the end she gave up trying and dried herself. She wrapped a towel around her and listened at the bathroom door. There was no sound. He might, of course, be waiting quietly, standing by the window, looking out into the night as his garden was blanketed with snow. But she couldn't hide in the bathroom all night, and if Claudia was launching a hue and cry for her, the sooner she appeared the better. Claudia. With the unexpected arrival of her sister she was under no illusions. Life was about to become even more complicated.

She had scarcely registered Luke's bedroom as she had bolted for the bathroom. Now she looked about her. It looked somehow different from the way she remembered it, the colours darker, the furniture heavier, grander. Rich velvet curtains had been drawn over the windows, shutting out the night, and even the four-poster with its heavy drapes seemed larger in the soft shadows thrown by the lamplight.

And it was all painfully redolent of its occupant: a pair of men's silver-backed brushes, discarded cufflinks, the box that had contained his shirt studs – all had been left on the great oak dressing table. There was no sign of Melanie's presence. Maybe she preferred to have her own room, somewhere softer, frillier, where her stuffed toys would feel at home and she wouldn't irritate Luke with her clutter. No, this was his domain, his alone, and he had been planning to bring her up here . . .

Fizz subsided onto the stool before the dressing table and regarded her reflection. Her cheeks were flushed, her lips beestung, her hair no longer sleek but tossed every which way by Luke Devlin's passionate hands. The look was unmistakable. She had been making love and, despite the most thorough application of soap and water, it showed.

Luke had left her small black clutch-bag on the dressing table, along with a large brandy glass filled a generous measure of the rich amber spirit. He doubtless thought it would give her the strength to face him. She didn't need brandy for that. Just guts. Or did he expect her to drink the brandy and wait for him to join her when he had made his excuses?

At the thought her heightened colour drained abruptly away. She opened her bag and began rapidly to repair the damage to her make-up in an attempt to recover the treacherous poise that had deserted her without a backward glance when she had most needed it. She combed out her hair until it glowed sleekly and made up sparingly, her lipstick helping to disguise the startling effect of Luke's embrace.

Then she dressed slowly, reluctantly, in her abandoned clothes. The elegant black gown was surprisingly uncreased, she thought, considering the abuse that it had undergone. But it had been made for a poised and sophisticated woman. Maybe that was one of the requirements.

He obviously hadn't found her earring, and she overcame the temptation to fling the other into the wastebin. She had made enough mistakes tonight and it would be too easy for Melanie to put two and two together if the housekeeper brought it to her, asking if it was hers. Especially if the other were later found on the study floor.

She put it into her handbag to be disposed of later, along with everything else she was wearing that evening. The dress that had given her such pleasure when she had put it on earlier that evening no longer had a place in her wardrobe. She wasn't poised, she wasn't sophisticated and it had been a terrible mistake to pretend she was. But pretend she must until she could make good her escape.

A final glance at her reflection satisfied her that she looked as nearly like the Fizz she knew as was possible under the circumstances, and with a little lift of her head she rose and let herself out of the room without a backward glance at the four-poster bed in which Luke had intended she spend the night. He had obviously tried it out for length and not found it wanting.

The main staircase descended into the large, panelled entrance hall. Luke was there, leaning against the mantle, every inch the urbane host as he and Melanie chatted to her father and sister. Only she would spot the less than perfectly tied black silk bow at his neck, that he wasn't wearing the same studs in his shirt and that, in his haste, one of them hadn't been fastened properly. With her sister standing so close to him, who would notice anything but how good they looked together?

Claudia was certainly too busy flirting, and her father too busy talking to Melanie. Luke, it seemed, had eyes for no one but Claudia, and who could blame him? With her hair blonde once more, rippling over her shoulders and down her back in tiny little waves that caught the light and shone softly as she turned to look up at him, she was enough to fill any man's eyes. And when, on top of all her natural assets, she wore a scarlet dress that skimmed her breasts and clung to her like a second skin all the way down to her ankles, no red-blooded male stood a chance.

Yet, despite Melanie's fresh and youthful charms as opposed to Claudia's more blatant attractions, there was no doubt about one thing. The Australian reporter in the clipping Jim had given her had been right. There was a likeness between the two girls. Nothing you could put your finger on. Nothing obvious. And Claudia's present colouring was not inherited but achieved at great expense in an exclusive salon in Knightsbridge. But it was there.

Her father was remarking on it as she approached them. 'What do you think, Fizz?' he demanded.

'About what?'

Luke turned abruptly, as if he hadn't heard her coming. But he had. She had seen his shoulders tense beneath the smooth cloth of his jacket, his jaw tighten. He was having to force himself to relax. 'Are you feeling better, Fizz?' he asked.

She turned a pair of expressionless eyes upon him. 'Better?' Better than what? she wondered.

'I was just explaining that the noise of the band had given you headache. Did the brandy help?'

'Brandy?' Melanie was aghast. 'The poor girl had a headache and you gave her brandy? I couldn't think of anything worse.'

'I don't believe there is anything,' Fizz agreed. 'But Luke has already told me that he's not cut out to be a nursemaid.'

He gave her a look that would have fried onions before offering the shrug of a helpless male. 'It seemed like a good idea at the time.'

'It's all right, Melanie, I didn't drink it,' Fizz reassured her. 'I'm driving, you see.'

'Well, can I get you an aspirin or something?'

'Nothing. Thank you,' she said, her conscience jabbing her painfully. 'A liberal application of cold water was all I needed to clear my head.'

'Very liberal. Your hair is damp,' Claudia remarked, her eyes full of mischief.

'And is it?' Luke enquired. She turned to face him and their eyes clashed over Melanie's head. Although the effort cost her dear, she raised one questioning brow. 'Clear?' he enquired.

'Perfectly. There's absolutely no chance of a relapse.'

His mouth tightened slightly, his eyes seemed suddenly colder than she remembered, but otherwise there was nothing to indicate that he had received her message loud and clear. But then with his arms full of Claudia he would scarcely notice her defection. And as if to confirm this he looked down and said, 'Perhaps you'd like to dance, Claudia?'

Claudia glanced at Fizz, then back at Luke, and with a little cat-like smile she snuggled against him. 'Love to, darling.'

'But I thought you were desperate to talk to Fizz,' Edward Beaumont interrupted. 'That's why I was so late,' he explained to his host. 'Claudia arrived just as I was leaving, but she was so desperate to see Fizz that I had to wait for her.'

'Fizz isn't going anywhere, Beau. And they're playing my tune,' Claudia said with a husky laugh, as someone opened a door and the soft strains of 'Lady in Red' filtered into the hall.

Beau. Fizz exchanged a look with her father. Beau was the affectionate nickname that everyone in the theatre world used for her father, and when she was working with him Claudia naturally used it too. But he wouldn't tolerate it at home – largely because she used it to rub in the fact that while she was a success in the family profession Fizz was stuck in Broomhill, running her tedious little radio station.

Despite the fact that she was all smiles and charm, her

use of it now was tantamount to hoisting a storm warning. She had obviously heard about Melanie's imminent arrival as part of the cast of *Holiday Bay* and she clearly wasn't in any mood to tolerate it.

Melanie's face betrayed her unease. 'Do you think Claudia will mind working with me?' she asked Fizz.

Edward roused himself from contemplation of Melanie's face. 'Why on earth would she mind? She's glad enough of the work when there's nothing else to be had.'

'Oh, but she's rather a grand actress. I saw her when she came to Australia last year.' She smiled shyly at Edward Beaumont. 'You too, of course. I thought you were both terribly good.'

'Did you?' Edward asked thoughtfully. 'Is your mother English?

'She was,' Melanie confirmed, a little sadly. 'She died last year. How did you guess?'

'The way you said "terribly good". You don't hear it much these days.' He took a deep breath. 'Will you two young ladies excuse me for a moment? I think I need a drink.'

'And something to eat,' Melanie exclaimed. 'Giving a party is such hard work. I'm positively starving.' She linked her arms through theirs and led them both into the drawing room.

'Are you all right, Dad?' Fizz asked quietly as Melanie led the way along the table, heaping food upon their plates.

'Me? Absolutely fine. It was just that something Melanie said reminded me of someone I once knew, that was all. Silly. It was years ago.' She wasn't shocked. Her father, after all, had never pretended to be a saint. That had been her mother's role.

'What happened?'

He shrugged. 'Your mother's accident. Poor woman – ' Fizz stopped him with a warning touch to his arm as Melanie reached the end of the table. 'We lost touch. She moved on. Found someone else, I suppose.'

He turned away as an acquaintance claimed his attention and she was left holding two plates of food that she didn't want. Spotting Andy sulking in a corner, she took one of them across to him. He didn't look as if he was enjoying himself any more than she was.

'You're an unlikely wallflower at a party, Andy, but since you're not dancing would you help me out with one of these?'

He took the plate she proferred and gave Fizz a tentative smile. 'Does this mean I'm forgiven for being an absolute heel earlier on?'

'No. It means I've been lumbered with a spare plate.' She gave him a look that betrayed her exasperation. 'You're handling this very badly, Andy. I know you're not used to having to make much of an effort, but Melanie Brett isn't your average girl.' She no longer felt the slightest guilt in urging Andy to woo Melanie away from a man who was clearly capable of such brutal infidelity.

'You've changed your tune,' Andy said with surprise. 'Anyway, Melanie's been told by that pompous great – ' He managed to stop himself before using a word that Fizz's expression told him he would regret. 'She has been told to be a good little girl and play hostess to her guests.

214

No dancing, no disappearing act. Not that he's making the same sacrifice, I notice.'

Fizz ignored this. Her own behaviour wouldn't bear close scrutiny and she certainly had no wish to discuss Luke Devlin's. 'You know, Andy, you could try using your imagination for a change.'

He gave her a long look. 'What is that supposed to mean?'

Advice to the lovelorn. It would make a good programme. Letters, music and advice. Maybe she could start a new career as an agony aunt. With a sigh, she buried her impatience. This was all new territory for Andy.

'You could try being a little less selfish. This is her party, so she can't just waltz off and have a good time. She has to make sure everyone else is enjoying themselves, see no one is left on their own. But I'm sure she'd love to have your company, your help – particularly with some of the locals. They are simply dying to talk to her but don't quite dare. Now, Luke Devlin can hardly object to that, can he? And I'm sure that Melanie will be very grateful.'

'How grateful?'

He was a slow learner. 'If you'll take my advice, Andy, for what it's worth, don't try and take it too fast.'

Andy grinned. 'You mean I should invite her to tea with my dear old mum?'

She shrugged. 'Why not? It's certainly original enough to tempt her.'

'Is that what it's going to take to woo you, Fizz?' he asked.

215

'I'm not in the market for wooing, Andy.'

He leaned across and kissed her cheek. 'That's a pity. You've a glow about you tonight. You haven't been on the Thunderbolt, have you?'

'You've used up your ration of cheek for this month, Mr Gilbert. I'd go and find Melanie if I were you, and give her a bit of moral support.'

She certainly wasn't getting it from Luke. His entire attention was directed towards making sure that Claudia was having a good time. Fizz watched as he directed her down the buffet, offering her a taste of anything she was uncertain of from his own plate, laughing as she pulled a face at something she had nibbled from the end of his fork. As a performance it was beautifully judged.

It was extraordinary, Fizz thought. For a man who hadn't had a good word to say for the Beaumonts a week ago, he was certainly going out of his way to cultivate their company tonight.

Jealousy was an unpleasant emotion. But as Fizz watched her sister flirting with the ease of long practice, and saw Luke Devlin responding, she knew the feeling that was twisting her stomach into knots could be nothing else. Jealousy. It wouldn't be so bad if the attraction was genuine, but even before she had seen the newspaper clipping she had suspected from his remarks that Luke had no great admiration for her sister. It could be, of course, that mutual respect had no place in his pursuit of women. It could be that he collected them in the same way he collected companies.

CHAPTER 9

'Fizz?' Andy took her arm, suddenly full of concern. 'Look, Melanie can wait. Would you like to go and have a dance or something?'

'What?' A dance was the last thing she wanted, but she could hardly get up and run from the room, which was what she wanted to do more than anything in the world. But neither could she bear to go on sitting there, watching the pair of them. 'Oh, a dance.' She gladly abandoned her untouched plate and allowed Andy to lead her across the room. No one, least of all Luke Devlin, took the slightest bit of notice. Once in the hall, however, she let him go. 'I don't think I want to dance after all, Andy. Go and find Melanie. She needs someone to look after her more than I do,' she said.

He hesitated, clearly torn. 'Are you sure?'

She forced a smile. 'Yes, of course. Don't waste time arguing, just go.' She gave him a little push back into the drawing room. 'And if you see Dad will you tell him that I've gone home?'

She found her cloak, swung it around her shoulders and shivered as she stepped out into a freezing night. It had stopped snowing, she saw with relief. There was just a light frosting, like the sprinkle of icing sugar on a sponge. And the clouds had rolled inland, leaving a frosty night bright with stars that threw a silver sheen across the quiet surface of the sea.

Behind her the noise of the party rose and fell, the thump of the band a solid underblanket of sound. Afraid that someone might have seen her, would come after her, she hurried across the ice-slicked gravel, the thin soles of her high-heeled shoes slipping treacherously as she found her way to her car in the darkness. By the time she tried to fit her key into the lock she was shivering so much that it took her several tries before she managed finally to open the door.

Once inside she made a determined effort to get a grip on herself. The car, in good working order despite its age, started immediately, and, taking enormous care in man-oeuvring around the dozens of cars parked along the drive, she made it without mishap to the road. The gritting lorries had already been out, she was relieved to see, and, automatically switching on the radio, she heard the late-night presenter warning drivers to take care on the narrow lanes that might not be reached until morning.

That was her life, she reminded herself. Her radio station, serving the community night and day. She had lost her head over a man once before. To risk it again over a man like Luke Devlin would be madness. Her sister could have him, and welcome to him. And as if to prove to herself that she didn't care one way or the other, she didn't go home, but headed her car towards the seafront and parked facing the sea.

It was dark but for the navigation lights of ships passing in the distance and the reflection of the line of lamps that punctuated the elegant wrought-iron railings of the pier. At the far end, the Pavilion lay like a ghost, reflecting the faint frosty starlight from its white domes.

Inside, the small night staff, fortified with endless coffee and sandwiches, would be keeping everything ticking over until dawn, monitoring the news bulletins, keeping the night owls fed with music and chat, and she suddenly had a great longing to be there with them. She needed to remind herself that just a few days ago she had thought getting her wings singed in Luke Devlin's flame would be worth the sacrifice if it meant she could hang onto this. So she got out of her car and, because it was locked at night, used her key to let herself onto the pier. Then she walked its silent length, her dark cloak billowing around her ankles.

She arrived home just before six the next morning, having preferred to stay with the night crew, sharing their coffee and their jokes, rather than return to her empty flat and face her thoughts. But when the day crew began to arrive, giving her curious looks, she realized it was time to leave.

Someone had been there before her. Luke. She immediately recognized the handwriting on the envelope propped up against the front door. She picked up the envelope and the delicate bunch of snowdrops that lay beside it. She lifted them to her nose and caught the elusive scent of cold woodland, smiling despite herself at the thought of Luke Devlin out in the freezing night picking snowdrops for her. Tying them up with a piece of narrow white ribbon. What on earth did he mean by it?

She gently stroked the satin, pulling it between her finger and thumb as if it might give her some clue. It sprang back into a slight kink. She looked at it more closely, saw the faint telltale buckling where it had been threaded through eyelets, and the smile abruptly left her face.

The ribbon wasn't new. Well, no. Where would a man get ribbon in the early hours of a Sunday morning? Easy. He would raid his lover's lingerie. A nightdress or petticoat. She couldn't believe the nerve of the man. To tie up snowdrops of all things! A symbol of everything that was brave and pure. She carried them into the kitchen and dumped flowers, ribbon and envelope straight into the pedal bin beneath the sink, letting the lid fall with a satisfyingly loud thunk. She didn't want his flowers, she didn't want to read his apology. If it was an apology.

Still wrapped in thought, she showered – using her own soap, with her own scent. And afterwards she walked along the cliffpath until the cold and the knowledge that her father would be expecting her for lunch drove her back home.

Sunday lunch was a time Fizz shared with her father whenever she could, although today lack of sleep was beginning to catch up with her. Or maybe it was the knowledge that Claudia would be there that made her feet drag. But when she arrived at her father's house, just before one, Claudia was still in her own apartment.

It was nearly one-thirty when she finally stuck her head around the door. 'Sorry, overslept. I was terribly late in.'

'Sherry?' Edward Beaumont was clearly irritated and Fizz held her breath. Her father didn't often lose his temper. When he did, the results tended to be spectacular. She had inherited her own short fuse from him. But Claudia was oblivious.

'Thanks. Wasn't it a wonderful party last night?'

'You certainly seemed to have difficulty dragging yourself away.'

'I didn't wake you up, did I?'

'Somebody did, and since we haven't been burgled I can only assume it was you.' Fizz watched them fencing with words, standing back like a child watching a game played by the grown-ups. 'Around four o'clock? Does that ring a bell?'

Fizz greeted the housekeeper's announcement that lunch was ready with relief, although it was short-lived as all through it Claudia waxed lyrical about Luke, Melanie and Winterbourne Manor.

'What a gorgeous house. And that four-poster bed!' She turned to Fizz. 'You've already seen it, of course.'

'Have you?' her father asked, surprised.

'Luke asked me to accompany him when he viewed some properties. Winterbourne Manor was one of them,' she replied, with every appearance of outward calm.

'Oh, I didn't know that,' Claudia said. 'I was thinking of your little, um, lie-down yesterday evening. I suppose your left early because of your headache. How is it this morning?'

'I'm quite recovered, thank you. I'm sorry I missed you, since you were so anxious to talk.'

'Oh, not to worry. We all went out into the snow. Quite silly, really. And since the gardens were just full of snowdrops we decided to pick some.'

'Anyone would think you'd never seen a snowdrop before,' Edward said, with a snort of disgust. 'The garden here is full of them, but you always complain about getting your feet muddy if you have to leave the path.' He turned to Fizz, clearly out of patience with his older daughter. 'Have you told Claudia about the changes to *Holiday Bay*?'

'Not yet.'

'I understand dear little Melanie is going to be given a part.'

Fizz gave her a long look, distrusting Claudia's smile. 'Yes, there's going to have to be a new twist to the storyline. I've called a script conference for first thing Monday morning. I'd like new ones written and re-corded as soon as possible.'

'There's no rush, is there?' Claudia asked casually. Too casually. 'I'll be here all next week.'

Fizz frowned. 'Will you? What about your chocolate commercial?'

'It's run into a bit of a problem. Apparently some of the Chocolate Company's shareholders objected to the slant the campaign was taking.'

'Which chocolate company?' Edward asked.

'No, that's it's name. The Chocolate Company. It's new, a bit upmarket, and they're launching in the autumn in time for the Christmas trade.'

'Oh, I see. Well, in my experience shareholders don't give a damn so long as the profits are rolling in and the dividends are up,' her father said cynically.

'There was rather a lot of publicity about the campaign,' Claudia said defensively. 'About it being sexy.'

'Yes, I saw some of it.' He leaned back in his chair. 'And now they've dropped it, you say? Well, it was nicely done. They've had their publicity for nothing and now they'll whip up another hooha about dropping the campaign. Advertising on the cheap. I hope your contract was signed and sealed this time.' He turned to Fizz. 'You heard about the Spanish fiasco, I suppose?'

'Of course it was signed,' Claudia said crossly. 'But I'll only get the flat fee agreed for filming the first episode.'

He snorted derisively. 'You've been had, my girl. They've used your name and your photograph to guarantee publicity for their product and they've paid you peanuts for the privilege. If they're lucky they'll get a re-run on the back of the cancellation of the campaign. I'd seriously consider changing my agent if I were you.'

'Wasn't it going to be one of those serial ads that run and run?' Fizz asked, concerned for her sister. 'Years of work?'

'I'll survive. To be honest, I'm not sure that I want to play a girl incapable of saying no if she's offered the right brand of chocolate.'

'Sounds like typecasting to me,' her father said unkindly. 'And you weren't so fussy when you thought you would have your face all over the television seven nights a week.'

Claudia pointedly ignored this. 'Well, it can't be

helped. And since I'm not working for a while, Fizz, it means I can stay in Broomhill. Get to know Melanie better. And Luke,' she said, with a teasing little smile.

But Fizz was tired of Claudia's game. 'Are you sure Melanie wants to know you? After what you said to that reporter in Australia?'

Claudia blushed. Fizz would have taken an oath that her sister had forgotten how, but there was no mistaking the real thing. 'How do you know about that?'

'Know about what?' Edward looked up from his roast lamb.

'Claudia wasn't very kind about Melanie. Unfortunately she was talking to a reporter at the time.' She looked at her sister. 'I wasn't sure if you'd seen it.'

Claudia glared at her. 'Of course I've seen it. But I didn't say anything like that.' She had. The colour in her cheeks could mean nothing else.

'What are you two talking about?'

'Nothing important, Dad. Would you like another glass of wine?' Claudia was suddenly all attention.

'I'd still like to get the recordings done as quickly as possible,' Fizz went on. 'Just in case you get called up for some fabulous part you can't possibly refuse,' she added, to soften her words.

'There doesn't seem to be much chance of that. I don't appear to be flavour of the month.'

Fizz frowned, but she knew her sister well enough to know when to let a subject drop. She didn't mention it again until after lunch, when their father adjourned to his study with the excuse of a heavy work-load. They both knew he was going to doze peacefully in front of the fire, but even Claudia knew better than to suggest as much.

'Claudia, have you had many parts suddenly disappear under your fingers just lately?' she asked. 'Anything else, I mean.'

She shrugged. 'Well, I thought I was going to get a part in a political drama, but it went to Marty.' She pulled a face and grinned. The two of them were always in competition for the same parts so that wasn't unusual. 'And there was an audition for a revival of *Private Lives* that fell apart for lack of backing at the last minute. One minute I didn't know how I was going to fit it all in, now all of a sudden work is decidedly thin on the ground. But it happens. You know that as well as I do. Why?'

Fizz shook her head. 'I don't know. We've had problems with sponsorship, you know, because of the Harries takeover.'

'Have you? Dad's worried about money too. Did you know that?'

'He's looked tired recently, I thought, but I've been so caught up with my own problems . . . Is it serious?'

'He had promises of finance for this television thing he's involved in. I mean cast-iron promises. Now a couple of his backers have dropped out when he's already committed to production. He's going to have to put in a lot more of his own money than he thought. And it's not a good time to be liquidizing assets.'

'I hadn't realized.' A three-fold lightning strike? Coincidence or design? Surely not. The fact that Luke had known what her sister was doing could be put down to the newspaper coverage of the campaign. But he had told her not to worry about Claudia's availability. And the letter she had picked up in his office had carried the Chocolate Company logo.

'Is something bothering you, Fizz?'

She met her sister's eyes and for a moment was tempted to blurt it all out. 'Oh, I don't know. Julian's probably right. I am getting paranoid.' Nobody would go to such lengths to avenge a catty remark made off the cuff to a reporter. 'It's just that ever since Luke Devlin arrived in Broomhill life has been . . . difficult.'

Claudia smiled. 'That's because he's way out of your league, little sister,' she said, curling up cat-like on the sofa. 'Better leave him to the big girls who know how to handle men like him.'

'The big girls are welcome to him,' she snapped. Then as Claudia's eyes widened thoughtfully, she rushed on, 'Frankly, I don't think he much cares what size they are, and it's none of my business, but he's treating Melanie very shabbily.' That was guilt talking, she thought. She hadn't given much thought to Melanie's feelings when she had stepped out of her dress, when his mouth had been doing indescribable things to her body.

'Is he?' Claudia seemed to find her indignant outburst highly amusing.

'For heaven's sake, you know as well as I do that he's living with the girl, but it doesn't stop him flirting with anything female that moves. That's bad enough, but when Melanie had the temerity to dance with Andy he hauled her over the coals like a naughty little girl.'

Claudia's eyes, wide and innocent as a puppy's, regarded Fizz with a provoking little smile. 'I know he's living with Melanie at the moment, darling, but it's purely temporary.'

'If he's told you that, he's playing with you.' The words were out before she could stop them and she knew instantly that she had made a mistake. Betrayed herself.

'Are you afraid that I'll take away your new toy, darling?' She laughed at Fizz's stricken face. 'I don't imagine you were worrying about poor Melanie when you were playing naughty games behind that locked study door, little sister. You can tell me about it if you like. I promise I won't be in the least bit shocked.'

'I don't know what you're talking about.' She bent over the fire, poking viciously at the logs in an attempt to hide the colour flooding into her cheeks.

'I'm talking about hidden doors and secret stairs.' A log split in two and flared, making Fizz jump. 'See what a state you're in? Just as well I arrived when I did and put a stop to whatever was going on. We really don't want a repeat of the last time you fancied yourself in love.'

'There's no chance of that, but let me return the compliment. You talk a lot about games, and you think I'm naïve and stupid where men are concerned, but I can tell you that Luke Devlin is trouble.' Just how much she wasn't sure.

Claudia, however, refused to he worried. 'Men like him are always trouble,' she said confidentially. 'But I can tell you they're worth it – ' She stopped. 'Hey, Fizz, I've just had an idea. We could help Dad out, you know.'

'Us? Haven't you been listening? I've got all the money problems I can handle.'

'No, listen. We could sell a bit of Ma's jewellery; we'd

227

hardly miss a piece each. You scarcely ever wear yours, anyway.'

'Oh, Claud.' Her sister was totally exasperating at times. She could be such a unutterable cow, but then she would do something warm, generous, thoroughly good-hearted . . .

'What? Fizz told her and Claudia's eyes widened. 'Copies? You mean we've been paying good money to keep copies in a security vault?' she demanded furiously.

'It would seem so.'

'But . . .' she frowned deeply, '. . . how on earth did you find out?'

'I told you – we've had sponsorship problems so I thought I might sell my jewellery. As you say, I never wear it and it seemed like a good way to raise the money to pay off my bank loan for the restaurant.'

'I thought Luke was taking over sponsorship of the station?'

'He is. But I had this feeling that something wasn't quite right. It wasn't until after I'd signed the agreement that I found out what you'd said about Melanie.'

'You're not really that worried about Luke sponsoring the station, surely?' Fizz didn't answer. 'I mean, what could he do? Make me write out five hundred times "I must not be a cat"? Apologize publicly before *Holiday Bay* is broadcast?'

Fizz was forced to laugh. Paranoia was something that happened inside the brain. Out loud her fears sounded ridiculous. 'I suppose you're right.'

'Of course I am. Now, tell me about the pawnshop. Was it terribly embarrassing?'

'On a scale of one to ten? Ten.'

Claudia reached over and clasped her hand. 'It's no good saying that you should have called me.' She gave an awkward little shrug. 'I've been staying with David. But I'm truly sorry you went through that alone.'

'Julian came along. He was a brick. Made me beans on toast and cocoa to comfort me.'

'Julian's your pet banker?'

'He's so sweet. I wish I could love him.'

'Like David.' Claudia was silent for a moment. 'You don't think badly of Dad, do you, Fizz?'

She shook her head. 'I was worried about you, though. You love wearing your sparklies.'

'Oh, but, darling, the relief! I lost an earring once, dropped it down the plughole in a ladies' loo at some swanky restaurant. Well, I could see the wretched thing glinting up at me from the murky depths so I thought I could rescue it. I unscrewed the thingie at the bottom – you know – with my nailfile, and water shot out all over the carpet and I still couldn't get at the damn earring.'

'Oh, Claudia!' Fizz stifled a giggle.

'Well, of course I had to confess what I'd done and pay for a plumber to be called out to dismantle the pipe properly, retrieve my bloody diamond and then put it all back. It took *hours*! And the restaurant sent me a bill for cleaning the carpet too. If I'd known it wasn't real I could have abandoned the wretched thing!' She glared at Fizz. 'It isn't funny!'

'Oh, God, I'm sorry, but the thought of you crawling about on your hands and knees . . .' She drew her knees up to her chin and buried her face in them, rocking with laughter.

Claudia choked back a giggle. Then exploded. They were still laughing five minutes later, when Edward Beaumont came to see what all the commotion was about.

The light on her answering machine was flashing when she got home. Fizz had a good idea who the message was from and she didn't want to hear it. But she might be wrong. It might be important. And a message couldn't hurt her.

'Hi, Fizz. It's Julian. I'm just checking to see that you're okay and to remind you that I meant what I said the other day. You obviously need a big brother to hold your hand and I'm happy to play the part. An offer, I have to say, that does not include your glamorous sister. If you need anything, you know where to find me.'

She smiled. He had really been a lot kinder than she deserved. The machine beeped, then cut off. Several times. Somebody had been calling but not leaving a message. Even without his voice she sensed Luke Devlin.

From the moment she had heard his name her quiet, very peaceful existence had been shattered. And right now Julian's gut feeling was developing out of control into a real sense of threat. Not just to her inward, personal peace, but to her entire family.

She picked up the telephone and dialled Julian's number.

'What's up, Fizz?' he asked, without preamble.

'Did you mean it? About helping me if you could?'

'Big brother at your command. Anything except

230

money. Unfortunately I won't have any until the old chap turns up his toes, and I'm not in that much of a hurry.'

'Actually, money won't really help now. I've already signed Luke Devlin's piece of paper, paid his money into the bank. But I need information.'

'Fire away.'

'Is it possible to find out the names of companies where Luke Devlin is a major shareholder? I mean, does he keep his certificates at the bank?'

'Christ, Fizz!' She had shaken him out of his easy manner. 'Are you trying to get me the sack? I can't go rooting through the man's personal papers. And even if I could, I would be in breach of just about every banking rule in the book if I passed private information on to you.'

'Oh, Lord, I'm sorry. I just didn't think. Forget I asked.'

'More gut feelings?'

'Is there anything stronger than gut?'

'Has something happened?' She told him about her misgivings. 'Well, I suppose if you had any particular companies in mind you could check the records at Companies House.'

'Could I?'

There was a pause. 'You mean, *Could you, Julian*, don't you?'

'Er . . . yes, I suppose I do. I would come up myself, but I've got a script conference tomorrow morning and the Pier Trustees' meeting in the afternoon. And I've a feeling that this is urgent.'

'You'd better tell me the names of the companies, then.'

'Have you got a pen?'

'Good grief, how many are there?'

'Just four. The Chocolate Company. Dicken Films. Hawkswell Productions. Carswell Holdings. I'm not sure if those last three are the full names of the companies.'

'As far as I know the Chocolate Company is the only one that's a publicly quoted company. If the others are private it will be a lot more difficult to get hold of the kind of information you want. It just depends if I can find anyone connected with them who might be prepared to chat over a pint. But I'll do my best.'

'Maybe I'm just being paranoid, imagining things, but I've sort of got a motive worked out as to why he might want to give Claudia a hard time. I can't believe he would really go as far as attempting to hurt Dad.'

'And what about you? Will he hurt you?'

'No.' She closed her eyes. 'No. He needs the radio station to get at Claudia; that's why he had to sponsor us. He didn't want it to go under.'

'Expensive weapon.'

'Am I just being silly?' How she would love to be told that. To be able to believe it. 'He couldn't do it by himself, could he?'

She heard the pleading note in her voice but Julian didn't offer her empty comfort. 'Shall we find out if there's any connection before we start asking ourselves how many beans make five? Haven't you got anything else to worry about?'

'Hundreds of things. Claudia and Dad suggested that I

hold a party at the new restaurant. A sort of launch, now it's been run in. Maybe get a mention or two in the Sunday papers' food guides. I suppose I should think about that. Of course, as the man with the foresight to provide the necessary capital, you are invited.' She paused. 'Claudia has promised to come.'

He chuckled. 'Is this your idea of a pay-off?'

'It's all I can afford. But I warn you, she collects charming young men like you and keeps them as house-pets.'

'If that's a promise my dear Fizz, wild horses couldn't keep me away.'

A long sustained ring on the doorbell brought the conversation abruptly to an end. She hung up and turned to stare at the door, and her skin prickled with gooseflesh. Luke. It had to be him. If she stayed very still, he might just go away.

'Fizz!' She flinched as his voice penetrated the door. 'Fizz, I know you're there; your light's on.' There was another ring. Then she heard her neighbour across the hall open her door.

'She's definitely in, dear.' Oh, Lord. Dear Mrs Pusey was as deaf as a post and shouted to compensate. 'I heard her come in about twenty minutes ago.' Deaf as a post, eh? 'Try the bell again,' she encouraged. 'Maybe she didn't hear you.' Didn't hear him? It was a wonder the entire street hadn't come out to see what was going on.

Fizz didn't wait but wrenched open the door. Luke Devlin, his face masked with tiredness and worry, leaned on the threshold. 'I want Andy Gilbert's address, Fizz,' he said. 'Now.'

Confused, not a little angry, Fizz stared at him in astonishment. Whatever she had expected him to say, it certainly wasn't that. 'Andy's address?' she demanded. 'What on earth for?'

'Don't play dumb, Fizz, you've been encouraging the pair of them since the word go. So you'd better give it to me right now, because I warn you, I'm in no mood to put up with any nonsense.'

'Oh, really! Well, let me tell you that nonsense is all you're going to get.' Furious beyond belief, she made a move to close the door. He blocked it. 'If there's anything else, Luke, I deal with business at the office, and you'll find me there tomorrow morning at nine o'clock.'

She remained at attention, refusing to look at him but holding the door open, inviting his departure. Luke ignored the invitation. Instead he unwrapped her fingers from the handle and closed the door, very quietly, still on the wrong side.

He still had her fingers grasped in his hand. It was desperately cold and she felt a momentary urge to warm it between her own before her instinct for self-preservation reasserted itself and she pulled free.

He dragged his hand over his face in a weary gesture. 'I understand how you feel, Fizz. Last night was a mess . . .' A mess. Well, that was an interesting way of putting it. 'I've been calling you on and off all day, whenever I've had a moment. I hoped the note would help . . . Where have you been?'

'Out.'

He took a deep breath, as if making a strong effort to control himself. 'All right. I'll leave us for later.

But I have to find Melanie. I need to know that she's safe.'

'Why shouldn't she be?'

'Fizz, please. I promised her mother I'd take care of her.'

'Her mother?' He expected her to believe that? 'She told me that her mother died a year ago.'

He looked for a moment as though she'd hit him. That she had the power to wound him was deeply shocking to Fizz. Her anxiety to protect herself had blinded her to the possibility that Luke might also be capable of deep feelings.

'I did suggest you took a bit more care of her last night, if you remember,' she said, more gently. She'd be a hopeless agony aunt, she decided. She dished out advice without listening to what she was saying. 'Just before you waltzed me into your study and locked the door.'

He made a weary gesture. 'Later, Fizz. You can tell me exactly how you feel about that later. But I've been at the factory since just after midnight and I'm not fit – '

'The factory?' Her voice wavered and finally she allowed herself to look at him. 'Why were you at the factory?'

'A couple of men who thought they were going to be made redundant got drunk and decided it would be a good idea to smash the place up. It took a bit of sorting out.'

'Oh, Lord. Was anyone hurt?'

'A machine fell on one of them. He's broken his leg, a couple of ribs. The other got away with a few scrapes and cuts. But it took a while to get hold of their families, discuss what was to be done with the union officials, organize a clean up.'

'But that's a major local news story. Why didn't we get any of this at the radio station?'

He gave her a deeply ironic look. 'Well, I'm sorry, Fizz. I guess we were all too busy to ring you.'

'Oh, look, I'm sorry – '

But he was already shaking his head. 'No, I am. That was a cheap shot. The truth is that I thought a little discretion was the best thing all round. Fortunately everyone else agreed.' He shrugged. 'Well, the police weren't very happy that I wouldn't press charges, in fact I was as good as told that if it happens again it's my own fault. But it won't. I'll make sure of it.'

'All that and you still had time to pick snowdrops?'

'Snowdrops?' There was the briefest pause, then he gave her an odd little smile. 'Well . . . I can always find time for the really important things. I did come after you as soon as I realized you'd left the party.'

'Why would you do that when you had Claudia to take my place?'

'Claudia could never take your place. And when your car wasn't outside your flat – '

'I went straight to the Pavilion.'

'Yes, I know. I went down to the pier, hoping that you were there and not in some ditch . . . but of course I couldn't get in, and short of calling out the lifeboat . . .'

'The lifeboat isn't a personal taxi service, Luke. If you plan on staying here for any length of time it might be wise to invest in a boat of your own,' she suggested. But not if he was to use it to lay seige to the Pavilion.

'Maybe I will. Anyway, I came back and left the note.'
He waited, clearly expecting some response, but it didn't
seem a good moment to confess to dumping his note
unread with the flowers into the bin.

'You've had an interesting night, one way and another.'

'That's certainly one way of putting it. And when I did
get home it was to discover that Melanie had gone
walkabout with Andy Pandy. So I really do want his
address, Fizz. Please.'

'I'm not so sure it's a good idea to give it to you.
Suppose . . . well, suppose you discover they're . . .'
Thankfully she didn't need to spell it out.

'Do hope they're not, Fizz, or you'll be looking for a
new DJ. You can't protect him. I'm not leaving until you
give me his address.'

He obviously meant it. 'All right, but I'm coming with
you. Despite your opinion of him, Andy is too valuable to
be knocked about.'

'Then we'll take your car and I can send away the taxi.
I'm a bit past driving.' He grinned quite suddenly.
'Picking snowdrops is hell.'

Being given them wasn't a whole bundle of laughs
either, so she didn't smile back. 'We don't need the car.
Andy lives just round the corner.'

They walked in silence along the street for a few
minutes before turning off. Fizz halted before a recently
constructed block of flats. 'This is it. It's number five.'
He looked up at the façade, apparently unwilling to go
inside. 'This is ridiculous, Luke.'

'I'm beginning to see your point.' Nevertheless, his

eyes narrowed dangerously as he caught sight of Melanie and Andy wandering down the street, arm-in-arm, heads together and laughing at some private joke.

'Luke!' Melanie's face lit up when she saw him and she pulled from Andy's arm to run and hug him. 'Are you all right? What happened at the factory?'

'A storm in a teacup. Nothing to worry about,' he said, holding her, giving her a little shake. 'The worst part was coming home and not knowing where you were.' Fizz felt the chill run right down to her bones.

'I was all alone in that huge house after everyone had gone. When Andy phoned to see if I'd like to have tea with his mother it was such a relief. I didn't think you'd mind.' Fizz coughed as Andy calmly met her eye. 'I did put it all in the note,' Melanie explained, with just a touch of reproach.

'What note?'

'It's pinned to the board in the kitchen. Oh, Lord, I don't suppose you've *been* in the kitchen,' she said comically.

'He doesn't consider the kitchen important enough,' Fizz agreed, but quietly.

Luke, his hearing apparently still wide-awake, gave Fizz a sharp sideways glance, then he returned his attention to Melanie. 'What time will you be home?'

'About ten. I know I was late last night, but we've hired a movie for the video and we thought we'd have a take-away.' She sounded like an eager teenager asking her father for permission to stay out late, Fizz thought. But she had no desire to dwell upon the peculiarities of their relationship. Melanie turned to her. 'Did you find the snowdrops?'

'Snowdrops?' She glanced at Luke, but he appeared to have spotted something far out at sea that required his total attention.

'I couldn't bear not to go out in the snow. Andy said it wouldn't last and it didn't,' she said sadly. 'Claudia came with me and we picked masses of snowdrops.' Well, what else would you do in the snow? 'She said she'd bring you some on her way home.'

'She did. Thank you.' And she hadn't said a word. She must have seen Luke's note . . . What a minx! And as for Luke . . .

Melanie, eager to be off, tugged at Andy's arm. 'See you tomorrow, Fizz.'

Luke gave Andy a hard look. 'Ten o'clock. Don't be late.' Then he stood back and watched as they disappeared into the block of flats. 'Tea with his mother?' Luke said faintly. 'Can you believe it?'

'Why not? You can hardly expect the girl to stay at home at your beck and call.'

'I don't. It's just that he's a bit older than her usual boyfriends,' he admitted, and stared at her in bemusement when she was forced to smother a slightly hysterical laugh. 'When I got back to find the house deserted I wasn't thinking quite straight . . . I just assumed he had carried her off last night.'

And serve Luke right if he had, she thought tetchily. 'Well, you're tired and probably hungry too. What have you had to eat today?'

'I don't know. Someone brought in some sandwiches this morning.'

'And now it's six-thirty,' she said, exasperated by this

evidence of the inability of men to look after themselves. 'Come on. I'll cook something for you.'

'That's the best offer I've had all day,' he said.

It's the *only* offer you're getting today, she said, but to herself this time, remembering just how acute his hearing was. 'And then I'll take you home.'

Five minutes later she opened the door of her flat, turned on the gas fire in the living room and shrugged out of her flying jacket on her way to the kitchen. 'You'll find some brandy in that cupboard,' she said. 'Frankly, you look as if you could do with one.' But he ignored her singularly ungracious offer of a drink and followed her into the kitchen, propping himself on a stool, watching her as she began to break eggs into a bowl.

'Fizz, about last night. You did understand, didn't you?'

She kept her eyes firmly on her task. 'I understood perfectly.'

'Then why are you so angry with me?'

'I'm not in the least bit angry,' she snapped as she dropped two slices of bread in the toaster.

'Is it because I didn't pick the snowdrops?' He looked around as if expecting to see them on display. 'I'll go right now and pick you a basketful if it'll make you smile.'

'Don't waste your time. I'd only put them in the bin with the others.' She turned away to the hob and began to beat the eggs over the heat. For a while the only sound was that of the balloon whisk rattling against the side of the pan. Luke was so quiet that she began to wonder if he was still there. She half turned, and as she did so the toast popped, startlingly loud in the quiet kitchen, and she nearly dropped the eggs. And Luke was still there, watching her.

Quickly, avoiding his eyes, she found a plate, buttered the toast and dumped the eggs on them. 'What would you like to drink? Tea, coffee?'

'Come here, Fizz.'

The width of the breakfast bar was between them and she intended to keep it that way. 'I've some orange juice, if you'd prefer.'

'Come here, Fizz, and I'll tell you what I want.'

'Salt? Pepper?' she continued on a sudden rising tide of panic. What on earth had made her bring him back to her flat? She should have put him in a taxi and sent him straight home. It wasn't as if she didn't know what to expect. The man had all the moral scruples of a tom-cat. They said women continued to fall in love with the same type of man . . . maybe that was a type she couldn't resist.

She held out the salt pot, relaxing as he gave a little shrug and reached for it. But he didn't take the salt, he seized her wrist instead, and before she could save herself he had whisked her around the breakfast bar and into the curve of his arm. 'This is what I want, Fizz. I've been dreaming of it since you left my arms last night.' And he kissed her.

For a moment she went quite rigid, then something sort of slipped sideways inside her as his mouth, warm balm to her jittery nerves, invited her co-operation and his arms offered her the kind of comfort she had always yearned for. By the time he finally raised his head, heavy

241

lids disguising the dark desire she had briefly glimpsed in his eyes, Fizz had become a more than willing accomplice to his blitz upon her senses.

'I . . . I . . . Your eggs are getting cold,' she blurted out guiltily, pulling away, turning to pick up the kettle, filling it noisily. She plugged it in and turned to ask him again if he preferred tea or coffee. But she changed her mind. They'd already had that conversation and just look where it had got her. Instead she busied herself on the far side of the small kitchen, keeping the maximum distance between the pair of them. She cleaned up, flipped the lid on the bin to drop in the eggshells.

'Thanks, Fizz. That was great.' His voice, too close behind her, made her jump, the bin-lid clattering down as she lost control and the eggshells went everywhere. He bent to pick them up and opened the bin, looked thoughtfully at its contents for a moment. 'The note too?' he said finally.

'Why don't you go and sit by the fire?' she said with forced brightness. 'I'll bring some tea through in a minute.'

His mouth twisted into an ironical little smile, but he didn't argue. But the fact that he left the kitchen without a further assault on her emotions didn't make her feel as safe as she had hoped.

But when, after endless delaying tactics, she had finally assembled the tea-tray and carried it into the sitting room, she discovered that her fears were groundless. He was stretched out on the sofa, cushion pillowed beneath his head. Fast asleep.

She put the tray down very quietly, so as not to disturb

him, and settled herself in the armchair angled to the side of the fireplace, watching the even rise and fall of his chest as he slept. The harsh lines of worry about the damage at the factory, compounded by Melanie's defection, had been ironed out by sleep. He looked younger, less threatening.

Sleep, Fizz thought, makes us all seem vulnerable. But with Luke Devlin she knew it was a dangerous illusion. Claudia might profess to revel in living on the edge of that kind of danger, and Melanie could certainly twist him around her little finger, but Fizz knew that she wasn't built for such games. If she didn't put a stop to what was happening to her, she might as well press a button marked 'self-destruct'. She had the uneasy feeling that she might already have left it far too late.

CHAPTER 10

Tearing her eyes from Luke, Fizz picked up a book and tried to read, but although the pages were turned with a regularity that suggested concentration, her eyes were just sliding over the words. She was merely keeping them busy so that they would not be tempted simply to watch the figure slumbering so peacefully on her sofa, apparently unaware of the confusion he had unleashed within her breast.

At half past nine she put the book down and walked across to him. 'Luke?' she said quietly. He did not stir. She would have liked to shout at him, bring him crashing painfully from sleep; that was what he had done to her. One moment she had been quietly cruising along, dealing with life's small crises, content in a career that she loved. Then she had lost her concentration for just a moment and hit the metaphorical brick wall.

But shouting at Luke wouldn't help. If her body marched to a different drummer from her head she could hardly blame him. So she resisted the urge. Instead she forced her reluctant fingers to gently stroke the warm curve of his ear. After a moment his eyes

244

flickered open, and she saw the blankness that betrayed the fact that he was not truly awake. She repeated his name. Then his eyes creased in a smile as he recognized her.

'Hello, Fizz. Did I fall asleep?' He sat up, rubbing his hand over his face. 'It's been a long day.'

'It doesn't matter. I wouldn't have woken you at all, but since you issued Melanie with a ten o'clock curfew I thought it would be too bad if you missed it yourself.'

He sighed. 'Melanie.' Then he gave a rueful little smile. 'To think that I could still have been sleeping peacefully on your sofa if I didn't have to worry about . . .' He stopped, raked his fingers through his hair. 'Well, perhaps it's just as well.'

More than perhaps. But even so Fizz leaned forward. 'Why do you worry about her?' she asked. He looked at her, clearly expecting more. Fizz, aware that she had probably said far too much already, gave an awkward little shrug. 'Don't you think it's time to let her go?'

'To Andy Gilbert?'

'She should be mixing with people of her own age, having fun. Not sitting at home like a ten-year wife waiting for her husband to come back and take some notice of her.' She stopped. 'I'm sorry. I shouldn't have said that.'

'No. You're right.' His brows drew down, creasing his forehead as he considered what she had said. 'I'm being over-protective, I suppose. I know she's nearly twenty and she's had loads of boyfriends. But she seems so vulnerable and I promised my sister I'd look after her. Frankly, it's harder work than I thought.'

'Your sister?' Fizz felt her blood chill. She shook her head a little, as if to clear it. It couldn't be true. She couldn't have made that big a mistake. But quite suddenly everything seemed to make a lot more sense. 'Melanie is your *niece*?' she asked woodenly.

'Of course she is. What else?' She tried to answer, even opened her mouth, but nothing came out. Luke's frown deepened. 'Fizz?'

'I . . . I thought . . .' She couldn't say it. She couldn't tell him the truly awful things she had been thinking. 'I thought you wanted to go home,' she said. 'If Melanie is there first you'll never live it down.' Her attempt at a teasing laugh was a dismal failure, and as she made a move to pass him he rose to his feet, blocked her way.

'Tell me what were you thinking, Fizz.'

'Luke, please.' But as she forced herself to meet his eyes she saw from the grim set of his face that he had worked it out for himself.

'You thought I was her lover, didn't you?' His voice was riven with disbelief. 'Good God, she's nothing but a child!'

'Hardly that. She's well over the age of consent. And she's very lovely . . . I mean, who would blame you . . .?' By way of justification it was hardly likely to improve matters. It didn't. The muscles in his jaw tightened and the skin drawn tight over his cheekbones darkened ominously. Fizz suddenly found the wallpaper behind his head utterly fascinating.

'You're right, of course. Which is why I'd rather she stayed away from Andy Gilbert.' For a moment, a single blissful moment, she thought he had accepted that she

246

had made an honest mistake and she eagerly sought his gaze. But his eyes chilled her to the bone. 'So, let's get this straight. I am supposed to be having the time of my life educating a girl young enough to be my daughter in the delights of sexual adventure?' He ground the words out. 'I'm not misunderstanding the situation? That is what you thought?'

'Luke – '

He had asked, but the question had apparently been rhetorical. No answers required. 'So what was going through your head last night, Fizz? You know, when you decided, entirely on your own initiative, to step out of your dress and tempt me into sex games on the study floor?'

'I don't think – '

'Had you been on the look-out for a likely tutor yourself, and I just happened to fit the bill? I know you live like a nun, but maybe you've decided on a change of lifestyle. Or did you just want to keep your sponsor happy? I'd be really interested to know.'

Fizz took a step back. 'I thought . . . I thought . . .' No, that was wrong. Thought had nothing to do with what had happened behind the locked doors of his study. She hadn't been thinking; she had been feeling. The world had been nothing but sensation and she had been reacting to his touch, his expert mouth, his teasing hands. Oh, yes, he could teach her everything she had ever wanted to know about herself. She didn't doubt it for a moment.

'Well? What were you thinking?'

She stirred, lifted her hand in a forlorn little gesture, then dropped it again. 'Perm any one from three, Luke,'

247

she said. And she saw, actually saw the moment when he made his choice, when his eyes turned to granite chips and her heart, her poor vulnerable, melted heart, disintegrated like a defrosted strawberry. But this time she didn't disintegrate with it. Instead she lifted her head and looked directly into his eyes. 'But you will remember that you were the one who locked the door.'

His face darkened as her dart found its mark, but she could see he wasn't in a mood to admit that he had played his part, to apologize.

'Yes, God help me. I locked the door. And then I kissed you. You did want me to kiss you?' he demanded. 'The signals seemed all set on go.' She didn't answer him; he knew the answer. But her silence made him even angrier. 'Answer me, damn you!'

'Yes.' Her throat was so tight that she could scarcely speak. 'I wanted you to kiss me.'

He nodded, satisfied. 'I just wanted to be sure I'd got it right. You accepted my invitation to join me in the study. You invited me to kiss you, then you took your dress off with breathtaking alacrity. And all this as a little offering of gratitude for my support of Pavilion Radio. Or did you think I'd change my mind before the next instalment fell due? No wonder you were so keen to get Melanie involved with someone else.'

Fizz welcomed the surge of anger that bubbled up from deep inside her, bringing the life flooding back into her veins. Anger would wash her clean. 'I just wanted to get her away from you!'

'Self-sacrifice? The noblest of all motives. I don't think so.'

She glared at him. 'Have you ever seen it in action? Up close, day after day? You wouldn't be so quick – '

'I've seen it, Fizz. Believe me, I can recognize the genuine article.' He shook his head. 'Did you know that everyone thinks your father gave you a job to keep you occupied because you can't do anything else? But they're wrong, aren't they?'

'Quite wrong.'

'You are a very talented lady indeed.'

'Not especially talented. I just work hard.'

'Well, you certainly could have fooled me. I'd have said it was all down to natural talent. It certainly ensured Michael Harries' generosity for the last five years.'

She suddenly realized that he wasn't talking about the fact that she ran the radio station. He was talking about something quite different, quite dreadful, and she gasped at such slander, but he was unimpressed.

'I trust Edward Beaumont is suitably grateful. It seems a quite remarkable sacrifice to make for any man's financial gain. I believe there's a word for it.'

Fizz. Bang. His head cracked back at the force with which she hit him, but apart from that there was no reaction. He didn't even raise his hand to the livid imprint of her fingers on his cheek. But his eyes cut her to ribbons with razor-edged scorn.

'Two actually. One for him and one for you.'

She swung again, her hand clenched into a tight little fist, but this time he caught her wrist. Her throat was finally released from the grip of pent-up tears that now began to flow silent and unchecked down her face, and she spewed out the bottled-up angry words.

'You're such a prig, Luke Devlin. It didn't take much to bring you to the boil, so don't you dare get sanctimonious with me! But you're like a child in a sweetshop. Not content with the toffee in your hand you've got to have the chocolate too. But then Claudia is some chocolate.'

'Chocolate?' He laughed, but it wasn't a pleasant sound. 'Your sister is as pink and obvious as a stick of Broomhill rock. And as hard.'

'But sweet, Luke. Sweet.'

'Jealous, are we?' His eyes were hard, dark as obsidian, his mouth a thin angry line. 'I flirted with her and you cared? Come on, Fizz, you thought I was living with Melanie and that didn't bother you one bit.' Oh, it had bothered her. It had bothered her a lot. 'And you see, poor saphead that I am, I wanted . . .' he seemed to have difficulty breathing '. . . I just wanted to protect you.' His laugh was harsh, humourless. 'You appeared anxious that your sister shouldn't know what you had been up to and it seemed to me that the easiest way to divert her was to make a fuss of her. She did seem to expect it.'

'In other words you were simply being a gentleman?'

'A gentleman?' he repeated dangerously. 'The gentleman and the whore. It would make a great title for a film, don't you think?'

'It sounds a touch clichéd to me. I do hope you don't expect me to be grateful?'

'Frankly, Fizz, I no longer care either way.' He finally dropped her wrist and she rubbed it in a vague, distracted manner while he stared down at her. 'It's extraordinary. My sister and I were such good friends that I'd never considered the possibility that siblings could dislike one another quite as much as you two seem to. I can understand you being jealous of her, but – '

'Jealous?'

'Of her success.'

Fizz walked across to the door and opened it. 'There's a taxi rank on the seafront, Luke. I hope, for your sake, that there's someone there this late on a Sunday, or you'll have a long walk home.'

He didn't argue, but picked up his jacket and slung it over his shoulder. 'Don't worry about it, Fizz. The fresh air will help to clear away the smell of the Beaumont family.'

Fizz resisted the urge to slam the door, closing it very carefully behind him and shooting home the bolts before leaning heavily against it, shaking from head to foot while all the terrible words that had been spoken spun around inside her head. Awful words. He had insulted her beyond belief. And her father. And poor Michael. And she had behaved so badly that she wouldn't want to look at her face in the mirror for a very long time.

But worse, far worse, was the suggestion that she was jealous of Claudia. And it wasn't true. It wasn't. God alone knew that they had no illusions about each other. She knew Claudia's weaknesses and Claudia understood her better than anyone else ever had. They had shared a strangely pampered, yet neglected childhood, shared the nightmare of their mother's accident, dark secrets. They cared for one another in a way no one else would ever understand. That was why Claudia hadn't told her about the snowdrops. Despite her cynical attitude, her warning that Luke was not for her, she had seen his note and left the flowers beside it, hoping to foster a little romance.

Turning up his collar, sticking his hands deep in his pockets against the biting wind, Luke took the hill at a punishing pace. Punishing himself. He had thought he was in control, perfectly safe flirting with Fizz Beaumont. When you'd made a lot of money as young as he had, it was essential to learn to keep your emotions under control, and he had learned his lessons well. He had never made the same mistake twice. But he had never fallen in love before, not like this. Which was why he hadn't recognized the danger signs.

Idiot! Just what had given him the impression that he could break Felicity Beaumont's heart at will? Why, indeed, had he supposed she would have one when the rest of the family had been so sparsely equipped? Phillip had warned him that revenge had an unpleasant way of backfiring. No doubt he would say that it served him right, but at least he would take no pleasure in it.

But how was it possible that he could have been so taken in? She was the one whose nerves had been in tatters, who had trembled when he touched her, who had melted so unexpectedly in his arms. He would never forget her face. The way she had looked then, her skin in the firelight. Even now he felt the tug of longing . . .

Could that really have all been just an act? He could scarcely believe it. And yet she had said as much, denied nothing. She had seduced him, drawn him in, had invited him to make love to her. And she had done it so cleverly that all the time he'd thought he was the one conducting the orchestra. And when Melanie had interrupted she had still been in control, had still been pulling his strings, because when he'd seen how upset she was, he'd had nothing else in his head but the desire to protect her.

Despite the cold he broke into a sweat as he recalled his gut-wrenching concern when he'd realized she had left the party without a word, his mad drive down to Broomhill, expecting at any moment to see that crazy old E-type upended in a ditch, his relief when he'd found her car parked on the promenade. And when he'd realized he couldn't get at her he had left that note. What an idiot he had been! Thank God she hadn't read it.

Then he stopped. Why had she thrown it in the bin unread? That was rather odd, surely? In her position most women would have wanted to revel in their triumph. Or maybe it just hadn't mattered that much to her. Maybe it was just business, sex as a reward for bailing her father out of a sticky situation, not, as he had so naïvely thought, simple, uncomplicated desire.

And instead of Fizz Beaumont's heart lying shattered in his hand, the trophy he had sought to place on his sister's grave along with Claudia Beaumont's brilliant career and Edward Beaumont's reputation, he was the one left feeling used and heartsore. Well, they would see. They would see.

'Luke?' He turned to regard the car that had drawn up alongside him and Melanie's concerned face looking up at him. 'What are you doing walking?' He didn't answer, and she opened the door and climbed out to stand beside him. 'Come on, get in.' She took his hand. 'You're freezing.'

'It doesn't matter,' he said absently. Then, 'But thanks for stopping.'

He climbed into the back of the car, saw Melanie and Andy exchange a glance. Then he shut his eyes and began to think again about Felicity Beaumont. If he had been that wrong, he decided, he had missed something. Something important. He would have to go back to the beginning. What had happened with Patrick March?

Luke looked up from the folder in his hand to the man sitting before him. According to the sheet of paper in front of him Patrick March was thirty-three years old, but he looked nearer forty. It took more than a salon tan to disguise a cocaine habit, alcohol abuse and a mouth that in repose wore a naturally bitter expression. Patrick, conscious of the scrutiny, shifted uneasily in his chair.

'It's a long time since you've done any film work, Patrick,' he said finally.

'I've never been out of work.' Luke waited. Fizz would have recognized the technique, although perhaps not the Australian accent he had adopted for the interview. 'Mostly in the States, of course. Sitcoms, adverts, summer stock.' Again the silence descended. 'I did a couple of films a few years back.'

'Is that why you stayed in America? In the hope of more film work? I have the press cuttings your agent sent me.' He looked up, his expression deceptively mild. 'Of course they're rather old, but they're very flattering. You looked set for big things, Patrick. What happened?'

Patrick's shrug was studied, diffident, the kind of

gesture to portray that there was something else, inviting the onlooker to probe a little deeper. Luke obliged.

'You did have a part starring in a film with . . .' He glanced at the papers in front of him. 'Felicity Beaumont?' He frowned thoughtfully, then wondered if acting could be infectious. It was hard to tell who was working harder at playing a part. 'Is she any relation to Claudia Beaumont?'

'She's her sister, her younger sister. Claudia's okay. I mean, she can act,' he said generously. 'I guess Fizz was given the part because –, well, I guess they hoped her name would ensure reviews, get plenty of publicity. "Another Beaumont takes the stage" . . . all that stuff.'

Luke buried his resentment at this man's casual use of 'Fizz'. 'It happens,' Luke agreed, apparently sympathetic. 'The film was never finished? Why?'

Patrick appeared to hesitate, a man apparently torn between gossip and discretion. It might have been genuine – Luke had no idea how good an actor the man was. It didn't really matter. He knew that Patrick March was desperate for work and that he would succumb to the need to justify what had happened, so he waited patiently until he gave a helpless little shrug and grinned. 'Oh, well, it was all a long time ago. The truth is Fizz had a bit of a crush on me.'

The grin gave him an oddly boyish charm. And Luke had seen the old publicity photographs. Even now, with the telltale marks of disappointment etched into his still handsome face, he could see how girls might easily have had a crush on Patrick March.

'A bit of a crush?' His manner suggested disbelief.

'A bit? Did I say a bit? The truth is it was off-the-scale crazy. I suppose I should have seen it coming. I mean, she was a good-looking kid, eager to learn, and I went out of my way to help her, but I had a steady relationship with one of the make-up girls.' He gave Luke a knowing look. 'I got her a job on the crew so that we could be together in Italy. Fizz Beaumont did everything she could to break it up.'

Luke felt his heart sinking. He had wanted to be wrong. He would have liked to look this man in the face and call him a liar. But Fizz hadn't been exactly subtle in her attempts to shoehorn Melanie out of *his* life. 'It must have been difficult for you,' he encouraged.

'It wasn't funny. She practically cornered me in my caravan, began tearing off her clothes, all over me like a rash. When I wouldn't play ball she had hysterics, refused to carry on with the film, acted just like the spoiled brat she was.'

Luke's mouth flooded with saliva, and for a moment he felt physically sick. It took all his will power to reach for the glass of water on the table in front of him and sip it while he carefully blotted out the memory of Fizz sliding down the zip of her dress, stepping out of it; throwing herself at him.

'The director even suggested I should play along with her – just to get the film back on the road, you know . . . Of course I couldn't. It wouldn't have been right.'

'No.'

'Poor kid. I felt sorry for her, really. Her sister had to

256

come and take her home and the whole thing was hushed up. Her father saw to that. They said she had developed a virus or something.'

'And the film folded?'

'There just wasn't enough money to start again from scratch.'

'That was very hard on you.'

'It didn't do her career much good either. At least I've been working. She's never set foot on a sound stage since.' He wasn't able to disguise his satisfaction.

Luke, too, discovered that hiding his feelings was increasingly difficult, that smiling was too much effort. Even talking to the man was more than he could bear. He stood up, indicating that the interview was over, but didn't offer his hand. 'Thank you for coming to see me at such short notice, Patrick. I'll be in touch if we decide to go ahead with the project. In the meantime Phillip will refund your expenses.'

'Well?' Phillip Devlin demanded a few minutes later, after he had seen Patrick March out of his office. 'Did you discover anything?'

Luke regarded his cousin thoughtfully. 'Only that talking to Mr Patrick March has left me with a very strong urge to take a shower.'

'Maybe that's enough.'

'Maybe.' Luke would have liked it to be enough. But he couldn't rid himself of the feeling that he had been listening to an eerie echo of what had happened at the party. Was that the reason Fizz had looked afraid when he had first met her? Why she seemed to veer between fire and ice? Did she have a terrible weakness that she tried desperately hard to control? And just occasionally something snapped? Fizz, bang.

'Maybe he just took a knock at that crucial moment when the scales are evenly balanced between success and failure. A well-received film, Phillip, an opportunity to show what he could do, and we'd have to join the queue and pay good money to see him perform. Instead it all went wrong. So now his agent will send him to talk to anyone about work, even an unheard of producer who hints at a minor role in an unlikely drama series set on the other side of the world. What expenses did he claim?'

'A first class fare from Perth.' Phillip smiled as Luke's eyebrows rocketed upwards. 'Perth in Scotland. According to Mr March, he interrupted a golfing holiday to see you.'

'How good of him. What else?'

'Overnight at Brown's and thirty pounds for taxis.'

'Only thirty pounds?' Luke smiled. 'I fully expected fifty. But added together not a bad fee for half an hour of his time. I do hope you didn't embarrass him by asking for receipts.'

'Perish the thought.' Fizz would have been surprised by Phillip's sudden grin. 'And this way he's left with the very unsatisfactory feeling that he might have got away with more. Are you staying in town tonight?'

'No, Phillip. I've got to get straight back. There are things to be done at home.'

'Home? Broomhill? You mean you're serious about setting up your headquarters there?'

'I've got to decide on somewhere; I've camped out in

your offices for long enough. And I want to expand Harries, develop the site to its full potential.'

'Is that altogether wise? I mean, will you be able to stay on after you've given the Beaumonts the *coup de grâce*?'

'I rather think it's a question of whether Edward Beaumont will want to remain in Broomhill, don't you?'

Fizz had arrived at the script conference hoping that the cast would be keen to proffer ideas about how best to use Melanie, because her own brain, deprived of sleep, seemed to consist entirely of cotton wool. Melanie had given her a strange look when she arrived, and once or twice since she had looked up from the pad she was doodling on to find herself the subject of further scrutiny. But nothing had been said.

The debate, fuelled by coffee, largely flowed over her until she was brought back from a distant and totally blank space in her head. The one place where she was comfortable. 'Fizz?' She roused herself. 'Can we go ahead with that? Or do you want to speak to your father about it?'

Fizz, who had once or twice nodded helpfully or murmured assent when it had seemed appropriate, had no idea what she was being asked to agree to. She discovered that she didn't care very much.

'Well, I think it's a brilliant idea. Edward will love it.' The old character actress, who had retired to the seaside and now supplemented her pension by playing a post-woman, a lady vicar and the mostly dignified but occasionally drunk wife of a publican in *Holiday Bay*, was adamant.

Fizz took her word for it. 'Then let's get on with it.'

There was a sigh of contentment from around the table and she looked up in surprise. It must have been a great idea. The husband and wife team who wrote *Holiday Bay*, another pair of retired thespians who had turned their hands to writing when work had been hard to come by, gathered their notes and, promising the scripts by the end of the week, threw her a smile before disappearing through the door.

The others lingered over coffee and, realizing she couldn't put it off, Fizz turned to Melanie. 'I don't believe I thanked you properly for the party. I'm sure everyone will be talking about it for months.'

'You didn't stay very long. I thought perhaps you weren't enjoying yourself.'

'Oh, I was. But the radio station is a bit like a baby. A seven-day-a-week job.' Melanie continued to regard her with big concerned eyes. 'I hope you beat the curfew last night,' she said, refusing to admit that she only wanted to hear that Luke had arrived home safely. Why she should care, she didn't know. But she did.

'Only just. We picked Luke up on the way. It was terribly cold to be walking.'

'He said he wanted to . . . um . . . get a breath of fresh air.' Fizz realized she was twisting her hair around the end of her finger, a nervous habit she'd thought she had grown out off. Self-consciously she tugged her finger free. 'I hope he didn't catch a chill?'

Melanie shrugged. 'I didn't see him this morning. He drove up to town first thing.' Fizz nodded, relieved that he was out of Broomhill, at least for the day.

'Fizz, did you two have a row or something last night?' That was the trouble with the young, Fizz thought. They didn't beat about the bush. 'I know I shouldn't ask, but I've never seen Luke looking like that before.'

Like what?

'I think "or something" would probably best cover it. Just a few crossed wires, nothing for you to worry about, Melanie. Really.' She made an effort to move the conversation into safer waters. 'Did you have a good time with Andy?'

'Oh, yes.' Her face relaxed into a smile. 'Luke says I shouldn't trust him further than I could throw him, but I think he's really nice.'

'Well, Luke may have a point . . . he's not *that* nice.'

Melanie laughed out loud. 'You don't have to warn me, Fizz. There isn't a man born who's *that* nice.' Then, more gravely, she added, 'Except Luke.' She looked suddenly shy and, dropping her eyes, gave a childishly awkward little shrug. 'I'd better go. Claudia said they are recording some more episodes today and I want to really get the feel of things before I jump in next week.'

'Of course.'

Fizz continued to sit in the conference room for some time after everyone had left. She couldn't get over the feeling that Melanie had, very gently, rebuked her for not driving Luke home. She sighed. Being an agony aunt was a thankless task, she decided. She remembered thinking that it might be a good idea to run advice slots, perhaps in conjunction with the lunchtime music programme. Cutting down on the music would help reduce the fees for broadcasting rights.

'If it's Monday it must be Money,' she wrote. Then crossed it out. She wondered if the dour Mr Nicholson at the bank could be flattered into taking part for free. No. That wouldn't do. It would have to be someone impartial. She threw down her pen in disgust. The trouble was, she really didn't care. For the first time since the station had been up and running she just didn't care.

She got up, suddenly desperate to get away, and blundered into Susie.

'Oh, here you are. There are a pile of messages on your desk.' Fizz didn't stop. 'Fizz?'

'You deal with them. I need some air.'

'You could open your window.' But Fizz was already halfway across the foyer. 'Don't forget the Trust meeting at two.'

Damn, damn, damn. She *had* forgotten it. And she couldn't miss it, they were going to discuss who should be invited to replace Michael Harries on the board.

She had been going to drive up to the Downs and walk. Instead she turned into the restaurant and found a table tucked away in a corner.

'Hello, Miss Beaumont. Are you going to help yourself from the buffet, or shall I ask John to whip you up an omelette or something?'

'Just a cup of tea, thanks, Janice. I've just come in to escape the office for a few minutes.'

'Right you are, dear. I'll take all this cutlery out of your way, shall I? That was a nasty old bit of weather we had on Saturday night. You don't expect it down here, do you?'

'No, I suppose not.'

'Although I expect our young Australian friend enjoyed the snow while it lasted.' She was looking out of the window, and with a sense of foreboding Fizz followed her gaze.

Melanie was laughing at something. Something Luke had said to her as they stopped by the window. She held her breath, uttered a short prayer – to no avail. Luke opened the door and something squeezed tightly in her chest.

'The kitchen . . .' she managed to croak out, scrambling to her feet as Melanie's voice drifted in on the wind.

Janice nodded. 'If you say so, dear.'

John looked up briefly from an omelette he was bringing to perfection but said nothing as she sank onto a chair set at a small table laid for one. He turned it onto a plate, garnished it with watercress and placed it on the hot counter, then he turned and gave her his undivided attention. 'Couldn't you wait for Janice to take your order?' he asked.

'I'm sorry to invade your kitchen at lunchtime, but I'm seeking sanctuary,' she said.

'Why, what have you done?'

'Done?'

'I thought criminals sought sanctuary in a church.'

'Two steaks, chef. Very rare. And green salad with dill dressing for Miss Brett,' Janice said. 'If it gets about that she's eating here regularly, it'll be good for business.'

'I'll put a sign up, shall I?' Janice flounced off to get the salad and John grinned. ' "Eat with the stars of *Holiday Bay* at the Pavilion Restaurant".' He looked at Fizz slyly. 'Or not, as the case may be.'

'I'm not avoiding Melanie.'

'No. I didn't think you were.' He picked up an alarmingly large knife and took two steaks from the fridge. 'I'm glad you dropped by, though. I was going to come up and see you later. This way we can have lunch together. I've already opened a bottle of my special reserve.'

'I hope that doesn't mean you're celebrating something.' He didn't answer. 'You're not going to give notice, are you, John?'

He finished trimming the steaks, and after dipping them in hot melted butter put them on the griddle. Then he fetched a bottle of red Bordeaux that he had opened an hour earlier in readiness for the peace that descended just after one-thirty, when it was suddenly just a bit too late to order lunch and still too early to think of tea. He poured Fizz a glass. It was warm and rich in colour.

'Now, tell me, what do you think of that?' he encouraged her as he turned the steaks and a moment later laid them on a plate. She obediently took a sip of the wine. 'Take a proper mouthful,' he advised, apparently capable of seeing through the back of his chef's hat.

'It's wonderful. Very warming.'

Janice collected the steaks, muttering beneath her breath. Quiet descended. Fizz took a another mouthful of wine.

'Now, what would you like me to cook for you? Some medallions of lamb? A chicken breast cooked in butter? Or I've some fresh halibut.'

'Nothing. Really. I'm not hungry. Come and talk to me, John.'

'It can wait; it's not urgent.'

'Tell me the worst, John.'

He fetched another chair, poured wine into another glass and savoured it for a moment. Then he said, 'An uncle gave me a case of this last week.'

Uncles. She was heartily sick of uncles. 'I congratulate you on your excellent taste in relations.'

'He's a wine merchant. My mother told him that he should call in and let me look at his list. He was so surprised by the place that I have the feeling he thought I was serving burgers and chips with the occasional can of lager on the side.' Fizz took another sip of John's uncle's wine. It really was very good. 'He stayed for lunch. On the house, of course. In return for the wine.'

'Of course. I hope he was thoroughly impressed.'

'Oh, yes. In fact he was so impressed with my cooking that he came back yesterday. He's offered to put up the money for me to open a restaurant of my own.' He made a little gesture that might have been apology or constrained triumph. 'I expect to be able to buy him out over five years.'

'You signed a contract for the season, John,' she reminded him.

'Would you keep me to it?'

She considered the damage a disgruntled chef could do and shook her head. 'That really wouldn't be very wise, would it? When will you go?'

'As soon as we can find the right premises.'

'Then you have my very best wishes.' He said nothing. 'I knew you wouldn't stay more than a couple of years, of course. You're far too ambitious to work for somebody else.'

'To be honest, I didn't expect an opportunity like this to come up so soon.'

'Where are you going to look for premises?'

'I hadn't given it much thought. I don't suppose you'll want me too close to the Pavilion.'

Fizz picked up the bottle of John's special reserve. 'Have another glass of wine.'

The wine, combined with two sleepness nights, was not the best preparation for a meeting. But Fizz took her place at the table in the boardroom promptly at two and managed to look reasonably alert as various matters were discussed. Michael had been chairman, but her father had taken on the role and was looking extremely pleased with himself, Fizz thought as the meeting progressed. A bit like a cat that had swallowed a canary and not been found out.

'Now,' he said as they reached the item concerning a new board member. 'You all know the circumstances that resulted in the resignation of Michael Harries from this board, and I know we are all agreed that he will be very much missed for his enthusiasm and help since the inception of the Trust.' There was a general murmur of agreement. 'I believe it would be appropriate if the Trust were to present him with a token of our appreciation, and if you agree I will solicit ideas as to an appropriate gift after the meeting.'

Agreement having been sought and obtained, they moved on to the question of who should be invited to join the board in his place. Edward smiled benignly around the table. 'I'm glad to be able to report that one of our members has been thinking on her feet in this regard.'

There were only two ladies present, and as Lady Stockley, the wife of the local MP, shrugged in a manner that disassociated herself from anything as dangerous as thinking, Fizz suddenly found herself the centre of attention.

'What?' she said.

'Fizz has apparently had the quick wit to suggest to the new owner of Harries Industries that he take up where Michael left off.'

'Oh, excellent.'

'Clever girl.'

'Will he do it?'

As the murmur of excitement flowed around the table Fizz went first pink, then white.

Edward Beaumont beamed. 'I take it everyone is in agreement? Can I have a proposer?'

'Oughtn't we to discuss it?' Fizz said quickly. 'I mean, we don't really know anything about him.' She was being stared at. 'I did mention it to him, but he didn't seem very keen. He has business interests all over the world. I'm not sure that he has any long-term plans to stay in Broomhill.'

'My dear girl,' Lady Stockley said, with the smile she normally reserved for election night successes, 'you obviously don't listen to your own radio station.'

'Not twenty-four hours day,' she agreed, and turned to her father for help.

'Jim interviewed Luke on the lunchtime news pro-gramme. Apparently there was a bit of bother over the weekend and he wanted everyone to know that Harries was safe, that there'll be no compulsory redundancies and that he'll be investing in plant and machinery. He's also approached the local authority about acquiring some adjoining land. He wants to expand the Enterprise Park. It seems he's decided to make Broomhill his headquarters.'

'No,' she said, rather loudly. The room fell silent and everyone waited for her to continue. She wanted to say that he was sucking them all in. That he was bad news. But she couldn't. He had sucked *her* in. He was *her* bad news. 'No, I didn't hear the radio broadcast.'

There was a general expulsion of held breath and laughter as relief rippled around the room. 'Then perhaps you would like to propose the motion, Fizz?' her father invited. No one waited for the formal proposition, which was probably just as well. The motion was seconded. Edward looked around. 'I take it the vote is unanimous? Excellent, Fizz, I think you should have the honour of inviting Mr Devlin to join us. He's waiting in the Green Room.'

CHAPTER 11

While he waited for the board of the Broomhill Bay Pier Trust to make their decision. Luke Devlin slowly traversed the four walls of the Green Room, absorbed by the dozens of photographs that lined it.

Most were of Edward Beaumont and Elaine French in roles they had famously played, individually and as the theatrical world's favourite leading twosome. More recent photographs included Claudia, alone and with her father. He had seen them in *The Merchant of Venice* when they had toured Australia – not his first choice for entertainment, but Melanie had asked him if he could get tickets and on an impulse he had telephoned and asked his sister if she would like to come too. Such a small thing to touch so many lives.

He moved on. Not all the photographs were theatre stills. A few were more personal family groups. The Beaumonts had put on their make-up and performed for their loving audience not just on the stage, it seemed, but in their personal lives. It was possible that their joint roles as the perfect couple and most loving parents had been Edward and Elaine's greatest triumph.

No one had ever questioned it – probably because most people had wanted the illusion to be true. Even now people still thought of them as the ideal couple, and Edward Beaumont, a good-looking man with charisma thick enough to spread on toast and the kind of temptation to philander that would have turned the head of a saint, was apparently immune to the usual newspaper tittle-tattle.

He stopped to look more closely at one photograph – Fizz and Claudia, little girls, building a snowman with their parents. It looked so natural, so perfect. Only a hardened cynic would notice that Elaine French was perfectly made-up, that her fur coat was worn casually open to display her perfect figure rather than bundled up for warmth, that the lighting had been used to flatter and enhance her beauty.

The door behind him opened and he turned.

Fizz Beaumont, framed in the doorway, looked white. Even her lips had lost their colour. She looked, he thought, as if she was just about to faint, and instinctively he moved towards her, a hand outstretched.

She stepped back so quickly that she stumbled and had to grab the doorframe to stop herself from falling, her eyes for a moment daring him to touch her. Then the heat died away, and without any expression in her voice she said, 'I've been asked to invite you to join us in the boardroom. Will you follow me?'

She didn't wait for his answer, but turned and walked around the ornate and theatrically gilded curve of the gallery to the boardroom. She had the kind of walk that men had dreams about; from the hip, slow and unconscious in its sensuality. Everything about her moved with natural grace, from the elegant black knee-high boots and the gentle swirl of the bias-cut skirt in heavy black wool, to the soft downy sweater with its enormous cowl neck in a colour reminiscent of a ripe peach which draped itself so enticingly over her body.

He had been absolutely clear in his mind as to why he had telephoned Edward Beaumont this morning after his meeting with Patrick March and offered to take Michael Harries' place on the board of the Trust. He knew they would fall over themselves to accept. They had been taking money from Michael hand over fist for years and they thought they would be able to take it from him. They were wrong, of course, but he was demonstrating to Fizz Beaumont that he could take the initiative, seize power in her little world, and that she could nothing about it.

But that awful lurch deep inside him as he had turned and seen her had been unexpected; the hot flood of desire, the urgent longing to pull her into his arms, hold her, take back every dreadful word he had said to her, was shattering. Well, he would deal with that. She had set him alight and she would put out the fire. If she didn't have a heart to break, there were other ways.

She paused in the boardroom doorway and looked back at him. She looked so utterly alone that for a moment his determination faltered. Then he gathered himself and followed her. The board members were all standing to welcome him. Edward Beaumont briefly introduced each of them, made a gracious little speech of welcome and then suggested they should all have a glass of something to mark the occasion.

'Actually, the meeting hasn't been adjourned.' Everyone turned to look at Fizz. She was still white, dark smudges beneath her eyes betraying a lack of sleep. Luke slammed the lid down hard on the longing to hold her, cradle her, tell her it would be all right, that he would make it better. He hadn't slept either.

Edward glanced at the agenda. 'Quite right. Keeping us on our toes today, Fizz.' He looked around. 'Is there any other business?' he asked, clearly expecting no response. 'If not, I think we can – '

'I have a proposal to put to the board. I'm afraid it won't wait'

She had made a mistake, Luke thought. Everyone had mentally abandoned the meeting, and didn't appreciate being jerked out of their celebratory mood and brought back to business. He took the seat that Susie found for him and watched with interest.

Edward Beaumont, impatient with her for taking the buzz out of the atmosphere, for destroying his scene, was not encouraging. 'Well, what is it, Fizz?'

'I have been approached by John Moore about the possibility of putting some kind of fast food outlet outside on the pier. Some of you may know that we had an invasion of teenagers a day or two ago, and they would certainly have welcomed the opportunity to buy a warm drink and something like a hot dog.'

'It isn't likely to happen very often, is it?' Lady Stockley asked, with every appearance of concern.

'Not quite on that scale. Although in the summer – '

'We have the restaurant for the summer visitors.'

272

'The restaurant is a year-round enterprise,' Fizz replied, clearly making a point.

For the board, or for his benefit? Luke wondered, but continued to doodle absently on the pad that had appeared along with the chair. The secretary, if not the chairman, had anticipated that the meeting might continue, but then Susie was in Fizz's confidence. He caught Susie's eye and smiled. She smiled back. Fizz continued.

'In the summer it is possible that the presence of Melanie Brett will attract more youngsters to the pier. Paying customers. They have to be catered for and I can't see many of them wanting to come into the restaurant, sit down and have a proper meal. I doubt if we could accommodate them if they did. But they won't be very happy if they have to go back into the town for a snack or drink.'

'There'll be a problem with rubbish. Paper cups and cans will be thrown into the sea and washed up on the beach.'

'The beach is swept early every morning in the season,' she said calmly. 'And I have yet to be convinced that youngsters are worse offenders with litter than anyone else.'

Edward frowned. 'I thought you sold cold drinks at the shop, Fizz.'

'We do, but there isn't the space to expand present sales, and frankly I would be happier if they could be moved outside altogether.'

'Is there room for competition?'

It was an interesting discussion, but no one was

addressing the real issue, Luke decided. He stirred, and asked of no one in particular, 'Who is John Moore?'

'He's the chef at the Pavilion Restaurant,' Edward informed him, before returning to Fizz. 'You can only sell so much – '

'Then it won't *be* competition.'

Edward abandoned his argument and gave Luke his full attention. 'What do you mean? Of course it will be competition for the shop.'

'The radio station runs the shop?' Edward nodded. 'The radio station owns the restaurant?'

'Yes, but – '

'The radio station apparently assumes it has the right to run the hot dog stall as well.' He flicked a glance at Fizz. She was staring down at the pad in front of her. It was blank. 'Three outlets, all controlled by the same organization would appear to be a monopoly. Or is that the way the Trust is run?' The room fell silent. 'Perhaps a little genuine competition would be good thing. It would keep the prices down and would surely be beneficial to the Trust.'

'In what way?' Edward asked.

'In every way. Mr Devlin is absolutely right,' Fizz said, rising to her feet, and Luke, about to explain that fast food vendors would pay a great deal of money for such a valuable site, found himself listening instead. 'When John asked me to approach you about a fast food outlet, explained how valuable it would be, I realized that it was something that you, as Trustees, should consider on a wider basis. The income would be most welcome, but if you are prepared to pursue this idea I know you will want to balance the needs of the pier with the demands of the vendor.'

'You don't think we should just accept the highest bid for the site?' Luke asked.

Fizz turned to him. 'I think . . .' She paused and indicated the others seated around the table. 'We have always taken the view that it is important to retain a special atmosphere on the pier.' There was a general murmur of agreement. 'But perhaps you would like to give us your own thoughts on that?'

Luke watched the betraying rise and fall of her breasts beneath the soft sweater. Everyone else was watching too, holding their collective breath, sensing something rather more than a run-of-the-mill tussle over finances.

'After all, none of us has quite your experience of the business world.' She made it sound like an insult. He smiled directly at her and she blushed. Definitely an insult.

'I think,' he said, weighing his words carefully, 'that the pier is a museum piece rather than an attraction. Broomhill pier was the liveliest and sauciest entertainment venue on the south coast in its day. Everything from "What the Butler Saw" machines and performing fleas to firework displays and a bandstand. It brought in over a million visitors a year. According to the local guidebook.'

'And all without the bother of Health and Safety Regulations,' she replied.

'Does the HSR have rules to cover performing fleas?'

'Don't you know?'

'You've only seen the pier in winter, Luke,' Edward

interrupted, before things got quite out of hand. 'In the summer we have live entertainers, jugglers, mime – that sort of thing. And the bandstand is in use most days. It really is very lively.'

'And the income from a fast food vendor would enable us to increase that entertainment,' Fizz continued smoothly. 'I would like to suggest that we invite local traders to put forward their ideas along with a tender for the space. And since the season will so soon be upon us we do not have the luxury of time if the Trust is to benefit from the additional income this year – which is why the matter has to be discussed today.' Then she turned and looked straight at him, and he saw with a slight shock the hint of defiance, even of triumph that had brought the colour flooding back into her cheeks.

Well, well. He would have given a good deal to know whether she was genuine, or whether she had realized she wasn't going to get away with pushing her plans through on the nod and had bluffed her way out of a sticky corner. Either way, it was an impressive performance.

It was extraordinary the way he continued to underestimate her. He would never have made the same mistake with a man. He would not normally have made the mistake with a woman, but he hadn't looked beyond the image of failed actress with a sinecure of a job in the family firm. Now he was certain that it was an image she had created herself, that it was what she wanted people to believe. Why? There had to be an answer. And Patrick March hadn't provided it. But then maybe he hadn't been telling the entire truth.

Suddenly all the trustees had something urgent to say on the question of renting space to a fast food outlet. Only Luke and Fizz remained silent, each a small oasis of thought as the debate rolled over them.

A decision was made to invite tenders, the meeting was adjourned and Edward invited everyone to join him in his office for a glass of sherry. Fizz, Luke noticed, took the opportunity to escape. His own presence claimed by Edward, he let her go. For the moment.

Fizz was consumed with anger, shock, waves of them leaving her shaking and weak. How dared he? How bloody dared he? He knew that her throwaway line about joining the pier trustees had been joke and he'd left her in no doubt at the time that it had been a bad one.

And he hadn't been in the boardroom five minutes before he was trying to make her look like a rapacious money-grubber who would use her position as a trustee to feather her own nest.

Well, she wasn't going to make his day by staying to make polite small talk while he smiled at her, emphasizing his triumph, relishing her discomfort, and she found it increasingly difficult to breathe. She would have preferred not to be in the same building as the man. In the same town. She staggered from the boardroom and took refuge in the ladies' loo. At least she was safe from him in there. But not from Susie, who found her sitting in the old basket chair that had been unearthed in the basement and staring into space.

'Well, that was the most entertaining meeting we've had since Ellie Stockley broke her false teeth on a ginger nut. Why aren't you knocking back the sherry with the rest of the gang?'

'I'm not in the mood to fawn at the feet of genius.'

'Oh. I see. You're hiding from the delicious Mr Devlin.'

'Delicious?' she enquired. 'Have you been licking – '

'Fizz Beaumont!'

' – his boots.'

Susie, tidying her hair, gave her a sideways look out of the mirror and changed the subject. 'Pity about the hot dog stall. John will be disappointed. Are you going to put in a tender for it?' she asked cheekily.

'One of these days you'll go too far, Susie.'

'One of these days I'll apply for your job. I get plenty of practice. I've been doing it all day.'

'Go ahead. You're welcome to it. But it's not all smiling over the boardroom table at Luke Devlin,' she snapped.

'Oh, come on, Fizz, lighten up. Luke Devlin spoiled your plan to make some quick money, so what? It was a chance in a million it would slip through unchallenged. Most of your fellow trustees have an axe of their own to grind.' Then she looked at Fizz more closely. 'Oh, I see. That isn't it. So what's the matter?'

'What could possibly be the matter?' Susie simply waited and Fizz sighed. 'I'm sorry. I shouldn't take my troubles out on you. I haven't been sleeping very well, that's all.' Susie's look suggested it was far from all, but Fizz ignored it. 'Was there some reason for you to come hunting me down?'

'Oh, yes. Someone called Julian says he has to speak to

278

you and that if you're in the building I must find you and get you to ring him straight back. He may just be an over-eager admirer who you're avoiding like the plague, but I thought I'd better find you and pass on the message.'

'Oh, heavens . . .' Fizz made a grab for her bag, fumbled and it fell over, spewing its contents all over the floor. She bent to gather up her scattered belongings and Susie joined her on the floor, retrieving a lipstick that had rolled beneath the table and then picking up an unopened envelope.

She held it out, slightly crumpled, faintly stained with some green stuff and the unmistakable touch of a teabag. 'Tell me, Fizz. Is the postman using the dustbin instead of the letterbox for your mail these days?' Fizz almost snatched the letter from her and stuffed it out of sight in her bag. She didn't know why she'd bothered the rescue the thing from the bin. She hadn't opened it. Had no intention of reading it. Ever.

'Actually, Susie, since you're obviously not busy –' she ignored the 'humph' ' – there is something I meant to ask you to start on when I came in this morning. Dad thought it would be a good idea to have a small party of some kind at the restaurant. A sort of launch. A buffet, I thought. Do you think two weeks on Friday is too soon?'

'What's the rush?' Susie held open the loo door for her. 'I mean, I can take a hint. If you don't want to talk about your letter just tell me to mind my own business. It is from Luke Devlin, isn't it? His handwriting is unmistak-able.'

'Mind your own business,' Fizz responded, leading the way up the stairs.

'And he delivered it by hand. Are you going to read it, or just carry it about as a trophy?'

'I knew you wouldn't take any notice.'

'Even so, planning a party simply to avoid giving me a straight answer is a bit over the top, even for you. Why don't you give the poor guy a chance?'

'He isn't poor and he doesn't wait to be given chances; he takes them. Remember that next time you're grinning at him over the boardroom table. And after you've organized the party, Susie, remind me to sack you.'

'You did that last week,' Susie reminded her with a grin. 'If you do it more than twice in one month I'll be forced to take you seriously.'

'Some hopes. The next time anyone in this office takes me seriously will be the first time,' she said, pushing open her office door.

'I take you seriously. In fact I'm beginning to take you very seriously indeed.' The smile died from her lips as she turned from Susie to be confronted with Luke's broad back silhouetted against the window. 'Come in, Fizz,' he said, without bothering to turn around. 'And close the door behind you. I want to talk to you.'

'Susie . . .' But Susie, like a rat deserting a sinking ship, had disappeared.

For a long moment Fizz was unable to speak, unable to move. Then Luke turned round to look at her, and the flare of passion that he hadn't quite managed to quench jerked a nervous, involuntary response from her. 'What do you want, Luke? I'm very busy.'

'Now, is that really any way to speak to your major sponsor?' he enquired softly. 'After Saturday night's little demonstration of how far you're prepared to go to keep me happy . . .' His shoulders lifted in an expressive little shrug that suggested he had every right to expect a warmer welcome, clearly trying to goad her into some unwise response.

She declined the invitation, took a shaky breath and wondered as she stretched her lips in an attempt at a smile whether the effect was more like a grimace. It certainly felt like it. 'If you would like to discuss sponsorship details then naturally I'm happy to see you, although it is wiser to telephone first and make an appointment.' The grimace stretched a little further. 'However, since you're here, please do sit down,' she invited, pointedly polite. 'Would you like some coffee?'

He ignored the chair she indicated. 'And if I wanted something else?' He regarded her from beneath heavy-lidded eyes with a look that suggested far more than his words.

The fixed smile disappeared and she flushed painfully, but she remained on her feet, her head high. 'If you'd prefer tea, Luke, you only have to say.' She made a move to pick up the telephone and summon Susie, but Luke's hand clamped down hard over hers.

'Don't play games with me, Fizz. You can't win.' Her dark blue eyes widened at the velvet threat of his voice.

'I'm not the one playing games. Why are you here, Luke?' she demanded.

'I came here to talk to Jim Ryan and to take up your invitation to join the Pier Trust. I do hope your bad temper is not because I spoiled your plan to recoup your fortunes with a hot dog stand.'

'It would take more than hot dogs to do that,' she replied. 'It would take hamburgers, ice cream and possibly candy floss as well.' A glint of amusement lit the depths of his eyes. 'And I am not in a temper of any kind. But I am busy. So, why are you here? In my office? Now?' she added, just to make sure he understood. 'If this is personal I believe we covered everything there was to say last night.'

'Did we?' He paused briefly, as if considering something, and she noticed the faint mark of a bruise on his cheekbone. He saw her look and with a tightening of the lines about his mouth that might have suggested a smile, or might not, he lifted her hand from the telephone and turned it over, lightly touching her finger, swollen and painful where a vein had been bruised when she struck him. 'Some things are better dealt with in an entirely businesslike way.'

'What things?' He didn't answer immediately. 'Well?' she demanded, furious that he was playing with her.

'Well?' He repeated, mimicking her with a cruel precision that should have been comic. But she wasn't laughing, and when he continued she knew she had been right not to be amused. 'Aren't you just a little concerned that I might want to forget all about sponsoring you?'

Of course the thought had crossed her mind, but it wasn't what had kept her awake most of the night. Luke Devlin had been responsible in one way and another for a considerable shortfall in her sleep during the last few days. 'You're not sponsoring *me*, Luke. You're sponsoring a number of programmes on my radio station. We have an agreement,' she reminded him.

'Pavilion Radio has an agreement with me,' he corrected her. 'Although you do seem to take it extremely . . . personally.'

Her heart was beating wildly out of control. The hand that had been clamping hers to the telephone receiver was now grasping her fingers in a gesture far too intimate for comfort, but to pull away would show that it mattered. That she cared.

'Yes,' she agreed quickly. 'Pavilion Radio. Of course that's what I meant.'

'Is it? I'm not entirely convinced that it is. You never discussed the details with your father, did you?'

She swallowed. He obviously hadn't wasted his time in those few minutes when he had spoken to her father at the party. 'He was very busy.'

'He seems to take a very relaxed attitude to his business affairs. Or maybe it's only the radio station. In all other respects I found him very astute.'

Fizz gave a little shrug. 'He leaves the day-to-day running of the radio station to me,' she confessed.

'Sponsorship?'

'Sponsorship,' she agreed.

'Finance?' She nodded. 'Staff?'

'Luke – '

'And the inclusion of Melanie in the cast?'

'I told him about it.'

'But you didn't seek his consent?' She didn't enjoy being found out in a blatant lie, but she didn't duck it. 'No.'

'So all the time this has just between the two of us?' He

was staring at her long, delicate fingers in a way that utterly unnerved her.

'Luke?' she prompted, gently tugging at her fingers.

He stiffened, released her hand. 'And since I've only given you the first month's payment – '

'I don't believe you would back out now,' she said.

'Your faith in my integrity touches me deeply, Fizz. Of course it also surprises me, just a little. Last night I received the very strong impression that there was nothing of which you thought me incapable.'

'Last night, in the heat of the moment, we both said things we have reason to regret. I made a mistake about your relationship with Melanie. It was an honest mistake, but I am prepared to apologize. I'm sure on reflection you would wish to withdraw your own remarks.'

'And if I don't?'

'Then I'm afraid I won't be able to accept any further sponsorship from you, or from any company with which you are associated.'

She had shaken him. Not that there had been any outward indication, but his eyes betrayed him. 'You'll go to the wall,' he said.

'If I can live with that, I'm sure you can. I'm sorry about Melanie, of course. She was so excited about working on *Holiday Bay*.' From somewhere she found a careless little shrug. 'She'll be terribly disappointed.'

'No, she won't. You are bluffing, Fizz, so I'm going to do you a favour and forget what you just said. But before I do, I'll offer you a few simple words of advice. I suggest you have them framed and hung where you can see them every moment of your working life.' He regarded her darkly. 'Never, ever, make a threat you're not prepared to carry out.'

'Who said I'm not?' she flared up at him.

'You've been running the promos all weekend, getting everyone excited. I think you should be the one worrying about whether I pull Melanie out, don't you?'

'You wouldn't do that, Luke.'

'Why not?'

'Because it would be self-defeating. You see, I know what you're up to.' She opened her desk drawer and produced the newspaper cutting, pushing it towards him. 'That is what this is all about, isn't it? Getting back at Claudia.'

He glanced at it, then looked up. 'How long have you known about this?'

'Unfortunately I didn't see it until after I had signed your agreement. When were you going to release that press cutting to the tabloids, Luke?' She waited but he didn't pretend not to understand. At least he didn't pretend.

'To coincide with Melanie's first broadcast, I thought.'

'Yes, I would have chosen that moment too. Let us hope that after so much trouble and expense it doesn't turn out to be a damp squib.'

'The tabloids will love it.'

'I'm counting on that, Luke, because the advertisers will love it too. There's nothing like a cat-fight between two actresses to raise interest. Hollywood publicists have been manufacturing them for years.'

'And you think that you'll be able to get by without my help?'

'I'm sure of it.'

'Are you? Then answer this. Did one of your major advertisers recently decide against renewing a contract with you?'

Fizz felt a cold, clammy hand clutch at her heart. 'It happens,' she said.

'Well, it could get to be a regular occurrence.'

'I see.' And she did. She would never distrust a gut reaction again.

'I'm calling your bluff, Fizz. And I'm raising the stakes. You see, I have this strange feeling that you would do anything to save this radio station from bankruptcy, and I intend to prove it.'

She was trembling. She couldn't take much more of this intense battering of her senses. 'What do you want, Luke?' she asked.

There was a long, painful moment while his eyes traversed the length of her body in a lingering survey of its curves. Then he took a heavy hank of her long chestnut hair, and, in swift gesture that wrapped it around his fist, he tied her to him, drawing her closer until her face was inches from his. 'You know what I want,' he said, with a quiet menace that struck her to the bone. 'I want you, Felicity Beaumont.'

Her heart, already pounding from his insolent inspection, now flared in alarm. 'I . . . I don't know what you mean.' At least she hoped she didn't know what he meant. The hope was short-lived as he wasted no time in removing any vestige of doubt as to his very precise meaning.

'Of course you do. The unspoken part of our agreement?' he reminded her.

'There is no – '

'You will discover for yourself whether the four-poster is too small. Shall we say the second Thursday of every month?' She started under his hand. 'I really can't bring myself to participate in ritual sacrifice more frequently than that.' She swore at him then, one single word to tell him what she thought of him. He didn't flinch, didn't appear to hear her. 'And on the Friday morning I will send the sponsorship cheque to your father, just in time to keep the bailiffs out. Would you like me to include a report on your performance? Do you earn a bonus for extra effort?'

The desperate plea wrenched from her lips made no impression on him. 'No, you don't earn a bonus? Or does that cry from the heart mean he has no idea just what kind of sacrifice you're prepared to make in order to protect his investment? How interesting.' He eyes gleamed thoughtfully as he considered her pale face.

'Luke, please!'

'Luke, please.' He repeated grimly. 'You do that so nicely. So convincingly. How can a man resist . . .? And without warning his mouth descended fiercely upon hers.

She could not pull away, though she tried, but his hand clasping her hair to the nape of her neck held her fast. And when she began to beat against his chest with her arms he simply caught her round the waist and jerked her tight against him, pinning them against his chest so that she was utterly helpless and had to endure that

287

punishing kiss. Except that held against his vibrant body, with his mouth doing impossible, exciting things to her, evoking a shimmering response that obliterated any desire to resist him, endurance was not the word that sprang to her mind.

'Luke.' She murmured his name as he finally lifted his head to gaze deep into her eyes, and, boneless, she leaned weakly against him. Then with an angry little hiss, he jerked away from her.

'I'll consider that a deposit on account, Fizz. And, of course, being such a thorough young woman, you won't need me to remind you that you're still one payment behind. I'll give you a call, shall I, when I have an evening free?'

She looked at him, her eyes pleading with his, unable to believe that he could do this to her. She met a blank wall. Obsidian, bottle-glass black eyes that held no expression. 'Yes, do give me a call, Luke,' she said. 'I'll look forward to it.'

The trouble was, Fizz thought miserably, she'd brought the whole thing crashing down upon herself. In the quiet peace of the dark harbour she wrapped her thick fleece-lined jacket around her, stuffed her hands into her pockets and stared down at the sea sucking at the ancient stone wall.

Given the right circumstances she would have surrendered all too willingly to Luke Devlin's embrace and thought herself redeemed by him. But not like this. On Saturday night, wrapped in his arms, she might have temporarily confused the hunger pangs of desire with

288

love to the point where nothing else had mattered. Not even Melanie. And afterwards, when she'd learned the truth of that relationship, she might so easily have been convinced that he felt something in return. Why else would he have been so angry with her? But not now. Now he had left her in no doubt about where his feelings lay. Desire was far too eloquent a word for what was, after all, nothing but a business transaction.

Her career or her honour. It was an extraordinary choice to have to make even once in a lifetime. It was a road she had travelled before, but this time it was different. She was older, stronger, and she had invested too much of herself in the radio station to let some man take it from her without a fight. But she didn't fool herself. There were some games where there could be no winners, only losers.

When she reached home, saw the flash of the answering machine, she suddenly remembered Julian and his urgent call. Quickly she called him back. 'Julian, I'm sorry. Things have been a bit hectic today.' Hectic? *Hectic?*

'Are you coming down with a cold or something?' His concern was immediate. 'You sound quite croaky.'

'I'm fine. Have you got anything for me?'

'Devlin doesn't have shares in the Chocolate Company.' Julian's excitement was palpable. There was definitely something. After today she scarcely doubted it. 'But he knows a man who does. He went to school with Richard Crompton.' Fizz waited. 'The Chocolate Company is Crompton's company.'

It was strange, but she discovered that she didn't want

Julian to know the truth. 'That doesn't mean anything,' she said with apparent carelessness. 'Some girls I went to school with I wouldn't cross the road to speak to.'

'Same here.' He hesitated. 'Well, actually I went to an all boys school, but I . . . well, you know what I mean.'

'I know what you mean, Julian.'

'But the thing is Luke Devlin flew from the west coast of America to be best man at Crompton's wedding a couple of years ago. And he stood as godfather to Richard's daughter just before Christmas.' Fizz didn't say anything. There didn't seem to be much worth saying. 'Fizz? Can I do anything?' Another long silence. 'Fizz?' A little more urgently this time.

She pulled herself together. It was decision time. And there really wasn't any choice. 'I'm sorry, Julian. Actually there is something you can do for me. Something I don't want anyone else to find out about.'

'Luke?' Melanie advanced deeper into the gloom of the study. 'Luke, what is it?'

He roused himself, looked at the girl standing before him, young, fresh, her whole life before her. 'Nothing. I was just thinking about Juliet, that's all.'

'Mum? What about her?'

'That aura she carried about with her. As if she knew something that no one else did. There always seemed to be a part of her that was just out of reach.'

Melanie flopped down beside him on the floor, facing the fire, her arms curled about her legs, her chin tucked on her knees. 'I know what you mean. She had a place inside her head where no one else was allowed.'

290

'Not even you?'

'I asked her about it once and she told me that every woman has a place like that, a place that she fills up with all the good things that have ever happened to her, special secrets, all the things she hoped for. It's somewhere to go when she's feeling a little bit alone, or frightened, or unhappy.' She turned and looked up at him. 'She said I'd understand one day.

'And do you?'

She hesitated just a second too long. 'Perhaps I haven't anything important enough to put in a place like that.'

'No hopes? No special secrets?'

'Special secrets are not for telling, Luke.'

'No, of course not.' But she didn't mention the hopes. He looked down at her with a kind of exasperation. 'You're just like her, you know.'

'Am I? She was very pretty.'

'Not to look at, minx. Except perhaps sometimes . . . something about the way you move, a sudden phrase said just the same way . . .' No. It was more than that. Directness. Courage. He hoped she would never be hurt the way her mother had been. Would never have to retreat into her head for memories instead of living every day of her life to the full. She was watching him and he grinned at her. 'Stop fishing for compliments.'

Melanie grinned back, then she put her head on one side. 'So, what about you and Fizz Beaumont, then?'

It was his turn to hesitate. 'What do you mean?'

She threw him a look full of mischief. 'I asked her if you'd had a row or something.'

'That was very rude of you.'

'Probably. But I wanted to know.'

'And what did she say?'

Melanie's eyes gleamed. 'She said "or something". Then she changed the subject. She was very polite, but she went off somewhere inside her head. She does that too. Have you noticed?' He had noticed. There wasn't anything about her that wasn't stencilled onto his brain.

'Well?'

His jaw tightened. 'What do you expect me to say?'

'You could tell me your side of it.'

'I don't have a side and I wouldn't dream of contradicting a lady. If she said "or something" you'll just have to be satisfied. Please don't let your imagination run away with the idea that there is anything else.'

'I'm not imagining this.' She held up Fizz's earring, dangling it tantalizingly in front of him.

He wanted to reach out and snatch it from the wretched child, but he didn't. He remained quite still. 'What is it?'

'An earring. Fizz was wearing it on Saturday – didn't you notice? Mrs Harris found it this morning. Under the rug.'

'If she only found one earring after Saturday it must be some kind of miracle.'

'It was the only one she found in here. Under this rug. After all, this room was out of bounds. Locked.' Luke maintained a dignified silence. 'Fizz has pierced ears and this is an expensive piece of jewellery. See – it has a little safety hook. I expect she lost it when she came down with that headache. Perhaps she took it off before she decided to lie on the floor and – '

'That's enough, Mel.' Luke leaned forward, twitched the earring from her fingers and slipped it into his pocket. 'I'll see she gets it back.'

'Good.' Melanie leapt to her feet. 'Shall I get you a drink? A brandy?'

For a moment their eyes met, and Luke knew she was remembering that he had given Fizz a brandy too, for her 'headache'. 'A very small one,' he said. 'Then, since I have it on very good authority that you are going to the cinema tonight, you can stop buttering me up and go and get ready.'

'I *am* ready,' she declared, outraged. 'Can't you tell?' She pirouetted for his inspection, displaying a down-soft sweater, a skirt so short that it defied its name and black boots that laced all the way up the front to her knees. Then, 'How did you know I'm going to the cinema?'

'Andy asked me if I thought it was a good idea. He didn't want you to be mobbed.'

'And you said yes?'

'I told him to ask you.' He shrugged. 'If you want advice about finance, contracts, your career, even, I'll do my best. But if you can't decide on a simple date for yourself – ' He left her to fill in the picture. 'Have fun.'

'Thanks, Luke.' She handed him a glass, then dropped a kiss on top of his head. 'You should try it yourself some time. You might like it. I expect Fizz would enjoy a night out too.'

As the door closed behind her his fingers fastened upon the earring he had pushed so carelessly into his pocket. He took it out and held it up for a moment so that it danced, a slender gold leaf, in the firelight. Then he closed his hand about it, his thumb rubbing against the smooth surface, warm to his touch, and he thought for a moment about doing something as simple as phoning a girl you liked and asking her to go to the cinema with you. And how sometimes life was very complicated indeed.

CHAPTER 12

Fizz had been through every emotion known to woman in the week since she had last seen Luke. Each time the phone rang she jumped. The sound of the doorbell put her through nightmares before she could bring herself to open it. And although she had warned Susie to keep visitors at bay she still felt particularly vulnerable in her office. But a whole week went by and he didn't ring, he stayed away from her flat and he didn't invade her cramped little office. So she began to hope.

When the tenth day drew to a close she was beginning to think that he had never really meant it. That it had all been anger, hurt pride. All those ridiculous macho things. Sinking down into the foamy water of a hot bath at the end of a blissfully peaceful day, she smiled.

The telephone began to ring. She had forgotten to switch on the answering machine, but she didn't get out of the bath. Whoever it was would ring back. She ran a little more hot water. The telephone continued to ring. It went on and on. No one let a phone ring like that unless they were sure someone was at home or unless it was urgent. It had to be the station, and finally she gave in and hauled herself dripping from the bath, cursing under her breath as she struggled with a towel. 'Fizz Beaumont,' she gasped as she picked up the receiver.

'Hello, Fizz.' Her knees buckled and she grabbed at the table, dragging in a breath. 'You sound . . . breathless. What were you doing that you took so long to answer the telephone? Or is it indiscreet to enquire?'

'If I had been doing anything that interesting, Luke, the phone could have rung until kingdom come before I answered it. In fact I was in the bath. I am, at this moment, dripping copiously onto the carpet, so I would be grateful if we could skip the small talk.'

'Were you going to have an early night?' he asked, his voice probing for weak spots, and finding them.

'I was hoping to.'

'Not too early. We've some unfinished business.'

More fool her for allowing herself to be lulled into a false sense of security by his silence. His intention, no doubt. 'You finally found a slot for me in your diary?' Her attempt at bravado was not entirely successful. If she could hear the shake in her voice, so could he.

'You've been sitting by the phone, waiting for my call?'

'I don't have time to waste sitting by the telephone, Luke, but I have to admit that under the circumstances your lack of eagerness is somewhat underwhelming.'

'I've been away.'

'For the good of your health?' she asked hopefully.

'For the good of my business. I can't regenerate Harries sitting on my backside in Broomhill, no matter how appealing the local attractions. Of course, if I'd realized you were so flatteringly anxious to hear from me, I promise you nothing would have kept me from Broomhill.'

Fizz pulled a face at the telephone. 'I thought when you left my office last week I had left you in no doubt about my feelings. I can see I'm going to have to try much harder.'

'I'm happy to give you the opportunity. I'll pick you up at nine,' he said, and she was pleased to note that the teasing note had abruptly left his voice.

'That's rather late.'

'It's the earliest I can manage.'

'What a busy life you do lead. Nine o'clock, then.' And as she replaced the receiver she thought she heard a crack as her heart broke. But then she realized that couldn't be right. If she didn't love him, how could he break her heart?

She returned to her bath, ran in some more hot water. There was no rush. She might have hoped he wouldn't ring, but she had made her plans anyway. Luke Devlin wouldn't catch her unawares again.

An hour later, Fizz checked her appearance in the antique cheval mirror that was one of her most prized possessions. Her make-up, her hair, her clothes were all pared to the bone, stripped of ornament and decoration, with Claudia's suit the final touch. A reminder to both of them that this meeting was purely business.

The bell rang promptly at nine o'clock. She smoothed slightly sweating palms over a neatly coiled chignon and straightened her padded shoulders before she opened the door. Somehow she had expected him to be dressed with equal formality, but Luke was leaning against her door-frame dressed casually in a well-rubbed leather bomber jacket, comfortable trousers and a open-necked shirt in some soft material. And hanging at his side, loosely held in his fingers, was a spray of white freesias.

'Hello, Fizz,' he said softly, and his mouth twisted in a smile that was pure self-mockery as he took in her appearance. 'It's odd, but I had been expecting you in something white. Sacrificial. But I should have known better. Since the first moment you stormed into my office you have never failed to surprise me.' He glanced down at the flowers. 'The snowdrops are over now; these were the closest I could get. They don't quite go with your outfit, do they?' With a shrug that spoke volumes he tossed them on the hall table. 'But then, what would?'

Flowers? How she hated him for that! How could he be so cruel, complicating things with such a mean-ingless gesture, as if this were some fairy-tale romance? And yet as the sweet scent filled the room she had to admit that they were heartbreakingly beautiful. And despite her determination to carry through this meet-ing with total formality she felt more like crying at the sheer idiocy of it.

'Shall I wait while you put them in the bin?' he enquired.

His voice brought her back to reality. Yet she still found it difficult to believe that he was truly intent on demanding his pound of flesh. Still hoped that he wouldn't.

Fool! she chided herself. But as the haunting scent of the freesias caught at the back of her throat she found herself blinking back a sharp prickling sensation behind her eyes. 'No. I don't want the scent in my flat.' She looked at them as if afraid they might bite her. 'There's a bin on the lamppost outside. Would you please dispose of them on your way out?'

'Way out?'

'Our unfinished business shouldn't take more than five minutes. Will you go through to the sitting room?'

His eyes narrowed. 'I thought we might go out.'

'Then you thought wrong.' She had expected him to resume his threats at this point. He didn't. Instead, deeply thoughtful, he closed the door behind him and walked through to her sitting room. It looked warm and inviting, lamps throwing soft pools of light, the flames of the gas fire flickering a welcome. 'Can I get you a drink? A glass of wine, perhaps? Or I have some whisky or brandy if you prefer?'

'Nothing. Thank you.'

'In that case we might as well get on. Would you sit down please?' She indicated the chair placed in front of her desk and seated herself behind it.

He didn't sit. She didn't push it. Instead she took her copy of the sponsorship agreement and a banker's draft out of a drawer and laid them in front of him.

'What is this, Fizz?'

'I am cancelling our agreement and returning your money. All that I require is your signature to say that you have received it.' She pushed a piece of paper and a pen across the desk towards him. He ignored it.

'You can't do that.'

'Oh yes, Luke, I certainly can do that. If you look at

the agreement I have marked the place. It's a fairly standard clause covering taste and decency.' He picked up the agreement, flipped over the page and read the place she had marked. 'I think it about covers the situation, don't you?'

'This refers to broadcasting.'

'Of course. That is *all* our agreement covered, Luke. But if you feel you've had a raw deal please feel free to sue me. I'll be more than happy to meet you in court.' She picked up the banker's draft and held it out to him. 'You were the one who called my bluff, Luke. But as you can see I wasn't bluffing.'

'Really?' He didn't sound convinced, and he made no move to sign the receipt or to take the draft. She placed it on the desk in front of him.

'Fizz – '

'One more thing before you go, Luke.' She dropped her eyes. 'I would like you to know that I have, in my entire life, had only one lover. It was a long time ago and he asked me to marry him.' There was a long silence. 'That's all.'

'Why didn't you?' She had been staring at her hands, concentrating so hard on what she wanted to say, that she hadn't anticipated questions. She had thought – hoped – that he would finally apologize for what he had suggested about her role in the procurement of sponsorship and leave. Get out of her life. 'Why didn't you marry him?' he repeated.

'I don't think that's any of your business.'

'I shan't go until you tell me.' As if to emphasize his determination, he finally folded himself into the small

300

chair she had placed in front of the desk for him. 'It was Patrick March, wasn't it?'

Her head snapped up. 'How do you know that?'

'I had a file on your family this thick.' He held up his finger and thumb, holding them a couple of inches apart. 'He was the only candidate.'

'Had?'

'I put it through the shredder this morning. Why didn't you marry him, Fizz? If he asked you?'

'You think I'm lying?'

'I've heard his side of the story and it varies in some of the details. He was very convincing.'

'He's an actor,' she said angrily. 'And a damned good one. With the right lines he could convince you black was white.'

'You're in the same game.'

'No, Luke. I stopped wanting to pretend for a living when . . . when . . .'

'When what? Tell me what happened.' She was still looking at her hands and he reached out and wrapped his own fingers about them. 'Talk to me, Fizz,' he said urgently.

'I don't think I know how.'

'Try.'

She had kept it bottled up for so long. She wouldn't have said anything to Luke, but she had to make sure that he understood what he had done to her. How insulted she had felt. She had never talked to anyone about what happened with Patrick. Never just let it pour out. Not even to Claudia. Only the bare bones when she had come racing to the rescue. Now she looked up into Luke's

301

unwavering eyes and knew that it was time.

'We were making a film together. Romeo and Juliet meet the twentieth century. Romance, violence, tragedy. Pretty corny stuff, but it was a good script. I was younger even than Melanie, and naturally everyone assumed I'd got the part because of my name. Perhaps that's what gave Patrick the idea.'

'What idea?'

'That marrying me would be a short-cut to instant stardom.' The words came out and she realized with something of a shock that it didn't hurt any more. She didn't actually care. 'He was really talented, Luke, but you're close enough to the business to know that talent isn't enough. Our marriage would have scooped all the publicity that goes with a fairy-tale romance. *Romeo and Juliet* with a happy ending. It would have ensured the film was a hit.' She looked up. 'I don't have to explain it to you, Luke. Your friend Richard Crompton recently pulled off a public relations coup using Claudia. Tell me, was it all just a cynical exercise in media manipulation, or did he drop the advertising campaign just to please you?'

Her attack took him by surprise and for a moment he gaped. 'I am godfather to Richard's daughter, Fizz. Do you really think I would ask him to get involved in something like that?'

'He's your friend.'

'And I intend to keep it that way. What happened with the commercial was pure coincidence.'

'But it wasn't all coincidence, was it, Luke?'

He took her hands in his. She tried to pull away, but he held her. 'Fizz, I'm sorry. I've done what I can to put

302

things right. I've spent the best part of a week sorting out the mess I made.'

'It was rather heavy-handed revenge for one catty remark, Luke. You could have made Claudia look silly without making Dad suffer.'

'I think you've suffered too.'

'That was my fault. I shouldn't have relied on Michael so much. I won't make the same mistake again.'

'Good.' He nodded as if pleased. 'I will explain, Fizz. Everything. But I have to talk to Edward first.' He waited for some acknowledgement that she had heard, had understood what he said. After a moment a shuddering sigh escaped her and she nodded, and when he squeezed her fingers gently she looked up and smiled.

'You still haven't told me why you didn't marry Patrick March.'

'Does it matter?'

'You *were* in love with him?'

'Of course I was in love with him. Half the women on the set were in love with him, and most of them were old enough to know better. I was eighteen and as green as grass; he was drop-dead gorgeous and clever enough not to be too obvious. He didn't even make a pass at me. He was the perfect gentleman.'

'How frustrating for you.'

She gave him a quick smile, grateful that he hadn't needed it spelt out in words of one syllable. 'Yes. I suppose he knew just how frustrating. He was light years ahead of me, in fact. Then we shot the first bedroom scene. Most actors get the giggles, you know. I mean, it's pretty ludicrous. There you are, stark naked, rolling about in bed with a lighting man holding a reflector six inches from your left cheek, a sound man leaning over to catch every sigh, the director piling in with his suggestions as to just where the leading man should be putting his hand.'

Luke didn't say anything. 'But I didn't even notice them. It was electric. First take stuff. I wanted him so much.' She lifted her shoulders. 'I suppose everyone knew what was going on. It was a director's dream. The real thing on screen. Afterwards, when I realized what it was all about, I felt so *used*. They were two clever, ambitious men who didn't think twice about what they were doing to me.'

'Not that clever. Neither of them got what they wanted.'

'No. I think perhaps that Patrick meant to keep me on the boil until he'd led me up the aisle.' She pulled her hand away, stood up, walked over to the window and stared out at the dark sea. 'But my name owes more to my habit of going off like a champagne cork under pressure than to my sister's childhood lisp. You may have noticed.'

He joined her at the window. Put his arm around her shoulders, smiled at down her. 'It's very . . . refreshing.' She smiled up at him briefly, then looked back at the sea.

'Yes, well. While my enthusiasm initially made up for my lack of experience, I don't suppose I was up to his usual standard.'

'Personally I'd have said you had natural talent.'

'Would you?' How odd. That was what they had said about her acting at RADA. That she had natural talent.

She shrugged. 'Then one day I left my script in his caravan. It didn't occur to me to knock when I went back for it. One of the make-up girls had taken my place. The sheets must still have been warm . . .' She stopped for a moment. No. It truly didn't hurt any more. 'It caused a bit of a problem with the filming. There were quite a few of those steamy bedroom scenes.'

'That must have been unpleasant for you.'

She looked up then, half a smile stealing across her lips. 'Not as unpleasant for me as for him. I'm afraid that after that I was sick whenever he touched me.'

'Sick?' He began to grin. 'Physically sick?'

'It wasn't funny at the time, Luke. Without me there wasn't a film. And I did try. The producer, poor man, was having kittens, and the budget was wildly out of control. But I just couldn't do it. The harder I tried, the worse it got. The weight fell off me; I looked dreadful. Someone must have telephoned Claudia and told her that I was ill. It might even have been Patrick. I didn't ask and she didn't tell me. I was too sick to care.'

His arm was around her, and the temptation to simply bury her head in his chest and go with the flow was overwhelming. But she drew back. 'Well, that's it. The cheap and sordid story of my one romance. Since then I've relied on my radio station to keep me warm on cold winter nights.'

'*Your* radio station?'

'Yes.' She lifted her chin. 'My radio station. It was my idea. I own it. I run it. Not many people know that. Jim, Susie, a couple of the senior staff who have been with us from the beginning.'

'But why? And why is your father's name on the franchise?'

'I prefer to stay in the background. Dad does the limelight bit so much better than me. And anyway, who in their right minds would have given it to a failed actress barely out of her teens? I mean, I didn't make a world-shattering impression on you as a businesswoman that first day in your office, and I've been at it for five years now.'

He laughed. 'If you knew exactly what kind of an impression you made on me that day, my love, you would blush.'

His love? 'Would I?' She turned to him. 'Well, I guess that makes us about even.'

'I suppose this is where I'm expected to apologize? Beg you to keep the money?'

She smiled slightly. 'Well, actually you missed your cue for the apology some time ago. And I don't want your money, Luke. I've made other arrangements to ensure the future of the radio station. All that's left now is to say goodbye.' She took a step back and offered her hand.

He took it, held it, pulled her closer. 'And what if I were to tell you that the balance of the sponsorship money was paid into your bank account just before close of business today?'

The tremble that swept over her came as a complete surprise. She had convinced herself that she had Luke's number, that there could be no more shocks. 'I would have to ask why you came here tonight if it wasn't to bear me away to your four-poster bed and have your wicked way with me? You certainly let me believe that was what you intended.'

'Maybe I didn't contradict the impression you had. But you didn't tell me you weren't prepared to go through with it, so I planned to give you a bit of a fright for being so damned stupid. Then I was going to take you to an attractive country pub Andy told me about, have a drink, supper maybe, talk certainly.'

'Well, we've talked. Maybe you'd like to change your mind about that drink?'

'You still haven't answered my question.'

'It was hypothetical. Have you really paid in the balance of the money?' He nodded – once. She couldn't believe the rush of joy that swept over her, leaving her weak, so weak that she simply leaned against him, laying her head against his chest. 'Then my answer, Luke, is that I would be very happy. Happy to know that you never meant to carry out your threats. Happy to accept a generous gesture. And more than happy to return the money to you the moment the bank opens tomorrow morning.' She felt suddenly liberated, light-headed, free of all the terrible tensions and anxieties of the last weeks.

'Return it? How? How have you found the money?' He gave her a little shake, demanding an answer.

'Don't worry, Luke. I promise you I didn't walk the streets.'

The colour drained from his face. 'I suppose I asked for that.'

'I suppose you did. Now, would you like a brandy? Or a glass of wine? There's a bottle in the fridge. You could always ring for a taxi if you're worried about driving.'

307

'Or I could sleep on your sofa again?'

'My sofa?' she murmured. 'Why on earth would you want to do that? I'm sure it isn't very comfortable.' *Certainly not as comfortable as my bed*, Fizz thought, and blushed.

'I'm open to alternative suggestions. In the meantime I'll accept your offer of a drink. But only if you take off that dreadful suit.'

'Take it off?' She looked down at it. 'Now, you mean?'

His cheekbones seared dull red as he realized what he had said. 'No!' But it was too late. She slipped the buttons of the jacket and let it slide onto the floor. Then she unhooked the waistband, slid down the zip of her skirt. It rustled over the black silk teddy that swooped over the flare of her hips, skimming her thighs to expose long legs clad in sheerest black stockings, before dropping in a crumpled heap upon the floor.

'No?' she queried softly.

For a moment there was a silence so intent that as they stood in the lambent firelight they could have heard a star fall a galaxy away. Then Luke dragged his eyes back to her face, and although his eyes were hooded, disguising his expression, she could feel the heightened awareness, the quickening of the tension that stretched between them like the gossamer silk of a spider's web. Barely visible, yet so strong that it bound them irreversibly together.

'Yes,' he said. 'Oh, God, yes.' And with a sound from his throat that was somewhere between a sigh and a groan, Luke reached out and tugged free the combs that fastened her hair. And as it uncoiled, thick and heavy, glowing the colour of chestnuts newly burst from the shell in the flickering flames of the fire, it spread about her face and fell over her white shoulders in a rich cascade. He lifted its weight in his hands, letting the silky length fall between his fingers. Then, without a word, he gathered her into his arms.

He didn't rush. He gave her time to say no, if that was what she wanted. But it wasn't. All the nightmares were over. It was time to say yes. She slipped her hands over his chest, sliding them beneath his jacket, pushing it off his shoulders. Before it hit the floor her arms were around his neck and she pulled his mouth down to her, letting her body and her lips and her hands say it for her.

As his mouth sought hers, the tip of his tongue and his teeth grazing her lips, her need for him filled her entire being, flooding through her body, heating her bone-deep until the desire that had been slowly building from the first moment she set eyes on him quite suddenly ignited. She wanted him, and as she felt his need for her, the rampant hardness of his body against hers, she wanted, more than anything in the world, to touch him. And since she was a natural, she did what came naturally.

He caught her hand. Held it against him for a moment before lifting it to his mouth, kissing her palm. Then without a word he picked her up and headed for the bedroom while she clung to him like a liferaft on a stormy sea, her nails digging into his shoulders.

Dusky velvet curtains were drawn across the windows, shutting out the dark night, the rest of the world. The lamp at the side of bed was lit, throwing a soft light across

309

the bed where the quilt was thrown back invitingly. He laid her upon it and was beside her before she could complain at their separation.

For a long moment he stared down at her, his eyes smoking with a desire that left her weak with longing, and she lifted her hands to his face, rubbing her palms over the faint stubble of his chin, murmuring his name.

He caught one of the narrow ribbons that held up her teddy between his long fingers. 'Black,' he murmured, his face all dark shadows. 'A little obvious?' He was teasing her. It was an intimate, intoxicating sensation and she loved it.

'If you don't like it, Luke,' she murmured in husky invitation, 'why don't you take it off?'

'Who said I didn't like it?' But he pushed away the ribbon, kissing her shoulder where it had caressed her skin, nuzzling the hollows of her throat, her neck, and she gave a little cry of pleasure as his lips brushed the soft cleavage. He stroked the heavy silk away from milky smooth breasts and for a moment his eyes lingered there. Then with the edge of his thumbs he teased their pink tips to a provocative invitation which he graciously accepted, drawing each delicately thrusting point into his mouth in turn, his tongue tormenting her to an exquisite agony of pleasure as she threaded her fingers through his thick dark hair, holding him close, offering herself to him.

'Fizz,' he murmured. 'Hold me now, touch me.' She needed no encouragement. Despite shaking fingers she swiftly unbuttoned his shirt, pushing it back from his shoulders over the iron-hard muscles of his arms until he could discard it and her hands could leisurely explore his chest, tease the broad expanse of his back with the tips of her nails, torment him in turn with her tongue until he gave a fierce groan and, seizing her, rolled onto his back so that she was lying above him.

'Witch,' he murmured softly. 'You must have me bewitched, because, God help me, I can't help myself.'

'Tell me to stop,' she invited with a crazy little laugh as she recognized her power over him and wildness seized her. She knew that he could not do it and she slid down his chest until she was confronted with the waistband of his trousers. She looked up then, her eyes indigo-dark. 'Just say if you want me to stop,' she repeated, 'and I will.'

But as she slipped the button, tugged down the zip, eased her hand inside the waistband to push down his trousers, his briefs, his only sound was a hiss of pleasure. Then he stilled as her tongue and her teeth followed the trail blazed by her hands over his abdomen, down the smooth skin inside his thighs and she felt him quiver with his need for her.

For a moment she knelt between his legs, just looking at him. He was beautiful. Lean, hard, with sculpted muscles that defined his strong neck, his wide shoulders, the flat plane of his stomach. She reached out to touch it, but he caught her hand, pulling her down on top of him so that her breasts were flattened against his chest and she could feel just how hard he was. All over. His eyes shimmered as he looked up at her, his lips curved in a smile of delicious anticipation.

Then without warning he tipped her over onto her

back, so that she lay against the pillows, her hair tumbled wildly about her face. 'Did you enjoy that, hussy?' he asked as he made a cave of his body over her.

'Why don't you try it and find out for yourself?' And she stretched out in invitation, smiling lazily up at him.

'Do tell me if you want me to stop at any time, Fizz,' he invited, confident that nothing would interrupt his slow exploration of her body as slowly, very slowly, he pulled the teddy down, lifting her to ease it under her hips, leaving a trail of kisses over her breasts, her waist, the gentle swell of her abdomen, down the smooth, silk-clad skin of her inner thigh and Fizz drew up her leg in response to the erotic charge that surged through her.

'How beautiful you are,' he said, propping himself on one elbow to lie alongside her, to look at her, touch her.

Fizz, desperate to feel his skin against hers, to take his weight, to know him, said, 'Tell me later. Right now I don't want talk.' And she turned to press herself along the length of his body. 'I want action.'

There was a moment when they just stared at one another, then his mouth swooped to plunder hers and he was pushing her back against the bedclothes, sliding his fingers into her. 'Oh, Fizz,' he murmured as he encountered the moist heat of her longing. 'I can't believe this is happening.'

Fizz arched her back, pushing against his hand. 'Now, Luke,' she demanded. 'I want you. Now.' And then she gasped as he drove into her, filling her, building the heat so that it was more than she had ever dreamed of, and she cried out, twisting in his arms, rising to meet his thrusts until something exploded. Fizz. Bang. A chorus of angels singing the 'Hallelujah Chorus' while Luke shuddered against her.

Afterwards it seemed very quiet. Luke, his head thrown back against the pillow, his neck corded in the shadowed light, lay perfectly still, holding her against him. Fizz did not dare move. Part of her was still in heaven with the angels, but part of her was afraid, terrified. He looked so distant.

Luke moved. Turned to her so that she was confronted with his chest. It was beautiful, as chests went. Sculptured, even. Not a lot of hair. She wanted to touch it, put out her tongue and taste his skin, take possession of him. The choir grew a little in volume. She had just decided that it would be safe to run her finger along the hollow of his collarbone when he brushed back the hair from her face and looked at her intently.

'I'm sorry, Fizz.' *Sorry?* The chorus stopped abruptly. The pain was instant, agonizing, immutable. 'I'm not usually quite that stupid.' *Stupid!* 'I don't know what came over me.'

'Don't you? Isn't there a word for it?'

He looked startled.

'Lust?' she offered.

'That wasn't . . . Fizz!' he protested as she flung herself off the bed. He came after her, rolling upright, reaching for her in a single movement, graceful, quite unconscious of his nudity. 'I did nothing to protect you,' he said, pulling her back into his arms. Then, thickly, 'And I'm pretty damned sure you haven't done anything to protect yourself.'

'Oh.' Even in her lust for Patrick she had never been

quite so lost to common sense. But then all those lectures Claudia had given her about safe sex had been so long ago that she hadn't for a moment thought about it. Even afterwards, up there with the angels, it hadn't crossed her mind.

She didn't doubt for a moment that he was right to be concerned. She just wished that for a moment he could have forgotten consequences and stayed to listen with her to the chorus. She shrugged out of his arms and crossed to the bathroom door, where she fixed a bright smile to her face before turning back to him. 'Well, it's too late to do anything about it now. I won't worry about it if you don't.'

He was across the room to her, grasping her arms, holding her at a distance before she could step back. 'Idiot,' he said, fiercely. Then, 'Marry me.'

She stared up at him, at the intensity of emotion knotting the muscles on his neck, his jaw. He was really concerned. Well, that was nice, but it wasn't enough. 'I think you're overreacting, Luke. You've been working too hard.'

'Idiot,' he said again, but gently this time. And then he kissed her. 'I love you, Fizz. Marry me. Please.'

That jolted her. 'And you have the nerve to call *me* an idiot? Lie down for a moment, take an aspirin.'

'I don't need an aspirin, I need you.'

She was almost convinced. 'Right now all I need is a shower, Luke.' She detached herself, switched on the shower and tested the temperature of the water.

'I mean it, Fizz.' The water was warm now and she stepped beneath it. He followed her.

'Luke!'

'Will you listen to me now?' He had her trapped, no escape. 'I want you to marry me.'

A smile, a real smile, began to form on her lips. She tried to stop it, but it had a life of its own. 'Will you pass me the soap?' she asked.

'I warn you I'm not going anywhere until you say yes.'

'Oh?' She held out her hand. 'The soap?'

He glared at her, then reached behind him, handed it to her. She worked up a lather in her hands, handed it back to him and began to circle her hands over his chest, over his shoulders. His skin was like silk beneath her fingers. She leaned forward, circling him with her arms, brushing his chest with her breasts, and suddenly it was Luke who was trapped. 'Fizz? What are you doing? I'm trying to talk to you.'

'Later. If you talk in the shower, you're likely to get soap in your mouth.' She lifted her fingers to his mouth, wiped foam across his lower lip. 'See? Now, do you want to play? Or do you really want to talk?'

She could still taste the soap when they finally emerged from the shower some time later.

'Shall I open that bottle of wine now?' Luke said, wrapping a towel around his hips.

'Mmm. There's some brie, if you're hungry. Or I could – ' She broke off as the doorbell rang. 'Who on earth could that be?'

'Do you want me to find out?'

'Dressed like that? If it's Mrs Pusey you'll give her palpitations.' Fizz grinned. 'You're giving me palpitations right now.' She pulled on a thick towelling robe and crossed to the door. 'You concentrate on the wine.'

The bell rang again before she reached the door. A long, urgent peal. And when she opened it Melanie flung herself at her. 'Oh, Fizz.'

'Mel, what is it? What's happened?' But the girl was shaking, tearful, and Fizz looked helplessly over her head to Andy. As their eyes met her insides contracted and twisted.

'I'm sorry, Fizz. It's Edward,' he said. 'They've taken him to the hospital.'

CHAPTER 13

'Fizz!' Luke called from the kitchen. 'I can't find a corkscrew.' He waited, but there was no answer and so, grinning in anticipation of another teasing game, he put down the bottle and walked to the door. 'I don't know what you think I'm made of, girl, but – '

Three pairs of eyes met his. Melanie, open-mouthed, appeared unable to speak; Andy stood still with a knowing look that took in the damp hair, the towel wrapped around his hips covering nothing but wet skin. Fizz was in shock.

'Funny time for a social call,' he said. 'What's up?'

'Edward collapsed at the studios about an hour ago,' Andy said, quickly pulling himself together. 'He's been taken to the General. Claudia asked us to fetch Fizz.'

'Collapsed?' His guts twisted, like spaghetti round a fork. 'Was it a heart attack?' Fizz uttered a brief anguished cry and Melanie began to cry.

'It's all my fault,' she sobbed, and for one sickening moment he stared full into the face of a nightmare of his own creation.

He had to get Fizz out of there before Melanie spilled

it all out, had to give himself time to explain. But she looked so fragile that when he touched her arm he was almost afraid that she might break. 'Fizz?' She stirred, looked at him with eyes that would tear a man's heart to shreds. 'Go and get dressed, my love. I'll take you to the hospital.'

'Yes. Yes, of course.' He watched her go, wanting to be with her, to hold her, to tell her that he'd never meant it to be like this. That he had never wanted to hurt her. But it wasn't true. His sole intention had been to hurt Edward by making his daughters suffer. He hadn't the right to tell her; it would be pure self-indulgence to unburden himself now. She was in enough pain. Instead he forced himself to give his attention to Melanie. It was barely a year since she had lost her own mother, since he had had to tell her about the accident, take her to the hospital to watch Juliet die.

'Why were you at the studios, Mel? I thought you and Andy were going into Brighton tonight for some concert.'

'Claudia has an audition tomorrow, something big. So she asked if we could record *Holiday Bay* this evening instead of tomorrow. Edward came back especially.'

An audition. The fork twisted again. An audition for a play he had agreed to back provided Claudia Beaumont was given the lead. Oh, God, the irony of it, the sheer bloody irony. The one thing he hadn't been able to fix, but hadn't worried about because there was no rush, because he could do it in the morning, had blown right up in his face. 'Can you tell me what happened?'

She sniffed a little, pushed the hair back from her face.

'Um . . . We'd done most of it before Mr Beaumont arrived. He only had a few words, right at the end . . . I don't think he'd even seen the script. He just took it, glanced at his lines, nodded and said we might as well go for it.'

'And?'

'Oh, he was wonderful. You'd have thought he'd been rehearsing all week. He said his lines, I said mine, and the recording manager nodded to say everything was fine. So we all started to talk at once – you know how it is.' Luke didn't, but had no wish to be told.

'What happened?'

'It was so odd. I turned round to speak to Mr Beaumont and he was staring at me so strangely. He just said, "Juliet?" That's all. He looked, well . . . haunted, almost. Then he sort of crumpled up – Oh, Fizz,' she said, breaking off as she saw her in the bedroom door. 'I'm so sorry. It was the name – I shouldn't have changed the name.'

'Mel,' Luke interrupted sharply. 'This isn't your fault.' She looked at him, her eyes full of tears. 'It's not your fault. Now, Andy will take you home.' He glanced at the other man. 'Will you stay with her until I get back?'

'Of course.'

Fizz had muddled the buttons of the thick padded shirt she was wearing, he noticed. It was such a childlike mistake, making her seem utterly defenceless. His heart just cracked with longing to go to her, to tell her that it would be all right, that he would put the world back together for her if she'd let him. But if Edward died . . .

319

'We'll go now. I'll ring as soon as there's any news,' he said, ushering them through the door, closing it behind them. He turned, slowly, because he didn't want to face this girl that he loved to distraction. Didn't want to see the accusation in her eyes. But when he turned he realized that she hadn't yet worked it out. He crossed to her. 'I'd better get dressed,' he said.

She didn't answer. He could almost see the cogs spinning in her brain. Then she took a deep shuddering breath, almost shook herself. 'Hurry, Luke,' she said.

He was already moving, relief that they had both been reprieved for the moment making his hands shake. When he rejoined her in the hall she was frowning. The cogs were busy clicking again.

'Are you ready to go, Fizz?' He kept his voice crisp, impersonal. She didn't answer, but picked up her bag and hurried down the stairs, leaving him to make sure the door was shut.

For a while they drove through the darkness in a silence so thick that he could feel it coming at him in waves from her. He stared ahead, his face fixed on the road, his hands grasping the wheel until his knuckles stood out, bone-white. Then she turned to look at him.

'You've done this, haven't you, Luke? That's what Melanie meant when she said it was her fault.'

'Fizz, I don't think this is a good time . . .'

'I don't know how, or why. But if my father dies you will be responsible.' He didn't deny it. Didn't make excuses. What excuses could he make? Phillip had warned him that revenge was a wild justice. Once set in motion the outcome could not be foreseen or con-

320

trolled. 'Will you be able to live with that on your conscience?' she asked. Not angrily, but as if she genuinely wanted to know.

And the answer was staring him in the face. No. He wouldn't be able to live with himself. He wouldn't deserve to. He simply prayed it wouldn't happen, and with some relief drew up at the entrance to the hospital. Fizz scrambled out, not waiting for him to open the door for her. 'I'll find somewhere to park,' he said.

'No. Go away, Luke. Go away and leave us all in peace.' She didn't wait to see if he had obeyed her, but pushed open the door and was immediately enveloped in the sterile, overheated atmosphere of the hospital.

For a moment he rested his head on the back of his hands as he gripped the steering wheel, wishing he could do as she asked. Give them back the peace he had snatched away. He would try. But if Edward died there would be no peace for any of them for a long time. For him, perhaps never.

Claudia was in the waiting room, pacing backwards and forwards. Jim Ryan was there too. He immediately went to Fizz, drawing her into the bulky comfort of his arms to hug her.

'What's happening? Why are you out here? Why isn't someone with Dad? Can I see him?' she said, the words tumbling over themselves, an antidote to the dreadful thoughts racketing around inside her head, too jumbled up to sort out right now. Or maybe she just didn't want to sort them out.

'The doctor's with him, Fizz,' Jim said quietly.

'They're taking blood for tests, that sort of thing. It'll be a while. Come and sit down.' He glanced up. 'Claudia, for goodness' sake sit down; you're wearing out the carpet.'

Claudia stopped pacing. 'Sorry.' She looked deathly pale beneath the glamour of her make-up and Fizz broke away from Jim and went to her, taking her hand, squeezing it.

'I just feel so bloody helpless,' she said. 'Now I know why people smoke. I'll be biting my fingernails next. There's nothing else to do when you're waiting.' She looked over the top of Fizz's head. 'Oh, Luke. I didn't expect to see you.'

'I drove Fizz to the hospital. What's the news?' Fizz didn't turn round, not quite able to face him. Or to face the fact that the man she was stupidly, crazily in love with, who had just made passionate love to her, who had just asked her to marry him, was somehow responsible for causing her father to collapse. He hadn't denied it when she had challenged him. But how?

'The doctor's with Edward now,' Jim said, filling the silence. 'Tests, that sort of thing. There's coffee if you want it.'

Luke shook his head. Claudia resumed her pacing. Jim helped himself to coffee. The hands of the clock dragged round.

'I can't stand any more of this,' Claudia said finally. 'I'm going to find out what's happening.'

'Claudia, they'll come for you – ' Jim began, but she had already pushed the door open and was striding down the corridor. Fizz wanted to go with her, run after her.

But she was afraid, terribly afraid of what she might find.

A few minutes later the door opened and a nurse stuck her head round it. 'Miss Beaumont?' Fizz spun round. 'Do you want to pop down and see your father now? Your sister is with him. No one else,' the nurse warned, looking around the waiting room as if anticipating a sudden invasion. 'He needs to be quiet.'

Edward Beaumont was white, hollow cheeked, with a drip-tube in the back of his hand and the constant bleep of the heart and blood pressure monitor a counterpoint to the low background hum of machinery. He still managed to raise a smile for his girls, lifting the oxygen mask so that he could speak. 'Sorry to give everyone such a fright,' he said, in a series of short, gasping breaths. 'I should know better at my age.'

Fizz leaned forward to kiss him. 'Don't talk,' she said. 'Save your strength.'

'I think perhaps you should let your father rest now,' a nurse advised.

'What's the matter with him? Can I speak to the doctor?' Fizz asked.

'I'm afraid you'll have to wait until the morning to see the doctor. We're having a busy night. Has your father been under a lot of stress lately?'

'Yes,' Claudia said. 'Quite a lot.'

'Then that may be the cause of his collapse. There doesn't appear to be any obvious sign of a heart attack, although until the tests come back we can't be sure. He's being given a clot-buster drug as a precaution, that's all.'

That's all? 'Can we stay at the hospital?' Fizz asked.

'There's no need. He's not in any danger. It's likely

323

he's just suffering from nervous exhaustion. We'll ring you if there's the slightest change. I promise.' But she'd been a nurse long enough to recognize their need to be close to a loved one in trouble. 'Look, why don't you stay until he's asleep? There's tea and coffee in the waiting room. Just help yourself.'

'But if we wanted to stay?'

'I won't throw you out, but I really wouldn't advise it. And it won't do your father any good if you wear yourselves out, will it?'

Luke and Jim looked up as they went back into the waiting room. 'How is he?' Luke asked.

Claudia looked at Fizz, obviously expecting her to answer, but Fizz was incapable of speaking. 'Stress, exhaustion. Hopefully not a heart attack. He looked done in when he came to the studios. I suppose after a day of meetings the drive back here in time to record *Holiday Bay* was just too much.'

'He didn't have to do that,' Fizz said. 'We could have edited him in tomorrow.'

Claudia glanced at Luke. 'He didn't want to disappoint Melanie. He knew how much she was looking forward to her big scene with him.'

'Big scene? I thought it was just a couple of sentences?'

'Yes, but *what* sentences. We've just recorded the *Holiday Bay* equivalent of the shooting of JR, the death of Grace Archer, *The Killing of Sister George* – '

'Who are we killing off?' Fizz demanded, horrified.

'Weren't you at the script conference?'

She knew Claudia hadn't been. 'Well, yes . . . but I wasn't paying that much attention, to be honest. I've had a lot on my mind . . .' She turned as the door opened behind her.

'Mr Beaumont is asleep.' The young nurse who brought the news blushed as she found herself suddenly centre-stage. 'I really do think you should all go home. You can ring any time. First thing in the morning, as early as you like – I don't mind.'

'And you promise you'll ring us if anything happens?' Fizz asked. 'Have you got a number?'

'They've got mine,' Claudia said.

'I'll ring, I promise.'

'Come on, Fizz, we're just in the way here. Jim, can you give me a lift back to the prom? My car's still there,' Claudia asked.

'I'll come with you,' Fizz said quickly, not looking at Luke. She couldn't bear to look at him. The intensity of both loving him and hating him were too much to bear. She sensed rather than saw his determined move towards her. 'In fact I think I'll stay with you tonight, if you don't mind?'

Fizz saw Claudia frown, glance at Luke, then decide not to say what she was thinking. 'Whatever you like.'

But when Jim dropped them at the pier, Fizz didn't get into Claudia's car. 'There's something I have to do.'

'Fizz – '

'Don't worry. Someone will run me home. Or I'll get a taxi.'

'I thought you were going to stay with me. Or was that just an excuse to avoid Luke?' Fizz didn't answer. Claudia sighed. 'Patrick March should have been horse-whipped for what he did to you. I let him off far too lightly.'

'Patrick?' No one had dared to say that name in her presence for years. Suddenly it was common currency. 'What did you do to him?'

'Oh, nothing much. Just a few well-placed rumours to make nervous producers back off. I couldn't have him rocketing to stardom while you were languishing with permanent stage-fright, now, could I? It wouldn't have been right.'

'But he had real talent. With the right breaks – '

'So did you, little sister.' She kissed Fizz on the cheek. 'And he didn't give a damn for your breaks, did he? He never did anything to put things right.'

'No, I suppose not.'

'Don't feel sorry for him, Fizz. You've worked hard to make something of your life, even if it does mean slaving away in that ghastly little office. Patrick March was pretty and he had talent, but he saw a short-cut and took it without a thought for what it would do to you. If he'd had half your strength he would have made it, no matter what.' Claudia reached out, rubbed absently at her sister's cheek. 'You could still be a star if you wanted it badly enough.'

Fizz could hardly believe her ears. Claudia had been the first to say she had got the film part purely because of her name and that she shouldn't let it go to her head because she was bound to make a mess of it. And the first to race to her side when the predicted mess had hit the fan.

'Do you want it?'

'Who'd run my radio station?'

'Good grief, who would want to? Well, don't work too hard, Fizz. I'll see you at the hospital first thing. Oh, and if Luke rings, I'll tell him I've tucked you up with a hot water bottle and a sleeping pill, shall I?'

'You can tell him whatever you wish.'

'I'll let you off the hook temporarily, little sister, but he's not going away and you're going to have to face him sooner or later. Unless you plan to spend the rest of your emotional life in hiding?'

Emotional life? What a joke. 'I'm not in hiding, Claud. Not any more.' She shook her head as she anticipated her sister's interest. 'There's something I have to do. It won't take long. I'll see you in the morning.'

The station was quiet, the offices empty and dark; only the newsroom and one of the broadcasting suites were occupied so late. Fizz went straight to the recording studio and turned on the light, which flashed momentarily and then flooded the room. As she had expected, abandoned scripts lay strewn over the table and the floor where the actors had dropped them as they had read their parts. Just so much wastepaper. She gathered them up into a heap and began to sift through them, looking for a complete set.

Then she sat down and read it through quickly, anxious to get to the last few lines that seemed to have caused her father to collapse.

It was a nice twist, she thought. The wedding had been on and off for so long that the listeners must be sure that something would go wrong. But so far it hadn't. The groom survived the stag night high-jinks. Just. The bride's last-minute nerves were dealt with. Everything, in fact, proceeded as smoothly as a well-oiled clock. The tension built. Something *had* to go wrong. And of course it did. Just as the bride – Claudia's character – and her father – played by Edward – were due to set off for the church, a pretty young girl arrived and in a strong Australian accent declared herself to be the illegitimate daughter of the father of the bride. The bride's father had a heart attack. Would the wedding take place? Would the father die? Was the girl telling the truth? Who was her mother?

Fizz wished she could be certain who had come up with that particular storyline, wished she had paid more attention at the script conference. But the small, cold spot in the pit of her stomach told her that she was clutching at straws; she let her mind drift back to the first morning that Melanie had visited the radio station and knew that the answer to everything had been staring her in the face all along.

When Fizz had shown Melanie around the studio that first morning she had taken every opportunity to probe for some clue as to Luke's motives in supporting the station, still not quite able to believe that Melanie was really keen to take part in *Holiday Bay*. 'I'm surprised you're so interested in radio,' she had said, angling for some lead.

'Oh, yes. My mother loved it, you see. No lines to learn, no make-up, wearing comfortable old clothes. It was all in the voice, she said.' Melanie's face had momentarily clouded. 'I have some recordings of her, Fizz. She was really wonderful. She was always being offered parts in films and on television but she wouldn't take them. She said she enjoyed the anonymity of radio. That's why I was so pleased to get the chance to try it for myself.'

'Was your father an actor too?'

Melanie's cheeks had flushed a little. 'My mother never talked about him.' She had seen Fizz frown slightly. 'They weren't married, you see.' Fizz, about to say something casual about such a thing hardly mattering these days, to cover the girl's embarrassment, had suddenly realized that to Melanie it did. It mattered deeply. 'I thought she might have been ashamed of him. I asked her once if that was the reason she wouldn't tell me who he was.'

Fizz, heartily wishing she had never brought up the subject, had been noncommittal. 'Did you?'

'I don't think I've ever seen her so angry. Then she cried a bit and then she hugged me and said she wasn't in the least bit ashamed of him. She said he was a good man, but it was impossible for them to be together. He hadn't abandoned me. He hadn't even known about me . . .'

'She never told him?' Fizz had been shocked.

'He had a family. A wife who really needed him.'

Melanie needed him too, Fizz had thought, with a cold anger at such selfishness. 'Is that why you've come to Broomhill? To look for him?'

Melanie had stared at her. 'Broomhill? Heavens, I shouldn't think he's here. I imagine he's in Australia somewhere. I mean, why else would she have gone there in the first place?'

Why else? 'Oh, look, I'm sorry. I thought Luke said

your family had come from this area. I must have misunderstood.'

Perhaps.

Fizz got to her feet. There was nothing here to explain her father's collapse. And yet standing in the doorway of her bedroom, listening to Melanie explain what had happened, she had been so sure that there was something. 'He just said, "Juliet?" . . . Then he sort of crumpled up . . .'

She paced the studio. Maybe it was nothing. Except she had been so certain that Luke was using *Holiday Bay* in some way . . . and tonight he had as good as admitted as much. Tonight. Her mind shied away from what had happened tonight. But it was a seriously elaborate exercise just to pay back a catty remark. Rather like using a pile-driver to crack a nut.

Juliet. Who was Juliet? She'd heard the name recently.

She went through the scripts again, certain somehow that the answer must lie there. Each of the actors had their own way of highlighting their lines and she automatically sorted them into individual characters. She realized that if there was any clue to be found on the scripts it must be on either her father's or on Melanie's.

Melanie had highlighted her lines in orange Dayglo, and they were easy to pick out, but the last page was missing. She looked around, saw the corner of white paper sticking out from beneath the piano. She pulled it out and felt her heart contract as she saw the alteration to the last line and everything finally fell into place.

Click. Luke's antagonism towards her father. The

remarks that she hadn't quite understood. References to the Beaumonts' lack of family values.

Click. The press cutting that Jim had given her. It wasn't Claudia's scathing remark about Melanie that was important. It was the reporter's comment. '*I was immediately struck by her likeness to our own sweet Melanie Brett . . .*' Her father had seen the likeness at once. Had seen it and remembered something, or maybe someone, that had sent him in search of a drink.

Click. None of this was about Claudia. Oh, Luke was happy to use *Holiday Bay* to embarrass her, make her pay for an offhand remark made in those vulnerable minutes after a performance when she had still been riding high on excitement and adrenalin. But she was just a sideshow to the main attraction. His real reason for involving Melanie in the show was to use the plot to expose Edward Beaumont not only as an adulterer but a man who would abandon his child.

She stuffed her fist in her mouth to stop the scream of anguish as she sank back onto the chair. '*I must have misunderstood.*' The words were a hollow echo in her head. She hadn't misunderstood. Had Luke meant to warn her when he'd told her that Melanie's family came from the Broomhill area? Or had it been a coded message that he had assumed she would pass on to her father along with the details of their discussions about sponsorship? Did it matter? She looked again at the paper in her hand. The name 'Jill Brady' had been crossed through. 'Juliet Carey' was written above it.

'I shouldn't have changed the name.' That was what Melanie had said. Fizz read the lines.

'Of course you knew my mother. Her stage name was Juliet Carey. And when she was pregnant you walked out and left her. Well, now she's dead and I'm here to tell you that I'm your daughter – and I'm going to make sure everyone knows it.'

Art imitating life, she thought as she remembered where she had heard the name. Luke's sister had been called Juliet. Juliet Carey? What else? And with the substitution of the name it was life that had imitated art, right down to the collapse of the accused man.

And now she had to come to terms with the fact that the man she had so recently made love with, the man who had brought her back to life so that she was still agonizingly aware of every nerve-tingling touch and caress, the obliterating joy when the final breach of all her defences had made them one, the man who had taken over her mind and stolen first her heart and then her body, had quite deliberately and callously put her father in hospital.

Revenge. It was all there, easy to see when you knew what you were looking for. Claudia's career. Her radio station. And her father's reputation. Even now she could not believe he had meant to risk her father's life, not if Edward was Melanie's father too. Even Luke couldn't be that cruel. Or maybe he could, because it was plain that Melanie didn't know. Luke had found out somehow, but he hadn't told his niece.

Fizz wanted to weep. Her eyes were hot and painful, but she couldn't cry, couldn't do anything to let out the hurt. Instead she put her head on her lap and covered it

332

with her arms and prayed. For her father. For Melanie. For some kind of answer.

'Fizz?'

She stiffened, but didn't move.

'Fizz, I'm sorry. I never meant this to happen.' He took a step into the room. 'You must believe me.'

'Must I?' She lifted her head with difficulty. It was so heavy as she turned to look at him, gaunt beneath the unforgiving lights. She loved him so much, wanted so much to believe him. But her father was lying in hospital with tubes in his veins and monitors bleeping all around him. And Luke had put him there. 'How did you get Melanie to change the name?' she asked.

For a moment he remained silent, then, with the smallest lift of his shoulder, he said, 'She was having trouble with the line. She said it didn't sound convincing enough. She wanted it to be perfect.'

'She's supposed to be an actress. Or did you put the doubt in her mind?' She regarded him steadily. 'It wouldn't have been difficult. She thinks you walk on water.'

He didn't answer. He didn't have to. 'I suggested a little method exercise – you know the kind of thing.' The dark hollows in his cheeks seemed to deepen as he remembered. 'I suggested she should try and imagine how she would feel if Edward Beaumont really was the man who had abandoned her mother, had abandoned her.'

'And so she changed the name in the script.'

'It worked so well that Mel telephoned the script-writers and asked if they minded if she kept it that way.'

And of course they would have been only too pleased to help. 'And if she hadn't made it that easy for you?'

'A resourceful man will always find a way, Fizz.'

'And you are surely the most resourceful man I've ever met.'

'Too damned resourceful for my own good. I didn't mean this to happen. The recording was scheduled for tomorrow afternoon. I thought I had plenty of time to see Edward. I . . . I left a message with his secretary to tell him I wanted to see him in the morning, that it was urgent. I was going to tell him everything.'

'And that makes it all right, does it?' she flared.

'Nothing can ever make it right. But will you try to understand? My sister died because she decided, in the end, that she had to see your father. Confront him, I suppose. We'll never know what she intended to say to him. She carried that with her to the grave.' He came into the room, crouched down in front of her. 'Will you let me tell you?'

'Why should I listen to you?' she said stiffly, withdrawing against the chair, pulling away her hand as he reached for her. She couldn't allow him to touch her. Not yet. She wasn't strong enough for that.

'Because I'll do everything I can to put things right. Because I – ' He stopped himself. 'No.' He stood up. 'You're right. I won't try to justify what I did. It isn't possible.'

'No, it isn't.' She closed her eyes, desperately, desperately tired, but knowing that there could be no escape from her nightmare in sleep. 'It was the newspaper, wasn't it?' she said. 'Saying how alike they were? I thought that was why you didn't like my family, because of what Claudia said to that reporter.'

'I didn't like *Claudia* because of what Claudia said, although I have to admit that she improves with acquaintance. It wasn't the newspaper article that gave me the link, Fizz, although afterwards it seemed to confirm what I already suspected.'

'How?' she demanded. 'How can you be sure it's true? Melanie told me that she didn't know who her father was.'

'She didn't. Still doesn't.' He hesitated. 'Look, can we get out of here?'

She lifted her head, eased her neck. 'I feel as if I've been beaten all over.'

'I'm not surprised. It's been quite a night, one way and another . . .' He stopped as she turned to look at him, her bright eyes dimmed with reproach.

'A triumph all round for the resourceful Mr Devlin.'

'A triumph suggests the attainment of every desire, Fizz. This . . .' He lifted his hand in a dismissive gesture. 'This is a Pyrrhic victory. Come on, I'll take you home.' He reached out to her, offered her a hand. But she didn't take it, and after a moment he let it fall and stepped back to give her room. 'You can't stay here,' he insisted.

'How did you know where I was?' she asked, getting to her feet. 'Did Claudia tell you?'

'No. She said you were tucked up in bed fast asleep. Somehow I didn't quite believe that after what had happened you would simply go to sleep. And you always come here when you're unhappy. Maybe that's why you spend so much time working.'

'Don't try to psychoanalyse me, Luke,' she said crossly. 'I came here to find some answers to the questions that have been bothering me ever since you came to town.' She frowned. 'How did you get in, anyway?'

'The tide's out. I went down onto the beach and climbed up the inspection ladder. That's why I'm in such a mess.'

She looked at him then, really looked at him, and saw the sand and green smears of sea slime on his hands, his jacket, his wet shoes. She had climbed the safety ladder once, when she was about ten, desperate to prove that she was as tough as any boy in town. She had made it, just, but she still remembered the mouth-drying terror as she'd had to let go with one hand and swing out into space to make a grab for the handrail.

'Idiot!'

His mouth twisted in self-mockery. 'I think we've already established that.'

Outside the night was clear and bright, the moon lighting a sea curled with tiny wisps of mist about the legs of the pier, and they walked its length in silence, a clear six inches of space between them.

Luke saw her into his car, taking pains not to touch her even though he wanted to grab her, hold her, promise that he would never do anything to hurt her ever again. It took every shred of self-control to stop himself, to wait. But self-control was all he had left and he didn't speak again until she had unlocked her front door, turning to bar his way as he attempted to follow her inside.

But he wasn't going to leave her. Not until she had heard him out. 'We have unfinished business, Fizz,' he reminded her, putting his hand out to stop her shutting the door. 'Go and sit by the fire – you must be frozen. I'll make you a cup of tea.' She glared at him, standing her ground. 'Or would you prefer something stronger? We never did have that drink.'

Fizz opened her mouth to argue. Then remembered boldly telling Claudia that she had stopped hiding. 'Tea,' she conceded.

Ten minutes later Luke put a mug of hot, sugar-laden tea into her hands, and when she had curled up in an armchair he took the one opposite. For a while neither of them spoke.

'Luke?' Fizz prompted him after a while, and was aware of him coming back from some distant place, far away inside his head, as he looked up, met her gaze. 'I think you'd better tell me the whole story.'

'Only Juliet knows the whole story, but I'll tell you what I know – why I believe Edward is Melanie's father.' He paused to gather himself. 'It began when Mel asked me to take her to see your father in *The Merchant of Venice* last year. When he toured Australia.'

'That's not much of a reason – '

'You said you'd let me tell you. This is the beginning.' He waited until he was sure she would listen. 'I was happy enough to take her to the theatre,' he continued, 'but since it didn't seem quite her kind of thing I teased her a bit about having secret ambitions to be a serious actress.'

'Why?' Fizz asked. 'Why did you tease her?'

He shrugged. 'Isn't that what uncles are supposed to do? I suppose it was dreadfully patronizing of me, but most of her contemporaries want to be pop stars. I'm afraid she rather floored me by saying that was exactly what she wanted.'

'To be a serious actress?'

He nodded. 'And in her eyes the very best was Edward Beaumont, which was why she wanted to go and see him. I professed surprise that she had even heard of him, and that's when she told me.' Fizz waited in silence for a long time.

'What . . . what did she tell you, Luke?'

He stirred. 'Apparently Juliet never missed him when he appeared on the television.'

'Juliet? Melanie's mother?'

'Yes, her mother. My dear, sweet sister. Apparently she watched all his old films, had videos of that drama series he did years ago that won him every award going. Melanie told me that whenever Edward Beaumont was on the television he moved her mother to tears, and if he was that good . . .' He looked across at her. 'Tell me, Fizz, *is* he that good? Really?'

She didn't answer. Her father had charm, charisma and a feel for good commercial drama that filled theatres. Olivier he was not.

'No,' he said, apparently satisfied with her silence. 'I didn't think so.'

Fizz turned away, unable to meet his eyes. 'It isn't my opinion that matters, is it? It was your sister who was his biggest fan.'

'Yes, unfortunately, and after Mel had told me how much Juliet liked him I thought she might like a chance to see him performing live. She lived a couple of hours' drive up-country, so I rang her and suggested she come down to Sydney for a few days. I said she could go shopping with Melanie, see the play – a treat from her little brother,' he added bitterly.

Fizz waited a moment, then, unable to contain herself, demanded, 'Well? What did she say?'

'She didn't say much at all. Just that she'd think about it and call me back. Then after a day or two she rang and said she had a lot to do and didn't think she could spare the time.'

'But I thought – '

'Then she rang again and said she'd changed her mind. I should have realized then that something was up. She sounded excited – like Mel. Like she used to be . . .' He stared down at his hands, as if seeking some answer in the bottom of his mug. 'After I bought the tickets she phoned again and said she was sorry, but she wasn't up to the drive. I offered to drive up and fetch her if she liked, but she was adamant that she didn't want to come and I thought that was that.' He made a small, lost gesture, full of unspoken regret. 'I heard the weather forecast – heavy rain, flash flood warnings – but I didn't pay much attention. There was no reason why I should.'

'Luke – '

He didn't seem to hear her. 'I had a late meeting so I changed at the office, picked up Mel and we went straight to the theatre. We met some friends there and went out to supper with them. When I finally got home the answering machine was flashing. It was Juliet. She'd changed her mind; she had to see Edward.' He looked up. 'Just "Edward". Not the play, you understand, and not

Edward Beaumont. "Edward". She said she'd meet us at the theatre.' The handle snapped off his mug. 'I don't suppose you've ever seen a flash flood.'

Fizz didn't think an answer was required, but she shook her head. 'No,' she said.

'It can be dry where you are. But up-country the rain will be pouring off the hills, with the ground too hard to absorb it quickly. It fills up the dry stream-beds and they funnel it into the rivers. Hundreds of thousands of gallons of water are channelled between steep banks, with nowhere to go but in a great tidal wave downstream, taking anything in its path with it. The branches of trees, old tyres, sheep, cattle. Inside a car with the radio on you won't hear the noise. The river might just be a little bit higher than usual at the ford, but you're driving a good four-wheel drive motor – no worries. Then the steering goes soft, and you turn and look, but by then it's too late. All you see is the wall of thick brown water as it hits the side of the car. And there is nothing you can do. Nothing.'

'Oh, Luke. I'm so sorry.'

'She didn't drown. When they found her the next day she was still alive. Just.' All the time we were sitting in the theatre watching your father and sister – Shylock and Portia – fencing with words in that witty, clever, appallingly racist play, she was sitting battered, semi-conscious, up to her waist in filthy water . . .'

'Luke,' she protested, going to him, kneeling in front of him and taking his hands, unable to bear to see him in such pain. 'Don't torture yourself. It wasn't your fault.'

'No?'

She remembered herself, pulled back, rose to her feet. 'It wasn't my father's fault either,' she said. 'It wasn't anyone's fault. It was an accident.'

'If I hadn't asked her . . .' He dropped the broken handle into the mug and put it on the table beside him. 'Perhaps I just needed someone to blame.'

'And my father was handy. There isn't a scrap of evidence to prove you are right, you know. It's all circumstantial – '

'Nothing that would hold up in a court of law, maybe. But your father collapsed when he was confronted with the truth. That puts it beyond doubt in my book.'

'Beyond doubt? Oh, come on, Luke, is it really enough to prove that Melanie is – ' She stopped, suddenly comprehending what proof would actually mean.

CHAPTER 14

'Melanie is my sister,' she said, staring at him. 'If it's true, Melanie is my sister.' She gave a little gasp of joy. Then, 'And you'd be – '

'Nothing,' he cut in rapidly. 'We're not related in any way.'

For a moment she stared at him while she tried to work it out. 'But, surely . . .' One dark brow kinked upward, pointedly, and she suddenly got the message. 'Oh!' she said, her hands flying to her face as the colour flooded along her cheekbones. 'Oh, no. No, of course not.'

'I'm glad we've got that straight.'

'But Mel . . . I can't believe it. It's so wonderful.'

'You're happy about it?' he demanded, shaken to the core by her obvious delight. 'Don't you care that your father had an affair with a young woman and then callously abandoned her and his child?'

His angry reaction brought her crashing back to reality. 'No,' she protested swiftly. 'Dad would never have abandoned her.' His expression suggested that she was fooling herself. 'No,' she repeated staunchly, defending her father. 'You might not think much of his morals, Luke, and I'm not making excuses for him. He's an attractive man with more opportunities to stray than most, and God knows no one had more cause to seek comfort elsewhere, but he has never walked away from his responsibilities – '

'You know that for a fact, do you? How old were you at the time, Fizz? Four? Five at the most? I realize that you feel obliged to defend Edward. He's your father and I wouldn't expect you to do anything else. But you know nothing about this,' he said fiercely. 'I was fifteen, Fizz, quite old enough to understand what Juliet was going through. After what he did to her she never formed another relationship, never had the kind of normal, loving family existence that she was made for. She just lived for Melanie.'

'But I thought she continued with her career? She did a lot of radio work, surely? Mel told me she preferred it because she valued her anonymity.'

'That's ridiculous.' He was dismissive. 'She still had a beautiful voice but she had lost that wonderful sparkle, that special confidence that every actress needs. You've seen Claudia put it on like a dress the moment she's got an audience. Juliet didn't want an audience; it was almost as if she was hiding . . .' Fizz gasped and his voice died away as he realized what he was saying.

'She *was* hiding, but not because she lacked confidence. If what you're saying is true, she didn't *want* my father to find her.'

He was by her side in an instant, louring over her, his fingers biting into her arm. 'And why wouldn't she want him to find her?' His voice had a dangerous edge, but she wasn't afraid of him. She put her hand over his and he immediately loosened his grip, tried to move back, embarrassed by the violence of his reaction. But she didn't let him go, taking his hand, holding it between hers. She had to make him see.

'Can't you see what happened, Luke? *She* was the one who ran away. She never told him about the baby.'

'But that's ridiculous . . . she needed all the help she could get. There was just our mother, and she was never strong. It was struggle enough for us, without the added burden – ' He made an oddly awkward gesture. 'She helped where she could, but it wasn't much, and I was still at school. Juliet knew that, so why would she have made things difficult by depriving herself of the support she needed and Melanie of her father?'

'Why, indeed?' Fizz asked gently. 'If the great, the glamorous Edward Beaumont, with his squeaky clean reputation to protect, was her lover, why didn't she demand it? She could have done. Oodles of support for herself and the baby. He would surely have paid up if it had been money she wanted.'

She saw him pause to reflect on the oddity of his sister's actions. But she didn't need to reflect; she knew why Juliet had hidden herself away, kept her secret. She had no doubts now that it was true, all of it. He wanted to know the truth? Well, she could tell him that.

'Juliet didn't demand help, Luke, because she loved my father so much that she wanted him to believe he was the one who was deserted. She let him go rather than put him through the agony of making an impossible choice.' He moved to interject, but she stopped him. 'Luke, nineteen years ago my mother was badly injured in a car accident.'

The time-scale was not lost upon him. 'Nineteen years?' he repeated, but she was barely aware of his voice as it all came flooding back.

'Elaine French. My beautiful, talented mother. I've been told that her walk was so graceful, so sensous that she could turn the head of a monk. After the accident she never walked again. Not because she couldn't, but because she refused to submit to the shambling limp that was all she could manage. And she hid herself away from all those adoring fans, the men who had danced attendance on her, fêted her with flowers and presents. She couldn't bear anyone to see her. The only person she would allow near her was my father, and she made him pay for that every day for the rest of her life.'

Luke was clearly shocked. 'I thought she just retired?'

Fizz closed her eyes briefly. 'No, Luke, she never retired. She never stopped performing. Drama was her life, the very air she breathed. She never, for one minute, stopped being the leading lady, the centre of attraction, the star. There are albums and albums of press cuttings up in the attic at home. Beautiful pictures of her with Claudia and me – taken before the accident, of course – with touching declarations that she was leaving the stage to devote her life to her family. Leaving the stage while they still wanted more. She was right about that. She received fan letters until the day she died. There are always fresh flowers on her grave and someone still puts a message in the *in memoriam* column of *The Times* every year on the anniversary of her death.'

'I had no idea.'

'No one did. And until she died she had to be content with Dad and Claudia and me as her audience. Some days she would be the dying Marguerite – pale, self-sacrificing. Some days she planned a triumphant come-back. Norma Desmond in a wheelchair. Some days she was Cleopatra, betrayed and noble. They were bearable. The terrible days were when she was just herself – unhappy, bitter, vindictive.' She drew a deep breath. 'There has been a lot of rubbish written about Dad's career sliding after she retired, about him never being quite as good without her. It's true that they were wonderful on stage together, but the fact is my father gave up some of the best offers he ever had to stay at home and nurse her. I never once heard him complain.'

He pulled away from her. 'She was his wife, for God's sake! For better, for worse – isn't that the way it goes?'

'Is that what you think? Well, Dad would agree with you, I suppose. He may not have been the most faithful husband in the world, Luke, but he stuck to the spirit of that vow when most men would have walked away. You see, my mother was with her lover when they crashed.'

'Oh, God.'

'No, not God. He just thought he was. He was a politician, a pillar of the community, a very publicly married man. He was driving my mother when the car overturned on a bend. He'd been drinking, of course; they both had. He escaped with barely a scratch to his body, and as for his reputation – well, I suppose he had powerful friends to hush things up.' She raised a rueful smile. 'I doubt he'd get away with it these days.' Then,

346

'He never went to see her in hospital. Never even sent her flowers in case he should be found out. The story was that she had fallen asleep at the wheel. Minor injuries.'

'And your father let him get away with that?'

'You wouldn't have, would you, Luke? Not your style at all. But Dad knew how much she would have hated the world to know that the superwoman image of loving wife, devoted mother, shimmering star, was all a sham. That her children were simply props to be paraded on appropriate occasions for the Press and consigned to nannies for the rest of time. That her marriage was a hollow farce. He always protected her – before the accident and even more so afterwards. No one ever knew about the terrible injuries she suffered.

'It wasn't just the wheelchair. She was dreadfully scarred. Mentally as well as physically.' She looked up at him. 'He was offered a knighthood that year. It gave him the utmost pleasure to turn it down. That way they could never say they had bought his silence. My mother never forgave him for that either.' She shrugged. 'It's the truth, Luke, but I can't make you believe it.'

Luke, remembering the photograph of Elaine French with her children in the snow, and his own instinctive feeling that it was a stage-managed media event, believed it.

'So that's why Juliet went to Australia after giving birth. She said she wanted a new start. I always assumed it was because she felt she was a drain on Mum and on me.'

'And you felt guilty.'

'Guilty for driving her away. And utterly helpless to

do anything about it,' he said, flaring briefly. 'But it wasn't anything to do with me, was it? She knew that if she'd stayed in England, in the small world of the theatre, she could never have kept Melanie a secret.' He dragged his hand over his face. 'Lord, how she must have loved him.'

'Luke,' she said urgently. 'He suffered too. It's too late to put things right for Juliet, but he'd want to know about Melanie. And she has a right to know who her father is. Straight away. Now.' She drew back a little. 'Just in case . . .' Just in case the nurse had been wrong. Just in case her father didn't make it.

'I always intended Edward to know that Melanie is his daughter, Fizz. But first I wanted him to work with her, get to know her – love her, I suppose. It's difficult not to.'

'And once you'd exposed him publicly, ruined his reputation, then what?'

'I wasn't going to expose him publicly. Financial ruin was all I had in mind, but first I wanted him to know what he had lost. I wanted him to suffer as my sister suffered.'

She drew in a sharp breath at the sheer arrogance of the man. 'Don't you think Melanie might have wanted a say in that? Or were you so bound up in revenge that you didn't care about hurting her too?'

'I wasn't going to tell her.' He looked down at her, then away, unable to face the accusation in her clear bright eyes. 'I was going to take his life away from him, piece by piece. His money. His radio station. His daughter's career on the stage.'

His radio station? Of course, Luke hadn't known that Pavilion Radio belonged to her. 'And me?' she demanded hoarsely. 'What were you going to do to me?' But she already knew the answer. He had been going to make her fall in love with him and then break her heart, treat her just as he believed her father had treated his sister. And in that one single intent he had achieved success beyond his wildest dreams.

'You trembled the first time I touched you. God help me, I thought it was going to be so easy. But you defeated me, Fizz.' He extended his hand. 'See? I'm the one trembling now.'

She lifted her face to look up into his. 'When you plan revenge, Luke, you don't do it by halves, do you?'

'I've never done anything by halves. Even falling in love with you. But perhaps that kind of love runs in the family.'

'No,' she said urgently. He had no right to talk of love. She couldn't bear it. 'I want you to go. Now.'

For a moment he looked at her, searched her face. Then he nodded, once. 'Yes, it's late, and Melanie will be anxious for news of Edward.'

She was unprepared for his acquiescence, expecting something more. A fresh attempt to justify what he had done. An apology. Even an ardent declaration of love, although the idea terrified her because she would never know whether it was true or some other devious game. She should have been relieved, but she wasn't.

'Are you going to tell her the whole story, Luke?' she asked. 'If you don't, I will.'

He leaned forward, touched her cheek with his hand

'Leave it to me, Fizz I'll clean up my own mess. I owe you that much.'

That was all? He'd come into her life, turned it upside down so that it would never be the same again, and now he intended simply to tidy up and walk away.

'*Owe* me!' she exclaimed, suddenly angrier than she had been throughout the entire revelation of his plans to avenge his sister. 'You don't owe me anything, Luke Devlin.' She looked around her, fit to throw something, anything, and saw on her desk the forgotten bank draft and the hated agreement. She seized them and thrust them at him. 'And you have no claim on me either.' He made no move to relieve her of the papers. 'Take them!' she demanded. 'I want an end to it.'

He took the draft, looked at it for a moment. Then he raised his eyes to meet hers. 'You couldn't raise this kind of money a week ago. Where did it come from?'

'I took the advice of the most ruthless man I have ever met,' she declared.

His mouth tightened, recognizing the intention to wound. 'And what advice was that?' he asked softly.

'To let someone else take the risk. You were right, of course, I should never have gone into the restaurant business. I've sold the lease on the Pavilion Restaurant and paid off the bank loan.'

His eyes narrowed. 'If you had done that I would have been told.'

'Would you?' Well, yes, of course he would have been told. She had anticipated that, which was why she had persuaded Julian to mislay the papers for a few days so that he wouldn't be able to interfere with her plans. 'If

350

you don't believe me, I suggest you check with your sources at the bank.'

'But you worked so hard for this . . . Is it too late to stop it?' he asked. When she didn't answer, he swore softly. 'Fizz, I'm sorry.'

'Are you? Well, I suppose it's just as well to get all your apologies over with in one day. But don't be too sad. John Moore, my chef, as I'm sure you'll remember, has been given family help to raise the finance for the lease. And he's negotiating for the spare space in the Winter Gardens too; he wants to use it for an old fashioned ice-cream parlour. You've actually done me a favour, Luke, because now I've got the best of both worlds,' she said, with just a touch of defiance, daring him to contradict her.

'Don't be kind, Fizz. I know what I've done.' He handed the draft back to her. 'And I'm afraid you have your sponsorship whether you want it or not.' As he pressed it into her hand he leaned forward, and for just a moment his mouth brushed hers before she gathered sufficient strength of will to step back. 'No strings attached,' he said. Then, turning swiftly, he headed down the stairs and out into the street.

She stared after him for a long time, then, shivering as the cold from the street door reached her landing, shivering with shock and anxiety and a cold, hollow feeling that chilled her to the bone, she rubbed at her arms and closed the door.

The freesias were still there, where he had left them on the hall table, their sweet scent reaching out to her. She couldn't leave them there to wither and die, and she couldn't, despite her declared intention, cold-heartedly dump them in the bin. So she put them in a silver bud vase and stood them on her desk beside the unwanted bank draft.

She looked at her watch. Four o'clock. Too early to ring the hospital, but she couldn't face her bed, sheets rumpled from the bittersweet moments of passion in Luke's arms. Instead, she curled up on the sofa and closed her eyes.

It was still dark when she telephoned the hospital. Her father had just woken and the nurse passed on his message that he needed a toothbrush and razor, his own pyjamas and a dressing gown – the blue silk Paisley one. Fizz raised a smile at that. He was definitely on the mend. Relief lifted her spirits a little, and after a brief hot shower to wake herself up she went to collect her father's things.

Claudia, who had also telephoned the hospital, was already packing them.

'Do you think they'll allow visitors in at dawn?' she asked Fizz, smothering a yawn as she folded the specified dressing gown into a bag.

'Just for a minute or two while we give him his clean pyjamas. We can go back later for a proper visit.' Fizz touched her sister's arm. 'Claudia, I've got something to tell you.'

She looked up, then straightened. 'Lord, Fizz, what is it?'

'I don't quite know how to begin.'

Claudia stared at her for a moment. 'No, you *can't* be pregnant. You haven't known him long enough.'

'How long does it take?'

'I'll rephrase that. You haven't known him long enough to be certain.'

Fizz felt the colour flooding to her cheeks. 'No. Well. It's not that. Look, I think we'd better sit down. This is going to take some time.'

So Claudia sat down and Fizz told her that they had a sister. That Edward Beaumont had his three daughters after all.

They arrived at the hospital just after seven and found Melanie waiting for them in the day room. She leapt up as they entered, clearly nervous of her reception, and there was a moment of awkwardness when no one seemed to know quite what to do. Then Claudia stepped forward to hug the younger girl. Fizz joined her, and for a moment everyone was overcome with tears and laughter.

'Mel?' They turned as one at the sound of Luke's voice. He looked, Fizz thought, as bad as any man she had seen who was still walking, his skin drained of colour, his eyes all dark hollows. 'Edward would like to see you.'

For a moment she didn't move. Then she turned to Fizz and Claudia. 'Do you mind?'

Claudia gave her a little push. 'It's your big moment, kid. Go take a bow.'

'I know it's stupid, but my legs won't work.'

'Come on. I'll hold your hand as far as the door.'

'After that I'm on my own?'

'On your own? Hey, you're a Beaumont,' she said with a broad grin. 'You'll never be on your own again.'

When they had gone, leaving her alone with Luke, Fizz shifted awkwardly, turning to the window to stare out at the sea.

'How is he this morning?' she asked.

'Sad to hear about Juliet. He talked about her. Wept a little. But to discover that he was loved so much, that they had a daughter – ' he raked his thick dark hair back from his forehead with his fingers ' – to discover that would, I think, be sufficient to put the life back into any man.' He looked down at her. 'Are *you* going to be all right, Fizz? You look tired.'

And he didn't? 'The station won't fall apart if I take a few days off to catch up on my sleep.'

'Won't it? I thought you were afraid it might disappear altogether if you weren't there to keep an eye on it twenty-four hours a day,' he said, trying to tempt a smile from her.

She half turned, looking down, avoiding his eyes. 'I thought you wanted the radio station. I was so afraid that you would try to take it from me that it blinded me to everything else. I suppose that's why I never saw the real danger.' She drew in a deep breath. 'No, that's not true. I always recognized the danger, but it was blurred, confused by . . . by everything. Last night was a mistake, Luke.' Her gesture, small, restrained, painful, needed no words. 'Now, I think I'd better go and find Claudia.'

Fizz had left all the arrangements for the restaurant launch party to John and Susie, and as a result discovered that there was nothing for her to do but enjoy herself. Unfortunately, enjoying herself was the last thing she was capable of. She felt lost and very alone, despite the crush of guests. Any sense of achievement in the restaurant had been leached away by the announcement of its takeover by John. The evening was his, and she did not begrudge him his moment, but it left her feeling superfluous, a hostess whose party had moved on.

She looked around. Edward, seated in state, still officially taking things easy, was enjoying the flattering attention of his new-found daughter and didn't need her. Claudia had spotted Julian the moment he arrived and, informing Fizz that she didn't know a good thing when she saw one, had appropriated him for herself.

Susie, she knew, had invited Luke, even though she had personally crossed him off the guest list. She had not seen him since their encounter in the hospital and she dreaded meeting him again, but as the evening wore on it seemed increasingly likely that even he would not put in an appearance to disturb the tedium of the occasion.

Then the door opened behind her and Fizz, not meaning to, turned. It wasn't Luke, but she still felt the sudden wobble of her knees. Her throat dried and her pulse was racketing like a drum. Not with excitement, not with desire, but with anger.

'Patrick March.' The words, though startled from her, had a dead quality, nothing of welcome. 'What are you doing here?'

'I asked Susie to send him an invitation.' And this time the knee wobble mattered as Luke closed the door behind him. 'I've suddenly become very conscious of the damage that can be caused by unlaid ghosts.'

'And, having finally laid all yours to rest, you're on a

crusade?' She lifted her chin, the sparkle back in her eyes.

'Something like that.'

Claudia appeared at her side. 'Well, this is a pretty gathering,' she said. 'Can I offer either of you gentlemen a drink?'

'Thank you.' Patrick March seized the opportunity with evident relief. 'A whisky. A large one.'

'I do hope you're not driving. Oh, no. Of course not. You lost your licence last year, didn't you?' Claudia didn't wait for an answer. 'Luke?' He shook his head. Fizz waited. Patrick fidgeted. Claudia returned. 'Whisky for you, Patrick. And I brought this for you, Fizz. I'll leave the target to your discretion.' She offered Fizz a bowl piled up with avocado mousse.

'Take it away, Claudia,' she declared crossly. 'This isn't a farce. Luke was right first time. It's a melodrama – a very bad one. Drink up, Patrick and start walking. It's a long way down the pier, but Luke isn't stopping either, so he can keep you company.'

'We'll go in minute, Fizz, but I brought him with me because he has something to say to you,' Luke insisted quietly.

'Nothing I want to hear.'

'Fizz, please,' Patrick pleaded. 'Listen to me, please. I have to . . . want to tell you how sorry I am for what I did to you. Truly sorry. I used you without a second thought. When I asked you to marry me I was thinking only of myself, of what marrying you would do for my career. The worst thing was not coming clean, pretending that it was all your fault. I was still lying about it even

356

a couple of weeks ago, to Mr Devlin. He's made me see how wrong it is.' The room had fallen silent; everyone was looking in his direction. 'There are no excuses. I don't expect you to forgive me. I just wanted you to know that I'll do whatever you want to put things right.'

The silence stretched endlessly as the second hand ticked around the clock. Then Claudia touched her arm and Fizz stirred. 'Very pretty,' she said. 'I hope your speech-writer was well paid.'

'Fizz,' he protested. 'That came straight from the heart.'

'Did it?' Perhaps it had. But that convincing sincerity had once been his stock in trade. He had missed his vocation when he took to the stage. He would have made a far better politician. 'If you say so.' She looked at his empty glass. 'I'm sure you could do with another drink after that ordeal.' She made a gesture towards the bar. 'Help yourself.'

The other guests let out a collectively held breath and Patrick was absorbed into a crowd that began to buzz with excited conversation. Then Julian appeared at her side and glared briefly at Luke before saying, 'Can I do anything, Fizz? Throw anyone out? Hit anyone? You only have to ask.'

Luke glared him. 'Do I know you?' he asked.

Before he could answer Claudia pulled him away. 'Come and dance, darling, before you get into trouble.'

Fizz waited in the quiet space that surrounded the two of them, and finally Luke broke the silence. 'If I come back in seven years, Fizz, will you be as generous to me?' He looked across the room to where Patrick was helping himself to food from the buffet.

'Seven years? A century wouldn't be long enough to atone for what you tried to do, so very nearly *did*, to my family.'

'You hate me that much?'

'Hate you? If I could hate you, Luke, I could anticipate that one day I might be able to feel what I feel for Patrick. Nothing. But you came here to make me fall in love with you and you succeeded beyond your wildest dreams. That I cannot forgive.'

'But you loved Patrick once – ' he began.

'I thought I loved him, but it was just infatuation.' She'd had two weeks to think about it, to compare the pangs of calf love with the real thing. 'No doubt I'd have got over him in a few weeks if he hadn't betrayed me quite so brutally, if I hadn't been quite so young. But I shall never get over you.'

He looked at her for a moment before nodding, accepting that she meant precisely what she said. 'Then we must both suffer for my mistakes. If you need anything, Phillip will be taking over here. Just call him.'

'You're going away?'

'Oh, yes. Unless you call me back, Broomhill has seen the last of me.' He waited a moment. 'Goodbye, Fizz.'

'Goodbye, Luke.' She was still staring at the door when Claudia, taking pity on her, put her cloak about her shoulders and took her home.

'Fizz? It's on. We're going to do it!'

She looked up from her desk as Claudia bounced into her office and plumped herself down on the sofa. She had moved into her father's luxurious suite on the mezzanine floor and she was busy preparing to do battle for the retention of her franchise, well aware that a rival was preparing to try and outbid her. But she sat back, ready to listen to her sister's news. 'What are you going to do?'

'*Private Lives*! Amanda for me, Sibyl for Melanie, with Dad directing. I can't believe our luck.'

Fizz sighed. 'Oh, I'm sure you can, if you think about it. Luke is using his money to put your lives back together. Money is all he has left.'

'Don't be paranoid, Fizz. It's being backed by a well-known theatrical entrepreneur.'

She shrugged. 'If you say so. But I wouldn't have expected him to be obvious about it; he's far too clever for that.'

'Have you heard from him?'

Fizz shook her head.

'Do you expect to?'

'Not this side of a hundred years.'

'A hundred years? Is that the time-scale you've laid down for forgiveness?'

'I didn't want him to be in any doubt.'

'But he loves you.'

Fizz raised her brows.

'He would have stayed if he didn't,' Claudia said. 'You must know that.'

'I know nothing of the sort.'

'And it will break his heart not to see Melanie make her West End debut.'

'The more so, I imagine, since he's footing the bill.'

'It'll be a sell-out. He'll get his investment back and a handsome profit.'

'Then nothing much has changed, has it?'

Claudia stood up. 'Nothing at all. You've wasted seven years because of that bastard Patrick March and now you're doing it all over again. This life isn't a rehearsal, Fizz, you only get one crack at it. And it's all your baby will have. Perhaps you should ask Melanie what that feels like.'

Fizz flushed. 'How did you know I was pregnant?'

Claudia smiled, turning in the doorway. 'You're my sister. I know *you*. Of course, the fact that you've been regularly rushing out of meetings to throw up hasn't gone unnoticed either,' she added.

'I haven't!' Fizz stared at her sister. 'Are you telling me that everyone knows?'

'Everyone except the father. Melanie wanted to write and tell him, but I told her it was better not to mention you at all in her letters. I thought the silence would drive him crazy and he'd come back all the quicker.' She shrugged. 'Of course, I didn't know about the hundred-year embargo.'

'No one is to tell him anything,' Fizz said.

'Oh, I agree. That's your job. But I wouldn't leave it too long,' she added, eyes full of mischief, 'or he won't be around to rub your back when you need him most.'

After Claudia had gone Fizz sat for a long time staring out of the window. A warm Easter had brought the crowds flocking to the sea and the pier was thronging with hordes of happy visitors. The restaurant was busy, the shop was selling stock as fast as it could be put on the shelves and advertisers were clamouring for air-time because of the publicity about Melanie. She should

360

have been happy. She put her hand to her waist. She was happy, she told herself. Perfectly happy.

'Perfectly happy,' she said out loud, defying anyone to contradict her. No one did, because her office, like her life, had only one occupant. Claudia was right; without Luke neither her life nor her baby's life could ever be truly complete. If only there was some way to know how he had felt about her before his guilt and her pride had got in the way.

Susie put her head around the door. 'Are you feeling generous? I'm collecting for a wedding present for Jim and Maggie.'

Fizz reached for her bag and took out her wallet. 'Here,' she said, stuffing a note into the big brown envelope. 'What are you getting them?'

'We thought a pram.' Susie grinned. 'They do say it's catching,' she added cheekily.

'They do say everything comes in threes. I'd be careful if I were you,' Fizz warned as Susie beat a hasty retreat.

Fizz pushed her wallet back in her bag. Stuffed to the seams with receipts and bills, it protested, and she sighed, pulling out a handful of paper to sort out – some to be passed to Accounts, most to be tossed in the bin. She was sifting through them when she came across the letter that Luke had left on her doorstep weeks earlier, the night of the party at Winterbourne Manor. The night she had fled the scene of her embarrassment and he had come after her.

It was creased, stained, still unopened. She laid it on the desk in front of her. She wanted to know how he had felt, really felt, before they had so briefly become lovers, before her father had collapsed. Could this grubby envelope possibly give her the answer?

Her heart beating too fast for comfort, she pushed her thumb under the flap. The single sheet of paper didn't say much, but the few words were enough: 'Tonight was real, Fizz. Whatever happens I want you to know that, Luke.'

Whatever happens. The words were scrawled, hurried, with nothing studied or careful in their composition. And everything about the groundwork in his plans to destroy her family had been both those things. Nothing had been left to chance. He must have been so relieved when he realized she had thrown this note away unopened.

She picked up the letter and laid it against her cheek, laughed a little, then wiped away a tear with the back of her hand. She knew it was genuine for the simple reason that he would have taken so much more trouble if it had been his intention to deceive.

CHAPTER 15

Luke saw the long plume of dust turning pink in the setting sun long before he could hear the complaining note of the Jeep as it climbed the long, slow rise to his campsite.

He stood up to poke his fire into life, threw on some more wood and set a billy to boil. Visitors were rare this far out in the bush, and even if not particularly welcome the civilities still had to be observed. He glared down at the trail before turning away and ducking inside his store tent to pick out a couple of extra tins for supper. There wasn't much to choose from. He'd have to head back to civilization soon. But what then?

Melanie had a new family, her letters were full of them – at least full of Claudia and Edward. They were tactfully silent on the subject of Fizz. Another couple of weeks and she'd be opening in the West End of London, and he wouldn't even be there to see her.

His plans for Harries were in Phillip's capable hands. He wasn't needed in Broomhill.

He looked around the tent and thought briefly, painfully of Winterbourne Manor. He'd made an offer for the place, had planned to lay it in Fizz's lap as his wedding present.

His mouth tightened. Everything he had striven for, worked so hard to achieve, had been thrown away in a mindless, stupid act of revenge. He might have all the wealth he would ever need, but in his heart he was right back where he had started all those years ago, when he had followed Juliet to Australia after their mother had died. Only then he had had a goal, ambition. What was left to him now but to make more money? A man needed more than that.

He thought of Fizz, wondered what she was doing. He half smiled. He knew. He could see her shivering in that poky little office at the top of the Pavilion, worrying away at a column of figures. She needed more than that too. Love, a family of her own.

He laughed out loud. God, what was he thinking of? Nothing to strive for? When she was there, in Broomhill? Damn it, he'd go back and convince her. Lay siege to the pier for every day of her hundred years if necessary. Refuse to take no for an answer.

He tossed up a can of beans, caught it, added a can of stew. The decision had been made, and a great weight lifted from him as he backed out of the tent prepared to offer his unexpected guest a very warm welcome. He was halfway through the flap when he saw something small and bright glinting in the sand.

He stooped to pick it up and held it towards the slanting rays of the sunlight. It was a small gold leaf, spinning and dancing as it hung from his fingers. The earring Fizz had lost in the study at Winterbourne. It must have fallen out of his wallet when he had taken out Melanie's last letter to read again, hoping, as always, for some hidden message between the lines. Some indication that there was hope.

And suddenly, quite suddenly, as the Jeep breasted the rise, even before he turned round, he knew who it was.

He turned as the engine stilled and she was there, her eyes echoing the deepening blue of the evening sky as she regarded him gravely, quietly waiting for him to speak. His heart felt so big that he thought it might burst at seeing her. He couldn't move. He couldn't speak.

'Have you a spare bed for a weary traveller?' she said at last.

'Not spare,' he replied hoarsely. 'But you're very welcome to share my sleeping bag.'

'Am I? Truly? After all the things I said?'

He crossed the hard ground to her then, wrenched open the Jeep door and took her into his arms. 'Oh, my dear, my lovely girl. Will you let me show you just how welcome?'

She held him back a little, her manner reserved, uncertain. 'I haven't come alone, Luke.' His brows drew into a sharp frown and he glanced behind her. Then he saw the unconsciously protective gesture to her waist and he understood.

'You're pregnant?' His joy was short-lived. 'Sweet Jesus, you're pregnant!' He was so angry he could kill. 'Just what kind of an idiot are you? Driving out here by yourself! Another day and I'd have been gone. Anything could have happened to you.' He stared down at her. 'To our baby.'

'I didn't drive all the way. I flew to the nearest sheep station,' she said.

'Flew! Is that a good idea?'

'I thought so. I used a regular aeroplane. It had an engine and everything.'

'Two.' He looked distraught. 'Please tell me it had two engines.'

'I didn't notice. And the station foreman was coming this way, so he pointed out your camp. He loaned me the Jeep and said he'd watch out to make sure I made it.' A smile widened her beautiful, enticing mouth. 'I expect he's got a pair of glasses trained on us right now, and if you don't kiss me within the next ten seconds he'll come roaring up here to take me back with him.'

Luke Devlin put his arms around the girl he loved and for a while had been certain that he'd lost. 'Let him try,' he said, gathering her to him. 'Just let him try.'

'Luke,' she said a long time later, as they lay under the brilliant starscape. 'Where were you going tomorrow?'

'Tomorrow?'

'You said that you wouldn't have been here tomorrow.'

'Oh, tomorrow.' She heard the laughter in his voice and dug him in the ribs with her elbow. 'I was going home,' he said. 'To Broomhill. To lay seige to a particularly stubborn woman I happen to love.'

'To lay seige?' It was her turn to laugh. 'How?'

He began to quote softly. ' "Make me a willow cabin at your gate, And call upon my soul within the house; Write loyal cantons of contemned love, And sing them loud even in the dead of night – "'

'Stop! That's enough. My neighbours would never stand for singing, particularly in the dead of night.'

'Then move out. Marry me and you shall live in Winterbourne Manor.'

She didn't answer immediately. 'You don't have to marry me just because I'm pregnant, Luke. I didn't come for that.'

'Didn't you?' He pulled away from her, sat up, his back hunched to her. 'Then why did you come, Fizz? To inform me of the good news and tell me how much child support you expect?' He glared at her, his eyes glinting dangerously in the starlight.

Fizz just grinned back. 'If I'd just wanted money I wouldn't have come all this way, I'd have gone to Phillip. That was what you meant, wasn't it?' He didn't answer and she reached out, slid her hand over his back. 'What I want from you can't be handled by an accountant.'

He expression lightened. 'Are you telling me that you just want me for my body?'

'You don't think you're getting off that lightly, do you?' She pushed herself up beside him and nuzzled his shoulder. 'This baby is going to be a family concern, and you are going to have to do your bit.'

'Oh? And what exactly is my bit?' he said, rolling over, pushing her back against the thick down of the sleeping bag, trapping her there.

'Hand-holding, back-rubbing – and the books I've read about natural childbirth have whole chapters on the subject of panting. I think it might be a good idea if we go to classes – '

'We? You really mean that?'

She took his hand, could feel it trembling as she pressed it against her waist. 'This is our baby, Luke. A life we made together. Luke Devlin and Felicity Beaumont made into a new person – unique, special. I thought . . . I thought we'd call her Juliet.'

'You're that sure it will be a girl?'

'Positive.' Then her lips curved into a provocative little smile. 'Of course, if I'm wrong, we'll just have to keep on trying.'

He lifted her into his arms then, and held her. 'Fizz, I don't know what to say, how to tell you how much I love you. You are so beautiful, so good, so generous . . .'

She tilted back her head. 'And?'

'And sexy as hell,' he said, his voice husky.

Her teeth gleamed white in the darkness. 'Well, I did want to be sure I hadn't *imagined* how good it was.'

'And had you?'

'Oh, no. That's included in the job description as well.'

'I see. Well, Miss Beaumont, I have a job description for you. It's headed "Wife". If you want my body on a regular basis you're going to have to promise to marry me the minute we get back to Broomhill.' He bent his lips to the smooth contour of her breast, blushed pink in the dying firelight, teasing its rosy tip with his tongue until she was clinging to him. Then he raised his head. 'What do you say?' he asked.

'That's not fair,' she exploded. Then, as he began to pull away, 'I promise!'

'Cross your heart?'

'On one condition.'

'Anything.'

'When you buy Winterbourne Manor, will you make sure the four-poster bed comes with it?'

He laughed out loud. He'd always known the four-poster would get her in the end. 'Whatever it costs,' he promised her softly. 'But for tonight I'm afraid you'll have to make do with a sleeping bag on the hard ground.'

'If you were sharing it,' she murmured softly as she reached for him, 'I'd be happy on a bed of nails.'

As *Private Lives* came to an end the house erupted in wild applause – the curtain-calls going on, it seemed, for ever, the flowers arriving on stage for Claudia and Melanie extravagant by any standards, and the appearance of Edward Beaumont as the director of the play bringing forth a renewed round of cheering.

Fizz and Luke, sitting in a box overlooking the stage, exchanged a glance.

'I was rather afraid that Claudia would wipe the floor with Melanie,' Luke said.

'Were you?'

'It must have been tempting to try.'

'She might well have done, my darling, but for one small detail.'

'Claudia took it easy on her because she's family?'

'No, love, she simply recognized the quality of the opposition. Melanie is a Beaumont, after all, and Beaumonts are born to the limelight.'

He saw the excitement shimmering from her, lighting her eyes, and something very like fear clutched at his heart. 'You're a Beaumont too. Don't you long for that acclaim?'

She must have heard the odd note in his voice because she turned and looked up at him. 'I'm into production these days,' she reminded him, patting the barely visible swell of her body where their baby was growing.

'And afterwards?'

'Shh, darling . . .' She put her hand on his arm. 'Dad's going to make a speech.'

And while the audience listened, held in the palm of his hand, Edward Beaumont told the world he had found a daughter so long lost to him. For a moment there was stunned silence, then the crowd rose to its feet as Claudia and Edward Beaumont presented Melanie Brett Beaumont to them.

'The man's a genius,' Luke said with genuine admiration. 'Seats have been selling like crazy because everyone wanted to see Melanie make a fool of herself. Now she's a triumph. More than that, she's a Beaumont. She'll be on the front page of every newspaper tomorrow and tickets for the show will be like gold-dust.'

'And Claudia, despite being leading lady, is having to take a back seat? Was that part of your plan, too?'

'No, my love. I've no plans for anyone but us.' He looked back at the stage. 'And I'm sure Claudia's graciousness in giving her new sister centre-stage on her West End debut will be given generous mention.' He stood up, drew back Fizz's chair, and as she turned to him smiled. 'Not that either of them can compare with the beautiful Felicity Devlin.' He took her hands in his. 'You do know how much I love you?' he said urgently.

She laughed softly. 'I promise I'll never tire of hearing you say it.'

'I love you. I love you. I love you.'

'Don't stop!'

'I'd rather show you,' he said, his voice husky with longing. 'Right now.'

'But if we don't make an appearance at the party people will talk.'

'Oh? And what will they say?' He was delighted to discover that he could still make her blush. 'That Devlin couldn't wait to take his lovely wife home to bed?'

'Something like that.'

Luke grinned. 'They'd be right.'

'Well . . . I suppose if we go backstage now, and tell everyone how absolutely fabulous they were, we'll have done our duty. They'll be so high on adrenalin and excitement that they won't remember whether we went to the party or not.'

But the moment they walked in to the dressing room Claudia rushed across to them. '*The Three Sisters*, Fizz,' she exclaimed. 'Dad says he'll do it next year if you'll take part.' Linking her arm with Fizz, she turned to Luke. 'We can't leave her out of all this excitement, and she deserves another chance to show what she can do. You'd never guess it to look at her, but underneath that cool, touch-me-not exterior she positively smoulders with repressed passion.'

'Does she?' he enquired, with studied surprise.

Claudia laughed as her sister coloured. 'I'm all technique and sex appeal. As you've obviously discovered for

371

yourself, Fizz is the real thing.' She touched his arm. 'You wouldn't mind, would you, darling?'

He would mind. He would positively hate it. But he'd seen the way Fizz had lit up in the atmosphere and the excitement of the theatre. She had been robbed of her chance to become a star once. If she really wanted it, he would not do anything to stop her. 'Fizz is quite capable of making up her own mind, Claudia. Whatever she does, she knows she'll have my support.'

'There you are. Say you'll do it!'

'Don't be silly, Claud. I'm going to have a baby. That's a full-time job.'

'Rubbish.' She appealed to Luke. 'She can have a nanny, can't she?'

'She can have anything she wants.'

But Fizz started. 'A nanny?' For a moment, for just a moment, she been dazzled by the lights, the excitement, and she had been tempted. But remembering the confusing procession of nannies who had tried to provide a little love and warmth until her own mother could find a few spare moments for her daughters, she blenched.

Claudia saw her face and remembered too. Impulsively she flung her arms about her sister and held her for a moment. 'No. Of course not. Silly of me.' Then she stepped back, quickly blinking away a tear, to flash a brilliant smile. 'For goodness' sake take her home, Luke. Back to the real world. It's where she belongs.'

In the limousine, gliding quietly through the empty London streets, he held her hand. 'Are you sure, Fizz? For a moment I thought you wanted it.'

'For a moment, so did I.' She turned to him. 'But I

don't. All I want is you and our baby. I've never been surer of anything in my life.'

He took her in his arms then, and held her. 'I suppose I still can't quite believe you're mine. After what I did.'

She placed her fingers lightly over his mouth. 'That's all over, Luke. Forgotten.'

'I'll always be there for you,' he said, suddenly fierce. 'Always.'

Her lips widened in an inviting smile. 'Show me.'

He was still showing her when the porter smartly whisked open the car door as they drew up in front of their hotel. They didn't even notice when he closed it again much more gently and, with a smile, gave a signal to the driver to take them once more round the block.

We hope you've enjoyed Fizz and Luke's story. You'll be pleased to hear that Liz Fielding has written two more **Scarlet** *novels featuring the delightful Beaumont sisters. On the following pages, you'll find an extract from* WILD LADY, *Book II of the 'Beaumont Brides Trilogy,' which we know will leave you wanting more!*

Look out for Claudia's story early in 1997 . . .

WILD LADY

When Claudia Beaumont, late and pushing her new sports car hard in the narrow Berkshire lanes, finally spotted the entrance to the airfield, she experienced two distinct and warring emotions. Relief and dread. And dread was winning by a country mile.

But she knew that the letter was simply the product of a sick mind. Someone was trying to frighten her, make her look feeble, and if she backed out now her anonymous correspondent would have succeeded. For heaven's sake, she expected to be frightened. Who wouldn't? And who was she to deprive millions of television viewers of a vicarious thrill? She slowed and turned into the gate. There had damned well better be millions, or she would want to know the reason why.

The security guard checked her car registration against a list he had on a clipboard, then directed her to the far side of the field where the OB unit was set up beside a large aircraft hangar.

Even at a distance the scene gave the appearance of organized chaos. Excitable men and earnest young women were milling about in an attempt to give an

374

impression of their own enormous importance, heavy cables were snaking through the grass, vehicles were everywhere, and the essential catering truck was doing a roaring trade in coffee and bacon sandwiches.

And a small aircraft, a very small aircraft, was parked on the apron in front of the hangar, waiting to take her several thousand feet into the air so that she could jump out of it for the amusement of the vast audience of Saturday night viewers.

'Do the show, darling,' her agent had coaxed. 'It's popular family entertainment, not in the least bit tacky. All the money the viewers pledge goes to a charity of your choice. And we'll get a big plug for the new television series.'

He'd forgotten to mention the fact that one of the guests on the show would be landed with an amusing little forfeit. And with three envelopes to choose from she'd managed to find the parachute jump. It was quite possible, she realized with a belated flash of insight, that they had all contained the same forfeit. It was highly probable that she'd kill her agent.

'You'd better put your foot down, miss,' the security guard advised. 'The weather looks as if it might be closing in, and if you don't get off the ground soon you'll have to come back another day. And that won't please Mr MacIntyre.'

It wasn't her eagerness to please Mr MacIntyre – whoever he was – or to get on with the jump that sent her little car leaping forward. If the film crew had a wasted day because she was late, Claudia knew she would be about as popular as an outbreak of rabies in a boarding kennel.

There were a number of cars parked in a neat line facing the hangar. Her car was lipstick-bright against the greyness of the morning and, aware that every head had turned at her approach, she did a slick change-down as she drove onto the grass, planning to slide neatly into the space between a gleaming black Landcruiser and the silver Porsche that she recognized as the pride and joy of the show's director.

There was only one problem. When she put her foot on the brake it went straight to the floor without resistance. For a split second she froze. It couldn't be happening. Her car was brand-new. Two days old. But it *was* happening. And she was heading straight for Barty's Porsche.

She wrenched hard on the steering wheel, somehow expecting that it, too, would fail to respond. It didn't fail. It responded with fingertip precision. And after that everything seemed to happen at once. The jolting tango along the black bulk of the Landcruiser, the bruising jerk as her seat belt locked and bit into her shoulder, the airbag exploding into life. The final nightmarish sound of rending metal as she collided with the hangar.

Then everything went very quiet for a moment, before the door beside her was wrenched open. If she had had the time to anticipate any reaction from the horrified onlookers she would have expected sympathy, concern, even worry that she might not be able to go ahead with the planned jump.

What she got, apparently, was a bear with a sore head. And he was growling at her. 'What the hell do you think you're playing at?' Definitely a growl. The kind produced by low, controlled anger. It seemed par for the day, Claudia thought, that the gap between expectation and reality should be so vast.

She turned, unhurt, but somewhat dazed by the rapidity with which events had overtaken her, and was confronted by a pair of large boots, combat trousers that seemed to ascend into the stratosphere and the kind of taut, aggressive hips that would normally have given her a pleasurable tingle of expectation. The voice, however, did not encourage her to expect anything except . . . well, aggravation.

At a disadvantage in the near ground-level car, she unfastened the seatbeat, leaned out and looked up. She had been right about the stratosphere. Wrong about the bear. But not that wrong. The man went up a very long way before widening out into a pair of shoulders that would have done justice to a barn door. He also had a thick pelt of black hair that would have curled had it not been ruthlessly trimmed into submission and the kind of blue eyes that any girl would gladly die for. Judging by the expression in them, she thought, this girl just might be required to. But she didn't like his immediate assumption that she was to blame for the accident. She would go down fighting.

'Playing at?' she enquired, determined to show him that she was not in the least bit intimidated by his size, or his damped-down anger. Or by his eyes. 'Why, musical cars, of course,' she said, with a careless wave of her hand. Her shoulder complained but she ignored it. 'Care to join me?' she invited.

It was perhaps fortunate that at that moment they were

inundated by near-hysterical television personnel. 'Claudia! Darling! My precious girl, are you all right?' Barty James, the programme's director, waggled his hands dramatically. 'Shall we call an ambulance?' He turned to his harassed assistant. 'Shouldn't there be an ambulance standing by? Isn't there supposed to be a doctor – ?' He began issuing a tirade of instructions, sending minions flying in all directions, but mostly for cover.

Claudia, used to theatrical hysteria, took no notice. Instead she swung long, silk-clad legs out of the car and waited for someone to help her to her feet. Barty was still busy berating his hapless assistant for the lack of an ambulance. Blue-eyes had swiftly removed himself from the scene and was now more concerned with the damage to the Landcruiser. Abandoning all hope of immediate aid and succour, she climbed from her car unaided and joined him.

His concern was well placed. The damage, although superficial, was widespread. She had scraped and dented every panel, leaving streaks of scarlet paint like careless kisses along the entire right-hand side.

The hangar didn't look much better. She hadn't hit it hard, but had still managed a pretty spectacular job of buckling and splitting the elderly corrugated metal.

But her lovely new car had by far the worst of it. The left-hand side had suffered horribly in its encounter with the Landcruiser, and the bonnet now looked as if a very heavy-footed figure skater had been practising triple toe-loops on its glossy paintwork. It was not a pretty sight, but as she turned to Blue-eyes she managed a smile, quite prepared to be brave about it although under the circumstances hysterics would have been quite permissible. Blue-eyes was unimpressed.

'I do hope you're properly insured, Miss Beaumont,' he said curtly, in case she had missed just *how* unimpressed he was.

Claudia, who could usually reduce a man to stuttering incoherence in less time than it took to say it, was seriously shaken at discovering that this man was quite immune to her particular brand of magic. Insurance? That was all that bothered him? He wasn't in the least concerned about her health? The fact that she might have broken her neck?

Apparently not. As their eyes met across the wreck of her car she received the very strong impression that he was quite prepared to break it himself. Well, the day was still young, and, if her anonymous correspondent was right, he might yet get his wish. The thought was enough to drive the smile right off her face.

'Why wouldn't I be properly insured?' Her premium was, in her opinion, large enough to insure any ten cars. 'But if you think I'm paying for this, you can forget it,' she said, nettled by his manner into displaying a little irritation on her own account. 'For your information my brakes failed, and since this car is only two days old it's going right back to the manufacturer. I suggest you call them and tell them your troubles.'

'The brakes . . .' There was a twittering of excitement from the watching television men.

Blue-eyes didn't twitter. 'You really expect me to believe that?' It was quite obviously not a question to which he expected an answer. He had made up his own mind and disbelief was written in every tightly controlled line of his face. 'You were showing off and driving too fast for the surface. Damp grass is like ice if you hit the brakes too hard.'

'Is it? And if you hit the brakes and nothing happens?'

'You lost control. If your brakes had simply failed you wouldn't have hit the Landcruiser, you'd have hit the Porsche.'

'I *know* that. That's why I swerved. I didn't want to hit Barty's Porsche . . .' Something in his expression warned her that she wasn't helping matters and her voice died away.

'Are you saying that you hit my car *on purpose*?' He spat out the words, one by one.

'It seemed like a good idea at the time.' She glared at him. 'It still does.' Then she threw up her hands in despair. It had been a bad day from the moment she had got out of bed and found that horrible anonymous letter on her doormat. 'Is there any chance of a cup of coffee around here?' she demanded.

'Claudia, darling, why don't we forget this for today?' Barty intervened quickly. 'You're overwrought. It's quite natural,' he added hastily, as she glared at him too. 'I'll run you down to the local hospital for a check-up. Since you've had an accident we'll be covered by insurance, and we don't want to take any risks, do we?'

'Don't we?' Claudia asked. Blue-eyes was giving her the kind of look that suggested she might have manufactured the accident simply to get out of the jump, and she didn't like it. 'Oh, for heaven's sake, Barty, I'm not made of glass. Let's get all my bruises over with in one day.' She looked around. 'Where's Tony?'

Tony was the one bright spark in this entire fiasco. Her role in *Private Lives* kept her on stage until eleven every night, but it had still been worth dragging herself out of bed first thing for Tony's training sessions – even under the watchful eye of the television crew. They had filmed her swinging gracefully from a tower in a harness under his careful instruction, learning how to fall, even packing the parachute she was to use.

Today they were going to celebrate her maiden jump. Without the cameras.

'Tony's wife telephoned this morning to cancel.' Blue-eyes regarded her steadily. 'Apparently he's feeling a bit under the weather. She didn't think it was a good idea to take any risks with him.'

Wife? He was married? The low-down sneaking rat. Some days it was just not a good idea to get out of bed.

'His wife?' she enquired coolly. Being an actress had its advantages. The ability to hide feelings was one of them.

'She's expecting a baby next month.' He punctuated the remark with a speaking, one-shouldered shrug. 'Didn't he mention her?'

No. He seemed to have overlooked that minor point. After all actresses were notorious, for sleeping around so it didn't really matter, did it? *Like hell it didn't.*

'Not that I recall,' she replied.

'Perhaps he didn't think it was important. But don't worry, Miss Beaumont. I'm here to take care of you in his place.'

Now, why wasn't that a comfort?

'Really?' she said. 'And who the devil are you?'

His face finally cracked into something that might have been a smile, although she could see that his heart wasn't really in it. 'Gabriel MacIntyre. But Mac will do.'

He didn't offer his hand, instead his eyes made a rapid transit over the space between her feet and her carefully tousled blonde hair, making an instant judgement on her short, flirty little skirt and loose silk jersey top. She had dressed to spend the day with Tony, not for a parachute jump, and he knew it.

'And you are the glamorous Miss Claudia Beaumont,' he said pointedly. He seemed singularly underwhelmed by the fact.

'I know that,' she informed him crisply. It was odd how very *crisp* she was feeling, considering the fact that she'd just run into the side of an aircraft hangar. The man had much the same bracing effect as a blast from a bottle of smelling salts. 'But please don't stand on ceremony,' she added. 'Miss Beaumont will do just fine.'

'Darling, don't be naughty!' Barty, his thin body encased in a close-fitting silk shirt, a toning scarf knotted with studied carelessness around his throat, intervened nervously, throwing a jittery look in the direction of Mac. 'Mr MacIntyre will think you don't like him.'

'Then he'd be right. I don't.'

'Claudia!'

'Well, what do you expect? I told him that my brakes failed, and without the slightest evidence to back him up he chose to believe I was lying.' It was clear that he believed a lot of other things about her too. None of them were true either.

Mac 'Blue Eyes' was unrepentant. 'I saw the way you were driving.' Barty was beginning to unravel. 'Are you quite sure you want to go ahead with this, Claudia, darling?' He pulled her aside, lowering his voice to a whisper. 'We'd all quite understand . . . shock, what have you . . .'

Claudia realized the crew were looking at her expectantly. Things had changed. With the insurance company paying, they'd all have an extra day's work if she decided to throw a wobbly and put the stunt off until a later date. But they didn't have to jump out of an aeroplane for the titillation of all those millions of television viewers, every one of whom was no doubt hoping to see her fall flat on her face. Especially the one who had sent her that nasty little note.

'We do it now, Barty, or not at all,' she announced. This was not a day she wished to repeat. She turned to Gabriel MacIntyre. 'Come on, Mac. I can see you can't wait to push me out of an aeroplane. Lead me to my overalls and let's get on with it.'

It gave her considerable pleasure to see that she had taken him by surprise. Although he didn't flicker so much as a muscle, Claudia knew that he'd been convinced she was going to bottle out. She would rather die than give him that satisfaction.

Slowly, and with obvious reluctance, he jacked up the smile. If he ever made an effort, she thought, he might be dangerous. There didn't seem much likelihood of her finding out.

The equipment was laid out on a trestle in the hangar: a pair of bright red overalls with her name printed across the back because they looked good in the ground shots – And it would make identification easy, she thought with a wry little smile, if she simply ploughed straight down into the nearest field – Then boots, her helmet next, with mini-camera and microphone already attached and ready to be hooked up to the power-pack she would wear at her waist, then goggles, and finally the parachute that she had packed herself, under Tony's supervision.

The crew were already suited up, running last-minute checks on their cameras and microphones with the OB unit.

'Is there somewhere I can change?' she asked.

Mac's eyes flickered over her unsuitable clothes. 'I hope you're wearing warm underwear,' he said. 'It'll be cold up there.'

'I've a nice line in silk thermals. Would you care to check them out?' He handed her the overalls and pointed her in the direction of the office without another word.

Claudia strode off jauntily enough, but once the door was shut behind her she let out a deep breath and sank into a chair. She was beginning to shake, and she wasn't sure whether it was reaction to the shunt with the car or whether she was just plain scared.

She shed her skirt, her top, her tights, then retrieved from her bag the thermal vest and long drawers that Tony had advised, pulling them on as quickly as her shaking fingers would allow. *Damn Tony and his boyish charm*. He could have got her through the next half an hour without a qualm, unlike Mr MacIntyre. At least she had nothing but a few stolen kisses to reproach herself for. Although why she should reproach herself for anything when *he* was the cheating bastard, she wasn't quite sure. But she did. And so did Mac.

By the time she came to fasten the front of the jumpsuit her fingers were shaking so much with a mixture of nerves and anger that she couldn't keep hold of the zip-pull. A sharp rap on the door, making her jump, was the last straw and she gave up trying.

'We haven't got all day, Miss Beaumont.' *Miss Beaumont.* He made it sound like an insult.

Clutching the overalls together at the front, she emerged from the office. 'I'm having zip trouble,' she said loftily. 'It seems to be stuck.'

Mac didn't say a word. He simply took hold of the pull and the wretched thing slid smoothly up to her neck. Then he pushed down the Velcro flaps. 'You should have asked for help sooner,' he said when he was satisfied. 'I told you I'd take care of you.'

She cleared her throat nervously. The crew had moved outside, leaving just the two of them in the hangar. 'So you did,' she said.

'Is there anything else?'

'No.' She reached for her helmet and tugged it on. 'I can manage now.'

'I hope so. We've all been waiting quite long enough. You were very late.'

She tucked in her long blonde hair. It seemed to take for ever, and he finally lost patience, finishing the job for her without much care for her scalp. Then he fastened

385

the chin-straps. 'I couldn't find the airfield,' she said. 'It's not exactly well signposted.'

He ignored the implied criticism and picked up her 'chute. She flexed her shoulders and held back her arms for him to lift it on. He didn't.

Now who was wasting time? 'What's the matter?' she asked, looking behind her.

'Nothing. I'm just going to change this 'chute.'

'What's wrong with it? I packed it myself and Tony said I'd made a perfect job of it.'

'Then Tony must have had his mind on other things. I'll get you another one from the store. Why don't you wait outside?'

She glared after him. It wasn't such a hardship. He was six feet two inches of unadulterated masculinity. He might raise her hackles, but after the narcissism and hot-house atmosphere of the theatre she had to admit that there was a rough-hewn, unfinished freshness about the man. Not that he was her type. She liked sophisticated, well-groomed men who knew how to treat a lady. Gabriel MacIntyre appeared to be the kind of old-fashioned chauvinist who preferred his women barefoot and pregnant. He probably had half a dozen baby MacIntyres to prove it.

And she made it a rule never to play house with other girls' husbands. But men didn't make it easy to be noble. Tony – lying and potentially cheating Tony – for instance, had looked as if butter wouldn't melt in his mouth. At least Gabriel MacIntyre wore a wedding ring.

Ten minutes later, buckled, fastened, and wired for sound so that every gasp of fright could be experienced vicariously by the television audience, Claudia was hurtling down the runway in a noisy, comfortless aircraft. She forced herself to smile. The fuselage had been fitted with tiny cameras to catch every fleeting expression and she was supposed to be enjoying herself. This was all good, clean *fun*.

Ideally they should all be chatting and laughing, but thankfully it was too noisy. No doubt someone would add on the kind of jokey commentary that would make the studio audience roar with laughter. She smiled harder, hoping that she hadn't chewed all her lipstick off. It was the performance of a lifetime.

Nothing could go wrong.

The cameramen, all experienced freefallers, were relaxed as they circled the airfield, gaining height, double-checking their camera equipment with the OB crew on the ground.

Mac was standing behind the pilot, waiting until they reached the right height. He turned for a moment and stared at her, his eyes thoughtful, his forehead creased in a deep frown. It was unsettling, but she met his gaze, challenged it. Then the pilot shouted something to him and he looked away.

Claudia tried to remember everything that Tony had told her. But her mind was a blank. And then, in the noisy, cramped space of the aircraft, with the jump only minutes away, the letter that had been pushed through her door in the early hours of the morning floated back to the surface of her mind and began to fill the vacuum with its insidious poison.

What kind of sick mind did it take to do something like

387

that? To take so much trouble to find all the right letters in a newspaper, cut them out neatly and then arrange them precisely, sticking them down one by one? She tried to blot it out.

It was rubbish, nonsense, some sick person's idea of a joke. Any successful actress was bound to provoke jealousy. It was inevitable. Especially when her path was perceived to have been eased by famous parents – a mother who had been a legend and a father who had directed the play she was appearing in right now. The letter was nothing. She had torn it up and thrown it in the bin with the rest of the rubbish.

Everything had been checked a dozen times. She was jumping from a static line. The 'chute would open automatically. All she had to do was go through the drill Tony had taught her. It was no big deal. She looked up as Mac tapped her on the shoulder. It was time to go.

Nothing could go wrong.

But her skin was slicked with sweat as she watched the camera crew jump out of the open doorway, move away from the aircraft, get into position to film her own exit from the plane. They made it look so easy. It *was* easy. She adjusted her goggles.

Nothing could go wrong.

Mac hooked her to the static line then guided her into place in the doorway. Below her the ground was like a picture from a storybook. Small, clean, beautiful. The rushing wind tugged at her, eager to suck her into the void, but she held on, waiting for Mac's signal. It seemed for ever coming, and she glanced at him. He smiled reassuringly. He'd picked a hell of a time to decide to be friendly, she thought, as at last he slapped her on the shoulder with sufficient impact to ensure that she didn't change her mind and mess up everyone's day.

Then, as she plunged towards the Berkshire countryside, she quite suddenly recalled that Gabriel MacIntyre had changed her carefully packed parachute at the last minute. And no one else had seen him do it.

The fields, the hedges, the silver ribbon of river all seemed to merge and resolve into a sheet of cheap lined paper covered with a jumble of newsprint:

I'VE FIXED YOU, DARLING CLAUDIA. OR RATHER I'VE FIXED YOUR PARACHUTE. ENJOY YOUR JUMP. YOU WON'T BE MAKING ANY MORE.

THE EXCITING NEW NAME
IN WOMEN'S FICTION!

PLEASE HELP ME TO HELP YOU!

Dear *Scarlet* Reader,

As Editor of *Scarlet* Books I want to make sure that the books I offer you every month are up to the high standards *Scarlet* readers expect. And to do that I need to know a little more about you and your reading likes and dislikes. So please spare a few minutes to fill in the short questionnaire on the following pages and send it to me. I'll send *you* a surprise gift as a thank you!

Looking forward to hearing from you,

Sally Cooper

Editor-in-Chief, *Scarlet*

P.S. Only one offer per household.

QUESTIONNAIRE

Please tick the appropriate boxes to indicate your answers

1 Where did you get this Scarlet title?
Bought in Supermarket ☐
Bought at W H Smith ☐
Bought at book exchange or second-hand shop ☐
Borrowed from a friend ☐
Other _____

2 Did you enjoy reading it?
A lot ☐   A little ☐   Not at all ☐

3 What did you particularly like about this book?
Believable characters ☐   Easy to read ☐
Good value for money ☐   Enjoyable locations ☐
Interesting story ☐   Modern setting ☐
Other _____

4 What did you particularly dislike about this book?
_____

5 Would you buy another Scarlet book?
Yes ☐   No ☐

6 What other kinds of book do you enjoy reading?
Horror ☐   Puzzle books ☐   Historical fiction ☐
General fiction ☐   Crime/Detective ☐   Cookery ☐
Other _____

7 Which magazines do you enjoy most?
Bella ☐   Best ☐   Woman's Weekly ☐
Woman and Home ☐   Hello ☐   Cosmopolitan ☐
Good Housekeeping ☐
Other _____

cont.

And now a little about you –

8 How old are you?

Under 25 ☐   25–34 ☐   35–44 ☐
45–54 ☐   55–64 ☐   over 65 ☐

9 What is your marital status?

Single ☐   Married/living with partner ☐
Widowed ☐   Separated/divorced ☐

10 What is your current occupation?

Employed full-time ☐   Employed part-time ☐
Student ☐   Housewife full-time ☐
Unemployed ☐   Retired ☐

11 Do you have children? If so, how many and how old are they?

_____

_____

12 What is your annual household income?

under £10,000 ☐   £10–20,000 ☐   £20–30,000 ☐
£30–40,000 ☐   over £40,000 ☐

Miss/Mrs/Ms _____

Address _____

_____

_____

_____

Thank you for completing this questionnaire. Now tear it out – put it in an envelope and send it before 28 February 1997, to:

Sally Cooper, Editor-in-Chief

SCARLET
FREEPOST LON 3335
LONDON W8 4BR
Please use block capitals for address.
No stamp is required!   WIJUS/8/96

Scarlet titles coming next month:

CARIBBEAN FLAME Maxine Barry
Revenge is what RAMONA KING wants and she'll allow
nothing to stand in her way – until she experiences true passion
for the first time in her life. Damon Alexander can't resist
Ramona, even though he already has a mistress and 'Alexan-
dria' is far more demanding than Ramona will ever be . . .

UNDERCOVER LOVER Sally Steward
Allison Prescott knows one thing for sure: the person with
the wealth calls the shots. Never again will she allow a man
to take over and dictate how she should live. So she needs
money – lots and lots of lovely money! What she *doesn't* need
is a man like Brad Malone! Brad, too, has other priorities
and they sure don't include falling in love with a woman
who has dollar signs in her heart.

THE MARRIAGE SOLUTION Julie Garratt
When Amy Weldon discovers that her uncle expects her to
marry a man she's never met, she's understandably reluctant. Then she meets Richard Boden and her uncle's plan
suddenly seems very, very desirable.

WIVES, FRIENDS AND LOVERS Jean Saunders
Take three friends: Laura had married Nick Dean after a
whirlwind romance and was still madly in love with her
husband . . . or was she? Gemma wanted stardom at all costs
. . . even if it meant denying her love for the one man who
was perfect for her; while Penny longed only for success and
had no time for romance at all. Friendship, love, marriage or
ambition . . . the choice was vital for all three women.